## PRAISE FOR THE CIVIL WAR CHRONICLES

'Arnold conveys the characters' befuddlement and terror, without losing his grip on the greater ebb and flow of battle . . . masterfully done.'

*The Times*

'Mike Arnold hooks the reader with the clash of steel and the roar of gunpowder. Rollicking action and proper history combine in this cracking series.'

Anthony Riches, author of the *Empire* series

'If you like Cornwell you will like Arnold.'

*Historical Novels Review*

'The enigmatic Stryker promises much entertainment.'

*The Sunday Times*

'A thumping good read. With considerable skill, Arnold has reached back in time to create a living, breathing depiction of 17th century England. From his vividly described battle scenes to the richly drawn descriptions of everyday life, from the earthy vernacular of its characters to the precise details of military equipment, every last part of this book oozes authenticity. Fans of Cornwell's Sharpe novels will love Captain Innocent Stryker – he's uglier, meaner and cleverer than Sharpe. Tremendous!'

Ben Kane, bestselling author of The Forgotten Legion Chronicles

'Arnold has joined the ranks of Cornwell and Sansom'

*Battlefield*

'Crackling with the sound of musket fire and punctuated with the roar of cannon, this book brings the Cromwellian conflict to life in an intense battle of wits and weaponry'

*Press Association*

## About the Author

Michael Arnold lives in Petersfield, Hampshire, with his wife and children. After childhood holidays spent visiting castles and battlefields, he developed a lifelong fascination with the Civil Wars. *Marston Moor* is the sixth in a planned series of over ten books that will follow the fortunes of Major Stryker through one of the most treacherous periods of English history. The first five books in The Civil War Chronicles, *Traitor's Blood*, *Devil's Charge*, *Hunter's Rage*, *Assassin's Reign* and *Warlord's Gold* are available in paperback and eBook.

### Also by Michael Arnold

Traitor's Blood
Devil's Charge
Hunter's Rage
Assassin's Reign
Warlord's Gold

*eBook Short Stories*
Stryker and the Angels of Death

# MARSTON MOOR

## MICHAEL ARNOLD

HODDER

First published in Great Britain in 2015 by Hodder & Stoughton
An Hachette UK company

First published in paperback in 2016

1

Maps drawn by Rodney Paull.

A CIP catalogue record for this title is available from the British Library

ISBN 978 1 848 54767 4

Typeset in Bembo by Hewer Text UK Ltd, Edinburgh
Printed and bound by Clays Ltd, St Ives plc

Hodder & Stoughton policy is to use papers that are natural, renewable
and recyclable products and made from wood grown in sustainable forests.
The logging and manufacturing processes are expected to conform to
the environmental regulations of the country of origin.

Hodder & Stoughton Ltd
Carmelite House
50 Victoria Embankment
London EC4Y 0DZ

www.hodder.co.uk

*To my nephew, Ben*

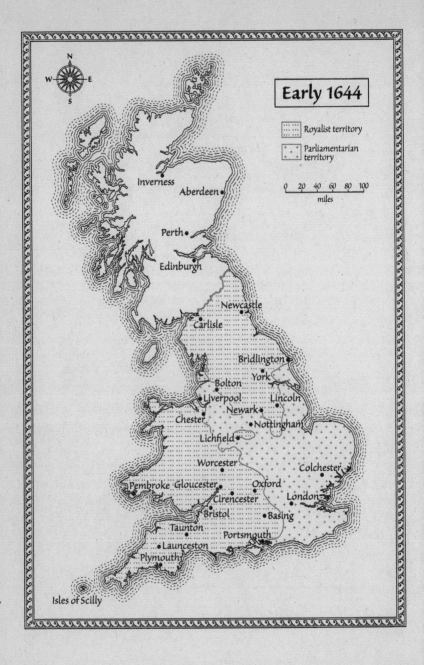

# Early 1644

- Royalist territory
- Parliamentarian territory

0  20  40  60  80  100
miles

N
W—E
S

Inverness
Aberdeen
Perth
Edinburgh
Newcastle
Carlisle
Bridlington
York
Bolton
Liverpool
Lincoln
Chester
Newark
Nottingham
Lichfield
Worcester
Colchester
Pembroke
Gloucester
Oxford
London
Cirencester
Bristol
Basing
Taunton
Portsmouth
Launceston
Plymouth
Isles of Scilly

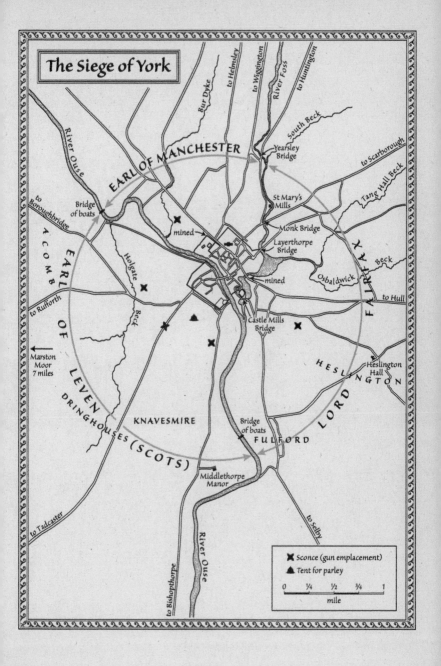

# PROLOGUE

*Near Tockwith, Yorkshire, 2 July 1644*

The stalks, a pale green blanket pearled in raindrops that shimmered in the fleeting moonlight, grew thick.

Deep within the green shroud, the young man shifted an arm to stave off numbness, wincing as the bean pods rustled overhead. He gritted his teeth until his jaw ached, waiting for the cry of alarm that would signal his discovery. The plants were heavy with a summer's bounty, a dense maze that concealed him well enough, but the season had been wet and the drooping stems were stunted, forcing the fugitive to lie completely flat.

The cold seeped into his marrow, and the soil tainted his lips. He let out the breath that had grown to flame in his lungs, and shuddered into the sodden mud. He was lying face down, clothes filthy, yet he prayed thanks all the same. He was still alive.

The pungent stench of roasting meat wafted through the crop. His mouth filled with saliva and his stomach cramped painfully. He knew the flesh sizzling out on the moor would likely be that of a thousand horses, but hunger overrode any qualm. He closed his eyes and tried to imagine a hearty repast. All he saw in the blackness were faces. Lily-white corpses staring at him in mute condemnation. He saw his dog, his beloved companion, gone now, rotting out on the cursed plain. He saw his uncle, delicate features screwed into the sour anguish of betrayal, his eyes – dark and wide – questioning how such misfortune could come to pass.

★    ★    ★

A shout in the dark. He froze. Horsemen were gathering beyond the bean field, out where pyres blazed and wounded men still moaned. He could feel the stamping of their hooves through the earth, could hear the chatter of voices and the jangle of armour, tack and weaponry. He eased his chin up from the sticky soil, squinting into the stems, but he could see no further than a yard or two. He prayed harder than he had ever prayed before.

An order broke out from amongst the unseen troop, shrill and stark above the murmurs of a victorious army making camp. The hooves rumbled again. The young man braced himself. He felt sick. Then the vibration faded to nothing and he was left alone once more. He began to shuffle backwards, slithering on his belly like a serpent, pushing further and further into the embrace of the crop. There was nothing left for him here. Escape was all he could hope for. He had to survive, to find his friends and rebuild his army, for on a moor in Yorkshire the world had been flipped on its head and suddenly everything had changed.

# CHAPTER 1

*Berwick-upon-Tweed, 19 January 1644*

The River Tweed marked the frontier between the two king-doms. It gleamed in the weak dawn sun, a thick crust of ice transforming it from barrier to opportunity. The stone crossing remained, its arches looming large above the river, but it was no longer the only gateway to the south; a bitter winter had seen to that. The cavalry clattered over the bridge, three thousand lances – peculiar to this part of Britain – bobbing with the rhythm of hooves to turn the column into a never-ending Leviathan of wickedly glinting spines. Artillery and baggage trains would follow, bringing one hundred and twenty heavy pieces of ordnance to the invasion, too heavy and cumbersome to brave the ice. Meantime the rest, thousands upon thousands of pikemen and musketeers, all clad in suits of Hodden grey broadcloth and voluminous lengths of plaid, slipped and slid their way across it as they fought to keep step with the incessant drums. Each unit safely across re-formed behind their colours – flags that bore the cross of St Andrew, rather than St George – held aloft by ensigns to bob like the prows of warships in the last tendrils of mist. The officers barked orders, their sergeants transformed the barks to snarls and, one after another, they tramped over the frost-silvered grass and on to the wide road.

A group of horsemen watched the procession from the north bank of the Tweed. They were clustered around a man perched on a dappled grey mare. His face was deeply lined, his red hair and whiskers shot through with veins of slate, so that he could not hide his advancing years. And yet they regarded him with reverential silence. The man shivered, glancing down to fasten the last of the silver buttons that brightened his black cassock. '*Alea iacta est*, Davey.'

The man mounted to his side was younger, leaner and heavily wrapped against the cold. He let out a lingering breath, studying the bilious cloud of vapour as it rolled from his nostrils. 'Will they stand?'

The older man looked across at his companion, blue eyes narrowing. 'They'll fight, and they'll stand, and they'll die if I say so.'

Davey shook his head. 'Not our lads, Sandie. The English.'

The general gazed back at the army that rumbled inexorably across the Tweed. He wore a wide, dark hat with a single blue feather, which he tilted down against the biting wind. 'They'd better,' he replied, and he said it with feeling, because his name was Alexander Leslie, First Earl of Leven, and he was commander of the Army of the Covenant; the best, hardiest, most fearsome army to be found anywhere in the Stuart dynasty's three kingdoms. But they could not win this war on their own. They would need the English Parliamentarians to grow a backbone for the new alliance to bear fruit. He eyed a company of foot as they slewed awkwardly across the river, their blue bonnets bright against the pale frost. 'That ice had better not break.'

'It is as thick as castle walls,' Davey replied.

Leven cast him a withering glance. 'Castles crumble with enough pressure.'

Davey offered a shrug. 'You wanted speed, Sandie. At this rate we'll be half the way to Alnwick before the buggers know we've marched.'

Leven knew he was right. The crossing, precarious as it was, had seemed a risk worth taking. God had sent the cold, and with His touch the bottleneck of the bridge had been negated. It would be foolish to ignore such providence. 'I want a proclamation,' he said after a short time.

'A proclamation, my lord?' Davey was nonplussed.

'Proclaim throughout our ranks, Lieutenant-General, that plundering, ravishing and whore-mongering are forbidden.'

David Leslie, Lieutenant-General of Horse, screwed up his thin mouth. 'Forgive me, my lord, but that'll be a tall order to—'

'And lewd language,' Leven went on as if his second in command had not spoken. 'I'll have none of that in my army. Make no mistake, Davey. We are foreigners here. We share a king with the English, but not a kingdom.'

'Foreigners in England are myriad, my lord,' Leslie argued. 'Fortune-seekers from the Low Countries. You and I both fought with them in the Swedish service. And what of the Welshmen who fight? Celts crawled down from their mountains. Or the Cornish?'

'Trickles in the face of a flood,' Leven answered. 'We outnumber Herbert's Welsh division tenfold, and the Cornish many times over. Besides, the Cornish have slunk back into the southwest. They do not lance the heartland of their enemies. But we? We are vast, and we are here to stay. The common sort will not find comfort in our presence. We must, therefore, behave impeccably. They must welcome us at their hearths or we will not survive the winter.'

'Very well, my lord.'

'Derogatory remarks, Davey,' Leven added.

'My lord?'

'Referring to His Majesty. No word of irreverence or insult towards King Charles will pass a Covenanter's lips. He remains our king. We are nae here to topple him, but to aid the English in extricating his person from the smooth-tongued advisers he so calamitously admires.'

David Leslie nodded. 'I'll see it done, sir.'

The Earl of Leven touched his spurs to his snorting grey's flanks so that she skittered forward. He drew her up at the edge of the frozen river. On the far side his formidable force was rapidly assembling in the hoary dawn. He had more than twenty thousand men in all. Many were veterans of the European conflict; more still had served with him in the Bishops' Wars, where the king's army had been trounced and humiliated. They were granite-hewn, experienced and godly. And they were ready for a fight.

Yes, thought the Earl of Leven, the die was indeed cast. The Army of the Covenant had finally crossed the frontier. They were in foreign territory, marching south to crush the malignant Royalists and end a war. The invasion of England had begun.

# PART 1

# GENEVA OF
# THE NORTH

# CHAPTER 2

*Bolton-le-Moors, Lancashire, 28 May 1644*

The steep-banked clough carved a ragged gully to the east of the small town. At the ravine's deepest reaches the River Croal swirled and bubbled between reeds stooped against driving rain, a glassy streak overlooked by the timber-framed houses clustered on the flatter terrain along its west bank. The mosaic of woodland, pasture and meadow that fringed Bolton was swollen with springtime bounty: hedgerows were bursting with berries, woods were thickening and luscious; even the wide, desolate gritstone expanse to the north seemed greener than ever before. It was an Eden nestled on the edge of the great moors.

And yet, on this drizzle-dampened afternoon the place reeked. Buttery smoke wafted on the breeze, its sulphurous fingers creeping gently, groping alleyways and thatches, barns and carts, curling about the marketplace, meeting and mingling in ominous skeins above the heads of frightened folk.

The streets were empty of all but those bearing arms. Women and children, the elderly and infirm, had long since gone to ground, hiding in cellars and churches, in back rooms and attics, leaving their men to find what tools they could. Those men, five hundred in all, had mustered with the two thousand regular soldiers that had marched through the gates that morning, and already they had been compelled to fight. Because a multitude had come from the south and west, emerging from the rain-blurred woods in dark, dense blocks of horse, pike and shot,

9

marching to the thrum of a hundred drums to converge like a swarm of demons.

The attack had come at just after two o'clock. Four regiments of foot detached themselves from what might have been twelve thousand in all and assaulted earthworks carved from soil and capped in turf. They had advanced in bristling battalions, musketeers flanking a centre of grim pikemen who jabbed up at the defenders on the muddy rampart with their long spears, the height of the work being less than the length of a pike. But the rain had played havoc with the assault, turning powder to black broth and cooling resolve, and the battalions had faltered. Engaged by men protecting their homes and families, they had been found wanting in the murky afternoon, and had been repulsed and humiliated.

The defenders had cheered as the last life evaporated from the glazed eyes of corpses left along the wall, dangling from sharpened stakes like string-cut marionettes, or dumped like sacks in the filth of the outer ditch. They had taunted their persecutors from the slick palisade, given thanks to a shielding God, and prayed that the enemy would skulk back into the woods. But passions were running high. Crazed with zeal from their modest success, Bolton's defenders had wanted to make a statement. It was a famous town; prosperous as a centre of the English textile industry, it was so well known as a bastion for austere Puritanism that it had been garnished with the moniker 'Geneva of the North'. It was a Parliamentarian stronghold transformed into a fortress by circumstance, and they had all seen the standards outside, though the gaudy cloths hung limp in the rain. Those colours, adorned with crosses of St George, with badges of heraldry, with Latin inscriptions and with passages of Scripture, left the defenders in no doubt as to who they faced. This was a Cavalier army. Tyldesley's were here, Broughton's and Molyneux's too. Vaughn's, Tillier's, Pelham's, Gibson's, Eyre's and so many more. And at their head rode the very talisman of the Royalist cause.

'This one's for Rupert of the Rhine!' the sergeant had snarled as he nodded to the team of musketeers clutching the thick rope. 'And may his privy member be soured by pox!'

His men had wrestled in their villages' tug-of-wars; they were strong men with calloused fingers and knotted shoulders, and they grinned as they hauled. But there was no team of ale-drenched opponents on the other end of the rope. Instead, it was slung over the branch of an ancient tree that sprouted, canted and gnarled, from the high bank above the gushing Croal on the town's eastern flank. There was no wall or ditch here, for the river and clough did that work well enough, and it meant that the tree was visible from a long way off, its branches clawing above the palisade that traced the line of the natural embankment. It was the perfect place to make clear their declaration of loyalty to the rebel parliament, and so they dragged back the rope and the man standing bound and noosed below the branch was hoisted into the air with a sickening jerk. He was an officer of Thomas Tyldesley's regiment, captured in that brief, white-hot skirmish that had proved to the defenders that they had God on their side. And that Tyldesley's regiment, like the colonel himself, was full of Papists. What better kind of declaration could be made than stringing one of those Rome-lovers up for the Almighty to see?

The wretched officer had taken a long time to die. He had writhed and kicked, danced a piss-drenched jig with wide, blood-shot eyes and a tongue that lolled purple and huge between wintry lips. In the end he had bitten that tongue off, and a lone crow had been brave enough to swoop for the plunder. Faced with the sight, even the sergeant whose laughter had accompanied the lynching had fallen to pasty-faced silence, as if, with the grotesqueness of the death, the bubble of their zeal had been burst.

And the vast Royalist army, including Prince Rupert of the Rhine, had witnessed it all.

Now, as the corpse turned slowly above the River Croal and the crows circled above the powder-flecked mist, the defenders of Bolton-le-Moors held their breath.

\*     \*     \*

Private Acres was a patch of land to the north-west of the town, a place of ramshackle shepherding hovels and leaky outbuildings thrown up beyond Bolton's limits. It was where sheep could be corralled when brought down from the moors, and where the accoutrements of the wool trade – rope and shears and fodder and wattle fencing – could be temporarily stored; a dilapidated warren grown out of convenience and now resembling a full suburb of untidy lanes clustered flush against the outer edge of Bolton's earthen rampart.

'This way,' the guide hissed, beckoning a troop of men and horses through one of the narrow lanes.

The man leading his large reddish stallion immediately in the guide's wake tapped him hard on the shoulder. 'You're certain?'

The guide paused, glancing left and right. 'I live here, sir.'

The fellow with the red horse did not return the smile. 'If you play me false, Master Grabban, I'll pull your heart out through your nose.'

'If he's playing us false,' another of the party – a head taller than the rest and shaven-headed, with dark, cavernous eyes – droned sardonically, 'then we're all bleedin' dead.'

Grabban kept his gaze on the leader. The man was a fiend, he felt sure. The Parliament news-sheets never exhausted their reserves of vitriol, branding Cavaliers Satan-lovers, pope-turds and warlocks. But now that he had finally met one, his natural cynicism was in danger of fraying. The soldier, a major, was dressed completely in black, save for a scarlet ribbon tied at one wrist. He had long, black hair, a thin layer of black stubble at cheeks and chin, and his wide hat was black too. That was enough to frighten most God-fearing men, except that the soldier's face made the rest of him pale in comparison. It was a granite scarp, ragged and rugged, lean and weathered. One eye was gone. Torn or gouged or burned to nothing, just a ruined socket of mutilated scar tissue remained where once it had been. The other eye glimmered, lonely and feral. It was grey, flecked with silver, and it never seemed to rest. Perhaps, Grabban thought, Prince Robber and his friends really did consort with the powers of darkness. He forced himself to look away, pointing at a row of rot-slanted shacks that ran north to south directly across their path. 'There. Behind them sheds. Outer ditch runs right behind it.'

The major followed his gaze. 'How are they disposed?'

'Rigby's Foot number a thousand or two,' Grabban answered.

The tall, bald-headed fellow spat at Grabban's shoes. 'Nowt like a good intelligencer.'

Grabban ignored him, scratching instead at the burning itch that ever afflicted his stones. 'Rest are clubmen. Locals.' Bastards to a man, he thought, deserving of everything that was to come. He walked on, the long line of men shifting into motion at his back, their progress concealed by the leaky rooftops of the tumbledown suburb. In moments they had reached the entrance to one of the shacks. The double doors were open, hanging at awkward angles from broken hinges and providing ample room for the first dozen men and their horses. There was a door on the far side that was closed and barred on the inside. Grabban stood beside it as his charges mustered beneath the low rafters. 'They'll have watchers on the wall, but most are to the south, near Bradshawgate. Your fedaries will come north from there.'

The major wound his horse's reins around gloved knuckles. He threw his grey gaze at his men. 'We will crush them between us. Have they harrows on the roads?'

'Chains,' Grabban said. 'Have you cutters?'

'Aye.'

'And the reward?'

The major coaxed his mount to the door. 'Will be paid upon the success of our enterprise.'

Grabban did not bother to stifle his smile as he hurried to lift the bar clear. 'Then God preserve you, Major Stryker.'

Stryker pushed the doors open with his boot and led the snorting horse out into the drizzle. 'We take the town,' he commanded, swinging up into the saddle as soon as man and beast had cleared the lintel. 'Offer no quarter to any person discovered under arms. By order of the Prince.'

It was not the most intimidating earthwork Stryker had ever seen. Indeed, he had been present at Newark Fight in March, and that circuit was a far more imposing sight. But Bolton's ditch would swallow all but the tallest man, and the heaped bank of mud climbing on its far edge – two yards thick and the same in height – was crested with a wooden palisade, below which horizontal storm poles jutted from the outer face like teeth, turning the whole structure into something akin to a gaping maw. Moreover, there were men stationed at intervals along the wall. Not many, for the garrison and militiamen were spread thinly right around the perimeter, but even a handful of eagle-eyed musketeers could bring slaughter from such a vantage.

Which was why the Royalists had crept through the Private Acres, and why the cavalrymen, famously so ill at ease on terra firma, had dismounted, and why they had entrusted their lives to the avaricious stoat, Grabban. Because there was one weak point in the perimeter. Here, behind this dilapidated run of musty, mouldering structures, the ditch was not so deep. The defenders had evidently bargained on the buildings themselves providing obstacle enough. Which was true, so long as they could guard those dung-carpeted rooms. But Rigby did not have enough men for such a task. Indeed, he had only marched into town that morning, and might not even know about the secret corner Bolton's engineers had cut.

But Grabban knew. Thus, for a bag of gold coins, Prince Rupert of the Rhine had been informed. And Prince Rupert had witnessed the twitching death of one of his officers above the banks of the River Croal. If the gesture had been designed to enrage the young General of Horse, it had worked. The king's nephew was incandescent with fury, and he had sent his best men to find a way into the defiant rebel nest.

Stryker drew his sword as Vos, his sorrel stallion, crossed the shallow ditch and raced up the bank on the far side. There were no storm poles here; the palisade was a rudimentary barrier of latticed wattle that thrashing hooves turned to splinters in a trice. The few defenders manning the rampart to their left and right began to scream. They swung their muskets up, ripping off the oiled rags that shielded charges from the rain, and blew hastily on their matches, but they were too few, too bewildered, and the sporadic shots flew harmlessly high and wide. Already more horsemen were over the earthworks, clattering down in a storm of hoofbeats and bellows. These were Rupert's harquebusiers, the cream of his light cavalry, and they needed no direction.

'Kill dead!' one of the troopers shouted from behind the three vertical bars that encased his face. 'Kill dead!'

Stryker lifted his sword high so that the ornate basket hilt glittered in the weak rain, and repeated the general's decree: 'Kill dead! Kill them dead!'

But there was hardly anyone left to kill. The defenders were running. There were not enough of them to form the kind of cohesive unit required to counter cavalry, so they bolted, heading east or south into the town, desperate to be away from the vengeful horsemen bearing down. But the men with the cutters, a pair of gentlemen troopers from Rupert's own regiment of horse, had made short work of the first chain strung across the road. It rattled as it hit the cobbles, and the way was clear. Stryker raked his spurs and clung tight as Vos gave chase.

The Royalist infantry were already in the streets. The regiments of Tyldesley and Broughton had advanced against the southern earthwork at the same time as the clandestine manoeuvre by the horse, and Stryker guessed the appearance of cavalry at Roundhead backs had precipitated the abandonment of the wall. The rebels had fallen away from the rampart in every quarter, making for the dubious safety of the market square and leaving the attackers to clamber over the battlements with only the slick mud as hindrance. Now Rupert's forces were pouring in at every point. There were four main arteries spurring off Bolton's market cross, and the rampant assault troops swarmed along them, swords brandished, muskets firing at anything that moved. When those pieces were spent, while smoke still wisped from warm muzzles, the muskets were reversed so that their heavy wooden stocks could be employed as clubs, hammering and smashing at doors, windows and skulls.

Stryker was pushing eastwards with the harquebusiers he had led over the defences when they met their first pocket of resistance. It was a half-dozen musketeers, corralled by a stocky, snarling corporal into a tight alley between two rows of jettied houses. They backed into the space, shoulder to shoulder, like a dam in a stream, and prepared their weapons. Stryker dug in his heels, compelling Vos to an extra yard of speed, and he ducked low so that the coarse red mane brushed the tip of his nose. The volley came as expected, but the musketeers' powder was damp, and the charges fizzed weakly. The Royalists were on them, hacking down from their high saddles. The Roundheads broke, reeling away to flee down the alley, but there was not enough room for all and the slowest of them were felled like fresh saplings before the axe, cleaved at skull and neck and shoulder to turn the pooling rain ruddy.

Stryker broke away now, for there was no need to maintain formation. It was a rout, a cauldron of boiling, cacophonous chaos. His blade was red, and he wiped it on his thigh where the uppermost part of his long boot had been drawn back for protection. When he looked up he saw a surging tide of humanity; men, women and children racing pell-mell along the eastbound thoroughfare, shoes kicking off behind in their collective haste, bags dropped, contents scattering to be trampled by those in the rear. Screams echoed up and down the buildings. He saw children on some of the rooftops, shuffling on their backsides to perch on the apexes liked startled sparrows. He spurred into the midst of the mob, surprised to realize that he had reached a wide open area of neat cobbles that was marked by a large stone cross. Where were the regular soldiers? Rigby's foot regiment was two thousand strong, they had been told. It had already fended off a determined assault this day, killing upwards of three hundred

Royalists in the act, and yet they had dissolved like salt in a pot. The day was won. The way was clear, save only the horror-stricken tide of frightened townsfolk who poured to the north-east corner of the town. He looked up, scanning the skyline. Sure enough, a crenellated tower of pale stone poked sharply above the undulating horizon of thatch and slate. The fugitives were making for a church.

He kicked on. To his left a door was turned to shards by the butt ends of a trio of muskets, their owners smashing their way through to a chorus of shrieks from within. To his right a horseman trotted across the face of a large shop, using the muzzle of his carbine to casually put through every window-pane. When a cry of grievance came from inside, he pulled the trigger.

Stryker kicked hard, steering into the centre of the road to avoid debris flung from the buildings, and followed the flow of fugitives. The snorting beast had to vault the twisted body of a young man, face gouged by steel, but he did not break his stride, for he was as experienced as his rider, battle-hardened and unflappable, and soon they were coming to the very heart of the anarchy that was Bolton-le-Moors.

Grabban had described the lie of the land well enough for Stryker to ascertain that he was on Churchgate. This was the right-hand spur of the four main streets, and here, between the cross and the embattled crest of the riverbank, the houses were densely packed, the alleys dark. The whole area, Bolton's north-eastern quarter, was wreathed in smoke too thick to be born of black powder. Almost immediately he saw that three rooftops were on fire. Flames licked from the rafters beneath, pulsing through the damp thatch in lambent jets from eaves to chimneys. Soon they were dancing across to the adjacent buildings, lapping like huge orange tongues. The rain did nothing to slake their thirst. Steam drifted skywards to mingle with the noxious cloud, and the densely packed straw hissed and crackled, but the deeper layers of thatch were as dry as July kindling and the drizzle evaporated in moments. There were people on those roofs. Stryker could not see them for smoke, but he could hear their agonised wails: blood-freezing symphonies of pain and desperation.

All around him there were horsemen, both those who had crept through the Private Acres and those who had been following the fluttering cornets of Prince Rupert's Regiment of Horse. So they had crossed the wall behind the infantry divisions, and he now understood why the beleaguered defenders had cut and run. There were just too many Royalists inside the town now. Rigby's strong force had been slashed and shot from almost every side, and they had not had the stomach nor the numbers to resist. The only direction left open to them was the north-east, the warren around Churchgate, with the protection of the church beside the river. Some were making a stand. He could hear them; their orders, their cries of defiance, the cracks of their muskets. But the vast majority sought refuge, preferring survival to martyrdom.

Except that the choice was no longer theirs. The people of Bolton had defied a prince, fought off his first assault and executed one of his officers in cold blood. Stryker felt a pang of sorrow. Because there was no turning back. No forgiveness. Nowhere to hide.

He curbed Vos as he peered along the length of Churchgate, the market cross twenty paces behind, the church tower up ahead. On both sides, the suffocating passages between each terrace were stuffed full of people, some pushing through to find a way to the walls, others turning back, deciding to fight. Smoke drifted everywhere, roiling in poisonous black and yellow plumes, spinning in white coils, probing doorways flung open and windows obliterated. Soldiers displaying the red scarves and ribbons of the Crown were everywhere, entering homes, scouring each and every room. Men were dragged thrashing over thresholds into the road, cast down and run through, no consideration given to whether they were soldiers or civilians. Rupert, after all, had forbidden the offer of quarter to any found carrying a weapon.

'That one ain't armed,' a deep, sardonic voice rang on Stryker's blind left.

Stryker did not bother to turn to his sergeant. A young lad, probably not yet beyond his teens, was being dragged by the ankles from the smashed doorway of a smouldering cooperage. 'It will make little difference, Will.'

William Skellen urged his horse forward so that he was beside his commanding officer. He was staring at the mob of seven or eight musketeers who now kicked the boy as though he were a football. 'Different, sir.'

Now Stryker turned to regard him. 'Different?'

'This. You and me seen plenty o' sackings, sir.' He shook his head. 'But not in England.'

'Cirencester,' Stryker answered.

'A hard fight, sir, but not like this.' Skellen paused as the boy's attackers moved away, eyeing the new-made corpse impassively. 'This is bad.'

Stryker's natural response was to temper the sergeant's melancholy, not least because he did not wish Skellen to be overheard by the more zealous elements of Rupert's army, but he found he could not argue. This *was* different. The war had grown increasingly bitter after its first bloody year, and yet here, in this unlikely place, he too could see the telltale taint of brutality that had so blighted the European wars. He had fought for the Dutch and Swedes in the Low Countries. It had been a war of murder, of slaughter, of hatred, and always he had compared those dark days to King Charles's conflict with Parliament, consoling himself that England's tribulation held nothing of that continental calamity. But now he realized that things had changed. This Puritan enclave had enraged the Royalists – many of whom were Catholic – and now there was nothing but fury and revenge etched into the faces of the Cavaliers. There would be no mercy here.

From the house whence the dead lad had been hauled came the screams of women. Four were thrown bodily out into the street, laughter rolling in their wake as the soldiers kicked at them. Their exultant comrades were inside, and in moments their grinning faces appeared at the upper windows. Clothes were flung to the street below, bags and jugs, plates and sheets, goblets and papers.

'Stop them, sir?' Skellen asked.

'How?' Stryker said, hating himself, but knowing they could do nothing. The sack of a defiant town was the right of the victor, and he had no place meddling with a custom so long held.

'The women, sir,' Skellen said, a rare note of plea entering his habitually flat timbre. 'Chil'ens.'

'The Prince will bring them to heel,' Stryker said bleakly, knowing it was an empty assertion.

Musketry rattled again, thicker than before, and Stryker ducked instinctively. A new plume of smoke tumbled from the doors and windows of a substantial home some thirty paces along Churchgate. He glanced at Skellen. 'They're putting up a fight.'

They spurred on, reaching a close passage separating the gable end of the home from its neighbour. There they dismounted, leading the animals into the mouth of the murky channel, offering gentle encouragement as they were forced to edge around the twisted remains of a dead horse. Once they were away from the melee engulfing the road, they looped their reins through metal rings screwed into the gable's timbers and proceeded on foot, plunging ever deeper into the gloom. Stryker took both matched pistols from his saddle holster, thrusting one into his belt and cocking the other. He levelled it out in front, squinting into the shadows, and drew his sword. The darkness was almost impenetrable, and he tripped as he snagged his foot on the outstretched leg of a prone man. The fellow was long dead, his body broken at every limb, his skull misshapen where it had been dashed on the walls at either side.

'Rider,' Skellen said, flicking his pistol back in the direction of the dead horse. 'One of ours. Wonder how they got 'im off his horse.'

Stryker stepped over the corpse, his boot crunching on what felt like a pile of gravel. People ran past the entrance to the alley, their shapes ghosting through the smoke like dusk wraiths. A horse's whinny carried high above the thunder of hooves as cavalrymen clattered by in pursuit. He looked down and turned the ball of his foot gently, letting the stones scrape and grind under his boot. 'Slate.'

'Sir?'

Stryker looked up suddenly, straining his eye to examine the edges of the rooftops on either side. More smoke churned there, but it was brightened by daylight and he could see shapes above the eaves. 'Slate. They're tiles.'

Skellen swore filthily as half a dozen large rectangular project-iles crashed to earth, shattering into pieces around them. They leapt away from the middle of the alley, pushing hard up against the walls as more slate flew between them, splinters showering against their legs. They ran, howls from above accompanying every step, until they found a small door, perhaps a servants' entrance, set into the wall. The tiles spun above and behind, clipping both walls on their way down, and Skellen wasted no time, smashing through the door with two kicks and a driving shoulder. They dived inside, tiles still raining down, and suddenly all was quiet. They were in the kitchens, a wide, cool space of racks and shelves, ovens and tables. Along the walls there were stacks of trenchers and saucers interspersed with bowls large and small, and hanging from hooks ladles, knives and skimmers. The shelves were crammed with various types of jug and goblet, with pots and jars of spices arranged neatly in between. This was the heart of a grand home. Muffled musket shots echoed through the ceiling, and the pair exchanged a rapid glance before moving for the open doorway on the far side.

Two men – one large, one small – burst from behind those doors. The smaller, dressed like a musketeer, though missing his weapon, hurled a huge metal pottinger at Stryker as a fountain of obscenities poured from his black-gummed mouth. The pot-tinger clipped Stryker's temple. It was heavy, knocking off his hat and sending him reeling to the side and careening into a low table to collapse among a clanging pile of pewter chargers, which spun away in all directions. Skellen went for the assailant as

Stryker regained his balance, only to see the larger of the two men, bearded and grimacing above a long, blood-stained apron, bearing down, a hefty cleaver in hand. The blow came fast and heavy, a huge swat delivered with the full weight of the man, whose eyes were distended with rage. Stryker threw himself to the side, letting the brutal lump of rectangular steel scythe harmlessly past, and smashed the guard of his sword into the man's face. The beard was immediately wet with blood from ruined lips and teeth, but the big man did not retreat. Stryker shot him in the knee, stepping back to let his victim crumple with an incongruously puppy-like keening. Skellen was with him as he snatched up his hat and strode through the doorway. He supposed the soldier was already dead.

'Bloody butcher,' the sergeant muttered as they reached a broad staircase, musket fire ringing louder above them now.

'Aye, a butcher and a soldier together,' Stryker said. 'If the common folk fight beside Rigby's men, we'll have no choice. The order was to spare none caught under arms.' The thought made his heart ache. If the townsfolk had decided to stand with the garrison, then they would die with them too.

They took the stairs three at a time. The upper landing was almost completely dark and the air was clogged with acrid powder smoke. They moved along the creaking floorboards, more carefully now, voices wafting to them from beyond the panelled wall to the right. If Stryker's bearings were not thrown by the chaos, then the chamber beyond would face on to the street. He jammed his spent pistol into his belt, tugging its twin free and cocking it in one movement.

'Fire!' a disembodied voice bawled, and the building seemed to vibrate with a fresh volley. Screams carried to them from down on the street.

They felt their way along the passage until they found a break in the panels. An iron ring, cold and rough, betrayed the siting of a door. They exchanged a glance, checking firearms as Stryker said, 'No matter what we find, they cannot hold the high ground.'

Skellen nodded, grunting something grim below his breath, and lined his redoubtable boot up with the door's lock. A swarm of floating embers made him stop. At the far end of the corridor there was another staircase, and emerging at the top were at least a score of tiny, dancing flames. Skellen turned, Stryker too, and they stared as faces materialized from the gloom. The lights were the tips of burning matches, fixed and poised in muskets. The faces were those of soldiers. They hesitated when they saw the two men.

Stryker took a risk. 'King's men.'

The lead musketeer, a burly sergeant with a single, jutting tooth, quickly took in Stryker's red ribbon and expensive sword. He nodded curtly. 'Broughton's, sir.'

'To me, then, and be smart about it.'

They met outside the door. Stryker and Skellen stepped aside as the sergeant barked orders and several musket stocks turned the polished panels to kindling. And then they were inside.

More smoke greeted them. It was the swirling, choking cloud produced by many muskets discharged in an enclosed space. He pushed through the gritty pall, squinting hard through his stinging eye. A flash of a torso ghosted across his path. He fired his piece without thinking. It was blinding in the chamber, deafening. The men of Broughton's regiment poured their leaden fury into the bank of yellowish white, shrieks renting the stifling air in reply. A window smashed as someone tumbled through to the ground below. Stryker plunged into the miasma, lashed with the handle of his pistol at a man's chin, and stabbed deep into the belly of another with his sword. Figures moved on all sides, some wearing Colonel Broughton's ochre coat, others garments of black, brown, green, and he feared that these were not the fighters enlisted by Alexander Rigby, but were clubmen, or worse. Now the shots ebbed, for there was no time to reload, and the sickening thuds of musket butts against flesh and bone began to play out.

Another crescendo announced the obliteration of a second window, and this time the damp spatter of rain came in on the breeze. Out went the noxious mist, sucked into the ether in so sudden a gust that the Royalists found themselves in con-founded silence for a long moment. All around them there were bodies. One of their own was down, curled like a giant foetus as blood oozed from his cudgelled skull, but the rest were unscathed. Of the Roundheads there was only debris. Lead-pocked and battered bodies, scattered like old sacks all around what Stryker now saw was a floor rich in exotic pelts, now ruined by unspeakable stains and the black scorches of dropped match. He wiped his blade on a discarded hat and returned it to its scabbard, stepping over a corpse to come up against the sill of one of the shattered windows. He looked down at the road. It was almost empty. He leaned a short way forwards, craning out so that he could peer right the way down towards the church. Bolton's defenders still resisted, to judge by the gunfire that crackled from thereabouts, but they were hemmed in now, trapped in a single enclave of a town con-quered. Screams seemed to come from every house and street, and Stryker pushed back into the room, knowing that the real vengeance had begun.

People were pleading away to his blind left side, whimpering like scolded pups, and he turned to find the source. There were half a dozen prisoners, all kneeling, faces dipped, palms raised beneath the points of looming swords. He started towards them, made to speak, but the first blade killed the words on his lips as swiftly as it killed its victim. He heard himself protest as the rest of the captives were slaughtered where they knelt, but no one else heard him.

The toothless sergeant had given the order. He perceived Stryker with a surprised expression. 'Any found under arms, sir.'

And that was right. Stryker looked around the room, dumb-struck, as the stench of smoke was gradually replaced by the metallic hint of the shambles. None of the dead were Rigby's, he realized. Not one. 'Jesu,' he said quietly, as Broughton's mus-keteers filed briskly out.

★　　★　　★

'They spare none,' Skellen said.

They were walking up Churchgate, a road that in happier times played host to Bolton's vibrant market but which was now turned to a ruin of destruction and human misery. Shots still echoed in the houses, on rooftops and around the church, where the last rebels were determined to make a stand, but the battle was won. Already, Stryker expected, the unfortunate officer from Tyldesley's regiment had been cut from his noose, never to know the import of his death, and already the tide of retribution had turned the Puritan town into a vision of the hell their preachers so delighted in describing. There were bodies strewn all about, doors put through, belongings thrown from windows to be ransacked by crowing Cavaliers in the persistent drizzle that saturated but never cooled the skin.

'Any who fight are forfeit,' Stryker said as he reloaded his pistols. If anything, a town was more dangerous after its storming, for the sack made a man shift for himself and his plunder.

Skellen sniffed. 'You know that won't be true, sir.' Stryker looked up, and the sergeant swallowed hard. 'Forgive me, sir.'

'No matter.' In truth, Stryker agreed. Among the corpses littering the cobbles were women, and he had glimpsed the silver hair of the elderly amongst the dead. Perhaps they had been the folk flinging tiles from the roofs. He quickened his pace. 'We have our orders. They should not have denied the Prince.'

'They should not have hanged that fuckin' officer, sir,' Skellen said bitterly. 'Beg pardon. That's the cause. Now they'll pay dear.'

'The town is our prize. It has ever been thus. They do not slay the innocent in England.' Stryker had seen such things many times. If a besieged town or city refused to surrender, the possessions of its inhabitants would be forfeit when finally an assault broke through. It was an unwritten understanding that besieging armies, often forced to dwell behind filthy, disease-ravaged siege-lines for weeks, were due more than their pay after surviving the murderous gauntlet of an escalade. The reward for those privations lay in plunder and, in turn, served as a warning to the next place thinking to trust in its defences. In the conflict engulfing the Low Countries, that plunder had been tainted by wholesale massacres conducted in revenge. But such hatred had been engendered by reason of religion, which had meant, mercifully, that the darkest acts of a city storming had not been visited upon this new civil war.

'Until now,' the sergeant grunted.

Stryker stopped in his tracks, following Skellen's gaze. Slumped in the doorway of a smouldering shop was a woman in a torn dress, her auburn hair flowing free where her coif had been ripped away. Her face was black with soot, tears carving pale gullies down her cheeks. Cradled in her arms was a small girl, hanging limp and lifeless, blue eyes staring sightlessly at the grey sky. The two men exchanged a long, silent glance. Eventually Stryker stepped close to his old friend, deliberately crowding him. 'Have a care, Will. Do not be rash.'

Skellen was a hard man; a man raised in the dockside tenements and taverns around Gosport, where sailors, pirates and smugglers converged and schemed and whored and killed. But his real education, like that of his one-eyed officer, had been gained on the Continent, fighting in the cruel fields of Germany. Those formative years had inured him to so much and yet left in him a residue of deep pain, a cavernous rage, plumbed so infrequently it was easy to forget. Now, though, it was there, brightening the black core of his pupils like a distant torch. 'Rash, sir? Is it not a time for rashness?'

Skellen was gripping his sword, and Stryker noticed that his gnarled knuckles were bleached white.

'You are right,' Stryker admitted. 'It's as you said. This is different than before.' He glanced back at the dead girl. 'Greed does not drive them, but hatred.' Skellen's face tightened, and Stryker placed a hand on the taller man's elbow. 'But you will be the one to regret the day, should you meddle.'

Skellen's cheek quivered. 'Meddle?' He pointed at the girl and her weeping mother. 'This is slaughter, sir, plain and simple.'

'Search the dead,' Stryker said. 'Take what you will, and do not be foolish.'

'And you, sir?'

'I will find our billets.' Stryker moved away. 'Do not be foolish, Sergeant, or you will answer to me.'

Skellen nodded. 'Aye, Major.'

Stryker spent the next hour seeking the quartermaster to James Stanley, the Earl of Derby. The earl was the leading Royalist in the county, and, as host to Prince Rupert's army, it was his dubious honour to arrange quarters for the victorious troops. Of course, most would not require a place to sleep for hours, even days, so distracted would they be with the search for plunder, but Stryker had no yearning to immerse himself in the indiscriminate savagery. Both he and Skellen would be better off away from it.

When finally he discovered the quartermaster, he was directed to The Swan, a tavern on the corner of Churchgate and Bradshawgate, near the market cross, where most of the prince's staff were being placed. It was a strange thing indeed, to be classed as a staff officer after so long as a leader of men, but fate and a storm-carved sea had conspired to twist his fortunes during the bitter winter months. He had survived hardship and danger, impressed the grandees of the Royalist cause, gained the rank of sergeant-major, but lost his command. Now he and his group of mercenaries, the last of his company, were little more than Prince Rupert's hired swash-and-buckler men, fighters who drew steel on the whim of their Bohemian lord. Stryker had never felt more incongruous in a world to which he was otherwise so well suited.

He paced westwards along Churchgate, loosening his grip on neither pistol nor sword. There were fewer horsemen now, and he guessed they had left the town to their counterparts on foot, carrying the hunt for Bolton's fugitives into the surrounding fields and forests. The dead would be discovered in streams, under bridges and on the moors for weeks to come. There were bodies strewn here and there. Some were barely recognizable, mangled by hooves; the blood from their slash wounds seemed to have dyed every single cobble. There were women wandering listlessly in the street, stripped to their smocks and prodded at sword point by braying men who demanded plate and coin. The screams of children were smothered only by the sharp cracks of firearms. Stryker stepped round a party of grinning greencoats, presumably men from Tillier's regiment, as they dragged a hapless individual out through a doorway. He was a stick-thin, bookish-looking fellow, with red-tipped nose and thinning pate, who yowled as he was kicked to the ground. The greencoats stood around him like baying wolves as he hurriedly blurted out where valuables might be found. Whatever he said did not save his life.

Stryker was relieved when eventually his gaze fell upon The Swan; a large, slate-roofed affair of black timber and grubby whitewash. It had survived the fighting, and now enjoyed a heavy guard at its double-doored entrance. He was just about to make himself known to the sentries when his eye was drawn to a band of soldiers crowded around a young lad slumped in a pile of horse shit that still steamed. The boy, probably in his late teens, clutched his midriff, and Stryker, moving closer, realized that he was fighting a losing battle to keep his guts within his body. The boy was weeping as he groaned, calling for his mother, each cry eliciting a gust of laughter from the watching mob. One of the soldiers, a tall, thin-faced man with a prominent brow, a hunched back and severely hooked nose, stepped into the circle. From within the folds of a heavy, black-pelted cloak, he produced a pistol, which he discharged directly into the wounded boy's heart. The gut-sliced lad fell back, sighing up at the rain, but still his chest rose and fell in shallow pulses.

The shooter – an officer to judge by his fur cloak – turned like an actor playing to his adoring audience. 'Bless me, comrades! Yonder lies one of the strongest Roundheads that ever I did meet, for my pistol hath discharged at his heart and would not enter!' He paused, relishing the cat-calls of his men, before producing a second pistol. Spinning back with an acrobatic whirl that belied his crooked shoulders, he shot his victim again, bowing as the men cheered. 'But I think I sent him to the devil, with a vengeance, with the other.'

The boy was indeed dead. Stryker looked on as the fur-trimmed hunchback led a dozen of his crowing adherents into the home from which the disembowelled boy had been hauled.

—⁓—

The acid tang of vomit was ripe on Faith Helly's tongue. She swallowed it, stifling the urge to retch as it burned her throat. She feared she was suffocating. It was cool inside the clay dome, for the oven had lain dormant for the better part of two days, but the ash dust upon which she was curled had stirred into furious life when first Faith crawled inside, elbows and head disturbing more black plumes from the walls, and now it seemed there was no air left to breathe, her lungs becoming ever more clogged with each shallow gulp. She clamped her mouth as tightly shut as she could, leaving only the tiniest fissure between her lips through which she drew the foul vapour, feeling it rasp between gritted teeth. Her back ached and the joints in her hands were stretched to breaking point as she pulled her knees hard to her chest. She squinted in the darkness as her sight grew accustomed to the gloom, and angled her head so that she could see out through the mouth of the oven to the kitchen beyond. The larder on the far side of the room was firmly shut, and she stared hard at its doors, praying Master Sydall could sense her presence and feel shame in it.

She held her breath as laughter rang out from somewhere in the house. A man's voice chimed, recounting a ribald jest that had others guffawing and Faith aghast. She knew the words, but had never been in the company of men who used them with such flagrant contempt for decency. Soldiers. Her stomach churned, and she squeezed her thighs tight lest she soil herself for fear.

The men entered the chamber casually, as if their day's work was done, and even from Faith's poor vantage she could see their stained clothes and darkly spattered faces. It was all she could do to bury the scream that formed like a knot behind her ribs. They were laughing still, the soldiers. Perching on tables and ransacking cupboards, upending pots and rummaging through shelves, a flock of blood-drenched magpies seeking baubles for their greed. One man, a thick, russet moustache draping his upper lip and a horrific-looking three-bladed pole propped on his shoulder, found the cheese cratch and began stuffing tough scraps into his mouth. The others harangued him, wanting their share, but he snarled like a dog and the pack shrank gingerly away. In turn, the man with the pole-arm offered a deferential bow as another sidled in.

This newcomer, evidently the leader, was tall but strangely formed. His small head sat atop shoulders that seemed to be excessively round and slung in an unnaturally low position, as if his neck were too long. It put her in mind of a gigantic bird, his cloak – black as night and thickened at the collar by a luxurious black pelt – forming a strange plumage, the sharp features of his face and tiny jet pebbles of his eyes only adding to the avian appearance. Her father had often warned her of the dangers of witchcraft, that though its creeping, insidious talons dug un-noticed into every facet of society, every so often the minions of Lucifer became too strong to conceal their true nature and would crawl into the light for righteous men to see. It took the wisdom and guile of witch-hunters to weed out such men, drawing them to the light as a physic draws poison from an adder's bite, but her father had maintained that, on occasion, a creature of wickedness would walk in plain sight, too cruel and perverted to disguise. She shuddered as she watched him enter the room, dark eyes never resting, as if he weighed and measured the contents of each and every cupboard, somehow able to pen-etrate even the stoutest door. When eventually his gaze rested upon the shadowed corner where she knew Master Sydall and his family were huddled, it felt as though her heart would burst through her chest like a cannon shot.

'Valuables,' the bird-man said softly. He waited for a reply, but none came. 'Come hither, kind sir, and be Christ-like in your generosity.'

That provoked a response, as Faith knew it would. Master

Sydall, tall and broad like a great oak, rose from the dingy corner. 'You blaspheme, sir.'

The bird-man grinned. His teeth were huge, too large for his narrow mouth, and sharp, like fangs. 'There you are.' He whistled as he looked up at the man dressed in the simple breeches and doublet favoured by Bolton's strong Puritan community. 'Geneva of the North, they call this place. Cannot fathom why.'

Sydall was the larger of the two, and he stepped half a pace forwards as his wife, three daughters and one son edged out behind him. Faith did not like the man, but she could not help but admire his bravery. 'There are no riches here, sir. We are reformers. We detest wealth.'

The bird-man tutted, as if admonishing a child. 'Banbury-men detest greed, my friend, not wealth.' He tapped his boot heel on the floor. 'Glazed tiles. Very nice. Dutch? Flemish? It is not piety that pays for such things.'

'Never see a poor Puritan,' one of the other soldiers growled.

'Amen to that,' the bird-man chimed, his voice unsettlingly pleasant, made musical with the burr of the West Country. 'Where do you keep your plate, your coin?'

Sydall bristled. 'I command you to leave!' The old steel had returned to his tone. Faith hated that steel, that judgemental rhetoric that so often accompanied meals in this soulless home, and yet now she took solace in it, prayed the three girls clustered about their mother like a trio of chicks would feel the same. Young John, the family's beloved second son, moved to stand by his father. He was fifteen, the same age as Faith, and she felt a swell of pride.

Master Sydall's eyes drifted past the soldiers to the open doorway. 'Leave, you villains! My older son will soon be home, and—'

The bird-man's dark brow jerked upwards at that. 'Son? I killed a man outside, only moments ago. You must have heard the shots. A tough fellow, granted.' He glanced at the moustachioed subordinate. 'Did I not say so, Sergeant Janik?'

The sergeant grunted something in a foreign tongue.

The bird-man nodded happily. 'There, you see? Tough indeed. Took two bullets. Impressive, given his preoccupation with keeping his entrails off the road. Was it not?'

The sergeant nodded again.

Master Sydall buckled. He did not fall, but the great oak swayed as though hit by a hurricane. Behind him Mistress Sydall went to her knees and the girls, those poor girls, wailed for their brother. They were only young, eleven and thirteen and fourteen. Faith felt the tears dash down her own cheeks.

'King Jesus, I beseech you!' Sydall brayed. 'Smite these invaders, in the name of—'

'A final chance, sirrah,' the bird-man interjected calmly. 'Your goods. Your silver plate, and your golden flagon.'

That stopped Sydall in his tracks. The big man's eyes widened, cleared, as if observing the intruders for the first time. 'I understand,' he whispered. 'You will not succeed, Devil.'

The bird-man shrugged.

It seemed to Faith as if the massacre took a long time, though it can only have taken minutes. Master Sydall – the dour, grey-bearded ranter with the stentorian tone and accusatory stare – wailed like a lost boy as the heavy-set sergeant with the wickedly bladed staff took a surprisingly nimble stride forwards and swept his grim weapon in a scything arc just above the ground, slicing right through one of Sydall's ankles and cleaving a ragged chunk in the other. The women screamed. Young John flushed white, deposited the contents of his last meal on his boots, and seemed almost not to notice the short-hafted axe as it dashed the side of his stooped head to smithereens. At least, Faith thought, he died quickly, for the fate to which the women would be subjected was as horrifying as it was inevitable. The men laughed as they were thrown to the ground. They used small knives to shred the outer garments, tossing them away like rags. Faith clamped her eyes shut after that. But she could not move her arms to cover her ears. The sound was atrocious. The screams and the grunts. It went on for so long, each man taking his turn, each taking his time. Master Sydall, the granite-hearted reformer who kept his emotion so utterly in check, writhed like a hamstrung calf and sobbed like a babe. And all the while the bird-man, the black-pelted hunchback with the tiny, restless eyes, watched the spectacle with blank disinterest. He could have stopped it, but he chose simply to sit on a table and gnaw at a hunk of seed-speckled bread.

All the while, Faith Helly prayed, as Master Sydall had prayed, and knew she had been ignored as he had been ignored. God had abandoned them; abandoned Bolton.

When lust had been sated, Mistress Sydall was put to the sword. Faith did not see which man slit her throat, but she heard the gurgle, like a brook crossing a pebble ford, and let her eyelids part only to see the colour drain from the woman's battered face. The three girls no longer made a sound, so broken were they. Three mannequins, waxy and inert, lying limp on the cold tiles, blood streaking their thighs, tears streaking their cheeks. They died too, swords pushed quickly and deeply into their slim necks, thrust so hard that the tiles beneath cracked. More blood pulsed as the blades jerked free, pooling around the feet of the soldiers as they fastened their breeches and arched back cracking spines.

'Where is the horde?'

It was the bird-man who spoke. He repeated the question, and Faith assumed he was addressing Master Sydall, but as she watched she realized that he, too, had been butchered. She wondered if there was someone else. Another of the family she had yet to see. Her eyes raked the bodies, counting them again and again, always coming up with the same answer. Then the bird-man stood, stepping carefully over the fresh corpses, and Faith thought she might expire then and there. For his eyes – those twitching black nuggets – had rested upon the oven. Upon her.

She held her breath so that her chest burned. He leaned forward, just a yard or two from the mouth of the clay dome, and peered into her hiding place. He smiled broadly, teeth big and bright. Now she saw why they were so sharp: they had been filed to points. To Faith it looked like they belonged in the mouth of a mastiff, neat rows of beautifully white daggers, made all the more luminous set between the sharply waxed moustache and tiny wedge of beard, both as black as his hair and clothes.

'Come out, pretty thing.' He winked. 'We shall not harm you.'

The soldiers sniggered at that. Faith pulled her body tight, shrinking back into the ash-stained cave, knowing all was lost. Then hands were groping at her, clawing at her clothes, at her hair, hauling her from the oven with irresistible strength. She bit one of the hands, a man bellowed in pain and anger, then the fingers returned, balled into a fist, and stunned her as they cracked against her nose. She smelt blood, her own this time, tasted it, and then she was out, plucked into daylight and bundled to the floor. Immediately the blood of the Sydall children was on her hands and knees, smearing her. She tried to stand but slipped in the slick flood, yelping as she hit the tiles again with a wet slap.

Stryker stepped into a charnel house. There was blood everywhere, gleaming red in the depressed grid between the glazed green floor tiles, spattered up chair legs, dashed on shelves as though some unseen vandal had flicked paintbrushes around the expensively equipped kitchen. He had followed the crowing group of soldiers by a twist of instinct, and now, as he gazed down at the shattered remains of a family, he knew that he had been both correct and foolish. They rounded on him immediately, brandishing a formidable array of weapons, and he could see they were not raw recruits, flushed with success and brimming with ale, but men who knew their business.

From amongst the tense party a man pushed through to regard Stryker. It was the officer he had seen before, the fur-trimmed killer. 'And you are?'

He chose not to inflame the situation, leaving his hand resting on the pommel of his sheathed sword. 'Stryker.'

The thin face twitched in recognition. 'I've heard of you. Captain?'

'Major.'

The darkly protruding brow rose in slight surprise. 'My compliments. I am Captain John Kendrick. They call me the Vulture.'

'I have not heard of you,' Stryker lied.

That hit a nerve, for the muscles in Kendrick's pale cheeks quivered. He tried to hide his annoyance by scratching his chin with a left hand that Stryker now saw was encased within a blackened gauntlet. There were gadlings set on each metal knuckle, spikes that could shatter a man's jaw as sure as any cudgel. 'Then perhaps you have heard of my brave hajduks?'

Stryker's eye was instinctively taken by one of Kendrick's men. He was a sergeant, to judge by his halberd, but he noticed the man – leering behind a bushy moustache – had a long, curved sabre hanging from his baldric. He had seen such weapons before, fought against the men who carried them. 'Hungarians?'

'Some. Some English, French too. My faithful hounds, blooded on the flesh of Turks and barbarians.'

'And now tasting English meat.'

Kendrick smiled, revealing teeth filed for effect to wicked points. 'Come now, Stryker, you understand the rules of war as well as I.'

Stryker regarded those fangs, those cold eyes, the casual ease with which Kendrick held court in the midst of such carnage. He had never personally encountered the Vulture, but the man who had enlisted with the king came with a reputation as frightening as it was impressive. He wondered how he might extricate himself from this slaughter house with his skin intact. 'You address me as sir.'

Kendrick cocked his head to the side, as if Stryker's bluster simply intrigued him. 'Sir.' He looked at the red-stained floor. 'The fools refused terms. We took their stinking streets, and this is our reward.'

'Murder?'

'Plunder.'

Stryker shook his head. 'We are not to kill innocents.'

Kendrick scoffed derisively. 'None here are innocent, Major Stryker, you know that as well as I. They prayed for our destruction as we mustered beyond their walls. Beseeched God for our deaths. Their crimes are as heinous as those of Rigby's soldiers. More so.'

To one side of the mob Stryker could see the pale face of a young girl whose sightless eyes were staring directly up at him. He could see, despite the blood, that her skirts were bunched high at her midriff. 'The children?'

'Their defeat here would only inspire them to greater mischief.' Kendrick sounded exasperated. He looked back through the legs of his men to catch sight of one of the bodies. 'Take the boy; he'd be wearing a tawny scarf by summer's end. Or Scotch blue.' He spat suddenly, the final words particularly sour. 'And what are Puritan girls good for but whelping more Puritans? Exterminate the species before they may breed, Major. 'Tis the kindest thing to do.'

It was then that Stryker heard the mewing. Soft, barely perceptible, as though a kitten were trapped in one of the room's shadowy nooks. He took a half-step to the side, peering past Kendrick. Movement caught his eye beyond the palisade of legs. It was a girl. Young, he reckoned, for her frame was skinny and fragile. She was filthy, her clothes smudged black and the bare forearms curled protectively about her coiffed head like twin seams of coal.

'Have a care, Stryker,' Kendrick muttered, his tone low and dark. His metal-clad left hand clenched slowly, the vicious gadlings glinting as the knuckles shifted beneath. 'She is mine.'

Stryker realized his fingers had snaked around the rough shark skin of his sword's grip. He hesitated, seeing only stupidity in anything but a rapid flight, and then the girl moved again. Groaned. She lifted her head, pushed the escaped fringe of copper hair from her eyes. He saw that she was indeed young. No more than sixteen. She looked directly at him through the booted obstacles, holding his gaze with a look that seemed to grasp his very soul. And then the sword was hissing, easing up from its scabbard so that six inches of gleaming steel were exposed to daylight.

'Draw it,' Kendrick warned, 'and you're a dead man.'

Stryker drew it. 'Try me.'

Kendrick's face turned from warning to disbelief. 'You would die for this bitch?'

'Someone will die, Captain Kendrick,' Stryker said, levelling the tip of the blade with the Vulture's sternum. 'Of that you may be certain.'

Kendrick's narrow lips parted as he regarded Stryker. His tongue flickered, serpent-like, between the gaps in his sculpted teeth as he considered whether one more murder was due this day. From his belt he tugged a broad, bone-handled knife that was at least the width of a man's hand. He turned it slowly, examining the blade. 'A cinquedea, Major. Took it from a Venetian after a particularly heated altercation. I gut people with it.'

The deafening noise drowned Kendrick's words. An entire troop of horse, by the sound of them, reined in outside the house. Whinnies and shouts, clattering hooves and jangling armour clamoured in the melee of sound heralding their arrival. Orders were barked as the horsemen tethered their mounts wherever they could find a suitable place, and laughter burst in sporadic bouts as men jeered prisoners and celebrated so crushing a victory. They did not seem intent on entering the Sydall home, milling outside simply to tend wounds and inspect ill-gotten goods, but their presence startled Kendrick and agitated his men. Regardless of the day's merciless directives and cruel deeds, none wished to be discovered in this place with so many butchered folk at their feet.

Kendrick seemed to consider the paths open to him; he then slipped the dagger back into its broad sheath. With a jerk of his head, he summoned his men, who filed past Stryker with grunted threats, making rapidly for the door. The Vulture went last, taking his time to glance back at the moaning girl. When he reached the doorway, he stopped short, looking back. 'I'll be seeing you, Major Stryker.'

# CHAPTER 3

*York, 29 May 1644*

'Impressive, Captain, is it not?'

Lancelot Forrester, second captain of Sir Edmund Mowbray's Regiment of Foot, stared out at the sea of humanity that lapped against the lead-pocked defences of York. The city, proud, ancient capital of England's north, resembled something like an island. 'I'd wager these stout walls have not been so threatened since the time of the Danelaw.'

The man beside him, a small fellow with a puffy face, smoothed down an errant strand of heavily oiled hair with a chubby finger. 'But you survived the night's enterprise.'

Forrester noticed the lack of congratulation in his companion's voice, and he smothered a wry smile, instead plucking off his wide-brimmed hat to pick at flecks of grime that he noticed – with not a little vexation – had soiled the already dishevelled feathers. 'The sally was indeed a close run thing, Master Killigrew,' he said, staring out at fields that seemed never to be still, so crawling with activity were their hedges and furrows. 'We lost two men, captured some shovels and half a dozen axes.'

They were standing on the imposing edifice of Walmgate Bar, one of four great entrances into the city. Forrester replaced his hat, leaning on the crenellated stonework that crowned one of two massive towers looming over the walled barbican below. It was a truly formidable bar, set into the south-east corner of the circuit of thick stone walls, and yet even here, in this place of immovable strength, he felt vulnerable, because the armies of the new alliance had converged to conspire in York's demise. He scanned the units that moved below them, cavalry on patrol, pike blocks at drill, musketeers escorting wagons of provisions from one village to the next. So far their efforts had been limited to hemming in the defenders as far as was possible, to patrolling the countryside, harrying the closest pockets of Royalist strength in the region, and setting up breastworks from which their marksmen could peck at the ramparts. In return, the king's men had launched several small-scale sorties to disrupt the encroaching Parliamentarian lines, and it was one such endeavour that had occupied Forrester for half the night.

'A commendable effort,' Killigrew said in a tone that suggested he was not remotely impressed. 'But two losses? We cannot afford such a toll.'

Forrester kept his eyes on the Parliamentarian lines lest his temper bring him trouble. 'The enemy are prone to shoot at us, sir.'

'You took no prisoners?'

Forrester shook his head. That was why Ezra Killigrew was here, of course. 'My apologies, sir, but there are none for your rack.'

Killigrew affected a look of horror. 'The rack? I would never resort to such base measures, Captain Forrester.' He placed a hand against his breast, the smell of lavender wafting out with the motion. 'You know me better than that.'

Forrester disguised a rueful smirk by fiddling with the strands of sandy-coloured hair that sprouted from his hat to play at his temples. 'A jest, Master Killigrew,' he lied. Ezra Killigrew was well capable of stretching a man's joints, or plucking out his fingernails, or branding his flesh, if that man had information worthy of the pain. For all his meek appearance, the man wielded disproportionate power within the Royalist high command, serving as personal confidante to the king's nephew, Prince Rupert of the Rhine, until his recent arrival at York to advise the Marquis of Newcastle. Forrester's heart had sunk when he had first clapped eyes on Killigrew in the city, a man whose every

39

gesture reminded him of a greasy rodent, for acquaintance with Ezra Killigrew tended to court nothing but danger.

A horse thundered into the barbican below, its rider braying his credentials as the guards moved aside. A deep groan of levers and chains reverberated up in the tower as the portcullis juddered to allow safe passage into the city.

Killigrew waited until the portcullis had been set back on earth, its sharp teeth deep in their fixtures, the heavy wooden doors swinging shut to seal York once more. 'It has been six weeks.'

'Feels longer,' Forrester said grimly. 'The enemy came hither in April, but I have been in York since deep winter.'

'Ah yes,' Killigrew said with a twitch of his sharp nose. 'You were with that fool Belasyse.'

Forrester nodded. The Parliamentarians were strong in Yorkshire, with their northern army, numbering five thousand, commanded by Ferdinando, Second Baron Fairfax, and his son, Sir Thomas. The governor of York, John Belasyse, had long been requesting reinforcements to bolster his garrison, and with the advent of the Scottish invasion, led by the veteran Earl of Leven, a detachment, including Mowbray's Foot, had marched north to his aid. But to the collective relief of the king's forces in the county, the Scots – despite the formidable size and experience of their army – had barely limped southwards, hampered by vile winter storms, swollen rivers and mired roads. By March they had reached only as far as Durham, where William Cavendish, the Marquis of Newcastle, held them at bay with his seasoned troops. It seemed the initiative had been wrested from the enemy by divine intervention, and Belasyse had been keen to put the Yorkshire Royalists back into the ascendancy. He heard news that the Fairfaxes were due to rendezvous at Selby, and marched out with a large part of York's garrison to intercept them. What followed had been nothing short of disaster. The hitherto ebullient Royalists were crushed, and Belasyse himself captured.

'Selby changed everything,' Killigrew said bitterly. 'With the York garrison so weakened, the marquis was forced to abandon

Durham and garrison this place, leaving the cursed Scotch to march unhindered through the north.' He placed his hands on the rampart, staring down. 'And here we are.'

'Aye, sir,' Forrester said. Mowbray's regiment had not been at Selby. Thus they had been part of the beleaguered garrison that had welcomed the marquis's northern army. It might have been the height of spring, but York was cold, and Forrester felt himself shiver. The besieging armies had spread out across the fields for miles around, like diseased flesh radiating from a festering wound. Most of the enemy units had been quartered in the villages surrounding the city, though clusters of tents sprouted at intervals like toadstools, the telltale sign that not all the huge force could be accommodated, while parties of pioneers could be seen working furiously to lay planks over boggy tracks or cut holes through the hedgerows by which the Roundhead brigades might move. What always struck him was the sheer scale of the enterprise. He had seen large sieges before, been present as the king had attempted to bring stubborn Gloucester to its knees, and played a part in the defence of Basing House the previous autumn when Sir William Waller had brought his huge army to its walls. But this was on an entirely different scale. York did not face one malevolent army, but two. When the marquis had fallen back on York, the Scots had given chase, joined with the Yorkshire Roundheads, and, during the third week of April, the combined armies brought more than twenty thousand men to the walls of York.

'And that, my dear captain,' Killigrew said, 'is why I should like to speak with any man captured by our brave sally parties. The situation is dire. The weeks drag by, and all the while our enemy digs in. If we discover their weaknesses, then we may expedite victory.'

A short distance along the wall an artillery piece belched into sudden life, its colossal report echoing for several seconds. Smoke slewed across the rampart, mingling with the lingering dawn mist, and Forrester drew a long breath, savouring the bitter odour. 'We have other strongholds, do we not? The castle at Pontefract? Sandal, Helmsley, Tickhill, Knaresborough.'

Killigrew sneered, exposing tiny teeth. 'Mere outposts. The countryside is lost. The balance of power lies with the devil's alliance.'

'The Committee for Both Kingdoms,' Forrester said. Consisting of fourteen members of the House of Commons, seven from the Lords and four representatives from Scotland, the Committee had been created in the wake of the Solemn League and Covenant, the agreement between Westminster and Edinburgh, providing Scots military might on condition that the Scottish system of church government was adopted in England. The Committee for Both Kingdoms was empowered to direct the coordinated rebel strategy, and it was that body which ultimately controlled Parliamentarian machinery in the north.

'And the devil's alliance has another weapon to discharge, do not forget.'

'Sir?'

'The Earl of Manchester looms large, I fear,' Killigrew said darkly.

'The Eastern Association,' said Forrester. 'How many?'

'Eight thousand,' Killigrew answered. 'Perhaps nine.'

'But the Oxford army keeps him in check, does it not?'

'I pray so.' Killigrew licked cracked lips and smoothed down his hair again. 'But our defeat in the south makes matters a touch more fluid.'

'And if the Eastern Association come hither?'

Killigrew grimaced. 'It bears not consideration. We are well supplied here, thanks to the foresight of Belasyse and the preparations Newcastle has put in place. But our saving grace is the enemy's failure to circumvallate the city. They have a large army, make no mistake, but it is not large enough to completely enclose us. If the alliance is reinforced, then they will cut York off from the world, and then, eventually, we will all starve.'

Forrester stared directly into Killigrew's hard eyes. 'The Eastern Association will come.' He received a mute nod for reply. 'Is there any hope?'

'There is one.'

'Rupert.'

'The marquis brought four thousand good men to the city,' Killigrew said, 'but he had three thousand horse too. They left, of course, for there is not the fodder within these walls for such luxury.' He spread his palms. 'Where did they go, Captain Forrester?'

'To Prince Rupert?' Forrester ventured.

'Perhaps, even now, he is on his way,' Killigrew said, brightening.

Forrester chuckled mirthlessly. 'And if he is not?'

'Then York will soon be lost.'

## Bolton-le-Moors, Lancashire, 29 May 1644

The place seethed. Buildings had been fired during the night and still their embers smouldered, thin fingers of black smoke poisoning the air and smudging the watery dawn. The foul odour of charred death clung to everything. Cries of the wounded and the forlorn replaced the birdsong. Women cradled sons, husbands held wives, children scurried like rats in search of lost parents and scarce food. Soldiers were everywhere, on the corners of every street, in houses gutted and robbed, in the taverns and in every alleyway wide enough to provide shelter. They emerged now into the dawn, red-eyed and parched after a night of blood-stained revelry, many clutching bundles of linen they had stripped from beds, or piles of stolen clothes. Others carried plate, cookware, cutlery, cloth, weaponry. Fights broke out as men realized their snapsacks had been emptied while they were in their cups, hordes lifted by slight hands and greedy hearts. They blamed one another, bawled and cursed and drew blades darkly congealed from the night before. Some officers called for calm. Most ignored their men, for they were as ale-sick as the rest. Accompanying everything were the sporadic reports of gunshots, which echoed about the streets as survivors were pulled from their hiding places like weeds from a flower-bed.

Out on the moors, pistols cracked as cavalry units hunted those who had made it out into the wilderness.

Stryker was perched on the edge of a low stool in the yard of The Swan tavern. The enclosure itself was a potholed square of rammed earth pooled with rainwater and filled with men. These were the leaders of the enemy, Rigby's officers and those senior townsfolk marked as the mandrel upon which Bolton's defence had spun. Colonel Rigby himself had escaped in the confusion, galloped off to safety as his men had died, but the Royalists had taken hundreds of prisoners and dozens of colours, and now Stryker had the dubious honour of guarding the cream of them. He eyed the sooty, streaked faces, checking for signs of furtive whispering or grim determination, but there was nothing. The men were utterly deflated, resigned to their fate, and cowed by the sentries that lined the yard's edge. Most sat, despite the wet ground, while a few stretched their legs, milling listlessly like so many ragged sleep-walkers, pleased, he supposed, that they had at least survived the night. He glanced up at the clouds that drifted high on the nagging breeze. He guessed the rain would stay away for a time, so he drew his twin pistols, laying one on his lap, and fished an old, dry rag from his coat.

As he began to scour the grime from the pistol's frizzen a dark shadow snaked across him. 'Did you fare well?' he said, without looking up.

Sergeant William Skellen issued a noncommittal grunt. 'Well enough, sir.'

Now Stryker turned. 'Oh?'

Skellen had retrieved his fearsome halberd from their baggage wagon, and he jammed its butt end into the ground so that he could lean against it. In his other hand he gripped a visibly bulging snapsack. He shook it so that its contents jangled. 'I shall not bemoan the lack of pay for a while.'

'Taken from the dead, I trust.'

'None alive shall miss its shine.' Skellen's shady eyes moved to the captives, examining each stricken face. 'Sorry parcel, ain't they?'

'Sorry but alive.'

Skellen nodded. 'Aye, not scoopin' their guts off the street like some o' those poor bastards. What's to become of them?'

Stryker shrugged, returning to his pistol. 'Exchange. The gaols are full. We shall see our own officers released in return. Many were taken at Cheriton Fight.'

'And the commons?'

'Locked in the church, to be chained and marched far away to some dank hole.'

'Transport the buggers?'

'Perhaps,' Stryker said. The order that would seal the captives' fate had not yet been issued, but those corralled in the church, the lower sort of folk worth nothing in an exchange and expensive to feed and guard, might well be banished from the realm altogether. Especially, Stryker thought, given Bolton's reputation for zealous Puritanism. These were not the kind of men who would turn their coats and enlist with the prince's growing army. It would not surprise him if Rupert sold them into indentured servitude, slavery in all but name, and packed them off to work on plantations in those fever-ravaged islands across the ocean. 'They cannot be left to grieve and conspire.'

'How are the dags, sir?'

Stryker lifted the pistol, turning it for Skellen to scrutinize. 'Not failed me yet.' The matched small-arms, carved with images of malevolent skulls, had been purchased using part of the reward they had earned at Newark. The relief of that stubbornly Cavalier town – locked down by a strong Roundhead army – had been a magnificent triumph for Prince Rupert, and a significant boon for morale, especially given the defeat suffered by the king's army in the south only days later.

Skellen had purchased a new halberd with his share of the prize, and he absently twisted the ash shaft so that the blade – consisting of an axe, a spike and a hook – glittered for the prisoners to see. It was a weapon as ceremonial as it was practical, the object that marked a man out as sergeant, but in the hands of an experienced halberdier like Skellen, the bladed staff could cut a swathe through the enemy as sure as any well-aimed cannon ball. 'That young lass, sir,' he said after a short time.

'Safe,' Stryker answered abruptly. He had been acutely aware of wagging tongues as he had carried the battered girl from the home that had become a place of such slaughter. He had behaved appropriately, of course. Delivered her to the womenfolk who followed the army and were streaming into Bolton as its defenders streamed out. But that did not mean curious onlookers saw anything more than a victorious Royalist officer dragging away a legitimately won prize, and the thought made him uncomfortable.

'Women'll take care of her, sir,' Skellen said. They had not discussed the incident with Kendrick in any depth, but he had coaxed the salient details out of his friend. 'You've played your part.' He sniffed awkwardly. 'Which is just as well.'

'Go on,' Stryker said. He stood, thrusting the pistol into his belt. 'Well?'

'It's Lieutenant Hood, sir.'

'Spit it out, man.'

Skellen winced. 'Simeon's found him.'

The sound of flies was thick on the air as they entered the storehouse. It was a decrepit, single-storeyed structure of wormed beams and patchy daub that leaned alarmingly to one side. The space within was strewn with debris, barrels and shelves ransacked, tipped asunder, kicked and torn and taken. There were blood spatters on the walls, made visible by the light streaming through windows without shutters, and half a dozen bodies – some stirring, some clearly deceased – strewn amongst the wreckage.

'Where is he?' Stryker said, fanning his face with his hat to waft away the pungent stink.

From the shadows a small figure emerged. 'Down there, sir.'

Stryker followed the pointing hand to where a prone body, curled into the foetal position, nestled under a table. 'Dead or drunk?'

The figure, a man, moved into the room. He was tiny. Not a dwarf, per se, for his limbs were proportionate to his body, but his stature was that of a child, so that his head, at full height, did not reach beyond Stryker's sternum. Yet one could never mistake him for anything but a man of forty years or more. His clothes and weapons were especially made to fit his form, but his bald head, weathered skin and crooked, half-rotten teeth spoke of his true maturity. His eyes were yellow – not merely a jaundiced hue, but a brightly blazing shade that gave him the stare of a hunting cat – and his hands were gnarled and calloused. 'You know the answer to that, sir,' he said. His voice, inflected by the accent of Scotland, was severely constricted, as if he suffered garrotting even as he spoke.

'Thank you, Master Barkworth.'

Simeon Barkworth offered a short bow. With a sharp glance at Skellen, he followed the sergeant from the storehouse.

Stryker noticed a pail of grubby water and fetched it up. It slopped as he steadied it, rusty liquid leaking over the side and dripping on his boots. 'A soldier who fails to return to colours when called, is clapped immediately in irons!'

The body under the table stirred, emitting a low groan.

'Any soldier,' Stryker repeated the article, stooping to clear the table top, 'who should fail to return to his colour when called, will be clapped, Mister Hood, in irons!' He swung the bucket on the final word so that the putrid concoction dashed the suddenly animated body in a stinking wave.

Lieutenant Thomas Hood rolled out from under his makeshift shelter, groping for a sword that had long since vanished from its flaccid scabbard. 'Jesu!' he spluttered viciously. 'S' precious blood, you bastardly gullion! I'll gouge your eyes out, sir, I'll—'

He cut himself short when finally he braved the light to look into his persecutor's face. Fury turned to horror.

'Eye,' Stryker said. 'Another knave has saved you half the task.'

Thomas Hood pitched on to his front and vomited. When he was done, chest heaving, he risked a glance up. 'Christ on His cross.' He spat and wiped a dangling tendril of greenish mucus from his chin with a heavily stained sleeve. 'Major, I—'

'You are in your cups, Lieutenant.'

Hood blinked rapidly, looked as though he would vomit again, but managed to hold himself together. His long hair was sopping from the untimely bath, and he was forced to peel the strands from his cheeks. 'Nay, sir, not in ... not *in*.' He struggled to his feet, swaying as he finally stood tall. His face, ordinarily so fresh and handsome, was haggard. His eyes were deep red, his lips caked white with dried spittle. 'Have been in them, I admit freely, but no longer. Sober as a monk, sir.'

Stryker dropped the pail, Hood recoiling at the clatter. 'You know my rule.'

Hood dabbed his wispy beard with a sleeve. 'I was not drinking during the escalade, sir, 'pon my honour I was not.' He took a step forwards, then two in retreat. 'P'rhaps a sip, then, but no more.'

'Better a sip to get a man over the wall than sobriety see him cower in the ditch,' Stryker conceded. 'But after, Tom. I saw you. As the town burned.' Indeed, he and Skellen had stumbled upon Hood in the smallest hours, or, rather, Hood had quite literally stumbled upon them. The sack was in full swing, terror unleashed with free rein and a prince's blessing, and Hood had been sighted staggering along Churchgate with his sword in one hand and a blackjack full of wine in the other.

Hood set his jaw defensively. 'The fight was over. It was won. Was it not my right to make merry with the spoils?'

'You have the right to toast a victory, Tom, not to slump in a gutter like a common wastrel. You are an officer.'

A flash of defiance lanced across Hood's damp features. 'You are the arbiter of my revelry now, sir?'

'I am your commanding officer, Mister Hood. Your god-damned chief!' Stryker advanced angrily. Hood skittered back until he collided with the table. 'You may imbibe what you like, Lieutenant, so long as you return to quarters at dawn. Look at you. Where is your dignity? Jesu, man, where is your sword?'

Hood's hand went to the empty scabbard and the defiance left him. 'Bastards,' he whispered, evidently recalling something of the night. He met Stryker's hard gaze. 'Where is my dignity, sir?' He shrugged. 'What dignity?'

'You are an officer of the King.'

Hood's chuckle was mirthless, embittered. 'With not a kitten to command.'

'That is beside the point.'

'It is precisely the point, sir,' Hood answered hotly, insolence rearing within him again.

'Mind your tongue, sirrah,' Stryker warned.

Hood held Stryker's eye for a second, then broke the trance with a pitiful sigh. He studied his boots for a short time, breathing heavily as he steadied his anger. When he looked up, his expression was wretched with contrition. 'My apologies, sir. Sincerely.'

Stryker relented. He was angry at Hood, for the young officer was a good man, a competent leader, but his penchant for drink was beginning to be noticed in higher circles, something that would harm his chances of advancement. Hood was right, he had conducted himself no differently to the majority of Royalist officers in the wake of Bolton's fall, but Stryker would be damned before he saw the young man throw his prospects away for the sake of a fine claret. And yet, deep down, he knew that his interference only seemed to breed resentment. He made to turn. 'Clean yourself up. Meet me at The Swan.'

'Sir,' Hood said, though his watery stare had flickered to the open door.

Stryker caught the gesture and hooked the door with his foot, toeing it closed. Behind it, nestled against the wall, was a substantial flagon. He could see dark liquid just below the brim. Stryker looked back, saw the longing in Hood's eyes, noticed how the lieutenant's hands trembled.

The door swung open, concealing the flagon. 'Major Stryker? Is he present?'

Stryker and Hood both turned to the doorway. Under the rotten lintel, wreathed in sunlight, stood a tall, finely dressed man. He wore the caged helmet and russet breastplate of a har-quebusier, with lace at his falling band collar, a silver gorget at his throat, and a blue coat that was threaded in silver all the way down the sleeves.

Stryker squinted, but the light at the man's back turned his features almost black by contrast. 'He is, sir.'

'Ah, good,' the newcomer said, his voice loud and well edu-cated. 'Get him out here, would you? I have no wish to speak within these walls, for it smells like a latrine.'

'One of my lads claimed he'd seen you in there,' the dismounted cavalryman said as Stryker and Hood joined him outside. He breathed deeply and theatrically, and unfastened his helm, letting shoulder-length tousles of richly golden hair cascade around the leather straps running between back- and breast-plate. He tossed it to one of the troopers who ringed the group like iron sentinels, and smoothed his thin moustache between gloved thumb and forefinger. 'Seemed unlikely, but here you are.' His grin was permanent, etched by a sword slash that had left cleaved his mouth and healed in puckered lines so that his lips, forever upturned, appeared to stretch into his cheeks. But his smile was genuine in its warmth. 'Well met, Sergeant-Major. Ha! Major. A pleasure to name you by your new rank, sir.'

'Thank you, Sir Richard,' Stryker said, returning the smile. 'I am not entirely accustomed to it myself, truth told.'

Sir Richard laughed at that. 'And how does life treat you in your new role?'

In truth, life was decidedly more dangerous. Everything had changed. He was still a soldier, still bled for the cause of the king, and yet so much now was alien to him. The sea had changed all that. It had taken a ship called the *Kestrel*, tossed it and smashed it and turned it to a tangled wreck of floating rigging and splin-tered spars. On that ship had been Stryker and his company, sailing for the Isles of Scilly and a cache of gold, and they had been sucked into the icy depths with the stricken vessel. A handful – Stryker and Skellen among them – had been thrown up on a hostile shore, and though they had faced yet more tribulation before their mission was complete, they had been the fortunate ones. Stryker's Company of Foot had been shattered, and the remnants – both the wreck's survivors and those remaining in quarters with the Oxford Army – no longer amounted to a unit worth salvaging. They had been scattered, dispersed amongst the rest of Sir Edmund Mowbray's regiment, leaving the officers with nowhere to belong. The common term was *reformado*, an officer without a command, and that was the status under which Stryker and Lieutenant Hood had found themselves operating. The king's nephew – and his majesty's greatest warrior – had long meddled in Stryker's affairs, often dispatching him on clandestine duties in the face of Sir Edmund's understandable chagrin. Now Stryker had no colonel to tie him down. He was the prince's creature; his personal attack-dog, intelligencer and assassin.

Stryker looked directly into the blue eyes of Rupert's close friend. 'It treats me well, Sir Richard.'

'You'll have your own regiment next. Lieutenant-colonel follows major, as night follows day, and then full colonel.' He broke into a rueful chuckle. 'Particularly when one considers the rate at which our senior officers seem presently to expire.' Crane wrinkled his slightly crooked nose as he regarded the dishevelled form of Thomas Hood. 'You look abysmal, son.'

'It was a sleepless night, sir,' Hood muttered.

'That it was,' Sir Richard barked happily, twisting back to observe the troopers that still clattered into the area in his wake. A large pearl earring winked from behind his golden tresses. 'My brave boys have been a-hunting. The moors are infested with Roundheads. Still, we have cleared the way, have no doubt.'

Stryker had no doubt at all, because Colonel Sir Richard Crane was a killer. One of the king's true veterans, Crane was the younger son of minor nobility, destined for a life denied inherited wealth. Like so many of his kind, he had seen only two avenues left open: a career in the clergy, or a career at war. Having chosen the latter, Crane had seen service with the

Protestant armies on the Continent, returning when the Royal standard had been hoisted at Nottingham almost two years before. Since then his post as the commanding officer of a troop of horse had taken him across the country. Like Stryker, he had witnessed the opening salvos of England's tribulation at Kineton Field, and had been embroiled in the storming of both Cirencester and Bristol. But Stryker knew he had done so much more. Crane would have been at Chalgrove and Bristol, Newbury and Market Drayton and Chinnor and countless other fights. He was a man forged in the furnace of this civil war, because Crane's was no ordinary command.

Stryker stared up at the horsemen that packed the road. They were mud-spattered, their mounts' fetlocks wet and ingrained with grime, but their bearing, to a man, betrayed nothing of the hard riding to which they had been subjected. They wore scarves of ruby red at their waists, and every trooper's hair flowed long, framing lean, hard faces and restless eyes. These, Stryker knew, were the elite: Prince Rupert's Lifeguard, a troop of a hundred and fifty riders, gentlemen all, forming the razor edge to his Regiment of Horse. Sir Richard Crane had the honour of their command, and he revelled in it.

'Sergeant Skellen!' Crane bellowed, touching a finger to his temple in acknowledgement. 'You survived, I see.'

''Course, Colonel, sir.' Skellen, who had been waiting out-side the door with Barkworth, sidled forth and bowed low.

Crane beamed. 'If the world were to burn tomorrow, I do declare this man would come through the conflagration with nought but a singe.' He looked back to address his watchful horsemen. 'These men are to be afforded all respect, you rogues. They may appear to be a party of vagabonds, but they serve upon good Prince Robert's business, and they enjoy his protection.' He met Stryker's gaze again. 'I've not seen you since Newark, Major. What a day that was! His Highness would not have out-foxed Meldrum without you. Verily sings your praises!'

Stryker felt heat pulse at his cheeks and he stared hard at the ground. 'Kind of you to say, sir.' It was true that he had played his part in that unlikely victory, but the praise embarrassed him nonetheless. 'I did my duty.'

'You'd have been well employed at Cheriton, I suspect,' Crane went on, his tone turning sour. 'What a dungheap of a campaign that turned out to be.'

'I was at Cheriton.'

Crane's pale brow climbed to crinkle his high forehead. 'As bad as they say?'

Stryker thought of that race southwards through a newly secured Nottinghamshire still basking in the stunning reverse over Sir John Meldrum's superior force. He had been charged with delivering a message to Sir Ralph Hopton, commander of the king's army in southern England. Hopton was advancing rapidly, pushing through Hampshire with the objective of punching rebel London in her less fortified underbelly. But the man opposing him – his dearest friend and most dangerous rival – had marched to block that confident advance. Among the rolling fields east of Winchester, at a sleepy backwater called Cheriton, Sir William Waller, with his newly formed Southern Association Army, inflicted a resounding defeat upon Hopton. Stryker had been caught up in the fight, retreating with the battered Royalist force to Basing House, and had returned north almost immediately to deliver Hopton's doleful report to a prince incandescent with rage.

He met Crane's eye and nodded.

Crane pushed no further, absently twisting the pearl that hung from his left ear. 'That battle has ended the king's ambition to take the capital. Hopton's army is dashed to pieces, and Winchester has fallen to that dog, Waller.' He blew out his cheeks. 'A catastrophe indeed. The ghastly rebel news-books make merry with the fact. The Roundheads have their first decisive victory against us. Their tails are up. There is no turning back now.'

'The path has long been too narrow for this horse to turn,' Stryker said. 'All hope for peace was lost when the Scots crossed the Tweed. The Committee for Both Kingdoms will prosecute war. That is their mandate.'

'You are right, of course,' Sir Richard said. 'Thus we are squeezed to breaking. Waller in the south, the Scots and Fairfaxes in the north. Hopton will regroup, re-engage.'

'Leaving His Highness to deal with the northern threat.'

Crane's head bobbed. 'He marches imminently. Soon as he can rouse our brave drunkards from their cups.'

Stryker forced himself not to look at Hood. 'To where will he march, sir?'

'Bury, Stryker. A town just east of here, you know it?' The shake of Stryker's head did not appear to bother him. 'George Goring is en route. The Prince plans to muster there.'

'General Goring? He has the Northern Horse, does he not?'

'Indeed. Five thousand of Newcastle's very best cavalry. The only part not presently hemmed inside York's embattled walls.'

'Our army swells, Colonel,' said Stryker, his mind working through the numbers as he spoke. Rupert had eight thousand men with him. Goring's division would be a formidable addition.

'That it does,' Crane agreed. 'Lancashire will be subdued before long. We intend to take Liverpool. The port will be the ideal route by which our troops might return from Ireland. Then on to Yorkshire, where the villainous Covenanters await.'

'Forgive me, Sir Richard, but is that why you sought me?'

'Indeed!' Crane bellowed. 'Your task, Major. You will know that Lady Derby lately held Lathom House in her husband's name against Rigby's vile rebel horde.'

Stryker did. The Earl of Derby was the leading Royalist in Lancashire, but he had been away fighting when his house at Lathom had fallen under siege by Rigby's forces. The Parliamentarians had pressed it since January, its defenders led by the stoic Countess of Derby. Rupert's arrival in the region had not only conquered Bolton, but lifted the siege.

'Lord Derby would make his heroic wife a gift,' Crane explained. 'We have captured twenty-two Roundhead colours. Many of them, just three days ago, were proudly flourished before her house. They are to be thrust at Lady Derby's feet, so that she may trample them and know that God is truly with us. I am charged with the delivery of said colours, Major. Additionally, there will be a convoy of munitions in the rear, for the bolstering of Lathom's future defence, pray God it is never required.'

'And I, Sir Richard?' Stryker prompted.

'The high roads are not safe in their entirety. Not yet. Thus I require a sturdy fellow to oversee my munitions. I hear tell you are currently employed as Lord High Gaoler of Bolton. True?'

Stryker laughed. 'True.'

'You enjoy the duty?'

'Nay, sir, I do not.'

'Good. Then you, Major Stryker, will command my convoy.'

# CHAPTER 4

*Lathom House, Lancashire, 29–31 May 1644*

The candlelight was enchanting. It danced along the walls, casting tremulous shadows across the tapestries so that the colourful depictions of saints and sinners, monsters and heroes, seemed charged by magic to play out their scenes for the assembled throng. And a welcome throng it was, declared Charlotte Stanley, Countess of Derby, from her high seat at one of the great hall's soaring gable ends. Before her – beneath her – the audience tittered and clapped as she accepted their praise, one bejewelled hand twinkling as it waved, the other cradling a large goblet of spiced claret sent with the compliments of Prince Rupert of the Rhine. But it was her husband's gift that took centre stage. From her dais, the countess peered over a snub nose to regard the standards of Alexander Rigby's routed regiment, arrayed in two great columns at either side of the room, each held by a stiff-backed ensign. There were so many of the huge taffeta squares that her guests, Lathom House's most senior inhabitants, joined this night by Sir Richard Crane and the Lifeguard of Horse, were almost draped in the colours of Parliament.

Stryker, standing at the very rear of the richly upholstered crowd, allowed himself a wry smile as a servant filled his proffered goblet. The man, dressed in the Earl of Derby's livery, had been reluctant to approach, and now, as the last drips rippled the surface of the wine, he shied quickly away to meld into the rows of bodies.

'You frightened him, sir,' Thomas Hood, standing at Stryker's right hand, said in a low voice.

'I have that effect on folk.' He lifted the cup, gulping back the claret.

Another liveried servant appeared and handed Hood a goblet. He took it, looking furtively at Stryker as it was filled, then sipped with deliberate slowness. 'Lady Derby basks, rather.'

Stryker ignored the wine in his lieutenant's hand. 'She has earned it. The house has been under close siege for most of the year. She held it with honour. Fortified it well to resist bombardment.'

Both men raised their goblets as one of the officers at the front proposed what might have been the tenth toast of the evening.

'I thank you, sir, for your gracious words,' the countess said. She was probably in her mid forties, Stryker guessed. Plump and pale, with dark, determined eyes and black hair that was styled with ringlets in a pastiche of the queen. Indeed, she reminded Stryker a great deal of Her Majesty, Henrietta Maria, for the women both spoke with the exotic tones of France. 'Now I must make mention of Monsieur Tipper,' purred Charlotte Stanley, who had been born Charlotte de La Trémoille. 'You will know that my success is due, in no small part, to the militia of expert marksmen who garrison my home. Tipper is chief of them.' She raised her cup, nodding to a spot within the crowd where Tipper evidently stood. The audience drank and cheered.

'Does she not put you in mind of Madame Lisette, sir?' Hood said, tilting back his head to take a long draught.

Stryker did not drink this time, but left the rim of his goblet to brush at his bottom lip. He had tried to put Lisette squarely from his mind. Now, as the rich Gallic voice wafted around the rafters, mingling with the heady fug of woodsmoke, beeswax and lavender, the final word of the incantation had been articulated: her name. All at once she was there, hair like spun gold, eyes like flaming sapphires, her image crowding his mind's eye, unwilling to let him see anything else. There was nothing left but the memory. He blinked hard, grinding his lone eyelid down in a vain attempt to eradicate her. The servant drifted by, and Stryker thrust the vessel into the startled man's hand, pushing his way out of the hall.

Outside, the dying light and melding clouds had turned the world a uniform grey. There were small fires around the courtyard, but this time they had been lit for the warmth of sentries rather than the cooking flames of an entrenched garrison. Lathom House was more castle than manor, with a thick stone wall punctuated by eighteen imposing towers that provided plenty of billets for all the men. Stryker's group were quartered in a modest guardroom close to the armoury, where their trio of heavily laden wagons had been placed for the night. He made his way there, leaving Hood to doubtless sink well into his cups before the night was over.

A pair of musketeers watched him approach the armoury from up high on the rampart, and he plucked off his hat to acknowledge them. Even in the gathering gloom, they evidently recognised him, for both let him pass unchallenged through the archway below their feet. On the far side of the arch was a smaller yard serving the armoury rooms. His three carts were here, their stoic palfreys tethered to rings set into the stonework nearby. At dawn the vehicles would be unloaded, the powder barrels stored in the stout subterranean chamber serving as Lathom's magazine, while the firearms, musket-balls and coils of match would be carefully stacked in the armoury's cavernous rooms. It was much darker here, for the presence of black powder, despite the heavy, damp sheet that covered the cargo, made torches far too hazardous, and he had to speak softly to soothe the animals who scraped their hooves in agitation at his approach. His own mount, Vos, nuzzled into his touch. He was a powerful thing, a Dutch warhorse, trained to snap and kick at enemies and to ignore the thunder of cannon. He had been in battle many times, been shot at and stabbed, been captured at Newbury the previous March and liberated by Prince Rupert's genius. Yet even he, Stryker reflected fondly, needed reassurance on occasion.

'Evenin', sir,' Will Skellen's voice broke the quiet.

Stryker stared into the near impenetrable murk. After several moments, he caught the ghostly outline of a tall figure, slim and bald-headed. 'Sergeant.'

Skellen sidled out into the yard, his boots crunching on gravel. He wore nothing above the waist, revealing a bony frame that belied his immense strength. Stryker considered his sergeant as akin to a weathered tree, bowed and knotted and gnarled, but possessed of roots and boughs of seasoned toughness. 'Would you tell Jack Sprat, sir, that we're bound for the north?'

A second figure appeared from the doorway, as Stryker knew it would. He looked at Simeon Barkworth, childlike next to the gigantic Skellen. 'The north it is, Master Barkworth.'

'The north, aye,' Barkworth croaked, 'but to what end?' He thumbed the air between himself and the sergeant. 'This long streak o' piss claims we'll engage the Covenanters.'

Stryker shrugged. 'I know not, except that the Prince intends to relieve York.' The latest threat to the king's greatest northern stronghold had come almost immediately following the heavy defeat at the Battle of Cheriton. Though the respective crises came from opposite ends of the country, their combined effect had delivered a hammer blow against the hitherto ebullient Royalist cause, and late spring had seen the sovereign's forces frantically consolidating their positions, with a ring of new defences begun in order to protect the king's capital at Oxford, and Prince Maurice, Rupert's brother, charged with the swift conquest of the west. That left Rupert himself, who abandoned his operations in Wales and the Marches and set out from his base at Shrewsbury to assist the Marquis of Newcastle at York. But first they needed to secure Cheshire and Lancashire, for supply lines needed to be protected and, with just three cavalry regiments, five regiments of foot and a regiment of dragoons, reinforcements were crucial. Stockport – and its crossing over the Mersey – had already been taken, and now Bolton was in the prince's iron grip. They would move to the next town as soon as was practicable, and all the while their army was growing.

Yet the plan to relieve York was not as simple as had been first thought. Because a huge Scottish army waited for them. 'He will tarry in the west. Gather his strength while he captures Liverpool. Then perhaps he will take the risk.'

'Risk?' Barkworth spluttered. 'That's some risk, sir. His Highness would be mad as a sack of adders to take on Leven and Fairfax at once.'

Skellen sniffed noisily, spitting into the darkness. 'Think what you will. I say we cannot take York without fighting the Scotch. There's no choice in it. You got the stomach?'

'I've killed plenty in my time, you spidery bastard,' Barkworth said, his yellow eyes glowing.

'Plenty of your own countrymen?'

'They're no countrymen o' mine, lad. The only true Scot is one who bends his knee to the Stuarts.'

A sneeze ended the debate. The three men fell utterly silent, alert in the darkness. They twisted round, studied the pitch-black corners of the yard, checked the horses, stared up at the rampart, but nothing stirred.

'The Lieutenant returns?' Skellen whispered.

'With a gallon o' wine in his belly?' Barkworth shook his head. 'He'll make a din to wake the dead.'

They waited, ears straining against the suffocating silence. Another sneeze, louder this time. Stryker drew his sword as Skellen and Barkworth vanished into the guardroom, returning with daggers in hand. No firearms could be discharged here, unless they all wished incineration, for the intruder seemed to be ensconced somewhere near the wagons. Skellen went first, heading straight for the powder cart, for it was the only one that was covered, the only one in which a person could remain completely concealed, and took a fistful of the dense sheet. On the count of three, he ripped it back.

'You!' Stryker stared down at the stowaway. 'You stupid girl. You wish to be skewered?'

'Sir?' Skellen prompted, eyes darting between the girl – curled in a foetal position amongst the hogsheads crammed with explosive – and his commanding officer. 'You know her?'

Stryker stepped back, sheathing his sword. 'You stupid bloody girl.'

She began to sit up. Even in the darkness it was clear that she was ragged and bruised, her skirts ruined by blood stains that had bloomed like sinister petals, her red hair, unleashed from its blood-stained coif, tangled around her shoulders and plastered to the wounds on her cheeks. 'Bolton is not safe, sir,' she managed to say in a voice that cracked with dryness.

Skellen's dagger had long since disappeared, and he held out a hand. 'There's not a corner in England you might call safe, lass.'

'You do not creep into cartloads of black powder,' Stryker growled. 'You do not creep into castles garrisoned by king's men. You dally with death, girl! There are some here who would stretch your neck for a spy.' He looked at the others. 'This is the one.'

'From the house?' Barkworth asked. He lingered further away, perhaps aware that his appearance might frighten the girl.

It occurred to Stryker that she had already seen hell. A man with yellow eyes and a noose-burned neck would barely register. He just nodded. 'Aye, from the house.' Skellen had eased her upright and helped her shuffle to the edge of the wagon, which he had duly unhinged. He noticed she clutched a small, tattered book to her lap, and remembered that she had snatched a Bible from the house as he had carried her to safety. 'What are you about, girl? Speak quickly or—'

'Or?' she echoed, her voice stronger now, and suddenly bitter. 'Or it will be the worse for me?' She stared back, directly into his eye, challenging him. Her knuckles shone white in the darkness as they tightened around the Bible. 'You will rape me, kill me? That is what the king's men do now, is it not?'

'That is not what I do,' said Stryker.

'Then you have answered your own question, sir,' she said. 'You saved me in Bolton. Protected me. Where else am I to go but here?'

'You will go back to the women upon our return to the army,' he ordered. 'There are many goodwives marching with the baggage train.'

She shook her head. 'I will remain with you, sir.'

'You will do no such thing.'

'I will remain with you, Major Stryker.'

Stryker turned his back on her, grinding fingertips along the bridge of his nose as he paced. 'Christ, girl, have you cloth in your ears?'

'Lass,' Skellen interjected gently. 'What's your name, lass?'

'Faith,' she said, the rigidity in her expression melting a touch when she addressed the tall sergeant. 'Faith Helly.' She looked at Stryker. 'If you will not have me, I will go home.'

Stryker turned back. 'There is only death in Bolton. You said so yourself.'

'Not Bolton, sir. Sussex. A place called Warbleton.'

The pair had barely spoken a word when he had carried her, trembling and broken, to the army's womenfolk who filed into Bolton once the fighting had died, and he had not noticed her accent until that moment. 'The south coast?' he said in genuine surprise. 'How will you travel?'

She set her jaw. 'I shall walk.' The men glanced pointedly at one another, and she fingered the Bible as her agitation rose. 'You mock me?'

'No, lass,' Skellen said softly. 'But the roads are no place for—'

'A woman?' Faith retorted hotly. Tears welled at her eyes and glimmered in the feeble moonlight as they made tracks through her bloody face. 'A child?'

Skellen smiled. 'A lonely traveller.'

'I will survive,' she muttered, smearing the tears with her sleeve.

'The roads are dangerous,' Stryker said, holding up his hands to stay her expected argument. 'They were ever dangerous, aye, but this is war, Mistress Helly. In a time of war, they are more than that. War unleashes wickedness.'

Skellen nodded. 'The devils in men's hearts stretch their wings.'

'I will chance the road, thank you.'

'You will find only three kinds of folk abroad, girl,' Stryker snapped, letting his irritation get the better of him. 'Brigands, who will rob you; soldiers, who will rape you; and deserters, fearful of discovery, who will kill you to still your tongue.'

'Some'll do all three,' Skellen added.

Barkworth had vanished into the guardroom, returning now with a cup that he handed to Faith. 'Small beer, lassie. It'll wash the powder from your throat.'

Faith took the drink with murmured thanks and gulped it down without a breath. When she was done, she handed the cup quickly back so that she might cradle the Bible once more. 'I cannot return to the women. I do not feel safe with this army.' She glared at Stryker again, and, though the night shaded her eyes, he could read their fury. 'It was your army slaughtered Master Sydall and his family.'

The words fell dead on Stryker's lips. She was right. 'What brought you there?' he said, trying a different tack. 'What did Bolton hold for you?'

'I was to marry James Sydall,' Faith said. 'It was James's father's house.'

Stryker recalled seeing the corpse of a large, soberly attired man in the kitchen of that carnage-strewn home. 'I believe I saw him.'

She nodded. 'Hate-Evil Sydall.'

'Hate-Evil?' Skellen echoed with a soft whistle. 'A Banbury Man, if ever there was one.'

She glared at him. 'An austere man, sir. A godly one. And I am Fight the Good Fight of Faith.' She hugged the Bible as a drowning man would cling to a floating spar. 'You hate us all, I suppose.'

'No, mistress,' Stryker answered for his sergeant. He thought of the hermit he had met on Dartmoor the previous summer. That man had become a regimental priest, and one of the wisest men he had ever known. 'Far from it.'

'Little young for marriage, ain't you?' Sergeant Skellen asked.

'I have recently seen fifteen years, sir.' Her shoulders visibly sagged. 'It matters nothing any longer. My betrothed was dragged out into the road.' The tears came again. 'Killed like a dog.'

The memory flashed in Stryker's mind. A man, gutted and dying, slumped in the crimson mud before a baying crowd. The hunchbacked officer standing over him, shooting him twice in the chest. 'By Kendrick.'

'By that monster,' Faith said, wiping again at the smeared cheeks. 'Vulture, I heard him say.'

He nodded. 'John Kendrick is his name, and he is infamous for violence.'

She frowned. 'You said you had not heard of him.'

'I lied,' Stryker said, startled that she had remembered the exchange, given the circumstance in which it had come to pass.

'He will seek me out.'

The assertion threw Stryker for a moment, and he looked sideways at Skellen, who pulled a nonplussed expression. 'He has put you from his mind,' he said to Faith. 'Just as he has forgotten Master Sydall and his brood. Thus is the callousness of such men.' He stifled the pang of guilt that stabbed at his insides.

But Faith was not listening. 'I am in danger,' she said, and this time the words were firm, as if her mind had hardened with the recollection. 'That is why I am safe only here, with you. You saved me before, Major Stryker, and you will save me again. When he comes for me.'

'Mistress Helly. It is natural that you are shaken by your ordeal, but men such as Kendrick care nothing for their victims, nor any witness to their crimes. The sack of the town was lawful. Your survival will not trouble him.'

'Who commands the Vulture?' Faith asked.

'The King.'

'But who gives his orders?' she persisted. 'His daily orders, I mean.'

Stryker spread his palms. 'I know not. Why do you ask?'

'He was at the Sydall house by design.'

Skellen touched her shoulder with a shovel-like hand. 'It was a general sack, lass. Every man for his-self.'

She shrugged him off. 'You are wrong. He sought something. Asked questions.'

'He was after plunder,' Skellen countered gently. 'Riches. It is what every man seeks when a town has crumbled.'

For a moment it looked as though Faith would argue, but whatever point she was about to make slipped away silently on a lingering yawn. She eased back without warning, slumping heavily into Skellen's outstretched palms. He let her drop on to her back amongst the powder barrels, looking quizzically at Stryker.

'She is overcome,' Stryker said simply. 'No surprise in that. Bring her in, Will. We'll deal with her at first light.'

Lathom House glowed through the night, the light of hissing torches and braziers throwing glowering, sinister shapes across the rain-beaten fortifications. But few slept, the relief of the small garrison turning to a revelry shared by Sir Richard Crane's influx of troops. This was no Bolton-le-Moors, no stubborn oyster shell to be prised open in bitter struggle, the spoils within good only for devouring. This place, embattled for so long, was welcoming, ecstatic at their arrival and keen to celebrate. But during a night of high merriment, while Charlotte, Countess of Derby, presided like an exotic empress over music and dance, her subjects quaffing strong ale and rich wine as they crowed over captured colours and slaughtered foes, danger mingled with the heady fug of smoke and sweat and drink. Soldiers and alcohol made trouble, and Crane had asked a man he trusted to guard the treasure trove that lay within Lathom House's substantial armoury. Stryker naturally feigned reluctance, for here was not a place to exhibit the merest trace of sobriety, lest a man be accused of Puritan austerity, but the order had suited him well enough, for it meant that his young, vulnerable charge could snatch a night's rest while Stryker considered what exactly he was to do with her.

He was in the main bailey beyond the armoury when Faith Helly found him. He was squatting against the wall, back pressed against the cold stones, an oiled rag in one hand and his sword in the other. The girl stepped into his light, dimming it and forcing him to look up at her narrow silhouette.

'Thank you, Major.'

'I have done nothing.'

'You did not send me away.'

'Because we have not yet returned to Bolton.'

She gave a short laugh; it was the first time he had heard the noise. 'I woke amongst coils of match, sir, like a bed of pale serpents. One might expect you'd have found lodgings within the house, if your intention was to be rid of me.'

Stryker pushed himself upright, shoulders scraping and snagging against the damp, grey blocks. The night's rain, a fine spray that sheeted on the breeze and made every one of Lathom House's itinerant guests thankful for the plentiful billets and pulsing hearths, had abated by dawn, and the clouds were rolling away to shadow the hilltops. But the light remained dull, the air moist, and the ground, to judge by the hem of Faith's sopping skirts, fairly sodden. 'We must find you some new clothes.'

Faith inspected her tattered, bloodied, water-darkened garments. 'I had not considered my appearance,' she said, suddenly self-conscious.

Embarrassed, and thinking it politic not to mention the soot-streaked mess that was her face and hair, Stryker hurriedly looked down at the blade he still held, running the greasy rag along the razor edges so that his reflection emerged from the steel, distorted in the groove of the fuller, tinted by Faith's looming shadow. It was a perverted version of himself. He wondered if that was what people truly saw when they looked upon his ravaged face.

'I can stay with you?' Faith asked abruptly.

'You are an impudent child,' he said, without conviction.

'I was to be wed, sir,' she chided. 'Hardly a child. I say you are an honourable man, Major Stryker, despite the dishonourable company you keep.'

Now he stopped while looking squarely into her face. 'Have a care, Mistress Helly.'

'I'll have no care, sir,' she bit back, fierceness rising in her tone. 'None at all. The king's men are murderers. You saw.' She jabbed the space between them with an accusatory finger. 'You were there. You waded through the blood of the children. You saw what that demon did, what he did to the man I was to marry. You heard what he planned to do to me. That is why you will not send me away again.' She hesitated, her throat thickening to choke the words. 'Not again.'

'We'll see she's safe, sir,' Sergeant William Skellen's monotonous voice cut across Stryker's intended reply.

Stryker was suddenly aware of figures coming from his blind left flank. He turned to see Skellen, accompanied by Hood and Barkworth. 'How long have you been standing there?'

'Long enough, sir,' Hood said. He shrugged, glancing at Faith. 'We are reformados. None to command but ourselves. Are we not well suited to offering this lady protection?'

'If we are discovered with her—' Stryker protested.

'They will think you have taken your own strumpet, sir,' Skellen blurted, turning quickly to the girl, 'beggin' your pardon, mistress.'

To Skellen's visible relief, Faith laughed. Hood stepped forward a pace. 'He is right, sir. Is it not the proper thing to do?'

Stryker slumped back against the wall. 'Take her inside,' he said to Skellen, pocketing the rag and sheathing his sword. 'Find her some food.' He turned to Barkworth. 'Well?'

'The Vulture,' Simeon Barkworth croaked with unseemly relish. 'I asked around, as you ordered.'

Hood cleared his throat sheepishly. 'What is a vulture?'

'A bird,' Stryker said. 'They had them in Spain. Big, black things. Carrion birds, but with great talons and a terrible caw.'

'And beady eyes,' Barkworth added, his own glowing yellow in the dawn murk. He looked back to Stryker. 'Though he's not named for your Spanish buggers, sir, but monstrosities to be found in the New World.'

'He told me he fought Turks and barbarians.'

Barkworth nodded. 'Savages, aye. Sold his sword to the Colonies before he sold it to the Habsburgs.' He stared into the middle distance, picturing far-flung places he could only imagine. 'Out in those never-ending forests where even angels fear to fly.'

'What else did you discover?' Stryker asked curtly, snapping Barkworth out of his reverie. 'He threatened me, Simeon, and I would know with what I deal, should our paths cross again.'

'He is a *hard-man*,' Barkworth said, 'after the Croatian fashion.'

Stryker glanced at the returning Skellen. 'She is well?'

The sergeant said that she was. 'Stuffin' her face with bread and cheese.'

'*Hard-man*?' Lieutenant Hood interjected worriedly. 'Good God.'

Barkworth nodded vigorously. 'That's what they say, sir. One who claims invincibility. Our friend, the Vulture, believes he cannot be killed by mortal hand.'

Skellen whistled a lilting tune. 'Mad as a barrel o' bees.'

'There are many tales of the hard-men who fight in the Low Countries,' Hood replied with a wag of an admonishing finger. 'They exist, for certain.'

'Aye, sir, no doubt about that,' Skellen replied. 'I've killed a few myself.'

'This is nothing to be mocked, Sergeant,' Hood said. 'I have read plenty of tracts claiming—'

'It does not matter,' Stryker interrupted before the discussion could become heated. 'He has fought savages in the Americas and Turks in Europe. That makes him dangerous, whether you believe the hard-man tales or not. And he has hajduks in his pay. Hungarian bandits, mercenaries. They're ruthless.'

'Aye,' Barkworth agreed. 'The Vulture earned himself the name for his looks, but the reputation is through deed alone. And it is quite the reputation, make no mistake. The Crown pays a pretty sum for his services. He's worthy of it, for the sake of fear alone.' He scratched at the mottled skin that blighted his neck. 'Do you believe the wee lassie, sir? That he'll come lookin' for her?'

'No,' said Stryker.

'Strange, though.'

'What is strange, Master Barkworth?'

Barkworth performed a half-turn so that he could point at one of the towers that jutted from the curtain wall. A red flag dangled on a pole thrust through one of its upper loopholes. 'That's his mark. The Vulture appears to have flown to Lathom.'

Stryker had crossed the wide bailey before a thought had entered his mind. He stalked past the central structure of Lathom House, a crenellated keep known as the Eagle Tower, and pressed on towards the portion of wall on the far side from his own billet. It was there that the red flag hung limp from a stout tower, and he did not hesitate as he passed under it.

Inside was a simple chamber of plain walls. There were doors leading both left and right, and a spiral staircase climbing away immediately to his front.

'You wish to cross blades, Major?' a familiar voice rang out from somewhere behind. 'Here?'

Stryker turned back, stepping out into the open to see Captain John Kendrick's grinning face. 'Here.' He drew his sword. 'Now.'

It was folly, he knew. He was outnumbered, for groups of Kendrick's men were filtering back from all corners of the castle, hastening at the sound of this new commotion. No consideration had gone into the act, simply instinct. He had thought, in that heart-shattering moment, of the Sydall family, of their blood on his boots, and of the wretched girl he had saved, and there seemed no other course to follow but this.

Kendrick tutted softly. 'Sweet Jesu, Major, but I am glad to see you again.' His left hand was encased in its vicious-looking gauntlet, but his right clutched a pipe, the wooden bowl large, smouldering. From its sides glowered horrifying faces, like the gargoyles grimacing atop cathedral walls. He slid the stem between those sharply filed teeth, drawing on it with studied calm so that twin trails of smoke roiled from his hooked nose to cloud the thin face. 'I have thought of you often. Still, I am surprised to see you on this drab morn.'

Stryker watched as Kendrick shrugged off his thickly pelted cloak. 'I mean to gut you, as you gutted those children.'

'If you don't, sir,' the constricted words of Simeon Barkworth came from somewhere to his flank, 'then I will.'

'Hush, evil imp,' Kendrick warned, though he did not take his eyes from Stryker, 'lest I decide to teach you some manners.'

'Let's test your fuckin' wisdom then, teacher,' the firebrand Scot snarled.

'No,' Stryker ordered. 'You'll not touch an officer, Simeon.' He levelled the sword at Kendrick's breastbone. 'The Vulture is mine to pluck.'

Kendrick upended the pipe so that the ash could flutter to earth on the weak breeze. 'Carved from Virginia maplewood, Major. Exquisite, is it not? Took it from a painted savage. He had been decidedly reluctant to hand it over, so I gelded him for it.'

There were perhaps a score of onlookers now, grunting oaths and threats and encouragement as the pair circled slowly. Stryker caught sight of his three men, but the rest, he knew, would be Kendrick's. He was vaguely aware of horsemen further off, beyond the tense crowd, but they were too far away to make out.

Now, finally, Kendrick unsheathed his sword. 'How fairs your flame-haired punk? Ploughed her yet?' He swept the blade in two great arcs before his face, making the air zing and the onlookers cheer. 'A particularly sweet furrow, I'd wager.'

'They say you are a hard-man, Vulture,' Stryker said.

The thin lips turned upwards. 'You wish not to speak of her, eh?'

That was a shrewd thrust, and Stryker fought to keep his voice level. 'I know nothing of her.'

Kendrick's laughter was echoed by his men. 'You simply left her there to bathe in blood, did you? Ha! A man after my own heart!' He swept the sword again, cleaving great arcs that seemed to leave a blurred ghost in the dank air. 'Yes – I am a hard-man. You cannot vanquish me. It is impossible.'

'I will take the risk,' Stryker said, stepping in.

Kendrick let him come, then backed off quickly to maintain the distance. 'Many before you have embarked on a similar path, Major. The pagans of the New World took rather a dim view of my penchant for swiving their squaws. Lovely dark meat, you know. Yet still I breathe.'

Stryker attacked, and this time Kendrick held his ground. Blades crossed, clanged loud and crisp between them, the juddering vibration careening through fingers and wrists. Kendrick held Stryker firm, but Stryker was taller, stronger, and he shoved hard, pushing his opponent backwards. Kendrick kept his balance, lost no composure, parried the next crushing blow to the left of his chest, then sent a low strike bouncing away, twisting his sword so that Stryker could not let his keen Toledo steel slide all the way up to glance unpredictably off the hilt.

They parted, came together again, and Kendrick affected two low sweeps, only to attack with purpose towards Stryker's neck. Stryker blocked it easily enough, but the man's technique was unquestionably impressive, unhindered by the hunch in his shoulders, and he hastened to retreat out of range. They circled again. The horsemen seemed to be closer now, more numerous. Some were shouting, though he could not make sense of the words.

More thrusts came from Kendrick. He parried, flickering his own probing ripostes. Kendrick was not remarkably fast. Certainly Stryker had faced quicker swordsmen in his time, but the Vulture possessed a guile that made him wraithlike in his movements. His was not a technique of serpent strike attacks, but of feint and parry, disguise and intelligence, ghosting out of Stryker's heaviest lunges and letting the weight of the blow carry his opponent off balance.

When they locked together again, pushing apart with a guttural grunt and skittering boots, Kendrick smiled, deliberately parting his lips so that the sharpened spikes of his teeth were exposed to the sunlight. He winked, ducked low, like a cat poised to pounce, then retreated, trying to lure Stryker into a careless play that would see him wrong-footed. Stryker kept his feet, kept his grip strong and his knees slightly bent, his elbow loose and ready. He jabbed at the air between them, hoping to unnerve Kendrick, but his only reward was mocking laughter from the men who formed a ring around them. Kendrick swept his blade down, slicing the air, then quickly up, carving a blurred figure of eight between them in what was evidently his signature flourish, all the while shifting his feet carefully left and right, never leaving his stance flat. He raised his left hand and held it level with Stryker's face so that the brass gadlings shone bright and malevolent.

'Not too close, Major, or I shall take your other eye.' Kendrick flexed the iron fingers. 'Pulp it like a cider apple.' He patted the gently curved bone handle of the broad knife that jutted from his belt. 'When you cannot see, I will set my cinquedea to work. It will hurt a great deal.'

'*Hold!*'

The voice, a lone bark, was ignored as the duellists edged around their private circle.

'Hold, I say! Damn your insolent hides! Desist, or I shall have every man flogged from here to Dover!'

Finally the bolt across Stryker's mind slid back as the mob began to thin with the arrival of the group of horsemen. Kendrick lowered his sword too, risking a glance behind once he could be sure Stryker was keeping his distance.

'What the devil transpires here, sirs?' the barking voice came again, this time louder. One of the riders pushed out from the troop; he was a huge, black-haired man on a huge, black destrier. He wore the garments of a harquebusier – plate at back and breast, gloved right hand, gauntleted left, boots unfolded right up to his groin – but his buff-coat was trimmed in gold thread, his hat ostentatiously feathered, and his waist swathed in a rich red scarf that was tied in a deliberately large knot. He glowered at the two fighters, furious eyes dark as jet against pale skin blazing over a long, straight nose. 'By Jesu's wounds, speak quickly!'

Stryker bowed low. 'A matter of honour, Your Highness.'

Rupert, Count Palatine of the Rhine, Duke of Bavaria, First Duke of Cumberland, First Earl of Holderness, President of Wales and general of the king's forces in the region, also known as Prince Robber by his enemies and Prince Robert by his friends, threw a withering glance at Sir Richard Crane, who had reined in at his side, before fixing his imperious gaze upon Stryker. 'Honour?' He laughed with not a hint of mirth. 'A pair of my best officers think to murder one another? Tell me where I might find the honour here, sirrah.'

Stryker realized his blade was still exposed, and he sheathed it quickly. 'Highness, I—'

'Jesu, Stryker, but you'll not duel here. No, sir, you will not!'

'I beg forgiveness, Highness,' Stryker managed to say. His mouth was bone dry as he stared up at the general. Prince Rupert of the Rhine was still only in his early twenties, yet he had been in almost constant military service for more than a decade, and every man knew he was not one to be trifled with. 'He slaughtered a family.'

The prince did not flinch. 'Many terrible acts befall a town under sack, Major.'

'He raped the women.' He looked to Crane, but the blue eyes gleamed hard in the shade of his hat. 'Murdered children.'

Rupert's eyes swivelled to pinion Kendrick. 'Well?'

'He lies, Highness.'

If Kendrick was a vulture, hunched and glowering, then Prince Rupert had the noble ferocity of a hawk, and his unflinching gaze seemed to twinkle as he spoke words dripping with danger. 'This is Sergeant-Major Stryker, Captain Kendrick. A man of senior rank and dignity.'

Kendrick was not to be cowed, though the smirk had faded.

'He is Sergeant-Major with no command, Highness. A reformado.' He twisted his narrow face, as if the word itself brought putrefaction to his tongue. 'I bring sixty-three men to your army.'

'He is a particular associate of mine,' Rupert replied, 'and I can assure you, regiment or no, Stryker brings plenty to my army. Have a care with your accusations, Captain.' The eyes shifted, lancing Stryker. 'Major?'

'Highness.'

'This,' the prince said, nodding at the Vulture, 'is Captain John Kendrick. Also an associate of mine, and a very great leader of men. I need both of you. Have a care with your own accusations.'

Stryker gritted his teeth. 'Highness.'

'The fact remains,' Kendrick said, 'that he challenged me to armed combat.' He swept his brutish gauntlet across the hushed crowd. 'Witnesses aplenty. Honour must be served, Highness, do you not agree?'

Prince Rupert of the Rhine paused for a second, pursing his lips in thought. 'Very well, gentlemen,' he said eventually. 'Fight your damnable duel.' He patted the hilt of the sword that hung at his hip. 'My own blade awaits the victor. We are agreed?' He waited as the two men first glanced at one another, then back at him, their mouths firmly shut. Rupert flicked his reins. His black stallion shook its head as it turned away, nostrils flaring as it whinnied. 'I thought not,' he called over his shoulder. 'Back to quarters Captain, Major. I mean to march on Liverpool, and I would have you both with me!'

# CHAPTER 5

*York, 3 June 1644*

The Parliamentarian Army of the Eastern Association arrived on the outskirts of York as rain lashed the ancient city. It was halfway through the afternoon, but angry clouds had transformed the sky to a blanket of black, and out of the tempest, illuminated by jagged spears of lightning, marched the great warlike column that represented the third arm of Roundhead power in the north.

Lancelot Forrester stood on the fire-step of the shallow trench, well ensconced within his deep hood, rain sluicing in maddened rivulets off the oiled cloth swathing his shoulders. Around him his men were collecting the valuable tools of trench work – shovels, picks, dog carts – and preparing to abandon the flooded sap for the fortress looming at their backs. They chatted as they worked, cheerful in spite of numbed hands and feet, because blazing hearths awaited. But it was more than that, Forrester knew. He felt it too: a yearning to be inside the walls as this new threat surged up from the south. He would lead his men back to their saps, he felt sure. Creep out to dig deeper, strive further, set new pickets, place new marksmen. For now, though, they were best to get out of the way until they knew where precisely the Earl of Manchester's fresh forces would be allocated.

'If they've any sense, they will push around to the north,' Forrester muttered to no one in particular. 'Take up the final unguarded section.'

'The last stopper in our confounded bottle.'

Forrester glanced to his right, icy droplets skittering off the edge of his hood. 'Quite.'

Seek Wisdom and Fear the Lord Gardner was himself cowled, though his long, white beard extended beyond the reach of the hood so that raindrops gathered like dew on the wiry bristles. He shook his head. 'How many?'

'Six thousand foot, so says Master Killigrew.'

Gardner screwed up his craggy face. 'Killigrew spews more dung than a donkey's arse.'

Forrester grunted his amusement, though the sound was lost in a sudden clap of thunder. 'He is an intelligencer, Father, and that is the intelligence he imparts.'

'Horse?'

'They're detached. Ravaging the county this very moment, I shouldn't wonder. Three thousand, as I understand it.'

'What happened to the Oxford Army?' Gardner's voice was strong with the accent of the Welsh mountains. 'Don't like the rain do they, boy?'

'Perhaps,' Forrester mused, searching the storm-hazed horizon for regimental colours. 'Though I rather suspect the defeat at Cheriton has put the King on edge. He would rather lose York than Oxford.'

'If he loses York, he loses the north.' The old man hawked up a wad of phlegm and spat it into the swelling quagmire at his feet. 'If he loses the north, then we're all buggered.'

Seek Wisdom and Fear the Lord Gardner was the de facto preacher to Sir Edmund Mowbray's Regiment of Foot. It was a curious arrangement, for the man, who might have seen anything from sixty winters to ninety, was a Puritan. Or, at least, he had been in earlier days. Father Gardner, as they tended to address him, had been found by Stryker's company during their flight from a troop of enemy cavalry the previous summer. He had been living alone on Dartmoor; a cantankerous, foul-mouthed hermit, who appeared unable to maintain his sanity from one moment to the next. But the madness, it became clear, was a screen for an active and sharp mind, and Gardner had proved himself invaluable in the escape of Stryker's embattled force. His shrewd advice had resulted in Stryker's request for Gardner to counsel his rough, jaded men. It was an unlikely appointment, given the obvious scarcity of those with Puritan leanings amongst the Royalist faction, but Stryker had wanted it, and Mowbray had not demurred. The irony, of course, was that Stryker's company had lasted a matter of months before its obliteration, leaving Seek Wisdom with no home in an army generally hostile to his particular beliefs. But then the regimental preacher had died, his heart giving out one snow-sprinkled day in January, and somehow old Seek Wisdom had taken over his duties. He had been forced to tone down his austere rhetoric, naturally, and carry out some of the ceremonial tasks required by the High Church, but Seek Wisdom and Fear the Lord Gardner was a survivor, and he had done what was necessary. Now the short, wiry priest gave a cackle that was pitched high and nasal. 'If I'd have known how poorly your bastard army would conduct this war, I'd have joined the other side.'

Forrester looked down upon him with a baleful expression. 'You have time yet, Father.'

'I may agree with the dissenters, Lancelot, but I do not like 'em.' Gardner rocked back suddenly, tilting his head up at the violent sky. 'Do not like 'em, Lord, do I?'

'Oh?' Forrester prompted when the priest had finished staring at the roiling abyss.

'Gaggle o' dour old goats.' Gardner spat again. 'The Godly, as we call ourselves' – he shot Forrester an impish wink – 'are imbued with the fear of the Almighty, but such divine blessing does not always inspire us to nurture a love of His creatures.'

Forrester smiled. 'The man claiming spiritual infallibility for himself tends rather to think the worst of the man who claims nothing.'

'Ha!' Gardner crowed, staring heavenwards again. 'He has it, Lord! The dear captain is not as stupid as we thought!' He fixed Forrester with a lucid stare. 'The Godly, dear Lancelot, know that all life is predestined and unchangeable, that the baubles of Rome and Canterbury are nothing more than idolatry, that all wisdom may be discovered in Scripture and that the Papacy dances hand in hand with the great whore that sitteth upon many waters. But that does not mean we have to be arseholes.'

Both men laughed at that, and Forrester helped Gardner along the bottom of the sticky gully. 'Let us find some warmth, eh? And some vittels.'

Gardner glanced pointedly at the pewter buttons of Forrester's cloak, straining taut against his ample midriff. 'Think you only of your belly, boy?'

'It is not the courageous man who wins the day, Father, but the well-fed.'

'Greed is a sin, dear Lancelot.'

'So is nagging like a bloody fishwife.'

Gardner slipped, slid like a fawn on a frozen lake, and was only saved from planting all fours in the mud by Forrester's firm grasp at his skinny wrist. He let Forrester haul him up the side of the trench to ground level. 'I'm right, though, you can admit that much.'

'Right?' Forrester said, rearranging his baldric after the scrambled climb. Musketry began to ripple out from the walls above them. Newcastle's sharpshooters had evidently decided to harass the oncoming column of infantry. The range was too great and their powder would be damp, but sometimes men needed to show an enemy that they were willing to fight.

'About the war,' Gardner said when there was a lull in the sporadic shooting. 'This time last year we were all dancing a jig round our fires and chanting *hang up the Roundheads*. We were winning, boy. Now it's all falling apart.'

'The smallest worm will turn, being trodden on.'

Gardner twisted his mouth in distaste. 'Do not quote Cicero at me, boy.'

'It is Shakespeare, Father,' Forrester said, exasperated. 'Henry the Sixth, Part Three, act two, scene two.'

'Blasphemy,' Gardner retorted.

'They were trodden on,' Forrester persisted: 'the rebels, I mean.'

'Not hard enough, boy.'

'Precisely.' Forrester led the way back to the gates of the Walmgate barbican, their boots splashing as they went. 'They fought for their very lives, Father, for the existence of their cause. At Gloucester, at Newbury, at Cheriton.' He looked back, nodding towards the Earl of Manchester's huge force as it trudged along the shadowy skyline to join with two more armies in defiance of the king. 'Now look. The worm has turned, well and truly.'

'Except it is not a worm, boy,' Seek Wisdom and Fear the Lord Gardner replied in barely more than whisper. 'It is a viper.'

## Near Standish, Lancashire, 3 June 1644

The camp had been pitched where fields dipped to a shallow valley fringed by woodland. A brook babbled through the centre of the temporary settlement, providing a latrine for both man and beast as well as a rich source of clear, crisp water that would slake even the most arid thirst, so long as a man thought to trudge upstream to dunk his flask. The heavy horses of the Lifeguard whickered as the light faded, their muzzles foamed green with torn grass. The sounds of men singing drifted on the light breeze, accompanied by a tuneful fiddle that seemed to exult in the retreat of yet another day's rain, while foraging parties groped the countryside in every direction, stretching out like tentacles to gather food and supplies from disgruntled but cowed folk who wished to play no part in the games of kings and parliaments.

Stryker pulled on his boots and left his tent. He paced across the small encampment, weaving in and out of awnings clustered around flickering fires freshly kindled against the onset of dusk. Pots hanging above the flames sent delicious vapours into the dank air, and he breathed in appreciatively. He paused at the stream, arching his back, heard the satisfying report of a cracking spine, and leapt the chattering shallows in a single bound. Somewhere men jeered, and he saw a large, black-eared hare race in a panicked blur through a gauntlet of baying folk and grasping hands. The startled creature eventually made it to the open ground on the camp's periphery, and bolted up the slope towards the beckoning shadows of wind-stooped trees.

Somewhere a dog barked, one of the flea-bitten mongrels that could always be found scuttling in the wake of armies. It was abruptly silenced, a yelp and whine its pathetic retort. Meanwhile, up above, the splayed wings of a red kite turned lazily, the bird of prey circling silently, biding its time. Stryker watched it, a black silhouette against the grey sky, and thought of the vultures he had seen in Spain.

'How now, Sergeant-Major?' Sir Richard Crane strode out of the half-light towards him.

'Colonel.'

Crane was already smiling, for the leathery scar across his mouth made it impossible to do anything else, but his brilliantly white teeth shone as he lifted and replaced his hat. 'The pickets are set?'

Stryker scratched at the beard that had sprouted since Bolton. 'I go to check them now, Sir Richard.'

'Then I will not keep you long.' Crane glanced at the sky. 'Weather's as grim as ever. Still, it has shackled the Covenanters, God be praised.'

'They besiege York, Colonel,' Stryker said, a touch too sharply.

Crane seemed not to notice. 'Aye, true enough. And if the roads had been drier, they might well be knocking upon Oxford's gates by now. As it is, we can yet turn them back. As you know, the Prince has been busy at Bury, joining forces with Goring and the Northern Horse. They will return to Bolton on the morrow, then on to Wigan the day after.'

'By which time we will already be waiting,' Stryker said. The Lifeguard of Horse, under Crane's command, had been ordered directly to Wigan, rather than traipse all the way back to Bolton.

The infantry units, Stryker's group among them, had been told to accompany him.

'You have it,' Crane confirmed. 'We break camp at dawn, reach Wigan by end of day, and on to Liverpool once we have made the rendezvous with the main army. As soon as the port is in our thrall, it will be a swing to the north and east. After Lancashire, we take Yorkshire, that's the nub of the matter.' His face, handsome despite the sword-slash, darkened a touch, and he waved a cautioning finger at Stryker. 'A word of warning, Major. The Prince is not a happy man. He rides out to Lathom to pay his respects to the Countess, and instead discovers two of his best men duelling.'

Stryker found himself staring at the ground between them. 'I apologised to His Highness, Sir Richard. It is a matter of regret.'

'You are fortunate. Another man would have been flogged, or worse.'

'I believe it.'

'Good. He values you, Stryker.'

Stryker looked up at that. 'He values Kendrick.'

'He needs Kendrick,' Crane replied. 'To fight a brutal war he must have brutal men. To fight a fearsome foe, we must be more fearsome.'

'The world would be a more contented place if I wrung the Vulture's neck,' Stryker said.

Crane seemed amused, but jabbed with his finger again. 'Let the Prince be the judge of that, Stryker. And do not be so damnably foolish in future. You know he hates duelling at the best of times, let alone when it distracts from so vital a campaign.' The finger was removed to push a long, matted clump of hair behind his left ear, and he began to twist the dangling pearl earring as he spoke. 'The morrow, then. We shall soon feast our eyes on this newly grown army, and to hell with the Roundheads.'

The pickets were placed as Stryker had ordered. Crane was jittery Lancashire remained a divided and hostile county, and he had looked to his most senior infantryman – albeit a reformado – to secure the camp for the night. Stryker had set Hood, Skellen and Barkworth as watch commanders and then snatched several hours of much needed sleep.

A roughly shaken shoulder roused him and he peered blearily into the diminutive Scot's searing eyes.

'Enjoy it, sir,' Barkworth said with a relish designed to annoy, and Stryker clambered up from his nest of crumpled sheets to throw on his cloak. Barkworth, able to stand beneath the fluttering canvas, glanced at the lumpen form at the tent's far end. 'Like a log, sir. Good for her.'

Stryker, shuffling towards the flap on his knees as he fastened buttons at his chest, followed his gaze. 'She recovers, I think.' Faith Helly had stayed with him since her discovery in the ammunition wagon. He had found himself instinctively driven to protect her, as if events in Bolton had formed a bond between them. He had considered calling her his whore, so that questions of her presence would be easily swerved, but the notion did not sit well. Thus Faith had remained concealed in the wagon, though she donned the clothes of a smith's apprentice, and travelled with their baggage, curled beneath the sheet and praying none would discover her. 'Her life is altered irreparably, Simeon.'

'Aye, sir. War will do that. Poor wee bairn.' Barkworth went to the flap, pushing his way out as Stryker snatched up his hat and clamped it hard atop his head. 'Wishin' you a quiet night, sir.'

Stryker watched the Scot scamper to his own tent, and stepped out into a foul night of high winds and merciless drizzle. He went north, squinting at the sodden ground to keep his footing, intending to check on the sentries up on the low escarpment. When he had cleared the outermost row of tents, he caught sight of a tumbledown wall, all that remained of a shepherd's hut, or perhaps an ancient stable, long since plundered of its better stones. He pressed himself into the cold breastwork, a refuge from the wind, and swore as his numb fingers fumbled to fish a clay pipe from the folds of his cloak and dropped the pouch of sotweed that had nestled beside it. Eventually, he managed to pack the pipe, but realized that igniting it would be a far more tricky task to negotiate, and he resolved to wait until he was up on the hill, where he would find pickets with match-cord ready lit.

He saw the light when he moved out from the shielding stonework. It was small, a speck in the blackness about the size of the glow given by a burning match. It flared bright, ebbed for a moment, and then vanished altogether. He lingered at the edge of the crumbling wall, watching, waiting, as rivulets of water cascaded off the brim of his hat. The light flared again, and this time he remembered the pipe in his hand. He remembered, too, the huge bowl of carved Virginia maplewood that had belonged to the man they called the Vulture.

Captain John Kendrick drew long and hard on the pipe. He dug his nails into the clefts whittled by its Indian creator, the chin, nose and eyes of a ghoulish face that leered from the smooth wood. He liked those clefts, for they were the reassuring contours into which his fingers had pressed every day since the horrors of the Americas, the pipe itself a talisman of his survival. He drank of the fragrant tobacco again, holding his breath as its coals pulsed warm on his face. 'It will be a hard ride. The roads are ruined.' He leaned in, making certain the messenger could see his fangs in the gloom. 'Your mount had better be good.'

He was a stoat of a man, this messenger. Underfed, sallow, with a beard of wispy curls and eyes sunk deep in cavernous sockets. He nodded. 'He is good, sorr.'

Kendrick eyed his companion down his long nose, running the pipe stem over his teeth. The man's scabby face hardly instilled confidence, and yet his was a commission of trust, a role given by a master not likely to employ fools. Besides, he had seen enough of the enemies of Massachusetts and Virginia to know the folly of underestimating a man. So many of the painted savages that infested the New World had appeared to be nothing more than wild beasts, ill educated and witless. It had taken just one skirmish with them – an ambush, to be exact, that had erupted from the tree-choked slope of a sleepy creek – to rid Kendrick of that illusion. He had been young and guileless, reared on the lie of European supremacy in battle, eyes blinkered to anything but an easy existence where a man with a pistol could pick off his targets with impunity. Except the Indians had been stealthy, resourceful and as cruel as any white man. They might not have had black powder, but that mattered little when their rudimentary weapons could be brought to bear in silent raids, expedited by deviousness and shadow. Kendrick had learnt that life was brutal, death was unstoppable, and the wise man takes what he wants and all else be damned. He took another pull on the pipe. 'Ride fast, then, Master Greer. Tell him the quarry was brought to ground.'

'That I will, sorr,' Greer replied. 'On the Holy Mother's name, I'll tell him.'

'I suggest you keep your mouth shut if you are accosted,' Kendrick said, 'for the Crop-heads will string up any Irishers they find.'

Greer smirked at that. 'They'll not take me, sorr, so they won't.'

Clouds raced by, revealing a gibbous moon. Greer's eyes were bright blue, as gleaming as the rest of him was dull. 'Inform him that all the Sydalls, but one, are dead. The last remaining survivor is a mere girl, and she is here, with the army. Tell him I will get to her presently. Inform him that I will flay her alive if she fails to cooperate.'

'You know where this girl is?' Greer asked, glancing beyond Kendrick at the far off tents. 'He will demand to know all.'

Captain John Kendrick emptied his pipe and pulled his heavy, fur-collared cloak tighter. 'I have a suspicion, aye.'

### Middlethorpe, near York, 4 June 1644

'York lies at the confluence of two rivers, the Ouse and the Foss,' said Alexander Leslie, First Earl of Leven. He looked up from the huge map that covered almost the entire surface of the campaign table. 'Needless to say, her position makes her the key to the north of England.'

The men standing on the far side of the walnut expanse shared a brief glance, before one, taller than his companion by an inch, and more fancifully attired, cleared his throat. 'I am aware, my lord.'

Leven eyed them closely. For his part, he had entered military service with the Dutch, before transferring to the mighty Swedish army, with whom he had recorded various notable victories, including the bloody struggles at Stralsund and Wittstock. His continental odyssey had begun thirty-nine years before, and in that time he reckoned there had been few of life's hardships he had not witnessed. And that was why, as he folded his arms beneath the high, patterned ceiling, he considered himself the natural leader of the York allies. It was a thing of great annoyance that his fellow generals, mere fledglings in his eyes, appeared to consider themselves his equal.

'Of course, my lord Manchester,' he muttered grudgingly. 'But you have only recently arrived, and I would guide you through our strategy.'

Edward Montagu, Second Earl of Manchester, tugged at the lace fringing his cuffs and gave a pious nod. 'It would be our honour, I'm sure.'

'You know David Leslie, my Lieutenant-General of Horse?' Leven asked, indicating the man standing at his right hand. 'No relation, but a stern Presbyterian and a brave soldier.'

Manchester's hazel eyes crinkled affably as he offered Leslie his hand. 'Well met, General.'

'And you know Lord Fairfax?' Leven asked.

Manchester nodded, turning to bow low before the dowdy, lugubrious man who led the Parliamentarian army of Yorkshire, the Northern Association, with whom Leven's Scots had first allied. Ferdinando, Lord Fairfax of Cameron, was Leven's junior by a couple of years, but his rheumy eyes, saddled with dark rings, made him appear much older. Indeed, he was commander of his army purely by birthright, the day-to-day running of things falling squarely upon the able shoulders of his son, Sir Thomas, who now conferred quietly with Manchester's own subordinate.

'Here we are, then,' Lord Fairfax announced in a voice crackling with phlegm. 'Three generals and three lieutenant-generals, three armies and one objective.' He paused to lick his fleshy upper lip, leaving a trail of foamy spittle to glisten on the bristles of his bushy grey moustache. 'A grand alliance and a shared foe.'

The others gave their huzzahs appropriately. Leven grunted in sour annoyance and shifted forwards to regard the map once more. 'More light in here!' he brayed as he realised he could not quite make out all the lines and annotations. The manor house was dingy, as it was each grey morning he had been here. It had been converted from a hunting lodge, its stoic Yorkshire stone given decoration by red brick, limestone and blue-black diapering. Leven did not like the place, found it pompous, as the whole cursed country was pompous, but its position due south of York made it a reasonable headquarters, and that was all that mattered.

Eventually an aide scurried in with extra candles, setting them on shelves around the room. Leven glanced at the third spoke in the besieging wheel, the Earl of Manchester. 'We must set to work, my lord. Prince Robber is abroad.'

Manchester frowned. 'Where, Lord Leven?'

Leven jabbed the map with his forefinger. 'They were spread between Bury and Bolton, last we heard. Here.'

'How composed?'

'Mixed,' David Leslie contributed. 'Foot, horse, dragooners, ordnance.'

'Strength?' asked Manchester.

'Twelve,' Leslie suggested, 'perhaps fifteen thousand, in all. The Northern Horse under Goring and Lucas have joined with them.'

'Do we know the Prince's design?' Manchester asked. 'Does he march north?'

'Not yet,' Leven said. 'Some say he will come to break up our enterprise, but I rather fancy he would not risk such a thrust without first securing a line back to his reinforcements in Ireland.'

Manchester's hazel gaze flickered across the map, fixing on England's north-west coast. 'He must take Liverpool.'

'Precisely.'

'Then we have time to reduce York.'

Leven moved his hand across the paper until his finger rested on the irregular shape sketched in ink that denoted the city about which their forces gathered. The twin prongs of the rivers Ouse and Foss snaked through it, coming together just south of the city limits, while in several places there were thick crosses marking the placement of enemy batteries. He traced an arc with his fingernail around the area west of the city. 'My army controls the land from here to here.' The finger moved to the opposite side. 'Lord Fairfax and his son have the sector to the east. The north, betwixt the rivers, has hitherto been left open, for lack of available men.'

'They are strong in artillery?' the man at Manchester's side asked. It was the first time he had addressed the group, and Leven was taken by the voice: the easy drawl of flat Norfolk fields, yet deep, dominating the room.

Leven met his steady eyes and nodded. 'They have divers cannon placed right around the city, and a strong battery on Clifford's Tower.' Just then a great boom bellowed from the north. Leven forced a wry smile. 'Their culverins have ears, it seems.'

'I saw outworks,' Manchester cut in, 'did I not?'

'To protect the cattle in the pastures.' It was Sir Thomas Fairfax, lieutenant-general to his ageing father, who spoke. His voice, by contrast with the hard tone of his East Anglian counterpart, was calm and remarkably gentle. The common soldiers, Leven knew, called him Black Tom, and he could see why, for Fairfax's complexion was as swarthy as his father's was pale.

'They keep cattle?' Manchester's second in command blurted incredulously. 'Outside the walls?'

'Aye, General,' Fairfax said, unruffled. He moved to the map, leaned over it, and eyed the Earl of Manchester. 'Perhaps I might detail the situation for you, my lord?'

Manchester sucked at his teeth. After a long pause he nodded.

Sir Thomas Fairfax examined the map, his dark eyes screwed to slits. He drew a circle with his fingertip around the circumference of York. 'They have good, solid walls of stone that cover much of the city. At the south-west it is lower, less robust, but stout nonetheless.'

'Much of the city? There is a place without a wall?'

'Here,' Fairfax said, tracing a line that ran down York's western flank, 'between Layerthorpe Postern and the Red Tower, there is a gap.'

Manchester squinted. 'Is that supposed to be water?'

'Aye, my lord. The King's Fishpond. It is stagnant, and quite shallow, but a formidable obstacle for all that. It stretches a quarter of a mile, perhaps more. We cannot cross it easily.'

Manchester massaged his eyes with his palms. 'Can we come up against the wall? Throw up ladders?'

'The outer face of the wall,' Fairfax countered, 'is covered by a moat. Often dry, admittedly, but, combined with the sheer height of the rampart above, we could not easily make a successful escalade.'

'You mentioned the wall was lower in the south-west. What say we strike there?'

Fairfax ran his finger along the relevant black line. 'Between the Red Tower and Fishergate Postern, my lord, aye. But I must report that it is here, outside that weaker rampart, that the moat is deepest, and always filled.' He shrugged apologetically. 'One might see the moat as compensation for the wall.'

Manchester blew out his cheeks in exasperation. 'It seems York is stronger than I had bargained for.'

'There are towers set at intervals along the wall,' Fairfax went on mercilessly, 'and entry is gained only through the four great bars, Micklegate, Bootham, Monk and Walmgate. All four are heavily defended. Moreover, they have occupied a ridge of high ground to the west, erecting three stout sconces so that we may not take that vantage point. It is behind those sconces, before the walls, that they put their cattle to pasture.'

'How do we bring this stubborn city to heel?' Manchester said, looking at each man in turn.

His second stepped forwards, face grim, eyes blazing. 'God is with us, my lords. We must trust in Him! He will see this popish nest smote!'

Manchester placed a staying hand on his lieutenant-general's elbow. 'An escalade would be costly in the extreme. We must be cautious.'

'There is a patch of high ground to the west,' Fairfax said. 'At Hesslington. I would take it, for it would serve well as a gun emplacement.'

'Forgive me, my lord Leven,' Manchester began, 'but you have been at the task for some weeks, have you not?'

Leven gritted his teeth. It was all he could do to keep from giving the arrogant pup a good hiding. 'Without the resources to properly invest the city,' he said as levelly as he could. 'Now you are here, my lord, we may move things on apace. Your numbers make it possible to effectively circumvallate the city. We may finally conduct a close siege.'

Manchester indicated the area above York on the huge map. 'I have inserted my army into the north-western sector, as agreed. Here, between the east bank of the Ouse as it flows into the north-west of the city, and the west bank of the Foss as it flows into the east of the city. Let it be known that my headquarters shall be at Clifton Without. Would it please you, my lord, for our armies to cooperate in joint enterprise?'

Leven frowned. 'How so?'

'Here,' Manchester said. 'At Poppleton. I would construct a bridge of boats over the Ouse to link our respective forces.'

David Leslie, Lieutenant-General of Horse, moved closer to Leven and cleared his throat pointedly.

'Tell me, my lord,' Leven said, reading his comrade's mind, 'of the disposition of your men.'

'We have nine thousand,' Manchester replied, nonplussed. 'Six of foot, three of horse. Raised from the East Anglian counties, in the main.'

'Nay,' Leven waved the information away, 'that was not my meaning. Forgive me, but yours is an army of an *Independent* mind, is it not?'

Manchester exchanged a glance with his own lieutenant-general, then looked back at the big Scot. 'What do you imply, my lord?'

'My men are God-fearing,' Leven replied, searching for the most tactful route to tread, 'but simple. I would be reassured to know that their minds are not—at risk.'

Manchester's genial expression became strained. He folded his arms defensively. 'Mine is a Godly army, sir, and that is what is important. I am Presbyterian,' he shrugged, 'while others of my force are not. But we are all believers, all saved.' He nodded at his second. 'This man, the commander of my horse, is one such Independent. I assure you, my lord, that he will prove invaluable, despite your reservations. There will be no preaching by my men, sir. Is that not so, Oliver?'

The taciturn subordinate nodded. 'No minds will be manipulated, my lords.'

Leven found he could not look away from the horseman with the reverberating voice. His large eyes seemed to impale him like twin spears, and he was transfixed by the large wart that danced on the man's creased right brow. 'Then all is well,' he said eventually. 'Lieutenant-General Cromwell. You are to provide protective cordon for our entire alliance. Screen our troops, escort supplies, warn of enemy advances. Understood?'

Oliver Cromwell bowed. 'I will do my duty, my lord.'

Leven tore himself away, staring at the map to hide his discomfiture. 'We must bring matters close to their walls. Enough of this cannon-play, for it resolves nothing. We will begin undermining the defences as soon as is practicable.' He looked at the Fairfaxes. 'Sir Thomas, will you press against the gate in your sector?'

The younger Fairfax nodded. 'Walmgate Bar, my lord. I plan

to place a battery nearby, to entertain the enemy ordnance at Clifford's Tower. Once their focus is taken by that gun, I will send in my sappers.'

'I shall look to mine the north wall, my lords,' the Earl of Manchester added. He squinted at the map. 'What is this?'

He was examining the angled lines inked along the north and west limits of York. They were irregular, jutting out from the otherwise continuous circuit of the wall, bulging from the surface like the burl of a diseased tree. 'The Abbey of St Mary's, now known simply as the Manor. The church itself has been ruined since the Papists left, but the manor house stands strong nearby. They will have troops stationed therein. The grounds have their own wall, connected to the corner of the main wall.'

'In effect, it adds a compound to their circuit?' Manchester said.

Leven nodded, but urged caution. 'It is crenellated for defence.'

'But weaker than the proper wall,' pressed Manchester. He looked at Cromwell. 'What say you?'

Cromwell frowned. 'I know it, my lord. There is a tower set into the northernmost corner of the Manor boundary wall.'

Sir Thomas Fairfax said, 'St Mary's.'

Cromwell nodded, then looked at his commander. 'That is where we must mine, my lord.'

Then all was silent, save the bellowing of artillery that rumbled back and forth like a far-off storm. Alexander Leslie, Earl of Leven, stepped back from the map and set his jaw. 'Then we are agreed, gentlemen. We will close upon this malignant city, build properly fortified leaguers for our troops, squeeze her inhabitants and bring down her walls. God be with us.'

# CHAPTER 6

*Wigan, Lancashire, 5 June 1644*

Faith Helly could scarce believe the sheer scale of the army as it converged upon the small town. She had never seen so many folk in one place. There were men borne on the backs of magnificent horses, saddles heavy with weapons, bodies encased in metal. Some were dusty and grim-faced, others proud like cockerels, their hats and helmets resplendent in colourful plumage, defying the ominously slate-grey sky as if their very grandiosity kept the rain at bay. Men marched on foot too, slopping through the ankle-deep filth. They moved in great blocks behind bright banners of red and gold and green and blue, shifting over the mud in unison. Some of those formations bristled with long pikes so that it seemed to Faith that each block was not made of men at all, but was like some great beast: the Leviathan, made flesh by the sins of the time to crawl off the pages of Scripture. Master Sydall's Bible was close by, and she could not help but glance at it. 'By the greatness of this monster Leviathan,' she whispered the quote, 'God showeth His greatness and His power, which nothing can resist.' She felt tears prick her eyes. 'God showeth His greatness through this monster?' She blinked hard and stared back at the marching column, wondering how much sin must have washed over the earth for this to be the necessary correction. These warriors were the king's horde. The malignants, Hate-Evil Sydall had called them. The very personification of sin. She had questioned him then, but he had been right, so profoundly, horrifically right. One day in

Bolton-le-Moors had proved it. 'Not His greatness,' she said to the oaken trunk behind which she was concealed, 'but His judgement.'

'This is not God's doing, but that of man.'

Faith spun on her heels. 'Major Stryker,' she panted, hands clamped at her chest to quell the hammering of her heart. 'You startled me.'

The tall officer removed his hat. 'My apologies, Mistress Helly.' His long, grimy and matted hair flowed free, and he gathered the strands at the nape of his neck, tying them off with a piece of frayed string.

The effect was to expose the hideous scar that dominated the left side of his face, and she fought back the gasp that caught at her throat. Instead she offered a smile that she prayed would appear as genuine as it was meant. 'It is I who should apologise, sir. I spoke sharply before, I hate your king. I hate your cause. I do not hate you.'

Stryker nodded. 'You have suffered much, Mistress. And I have been unkind.'

She smiled. 'You are brusque, sir, but not cruel.' She went back to her tree, looking out at the road that still thronged with activity while careful to stay out of sight. 'But you are wrong. This is God's work. Everything is God's work, one way or another.'

### Near Wetherby, Yorkshire, 5 June 1644

Devlin Greer changed his horse at a sleepy inn called The Star. It hugged a bend in the winding River Wharfe, to the south and east of the town, and had once been a bustling haven for shepherds and farmhands. Now it was almost deserted, which suited Greer well enough, because fewer patrons meant fewer questions.

'And she's fleet o' foot?' he said to the stable boy when the grubby urchin had guided him to where his new mount waited.

'Fast as lightnin', sir.'

Greer led the bay mare out into the yard, patting her hard on the neck. 'She'd better be. There's hard riding to be done, so there is.'

The lad pushed lank hair from his eyes. 'She's the best we got, sir.'

'Good,' Greer said. He had been riding for two days, the route over the rugged hills virtually impassable in places, and always perilous. There was another day's travel ahead, and weariness was beginning to creep in. 'And my gelding?'

'In good hands, sir. I'll have him fresh for your return.'

'See that you do, lad. See that you do.'

The boy met his eye as he clambered up into the saddle. 'Beg pardon, sir, but—'

Greer raised his brow. 'But?'

'I've never been out o' the West Riding, sir.' His eyes, blue and bright, were lit with excitement. 'Are you a fighter, sir? Do you go to war?'

Devlin Greer tugged at the reins and the mare paced away. He twisted back once, to call, 'I go to the very place where this war will be won and lost. I go to York!'

## Wigan, Lancashire, 5 June 1644

'The Northern Horse,' Stryker said, going to stand beside Faith and briefly checking their dense shield of tangled foliage for prying eyes. 'They could do nothing for Lord Newcastle inside York. It was wiser to let them roam.'

The vanguard under Sir Richard Crane had been in Wigan since the previous afternoon, Crane leading his thundering section into the town unopposed. Perhaps the prior notice was why, with the arrival of the main field army, bolstered further by the troops they had gathered at Bury, the townsfolk now lined the road, casting flowers and green boughs to the sides of the filthy highway in welcome, cheering the Teutonic prince who had almost entirely wrested Lancashire from Parliamentarian control. Stryker wondered whether the war-weary folk truly meant this display, or whether it was done through fear. Either way, the night had slipped by uneventfully, with Crane placing his troopers in a well-appointed district around a substantial church, the householders promised compensation for their trouble, the horses stabled in the chancel and nave, while Stryker and his group had found quarters in a modest taphouse near the southern gate. Crane had ordered that he and Kendrick stay away from one another, and both had been true to their respective promises, keeping far apart during the march. Moreover, Stryker had heard that the Vulture's company were lodging on the north side of Wigan, and that suited him fine. He had noticed Faith Helly's disappearance after a brief visit to the latrine, and had initially panicked, but Barkworth assuaged his worry, explaining that he had escorted her to this hiding place so that she might watch the huge force enter town. Now here they were, in a tangled copse on the crest of a slight ridge, staring down at the tramping units as they turned the road to a quagmire. And Faith Helly, to his amazement, was smiling.

It was a strange sensation, witnessing that smile, as if he were seeing her for the very first time. She had been around him almost constantly since Bolton, looked after by Skellen, who made sure that she could wash, exchange her apprentice's garb for the clothes of a woman and keep her wounds clean. But now, in this instant, her smile transformed her into a real person, with real hopes and dreams. Skinny, freckled, with a nose that would have been dainty had not a gauntleted fist clubbed it to a swollen mess. Her hair, a mass of copper tresses, had been locked away in a new coif as soon as Skellen could locate one, which made her appear even more vulnerable. Her eyes were green, her mouth wide, and her skin was impossibly pale. Stryker wanted to place his arm round her narrow shoulders, and promise her she would be safe. He knew it would be a lie.

'Part of me feels lighter, somehow,' Faith said, looking back through the branches to view the spectacle down on the road.

'Lighter?'

'I did not wish James dead, never that, but I am free of a marriage I did not want. Is that wicked?'

Stryker did not know how to answer. 'Why did you not want it?'

'James was sweet—'

'But?'

'But Master Sydall was not. He did not like me.'

'Then why wed his son to you?'

She turned, casting Stryker a withering look. 'An alliance in the name of trade. But when the malignants broke in to Bolton, he cast me from his home, looking only to the preservation of his blood.'

Now it all made sense. Stryker had wondered how she had managed to survive until his timely interruption. 'That was why you were hidden in the oven?' he said, remembering the soot stains that had blighted her clothes.

She nodded. 'I was too frightened to stay on the street, so I crept through a window, crawled inside the oven. I thought I would be safe there.' She began to weep softly. 'How wrong I was.'

'The lad, James,' Stryker said, recalling the killing in the road that had provoked him to enter the house. 'He sought you in the street, yes? That was why he was out there alone.'

'Defied his father and was slain for it,' Faith said. 'I carry the burden of his death.' Stryker made to argue, but she waved him away, anger flashing across the green eyes. 'A man like you would not understand.'

Stryker retreated a pace. 'Like me?'

'A soldier.'

'You mean a malignant.' His voice was bitter. 'You would follow me, girl, be as a limpet on my arm, yet bear me ill-will?'

'You saved my life, risked your own in the saving, and for that I will ever be grateful.' The weeping had ceased, and she was older again, wiser and harder. 'But you are loyal to a tyrant, sir.

It was your army destroyed Bolton.' She looked quickly away. 'Poor, poor Bolton.'

'It is war, Mistress.'

She laughed, but there was neither warmth nor mirth in the sound. 'That was not war. You slaughtered women, children.' The words were tumbling now. They had avoided the subject, focussing on her recuperation, on keeping her alive while keeping her hidden. Yet the sight of Rupert's army had released the memories that set her jaw stiff and blazed in her stare. 'Men too. Not soldiers, Major, but civilians. Unarmed and fearful. Begging for their lives. Pleading for quarter and receiving none.'

'I, Mistress,' Stryker protested, 'slaughtered those found under arms, as was our order.'

'You follow every order?' she sneered.

'Of course.'

'Even those that would have you massacre a town?'

'The townsmen were called upon to surrender,' he retorted. 'If they had done so, they would certainly have been spared. Indeed, if they had surrendered after our first assault, terms would have been forthcoming. The Prince is not so evil as your news-books would have it.'

'Then why—' she blurted, but her voice wavered and cracked.

'Your halfwit friends strung up one of our officers. No forgiving that. No forgetting. The Prince understands courage. He understands pig-headed bloody Puritans. But he does not take kindly to the public and dishonourable hanging of an honourable prisoner. It was a grave mistake that could not go unpunished.'

Stryker's response was harsh, and Faith's bottom lip quivered, but she held his gaze stoically, unwilling to yield. 'You approve of such punishment?'

'I neither approve, nor condemn.'

'The coward's answer,' she hissed. 'You are not wicked, sir, but you consort with wickedness. Excuse it.'

He shrugged and rubbed his eye with a grubby palm. 'When you see what a man can do to another man,' he said, more softly now, 'you understand that we are all of us capable of terrible deeds.'

'I do not believe that,' she answered defiantly.

'Then you are a fool. All men have the seed of wickedness within them. That seed will grow if allowed. The cultivation is pure circumstance.'

'The seed will grow,' she said, calmer herself now, 'but a man may trample its dark shoots.' She went to the Bible, snatching it up, holding it out to Stryker. 'With God's help, Major, and only with His help. You saved me. You did not need to, but you did. King Jesus guides you.'

'I wish I could believe that, Mistress Helly. Truly.'

She kept her arm extended, offering him the book. 'God calls to you, sir, I know it. You hold not the hatred for the likes of Master Sydall – for the likes of me – that clouds the eyes of so many of your brethren. With His guidance you may choose the righteous path, Major. There is still time.'

'Hatred for your kind is often deserved, Mistress Helly,' Stryker said bitterly, regretting the tone as soon as he had uttered the words. He deliberately softened, adding: 'Your Puritan tolerates no other. They are a—*difficult* breed.'

She looked hurt. Her arm fell away. 'The Godly admit our own weaknesses, sir, for we know we are sinners. We have not the arrogance of others. Thus we accept all creeds.'

He laughed sourly. 'In my experience it is quite the opposite. Your reading of Scripture assures you of the guidance of the Holy Ghost in all that you do. Does it not follow that any man thinking differently could not, therefore, enjoy that same divine guidance? Thus you afford him no toleration, no friendship. You claim you have no arrogance. I say it is your arrogance that renders you so despised by the rest of the world.'

A group of harquebusiers cantered past following a bullet-holed blue cornet; too close for comfort, they both shrank back. Faith saw that Stryker was not about to take the Bible, and so she held it instead to her chest. 'I do not understand how you can fight on the same side as that man.'

He knew who she meant, and stared out through the foliage as he searched for the right words. He had not told her of the chance encounter in the rain-soaked field outside Standish. What had he seen, exactly? The Vulture drinking smoke as he met with another man? The fleeting moonlight had shown his companion to be a skinny youngster in a Montero cap; hardly a surprising scene in a camp full of soldiers. Yet something had not seemed right. The meeting was clandestine, and it had jarred with Stryker ever since. 'Kendrick and I fight for the King,' he said eventually. 'I do not have to like him.'

'In your heart,' she said, 'you know you follow the wrong banner.'

'A politicker as well as preacher,' he chided, secretly impressed by the girl's conviction. She reminded him of Lisette.

Faith's stare did not waver. 'Power, unchecked, can lead only to tyranny.'

'So say those who would steal power for themselves.'

'Steal?' she scoffed. 'Common men would only be His Majesty's lawful subjects, rather than his serfs.'

'And you speak for these serfs, Mistress?'

Drums boomed from the roadside. They were not played in unison, but for practise, each section hammering out a rhythm or one of the complex beats to communicate an order, so that a cacophonous melee reverberated all the way along the road, as though a storm brewed over the hills.

'Why not?' Faith asked, when the sound ebbed a touch.

'Forgive me, but yours are not palms accustomed to work, I'd wager.'

'How dare you, sir?' Faith retorted hotly. 'My father is a wool merchant, an occupation made untenable by a tyrant king. Do not presume to speak of that which you know nothing.'

Stryker held up his palms in placation. 'My own father was also a wool merchant, Mistress Helly. I speak as I find.'

The drums had ceased now, replaced by the stentorian shouts of sergeants and corporals as they saw their charges safely into Wigan to search for billets. Stryker froze. The trees, away to their left, were rustling. He cursed himself, for his lack of sight had compromised them. Faith had heard it too, and she instinctively moved behind him, shielded by his body. Stryker studied the trees on the shallow bank, hoping to see a deer or stray dog, perhaps even a pig, rooting through the undergrowth. They waited. Nothing emerged. Stryker could hear his own heartbeat pulsing in his ears. 'Clear,' he said after a long moment.

'The King,' she rasped, careful to keep her voice down, 'seeks to control God-fearing, honest men who would but put food in the mouths of their babes.'

Stryker felt the puckered skin of his damaged face pull taut as he raised his brow. 'Honest men? The merchants, the lawyers, the men of commerce? These are not common folk, but the middling sort. It is the middling sort who would paint His Majesty tyrant, for he would curtail their greed.'

'For his own greed.'

'For the good of his people, Mistress.' He was playing with her now, though he could see she was genuinely angry. In truth, he merely regurgitated the argument he had heard so many times since returning from the cruel conflagration that had consumed Europe. These were not his principles, for he had not been in England to witness the divisive parts of the Stuart reign, but it was impossible to resist baiting the girl. In her ire she was becoming whole again. 'Was it not the King who did force the price of wool to be kept low at home? Were it not for his intervention, the common folk would have frozen while the merchants counted their gold.'

'The King's meddling has done far greater hurt than good, sir,' she answered, levelling the Bible at him. 'The Parliament fought against his monopolies for the benefit of all England. In return it received aggression and threat.'

He laughed. 'You wave that book like a cudgel, Mistress. It transforms from olive branch to weapon.'

'Do not mock me, Major,' she warned, though a flicker at the corner of her eye told him that she began to mellow.

'Forgive me, but I believed I was protecting an innocent girl from a terrible fate. All the while I harbour a Puritan, a Roundhead and a traitor!'

The Bible retracted, vanishing within arms she now crossed over her chest. She looked him square in the eye. 'Then hand me to your king's judges, Major Stryker, and I will defend my treason *and* my God.'

'Never, lass,' Stryker said, still grinning. She seemed perplexed, and he took a step closer. 'Upon my honour.' His voice was serious now. 'Never.'

The tavern's air was grey and thick, its walls dirty and its beams black. It was raining heavily outside, the water thrumming on the tiles above and pooling in the road. The hearth roared to dry the soldiers' garments, and the taproom was muggy in the extreme. Men swilled ale in only their shirtsleeves, foreheads glistening as they cradled cards or sang to the fiddle's tune. The whole place stank of sweat and beer and tobacco. Three men quarrelled in a corner over a game of Irish, a pair of drunken corporals clasped palms over a bench, snarling spittle-sprayed oaths as they arm-wrestled for a pile of tarnished coins, and a serving-girl struggled from a cross-eyed pikeman's lap, slapping his pock-dented cheek with one hand and scrabbling at the loosened ties of her bodice with the other. He laughed, made a half-hearted grab for her departing rump, and made do with the blackjack she had discarded during their tussle.

Captain John Kendrick picked at his front teeth with a silver pin he had liberated from Bolton. He was one of seven men seated around a large circular table that was rough-hewn and sticky to the touch, and he eyed his companions as they craned over the curved edge, scanning the untidy piles of coins and gnawing lips as they considered their wagers. They chattered incessantly, placing side bets amongst themselves, taking odds and laying money according to how they guessed the throw would play out. Kendrick removed the pin, using its point to slide his own money into the playing area, and muttered his bet. The rest considered it, sucking pipes and quaffing drinks, and then more hands went to the table, pushing groats and pennies through puddles of spilt ale to chink in the crowded centre.

Kendrick sat back, adjusted the sleeveless buff-coat that he retained despite the warmth, and observed silently as the caster took the box in which the pair of bone dice rested. The man, one of Tillier's drummers, blew on the dice and took his throw.

Cheers and groans rippled around the table as the nuggets of finger-polished bone came to rest. Players and onlookers alike hurried to make the count and gauge the result. Kendrick drew breath through his nose with studied slowness, propped the pin between his lips, and reached out to gather his winnings. A hand fell firmly across his.

'Cheat.'

Kendrick looked up, tugging his arms away from the clammy pressure. 'A strong claim.'

The accuser, who had introduced himself as a dragoon, was a thick-set, balding fellow, probably in his mid thirties, with chubby hands and a pulpy face. 'You cheated, sir.' He fixed Kendrick with a blood-shot stare. 'We did not begin with these pieces.'

'You accuse me of trickery?' Kendrick asked, glancing at the table. 'Of conjuring dice anew?'

'Of *swapping* the fucking dice, aye!' the dragoon snarled.

Kendrick folded his arms, laughing scornfully. 'You are copper-nosed and dull-witted. Now shut your mouth and play.'

The dragoon shook his head. He was still leaning in, protecting the uncollected windfall like a guard dog. 'I'll not play with a cheat. Nay, I will not, as God's m' witness!'

The tavern was silent now, the fiddle and the song and the bawdy laughter having died away. Some of Kendrick's men had abandoned their own games to sidle over to the table. One of them spoke: 'You speak to an officer, you poxy cur.'

'Wait,' Kendrick ordered, not looking round. 'We are all equal at the hazard table, as agreed. But have a care,' he said, addressing the dragoon again, 'you stinking weasel, lest you cause a scene.'

The dragoon bridled, scraped his fat fingers over a chin of

stubble. 'I know you,' he said in a low voice. 'The Vulture, they calls you. On account o' that beak.'

Kendrick smiled, making certain that his carefully filed fangs were visible. 'I have not a clue as to the name's true provenance, but I'd be willing to wager my rather curious stature claims a hand in it.'

'*Ha*!' the dragoon brayed, looking to the men gathered just behind him. 'Bastard crook-back, lads!'

'There again,' Kendrick returned, ignoring the laughter that ensued, 'perhaps it is my lovely cloak, for the fur doth lend a man's mind to thoughts of black plumage. Of course, a country maggot like you would never have seen the bird in question. Would not know it if it did shit in your eye.' The mirth fell away, the dragoon's face was suddenly tense with the sting of the insult. Kendrick clicked his fingers and one of his men was at his flank, the heavy cloak he had shed for the game hanging in his grip. 'Nor would you have knowledge,' Kendrick went on, shifting in the chair so that the cloak could be draped over his shoulders, 'of the animal that really lent its skin to my garb.' Now he let his eyes rake over the rest of the dragoons. 'It is the pelt of a bear. A black bear.'

'Ferocious beast,' the strongly accented voice of Sergeant Janik intoned gruffly behind. 'Was bastard.'

'And what happened to that bear, Andor?'

Janik sucked his moustache theatrically. 'You open it from belly to ballock!'

Now Kendrick's men laughed. The dragoon and his friends kept their silence. 'Ah yes. That is what happened, truly.' From within the fur-trimmed garment, he pulled a huge knife, turning it slowly so that the flame's light danced on the broad steel. 'Opened it with this fine thing. My cinquedea. My pride and joy. All of five fingers wide.'

The dragoon made to speak, but Janik interrupted: 'I'd open mouth for nought but cocks if I were you.'

The pulpy cheek quivered gently. 'You do not frighten me. I have my own blade, and I knows how to use it well enough.'

'But will it do any good?' Janik growled from his place at Kendrick's shoulder. 'Captain, here, is hard-man. He has supped of magic brew.'

The dragoon forced a nervous chuckle, but went to grasp the nearest of the disputed coins. 'And my colonel's a forest faerie.'

'But you have heard of our creed,' Kendrick said, and he knew from the man's thickly laboured swallow that he was right. 'There is a certain herb of which the men partake. I had the honour of its consumption in my time skinning Turks.' He dug at a spot of grime beneath his fingernails with the tip of the knife. 'It makes us strong, this herb. Bullets bounce off our very skin.' He looked the dragoon in the eye again. 'But I have no need of such power here. My beautiful cinquedea will be more than capable.'

The dragoon stared at the blade, as if bewitched by it. 'Capable?'

John Kendrick rammed the cinquedea down as hard as he could. It pierced the top of the dragoon's hand easily, driving through flesh, snapping bone, and bursting out through the palm. The man stared in wide-eyed disbelief for a long moment, and then he screamed. His hand was pinned fast to the table top, the fingers of the other clawing at the inert flesh, desperate to release the bone-handled spear, and all the while his confederates were reaching for their weapons. Kendrick sat back, as if he were basking on a summer's day. His men crowded round, their swords scraping free of scabbards. He knew there were too many of them to be bested. More importantly, the enraged dragoons knew it too, and quickly their numbers ebbed as men made their own count and slunk towards the tavern door and a quiet night.

The wounded man sobbed over his stricken limb. Kendrick whistled a jaunty tune as he swept the blood-spattered coins into a rough heap and deposited them into a leather pouch that one of his men held open. Only when all his winnings were safely tied away did he collect the dice. He winked at the keening dragoon, produced the original bone chunks from between his thighs, tossing them to the table, and stood. With a quick jerk, he plucked the cinquedea free from hand and table, eliciting a high-pitched scream from the man who seemed to fold in on himself, cradling his ruined hand to his stomach and sliding to the floor.

Kendrick was just deciding whether to cut off the dragoon's nose or ears when he was disturbed by the mention of his name. He stopped dead, turning to see one of his officers stalk from the murk. 'News?'

The newcomer nodded rapidly. 'You were right, sir.'

'About?'

'The bitch.'

'Come.' Kendrick looked briefly down at the whimpering dragoon. 'Remember this moment. For it is the moment your life was spared by the Vulture. You are fortunate.' He walked away as the remaining dragoons fell to their friend's aid, and led the officer into the deepest corner he could find. 'Speak.'

'Saw her, sir. With that one-eyed bastard. The one you fought, sir.'

'Well, well, well …' Kendrick paused in thought. And the more he thought, the more it made sense. He had sent his men out into the burgeoning Royalist fold almost daily since the escalade at Bolton. They had first checked the Sydall house, but, though the cold bodies had been removed, no warm ones had apparently returned. Kendrick had spoken personally with the musty aldermen of the grieving town, to no avail, and it was only then that he had decided the devious wench must have secreted herself somewhere within the itinerant city that was Prince Rupert's army. The obvious place to look was amongst the blossoming ranks that accompanied the baggage train, that straggling band of wives and whores, wheelwrights and peddlers, snot-nosed children, smiths, sutlers, hawkers, cooks and quacks. She was not to be found. And now he knew why. 'I have been a fool.'

'Sir?'

'When the Prince ordered me to Lathom House, I was angry. It took us away from the search. But Stryker was too quick to fight me. Too eager. He is a veteran of the Low Countries, every man knows it. The things that grey eye must have seen.' Kendrick shook his head, for he had seen such things too, and those things had turned his soul black as night. 'Why was he so enraged when he saw our colour at Lathom? Why so determined for me to kill him? Bolton was not the first time he has waded through carcasses, I can assure you.'

'Then why?'

'The girl was with him. Her presence stirs him to vengeance.'

'He swives her?'

Kendrick shrugged, as best his shoulders would allow. 'Perhaps he does, perhaps he does not.' He gave a rueful chuckle. 'I should have known. Damn me, I should have known.'

'Shall I gather the men, sir?'

'And march upon his billet?' Kendrick scoffed. 'Your enthusiasm is commendable, Ensign, but your wit requires a whetstone. He is protected by our Bohemian peacock. If I attack him directly I shall swing.' He paused as thoughts tumbled in his head. 'We must prise the slattern away from him.'

'And if we succeed, sir. Will she know where it is?'

'Of course,' Kendrick replied, pacing out into the wet darkness. 'That Puritan prig would not have died without bringing his whelps into the circle. She is Hate-Evil Sydall's daughter. She knows.' He splashed through a deep puddle, brown water spraying up his breeches, but he barely noticed at all. 'We will take her, and then we will take the cipher.'

# CHAPTER 7

*York, 7 June 1644*

It was an hour past midnight and the clouds had fled over the moors to leave a glowing moon. It silvered the city and its walls, illuminated the earthworks as though they were immersed in a hard frost and lit the way for Captain Lancelot Forrester's Company of Foot. They trudged along the cobbled Tadcaster Road that ran out of Micklegate Bar, the imposing edifice of the sconce up ahead, occupying the ridge of higher ground that arced around the south-west of York. There were three such sconces covering the ridge, thrown up at intervals to prevent the Scots from taking that natural vantage point, and each was permanently armed and garrisoned.

Forrester saw the flag of the Marquis of Newcastle's Regiment of Foot as he climbed the final yards. Highlighted by the glow of a flickering brazier, it flapped in the wind while proudly displaying the three white crosses that ran diagonally through its field. The rest of the flag, though he could not discern it in the darkness, would be blood red, with the cross of St George in canton.

'Ho there!' Forrester called as his column, numbering just over fifty, came up to the rear entrance of the sconce.

Men moved above, spectral shadow puppets in the light of moon and flame. 'You are?' came the call.

'Forrester.' He glanced again at the company colour, noting the trio of devices. '*Second* captain; Mowbray's Foot.'

A pause, some muted chatter, and the wattle screen serving as back gate was scraped clear. An officer clutching a wickedly sharp-looking partisan strode a few yards down the slope. He eyed Forrester's own flag, held in the thick fingers of his brawny ensign, and offered a deep bow upon counting only two of Mowbray's diamonds. 'Welcome to the Mount, sir.' He moved closer, angling his body to the side of the pathway and pointing the steel-tipped staff in the direction of the gateway. 'Follow me, if you would.'

'Thank you,' Forrester said as his company juddered into life. He was close enough to get a good look at the officer now. The fellow was probably in his late twenties, wore a suit of fine blue cloth, a red ribbon at his sleeve, and a beautiful, if rather impractical rapier at his waist. 'You command?'

The officer, having fallen in beside Forrester, spluttered an apology. 'I am Captain Elias Croak, sir, and yes, this is my little kingdom.'

'A fine fort,' Forrester said truthfully as they filed into the interior, 'and a marvellous vista.'

The Mount sconce sat bestride the road. It dominated it, guarding both the southern approach to York and the open land between the ridge and Micklegate Bar. From here Forrester could see the flickering specks of fires lit by the Scots besiegers, and, if he looked eastward, to his left, more flames betrayed the second enemy army, local Parliamentarians under the Fairfaxes. Further in that direction were imposing silhouettes of structures that climbed out of the sodden soil, and he supposed two were windmills, while the third would be another of the Royalist sconces, perched on the most easterly point of the ridge. He turned back into the interior. The central enclosure was a square platform above a rampart that was, he guessed, around nine or ten feet high. The purpose of the place was entirely militaristic. There were no billets, nor home comforts of any sort, simply weapons stores, a pit that served as powder magazine, and coils of spare match. The garrison itself was strong. In the tremulous light of half a dozen more braziers, Forrester saw that there might have been fifty musketeers and several gun crews. The musketeers were easy enough to make out in the gloom, for they wore suits of white, the colour of the Marquis of Newcastle. Their nickname, he remembered, was the Lambs, and he could see why, though he knew the reference would be made with tongue firmly thrust in cheek. There was nothing innocent or vulnerable about this northern regiment. They had fought right the way across Yorkshire and Northumberland, first against Lord Fairfax's Parliamentarian faction, then the invading Scots, and had become a force to be reckoned with.

'And what can I do for you, Captain Forrester?' Croak asked.

Forrester left his men and beckoned Croak to the edge of the rampart, the extreme periphery of which was screened by a wicker trellis. There was a ditch on the sconce's outer face, immediately beneath them, which was spiked with stakes, and at each corner of the square there was a jutting horn, a corner platform on which at least one heavy gun was mounted. He pointed to the cannon perched on the outer point of one of the horns. 'Would you mind pounding an enemy look-out post a while, Captain? Down there, to the west.'

'I know the one.'

Forrester nodded. 'My fellows and I are to sally out and smash it up. If you'd soften 'em a touch, I'd be grateful.'

Croak's smile was pleasant enough, but apologetic. 'I think not, sir.'

'Not?'

'Seems the enemy are on the move, sir. See here.' He fished in his coat for a slim perspective glass.

'A fine piece, Master Croak,' Forrester said, taking the brass tube and noting the engraved script on the side. He raised it to his eye, trained the scope on the point indicated by the young captain's outstretched arm, and saw a large body of men on the move. There was a colour in the van, held aloft and whipped in a continuous figure of eight, and in its wake marched scores of men carrying muskets. 'What the devil are they about?'

Croak took back the glass. 'Tightening the noose, sir.'

'We are pressed at all quarters,' Forrester agreed. 'The Eastern Association moved into the northern suburbs yesterday. 'Twas a hot fight, with many wounded.'

'I heard they attacked to the east, too.'

'Aye. Defeated, but the buggers killed five of our men for no loss to their own.' A rueful chuckle rumbled up from Forrester's chest. 'Brazen knaves retired having purloined several of our cattle and a large cartful of digging equipment.'

'How close do they come in the north?' Croak asked, lifting the perspective glass to his own eye.

'Within pistol shot of the wall,' replied Forrester. 'We burned most of the houses without the city, to clear our line of fire and prevent the rebels from sheltering therein, but, by Jesu, they creep up to the gates regardless. They choke us like a damned garrotte.'

'Sir?' Croak said suddenly, his voice pitched high in alarm.

Forrester looked at him, then out into the black abyss, and finally back to Croak. 'What is it, man?'

Elias Croak's neck convulsed as he swallowed thickly, the brass instrument still pressed tight to his eye. 'Ladders, sir. I see ladders.'

And all became clear. Forrester did not wait to take back the glass, swivelling instead to regard his men. They were arranged neatly in line further back inside the enclosure, muskets to the front, pikes at the rear. 'Ensign!' he bellowed through cupped hands. 'Bring up the lads!'

Croak spoke at his side. 'They're looking for trouble, sir.'

Now Forrester turned, even as his men shook themselves into life. 'And they shall find it, Master Croak. They shall find it.'

'Have you pitfalls?' Forrester asked breathlessly as his men drew up on the south-western face of the sconce. They were quickly joined by members of the garrison, white coats a glowing contrast to the red of Mowbray's regiment. No reply came, and he shook Croak's arm roughly. 'Pitfalls. Have you dug any on the outer face?'

'No, sir,' Croak muttered, his eyes glazing.

'Then we must pour lead upon them as they hit the ditch.' He swivelled to address his company. 'Line the rampart! Make ready your weapons! Those with wadding; use it! Keep calm and do not fire till I tell you!'

He made to find himself a post on one of the sconce's angular horns, but was held back by Croak's hand as it gripped his sleeve. 'I confess I have not seen much of war, sir.'

The young officer's neck quivered as he gulped back a rising tide of bile. Forrester wanted to offer a word of encouragement, but there was no time. 'The men?'

'They are veterans of many a scrap, sir.' Croak's gaze fell to the ground between them. 'It is only their leader you will find lacking.'

Forrester took Croak by the arm and all but dragged him on to the nearest horn. 'Of all base passions,' he said as they reached the battery, 'fear is the most accursed.'

Croak's face brightened. 'Henry the Sixth, if I'm not gravely mistook.'

Forrester grinned. 'I like you already.'

They gave orders for the big guns to be prepared, and for the muskets to line the rampart along the south and west faces. Forrester's pikemen would wait in the rear, their huge spears ready to throw back any escalade, should matters come to that. And then they waited, scrutinising the fields and trenches and hedgerows and outbuildings for sign of an enemy advance. Nothing seemed to be moving at all. It was as if the night had swallowed whatever regiment had dared to be abroad under such a witching moon.

'I would string the lot of them up,' Croak said after an extended period of tense silence. He was kneeling beside Forrester, the latter sweeping the perspective glass back and forth across the inky horizon. 'Hang every rebel high and let them dangle till their bones fell through the noose. What say you, Captain?'

Forrester lowered the glass. 'I was once at a place called Magdeburg,' he said quietly, nerves still jangling as formless men whispered all around them. 'It was chaos. When the Imperial troops broke in, they were consumed with battle rage.'

'Battle rage?'

Forrester smiled sadly. 'You will soon know it, I am sorry to say. It is the fury that comes of danger, of gut-twisting terror, of the stink of blood and piss and shit that wafts across a battlefield like invisible gun-smoke. It is a powerful, heady mix, like the strongest wine, and it makes a man drunk on violence.' He paused. 'At Magdeburg they destroyed everything. Fired the houses, stripped it bare. We were in a church with thousands of others. More and more came in, pushing through the doorway, trampling their neighbours, their kin, underfoot like a fleshen carpet. So much screaming, I thought my ears would bleed. Then the enemy were among us. Poles and Spaniards, as I recall. Chopping. Always chopping. The bodies shoaled like fish, surging away from our laughing executioners. There was nowhere to go. All one could do was climb, so I climbed. Pulpit, a tapestry, an upper balcony. Before I knew it, I was on the roof, staring down at the carnage. Twenty thousand died that day, so I'm told. Took them two full weeks to be rid of the bodies. I never again wish to see such horror so long as I live.'

'I—' Croak made to speak.

'No matter,' Forrester cut him off. 'Would I execute every rebel? No, sir, I would not. I would win this war, and then I would make peace. And then, Master Croak, I would forget it ever happened and put my mind to the pursuit of thespian perfection.' He lifted the glass again. Down below he could see movement. Men were surging forth from trenches he had not perceived in the gloom, led by torches that made the faces in the front rank glower like ghouls. The tiny lights of match-cord flecked the dark like fireflies, marking the extent of the large force, perhaps as many as two hundred in all. They were headed directly for the Mount sconce. 'Here they come. Fire the cannon!'

'Christ Jesus,' Captain Croak hissed when he took the glass to see for himself. He scrambled to his feet, evidently intent on evacuating the fort. 'Christ Jesus, we shall all be slain.'

'Stay where you are!' Forrester snarled. He stood too. 'Aye, man, you may be right, and this may be the death of us. Then again, you may not. But what is certain is that we will surely perish if we run.'

Croak stole a longing glance over his shoulder at York's flame-lit palisade. 'We can make it.'

'Over that swamp?' Forrester said scornfully. 'They'd be on us in a trice. Here we have protection. Out there we have nought but mud.' He dropped his voice to a soft hiss. 'And would his grace thank you for surrendering this position so cheaply?'

Forrester found one of his men, a fellow he knew to be fleet-footed and dependable. 'Get back to the gate. Tell them to send reinforcements immediately. *Immediately*!' The runner nodded once and was gone. Forrester paced at the backs of the men, unconcerned as to whether they wore coats of white or red. 'Keep the fire steady. Steady, I say!' He held his breath as the only field piece trained on the approaching infantry exploded into life, coughing thick smoke and recoiling savagely on its carriage. He could not see whether it had done any damage, but at least it would show this new ally of Parliament that the men on the Mount were ready for a tussle. 'They look to break our nerve so that they may slash at our backs. It is not men they wish to fight, but conies, high-tailed and scattering. Keep the fire steady, my lads, that is all I ask. We will not run! They will run!'

He moved back to the jutting limb of the horn as the enemy came out of the mist, a great swathe of swords and halberds, pistols and muskets. They were Scots, Forrester reckoned, for though the dark concealed much, it could not hide the blue bonnets. He brayed at his charges to brace themselves against a tide of notoriously formidable warriors.

The Scots slowed suddenly, performing the manoeuvre with seamless ease, and their musketeers came smoothly to the fore. The first rank took a knee, angled their weapons up at the looming sconce, and without pause for instruction they fired. The muskets billowed smoke across their faces, individual clouds spiralling out to obscure the ranks behind, and then the next men were through, advancing past the shoulders of their kneeling comrades, and they fired too. More smoke, more noise.

Up on the sconce, men cringed, turning their bodies in profile as if they braced against a howling gale. Most of the bullets flew harmlessly high or smacked into the rampart to rattle its timber facings, but some thumped into the space just above the lip of the fort, tearing noisily into the wickerwork, which shook and splintered. Forrester crouched beside the large cannon, its barrel still warm. A leaden ball whined as it careened past his right ear, another showered slivers of wood from one of the gun carriage spokes. He gestured for the gun crew to retire, for they had no time to make the iron killer ready for a follow-up shot.

Another volley rippled up from below. Forrester rolled along the base of the wicker screen to take up position at the joint where the horn met the main rampart. He noticed that the screen was badly holed in several places and beginning to disintegrate, leaking shot so that the first screams of pain rent the night. Moonlight, smudgy as it was, lanced through to dapple his coat. Somewhere behind, a mattross — one of the gunnery assistants — was down and shrieking, kneecap shattered by a ball that would have flattened into a disc as it smashed through the joint, pulverizing bone and tissue until the limb was tattered and forever useless. Forrester nodded to a pair of men who did not have loaded weapons, and they slunk forward to drag the wretched fellow to the rear. An appointment with the chirurgeon's ravenous saw awaited him.

He risked a peek over the screen. The Covenanters were swarming forwards now, slogging through the mire behind a big banner that swirled high above a bulb-eyed ensign. A smattering of Scots carried round bucklers, others the huge claymores favoured by the men of the Highlands; almost to a man they were swathed in dense folds of plaid. The slopes of the two horns that formed the corners of this side of the sconce were almost sheer, far too difficult to scale in the wet, and so the attackers funnelled into the space between, aiming for the broad, straight face that formed the southernmost side of the square. They leapt into the ditch, waded through its saturated bed, and began to scrabble up the earthwork. Some had ladders, and these were tipped against the escarpment for the bravest souls to climb into the fray.

Forrester drew his pistol and eased the hammer to half cock. He felt the muscles in his face tighten as his bowels turned to water, and forced a grim smile for the others to see. 'Front rank!' For a dreadful moment he thought his charges might not obey, but to his exquisite relief they began to move, the first group shuffling up to the screen, flinching as more shots rattled against it. But those shots were sporadic now, for the attackers were too close to risk a pause for the reloading of muskets, and the lull was precisely what he had been waiting for. 'Hold! Hold, damn your eyes! Let 'em come close!'

A bullet punched a wide fissure in the entwined willow switches beside his head. He leaned in, pressing an eye up against the newly cleaved loophole. The first of the Scots were very close now, almost at the crest. But their ladders were not long enough and they stalled, scrabbling for purchase on the slick timber slats that formed the final few feet.

'Blow on your coals!' Forrester snarled. He looked back at the second rank. 'You too, you laggardly bastards!' He counted silently to five, swallowed hard, and filled his lungs. '*Fire!*'

The foremost musketeers rose as one, black muzzles swinging up and over the screen. The long-arms discharged together, a great roar rippling right the way across the palisade, clothing it in white, sulphurous smoke. Forrester still stared through his spy-hole, long enough to catch glimpses of men snatched back by the thick wave of lead, tossed like rubbish into the ditch. Then he was screaming at the first group to retire, for the rear rank to come up, and before the Scots could reach the tattered wickerwork his charges were bringing the next volley to bear.

The world exploded for a second time, more smoke gusted out and over the slope, and then the whitecoats of the Marquis of Newcastle and the redcoats of Sir Edmund Mowbray were standing together, muskets turned about, butt ends brandished like clubs. Forrester had his pistol primed and cocked, and he stood too, leaning into the creaking trellis and squeezing the trigger as his men hacked and battered at the heads of the few Scots who had somehow survived the leaden barrage. A third volley ripped the night, and at first Forrester thought it had come from the enemy, but he saw the smoke billow out from the gun battery on the horn that formed the spike at the opposite end of the sconce's southern face. The men had lined that platform, aiming along the face of the rampart, and their fire raked across the Scots' flank. In seconds the rampart was clear, purged of the enemy, scattered blue bonnets the only thing left on the slope. Forrester squinted into the gloom, only to see the beaming face of one Elias Croak. He felt instantly ashamed, for he had presumed the young officer had fled in terror.

Down below, the ditch was filled with dead and wounded men who writhed like a pool full of eels; they were trampled as the next wave came upon them.

'Pikes!' Forrester bellowed. 'Pikes!'

The pikemen came up, their musket-wielding comrades sliding back to the safety of the enclosure so that they might begin the laborious process of reloading their weapons. Scouring sticks plunged into barrels, scraping the clogging soot clear, while priming powder was carefully tipped into the pan of each musket. They needed wadding too, so that they might shoot down the slope without the ball falling out, and they hurriedly carried out each and every task as the seconds slipped by.

Forrester knew it was all taking too long. He reloaded his pistol and moved to the edge of the screen. The Scots were shoving and kicking their way across the ditch and hauling themselves up the slope using swords and dirks like climbers' picks. He glanced along his line of pikemen, gave the order for the spears to be presented, and the steel-tipped shafts went up and over, jabbing down to stab and topple the attackers. But there were too many Scots this time, and though several were thrown back to earth, some dodged the pikes while others grabbed hold of the long stems of ash and pulled, dragging the defenders over the rampart and down into the killing field. There were more ladders this time, passed up from the rear to slam on to the rampart, and the Scottish horde suddenly found their climb made easy.

'Fall back!' Forrester called. He could see that most of his musketeers were ready now, but it was far too late to staunch the blue tide as it surged up and over the edge, smashing through the wicker as though the interlaced switches were so many brittle twigs. The Royalist defenders formed up in the centre of the enclosure, pikes providing a shield, muskets beginning to offer sporadic fire. The Scots kept coming, more and more, scrambling into the inner sanctum and firing their weapons. When they were spent, they reversed them to be used as clubs, while their officers brandished swords for the kill.

There was nothing left to do but fight. Forrester levelled his pistol and drew his own sword. More musketry rattled all around, immersing the sconce in bitter cloud. Forrester raised his blade high, hoping his men could see, snarled an unintelligible challenge, and charged.

At first he saw nothing, but then two bulging eyes above a russet beard leered from the acrid fog. He shot the man square in the face, features wiped clean in an instant, the trunk never emerging from the smoke. He moved on, swatted another man with his sword and ducked below a scything halberd. He was vaguely aware that others had joined him in the melee, bellowing their defiance as they fanned out to protect the redoubt. He saw bodies strewn here and there, and though they were half devoured by the mist, it seemed most flashed white and red in his peripheral vision, glimpses that told him the fight was not going well.

Then he was crouching, scrambling over terrain churned to sludge, barrelling headlong into a buckler and bouncing hard off its iron boss so that he landed with his rump planted in the cold filth. He rolled, slid wildly as he regained his footing, and swung his blade as the opponent came on. The sword glanced harmlessly off the shield rim, so he jumped backwards out of range of the inevitable follow-up thrust. The tip sliced air just inches from his nose, clanged off his sword-hilt as he frantically raised the weapon to block, and then he was falling again, battered off balance by a man possessed of impressive strength. The next blow would have cleaved him in two had not a thin rapier appeared a palm's width from his face. The slender steel snapped as it parried, but it was enough, and Forrester was able to scramble clear to see Captain Elias Croak toss his sword-hilt away and shoot their shared enemy in the chest with a pistol. He gave a madman's grin, spattered as he was in blood, and howled at the moon, then he was gone, plunging into the fray.

Forrester panted like an exhausted dog as he rose to his feet. They were overwhelmed, defeated in all quarters, and he screamed the order to retreat. Perhaps a few would make it to the safety of Micklegate Bar. All around him the fight raged. A musket coughed somewhere to the rear, the air pulsing at his left side as the ball flew into the attackers. It snatched one of the Scottish officers clean off his feet. And the attackers stalled. They hesitated, faces deflating as they stared, wide-eyed at the Royalist lines. Then they began to judder backwards. More shots came from behind him, picking away some of the retiring Scots as they faltered. And the Royalists were cheering.

Forrester turned. The whitecoats seemed to have multiplied exponentially. Dozens of them ran to the battle, emerging like ghosts from the tumbling smoke, grimacing like so many gargoyles as they screamed their victory, and Forrester joined them, cutting down a stunned Covenanter and looking for the next. He felt the battle-rage surge through his veins, intoxicating him, and he heard himself crow with the exhilaration he would later regret but could not hope to staunch.

The runner had made it back to York. The reinforcements had come from Micklegate Bar, and in the cacophony of battle, Forrester could hear the low thrum of hooves, and he knew then that they would win. The marquis had sent horse as well as foot, and the Scots would not face such odds with no horse or pike of their own. And then they were breaking, running, cohesion dissolved, the heads capped in blue were turning away, bolting pell-mell down the slope and into the cannon-pocked wilderness that separated besiegers and besieged. Forrester bent double, planting his hands on his knees, and gulped the caustic air into his lungs. Then he laughed, in bitter, mad relief. It was over.

# PART 2

# EXTREME NECESSITY

# CHAPTER 8

*Near Liverpool, Lancashire, 7 June 1644*

The Royalist army moved westwards, bullied always by wind and rain. Talk was ever of York, of the fevered reports that spoke of an alliance of three vast armies, now fused into one. Men whispered of the inevitable collision with the feared Scots Covenanters in battle – a brew many of them had sipped in the Bishops' Wars of the late 1630s, and one they would never willingly imbibe again – and of the need to relieve the Earl of Newcastle's stubborn force that had been holed up in the capital of the north since April. But despite the talk and the bravado and the anxiety, they trudged in the opposite direction, Prince Rupert's gaze remaining firmly fixed upon the conquest of the north-west.

The raising of troops had been Rupert's priority in the days since the sacking of Bolton. With the arrival of the Northern Horse and efforts to recruit, equip and train as many Cheshire and Lancashire Royalists as possible, the army that marched out of Wigan, winding south via St Helens and Prescot, boasted some seven thousand infantrymen and more than six thousand horse. A drawn-out column of artillery, ammunition, stolen livestock, victuals and baggage formed the tail, shadowed, as ever, by as many camp followers as there were soldiers.

Stryker and his party were in the rear. They had been invited to join Sir Richard Crane and his Lifeguard at the very front, and it had taken some smooth diplomacy for the offer to be rejected without giving offence, but Stryker would not leave his baggage wagon and its secret cargo. Thus, they were forced to keep pace with the lurching vehicle driven by Simeon Barkworth, who swore viciously with each water-filled divot and rut. Stryker was pleased to ride, though the mud was fetlock deep, and even Vos seemed happy to brave the pelting showers. Hood and Skellen rode too, though the latter grumbled for much of the journey, his Monmouth cap stretched down as far over his ears as possible.

The going was slow but steady, the road a morass, but the drums and trumpets thundered and squawked so that the men kept rhythm as best they could. Packhorses whinnied as their hooves slid and slewed, soldiers – grudgingly suborned into driving cattle – spat threats and swung sticks at their lumbering herds, and all the while the north-west coast of England emerged out of the blurry deluge, inch by inch, mile by mile. First, the glistening expanse of a great river gradually resolved in the distance like a colossal gilt serpent, cutting a curve in the terrain to the south. It was the Mersey, and they had forced a crossing of the same river back at Stockport, a few days before their fateful arrival at the Geneva of the North. It had been wide enough there, its thrashing currents impossible to ford, yet this was something entirely different. The Mersey formed an estuary as it rushed out into the tumultuous waters of the Irish Sea, and here it was a titan, broad and glittering and mighty. The scouts up on a hill near a marsh-strangled village called Huyton reported it to be close to three miles wide at one point, and a new vein of fretfulness rippled up and down the meandering column as men wondered how they might possibly get across. So Prince Rupert himself galloped his great black destrier up and down the nervous army, bellowing for calm and for level heads, assuring the filth-spattered troops that there would be no perilous crossing this time. For it was on the east bank of the estuary that they would find the enemy stronghold, and the Royalist conquerors would hem Liverpool's garrison between the vast waterway and their heavy artillery, and crush the rebels like hazelnuts in a vice. Sure enough, after a morning spent climbing into the undulating terrain that fringed the town, the walls of the region's principal port seemed to blossom like grey petals, emerging from the bitter miasma as the storm waned to a fine drizzle. The army, tired and saturated, tramped into the fields to the east of their prize, even as the guns on Liverpool's crenellated rampart coughed their first warnings, the flat cracks echoing back and forth between the mountains and the sea.

They fanned out in the area immediately to the east of their quarry, where the road from Prescot dipped towards the Mersey estuary. The scouts set off to investigate the terrain, while quartermasters and their teams began the arduous task of finding billets for the men. In reality it was only the most senior officers who would find warm quarters, for the villages in the region were small and sparse, and it was clear that there would not be enough houses to sustain this new population. Those fortunate enough to have canvas began pitching their tents. Those without were forced into patches of forest to construct rudimentary shelters out of branch and bracken. For a while the deep rumble of ordnance bellowed at them from Liverpool's walls, but they were out of range and the guns soon fell silent.

It was around one o'clock when Stryker's party reached the sprawling encampment. Hood went ahead, returning a short while later having found a modest clearing in the centre of a birch and beech copse. Mercifully, the rain had stopped, and it did not take long to stake the flax canvas sheets over freshly cut poles and bring the cart into the green shelter of a soaring beech tree.

Faith Helly emerged from her hiding place just as Stryker was shaking the rain from his hat. She went to the edge of the tree line and he followed. They could just discern the town's outline from here, and he saw she was staring wistfully at it.

'It will fall,' he said.

She did not look up. 'Pray God it does not.'

'It will.'

'Like all the others.'

He nodded. She was vehemently opposed to the king's cause,

and nothing he could say would change that. Indeed, he found that he respected her all the more for it. 'The Prince will call on the garrison to surrender.'

'Then I pray they do, for I would not see them share Bolton's fate.'

Stryker wiped a gloved hand over his chin, pushing away the rain that had gathered on his short beard, and replaced his damp hat. 'I will ask Skellen to light a fire.'

She turned, touching fingers to his elbow. 'The men talk of battle.'

'We will storm the town, aye, if its governor is foolish enough to resist.'

She shook her head. 'Battle, Major Stryker. Real battle. They say you will soon fight the Scots.'

'And more besides.'

'Will you win?'

This was a question Stryker had suppressed thinking about in the days since he had learnt that the army of the Eastern Association had joined the siege at York. No one knew if they would eventually march to the Marquis of Newcastle's aid, but all suspected it. Now he imagined those combined forces. Twenty thousand? Thirty? Perhaps more. He looked her directly in the eye. 'Of course.'

She saw through the lie. 'What will I do, if—?'

'You survived Bolton, Mistress Helly. You will survive my demise.'

'Do you not fear death on those cursed fields, sir?'

'Idle armies breed nought but disease. I would rather face steel and shot on the field than plague in Oxford.'

'I do not want to lose you.'

He shot her a crooked smile. 'It gladdens me to hear it.'

'Look,' Faith said suddenly. Her gaze had returned to the town, and Stryker followed her pointing finger. Three figures were on the rampart; two women and a child, to judge by their coifs and the diminutive stature of the third. It was difficult to see what they were about, but the distinctive pose they each took up described a trio of archers. They held the bows high, aiming for the brooding clouds, and loosed, one after another. Stryker and Faith watched as the arrows careened skyward, vanishing to black specks, and then they were larger, darker, like diving peregrines on the hunt. Further out, in the open ground before the town where the beginnings of saps and gun batteries were being marked by teams of engineers, men shouted the alarm, but the arrows fell well short, thudding into the mud almost a hundred yards from any target. The Royalist teams jeered as they made obscene gestures at their would-be assassins, baring lily-white rumps to taunt the women, but the message was clear. The people within the town were not there under duress. There would be no repeat of Wigan's joyous celebrations here.

In reply, one of Rupert's small field pieces, a leather gun that was not part of the main train, spewed its murderous iron up at the walls, forcing the plucky archers to shy quickly away. The Royalists cheered again. And the siege of Liverpool had begun.

Prince Rupert's regiments began to set themselves up for a siege even before the first summons to surrender was rejected. The lie of the land told them that much, for Liverpool's western border was the Mersey, and on the east it was protected by a medieval wall, strengthened by mud and stake so that it was high and strong. A ditch ran in an arc around the landward side of the town, screening the looming stone from assault, and a stout castle dominated the southern approaches. In effect, she would not fall easily, and the men scattered around her likely knew it all too well. So after the tents came the latrines and the grain stores, the powder magazines, livestock pens and troughs for fodder. Foraging parties went out in search of berries and nuts, vegetables, wild watercress and meat, and all the while the engineers rode as close to the walls as possible to plot the points deemed most likely to degrade under heavy cannon fire. The prince himself – with his ever-present cavalry – was up on a high ridge overlooking the port. The slopes were capped by the emerald bands of mature hedgerow, while the summit was blotted by the stonework of some ancient monument.

'Beacon?' Skellen asked, as he came to stand beside Stryker. It was a murky afternoon, and they were out in the open, their copse behind, staring up at the ridge.

'Like as not. In readiness for invasion.'

Skellen grunted. 'By the Diegos, not the King.'

Stryker laughed. 'Aye, I suppose you're in the right of it, Will.' He studied the high ground. There was a village halfway up, its chimneys spewing smoke, and he presumed Rupert and his men would be billeted beneath those inviting thatches.

Skellen took a tight ball of something resembling grass from his snapsack and pushed it into the side of his mouth. He gave a green-gummed leer and thumbed the air in the direction of the trees. 'Brooklime and chickweed. Found it back there.'

'Cannot abide the stuff.'

Skellen shrugged, and stuffed some more past his lips. 'They told our herald to piss off, sir, beg pardon. We'll be here a while, methinks, and I've no stomach for an empty belly.'

The first summons had indeed been rejected, and the cannon had continued to fire from Liverpool's battlements. At least, Stryker thought, they had found a reasonable place to wait it out. He glanced back at the copse. The heady scent of wood smoke announced Simeon Barkworth's successful attempt to light a fire. They walked back, high-stepping over clawing brambles and stooped bracken, to discover Lieutenant Hood had returned from a sojourn to the main camp with a good slab of venison and a wolfish grin. He had had the gumption to pay the quartermaster a decent bribe. Faith sat with them as they ate, perched on a damp log, saying little and forever scrutinizing the trees for interlopers. When she had finished, wiping greasy fingers on the wet grass, she waded into the undergrowth with her Bible, keen to find somewhere quiet to read before the day faded to dusk.

'Never had children, did you, sir?' Hood asked.

The question startled Stryker. 'Not that I am aware of,' he said, then he realized he must have been staring at the girl as she disappeared into the trees, and was immediately embarrassed. 'I do not think her my child, Tom.'

'That was not my assertion, sir.'

'You thought it,' Stryker said. 'And mind your tone, lad.'

Hood, seated opposite Stryker at the far side of the fire, stared quickly into the flames. 'I apologize, sir.'

From the trees the whinnying of horses roused them, and as one they spun around to look. Skellen's mount, a bay mare named Bess, promptly lifted her tail and deposited a hillock of dung amongst the foliage. The men laughed, Bess trampled her steaming shit, and Stryker's irritation was gone. 'No matter,' he said to Hood. 'Her presence has set my mind to work.'

'You ponder what your offspring would be like?' the lieutenant ventured. 'With Mademoiselle Gaillard, I mean.'

'Fearsome,' Skellen muttered.

Stryker smiled. In truth he had thought of little else. Fight the Good Fight of Faith Helly was a firebrand, to be certain, and might one day be a rare beauty, but to him she was the rag doll he had scooped up in the charnel house that was Bolton. She was a child, to be protected, and he could not help but imagine how his own offspring might have been. There was small chance of such a thing, of course, unless he considered the bastard whelps of whores that might, even now, be living out their lives in Zeeland, Frisia, Pomerania or Saxony, unaware of whose blood might have given them raven-black hair, a long, straight nose, or grey eyes that shone silver when anger flared. But children with Lisette? He doubted she would ever want them. She was too damaged for that, her own childhood tale of horror putting paid to the ambition of bringing yet more young lives into the world. And besides, he was not so sure he would ever see her again. He had betrayed her trust when last they had been together. She had been under threat of rape and death, and he had given her tormentors the information she was prepared to die to protect. He had done it for love, and she would never completely forgive him.

'I should be pleased with children like her,' Hood said,

nodding towards the gap between two trunks through which Faith had walked.

'She is a rebel, Tom,' Stryker chided. 'Through and through. We should imprison her, rather than protect her.'

'She is courageous, sir,' Hood argued. 'Forthright. Educated.'

Stryker nodded. 'Aye, she is those things too.'

'What to do with her, though?' Simeon Barkworth said. He was kneeling before a pot to the side of the fire, preparing the pottage that he would cook for the rest of the day. 'We cannot see her all the way to Sussex. Not when we likely march north.'

'She stays with the army for the time being,' Stryker answered. 'That is all I can say.'

'What of the Vulture, sir?' Hood said.

'He cares nothing for Mistress Helly, believe me. He ravished the Sydall women, and would have ravished her, had I not stumbled upon his crime.' Stryker watched as Barkworth dropped various ingredients into his pot. 'She is right to be frightened of him, but there is no design upon her.'

'What of his clandestine dealings?' persisted Hood. 'That fellow he met with. You have not seen him since?'

'No,' Stryker said. The rendezvous in the field near Standish had unsettled him, but he had not witnessed anything of note, and had nothing to act upon. 'I would not know Kendrick's companion if he tripped over my boot, Tom, so dark was it. They were trading sotweed, for all I could tell.'

'What you got there?' Skellen asked of Barkworth.

The tiny man held up a bunch of sprigs. 'Wild fennel. Plenty to be had now that we're near the coast. Always better near the sea.' He glanced up at the covering branches of the magnificent tree. 'I'd like to use beechnuts too, but they're no ripe yet.'

Stryker followed his gaze. He guessed the ancient beech was all of ninety feet tall, the smooth silvery-grey of its bark soaring above their little encampment, pointed-oval leaves dripping water when the breeze shook them.

Barkworth cackled happily. 'Belittles the concerns of man, sir, does it not?'

'Aye,' Stryker replied, just as new raindrops began to spatter his face.

'Beechnuts taste no better than punk's piss,' Skellen said.

'You'd know,' replied Barkworth.

Skellen grinned maliciously as the fire hissed beneath the rain. He held out a spadelike palm. 'Miss Helly'll ruin her book if she opens it in this.'

Stryker found Faith Helly near the edge of the copse. She was perched within the cleft of a tree where the trunk split in two, hunched over the open Bible cradled in her lap. She looked up sharply when he stepped on a crackling branch.

Stryker held up placating hands. 'You cannot read in the rain, Mistress Helly. Not even Scripture.'

She closed the book. 'I seek comfort in His Word.'

'And the words will soon run off the page. Come back with me. Simeon is cooking pottage for later. Perhaps you might assist?'

Her eyes narrowed accusingly. 'Because I am a woman?'

'Because he cooks like a blind fool.'

She held her rigid stare for a heartbeat, then her lips melted into a smile. 'Then I will assist.' She slid down from her lichen-upholstered seat. 'He is a kind man.'

'Master Barkworth?' Stryker responded in mock surprise. 'There's many who'd tell you otherwise.'

'How was he hurt?'

He flirted with the fabrication of some heroic tale, but he knew she would see through him immediately. 'He survived a hanging, Mistress.' He paused. 'Do not be so alarmed, he is no demon. He was cut down by those who took pity. Simeon lived, but his voice did not.'

'What was his crime?'

'He may not be a demon,' Stryker said, 'but he looks like one. Some Bavarian folk took offence at those yellow eyes and strung him up.'

She shuddered. 'Poor man.'

'Save your pity, Mistress Helly, he will not thank you for it.'

'He is so small. Does he fight?'

He laughed at that. 'Constantly! And as well as any I've known. He was once the personal guard to the Earl of Chesterfield.'

'And now he is yours?'

'You might say that. Though he has no rank, as such. He lives on a pikeman's pay and whatever he may . . .' he tailed off, realising the foolishness of his words.

Faith looked straight into his eye. 'Plunder?'

Stryker nodded. 'Wages are irregular, even for officers. We take what we can, but only from our enemies.'

He thought she might admonish him, but instead she settled for a sour look and a change of tack. 'Do you have a woman, sir? A wife?'

'Lisette.'

'French?'

'Aye. She is away on Crown business.'

Faith seemed genuinely taken aback. 'A fighter?'

'Of sorts.'

Faith hugged the Bible tight to her chest as they picked their way over the tangled brush. 'This war has truly opened my eyes. Such people, Major. A warrior woman.'

He laughed. 'You and she are not so different.'

'And your giant, Master Skellen,' she went on, 'and a tiny soldier, and—'

'And a blind man in command.'

She blushed. 'That is not what—'

'We are an ill-fitting troupe,' Stryker said, 'I grant you that.' He turned away into a dense stand of bracken that concealed the main track back to the tents, but soon realized she had not followed. He called once, but Faith was staring, head cocked slightly to the side, like a hound heeding a wind-muffled horn. Stryker called again, though the rain reduced his words to whimpers, and he fought his way back to her side.

A pig rooted in the muck a short way off, ploughing up clods of sticky filth with its flaring snout, and at first he assumed she was looking at it, but then he saw them. Two figures had appeared below one of the beeches about fifty paces away, half concealed by the low hanging foliage. One of the men was heavy set, with a russet moustache and the curved sabre of Hungarian infantry; the other was thin and angular, pallid of skin, with a twisted back and a heavy cloak trimmed in a thick, black pelt.

Faith was already backing away. Stryker caught her by the elbows and moved around and in front of her, shielding her from the stares. She was murmuring something, mouthing over and over a single word like an incantation: '*Vulture.*'

Stryker placed his hand on the hilt of his sword. Beneath the branches of the leaning beech, John Kendrick smirked. His sergeant spat once, gripped his crotch with his great paw, and slid back into the branch-thrown shadows. Kendrick waited a second longer, smiling very slowly, gradually exposing his sharply filed teeth.

'I told you,' Faith Helly said. 'I told you.'

The Vulture winked once, and was gone.

Before evening, Stryker was ordered up to the ridge overlooking Liverpool. He left Faith under the protection of his three men, the Vulture's black silhouette turning like a whirlpool in his mind. Kendrick must have come upon them by accident, but Stryker was unsettled nevertheless. As he reached the summit, he thought of the look of terror etched across the girl's face and a shiver of fury ran through him.

The ridge was called Everton Heights, and it was the ideal site for Prince Rupert's headquarters, for it afforded an extensive panorama of the port, including a distant view of the Cheshire side of the River Mersey. Rupert had his billet in a comfortable house near the village green, his officers placed in homes around him, but it was at the beacon that Stryker finally reined in.

He dismounted, kneecaps groaning like rusty hinges as his boots squelched in the earth. Prince Rupert and Sir Richard Crane were already there, both on foot, and they nodded as he bowed low.

'Men settled, Sergeant-Major?' Crane asked.

'They are, sir, thank you.' Stryker stole a glance at Rupert, who was staring out over Liverpool, his handsome smile a grim slash across his narrow face.

'Good.' Crane pointed to the plain, square edifice that capped the ridge behind them. 'Shall we?'

Stryker followed the men as they strode the few yards up to the beacon. The structure itself was two storeys in height and built in dull, reddish stone. Narrow steps on the outside wall led up to the first floor, and then to the flat roof.

'They perform marriages here, Stryker!' Crane exclaimed as he climbed. 'Can you believe such a thing?'

'The clergy having been driven from the town?' Stryker guessed.

'You have it!'

Rupert abruptly stopped and the others shunted into each other. 'The indignity is astounding.'

'It is, Highness,' Stryker said quickly.

They were on the roof now. At the south-west corner there was a large cistern, empty and black now, half filled with water, where the wood for the old beacon would have been piled and lit. The rest was empty, an open platform, perfect for the prince's needs. Almost immediately he had his perspective glass in both hands, training it on the fortifications below. Crane had one too, snatching a look and then handing it to Stryker.

Stryker scanned the land before him. The rough slope ran steeply towards river and town, broken only by the glistening silver of a broad mere about a third of the way down. Some of the army's purloined cattle were watering there, several musket-eers placed in guard around them. He eased the scope further down towards the Mersey and the settlement perched on a swell of land against its east bank. He saw walls, earthworks, bastions and ditches. It was not encouraging. 'They will resist?'

'Not if they possess an ounce of wit,' Rupert snapped coldly.

'There are more than a thousand residents in the town, so we are informed,' Sir Richard Crane advised. 'And they are of a rebel disposition in the main. They alone would make for a stern test, truth told, but we have the additional obstacle of the governor and his garrison.'

'Colonel Moore.' The prince spat the words. 'Never did a more unconscionable rogue hold sway over so crucial a place.'

'Colonel Moore,' Crane said, choosing his words carefully, 'may be a rogue, Highness, but he has more than six hundred men under his command, supplemented, I dare say, by a goodly number of sailors.' He tapped Stryker's elbow. 'Look to the river, Major. You will see several ships. Many are men-o'-war.'

'Forgive me, Highness,' Stryker said, 'but I would not surrender, were I Colonel Moore.'

Rupert lowered the glass, his kidskin gloves pulling taut as he gripped the ivory tube hard. For a moment it looked as though he might fly into a rage, but instead he blew a blast of cold air through his long nose. 'But we must take it, Stryker. Liverpool is the most important port on this part of the coast. We need it to bring in supplies from the sea, and troops from Ireland.'

'How long have the rebels held it, Highness?'

'A full year.'

'Then they'll have it well fortified.'

Crane pointed out the targets to Stryker. 'The east side is protected by an inlet of the river, while the rest has a substantial mud wall and ditch, as you will see.'

Stryker pressed the cold metal of the perspective glass to his eye socket as he examined the town. Much of Liverpool's eastern extremity was covered by the spur of river that essentially formed a huge moat. At the north end, where the water did not impinge, there were the grey remains of an ancient stone wall, patched together by new works of mud and timber, while a ditch provided another layer of defence. 'Substantial?'

'Locals tell us the ditch is all of twelve yards across, and three deep.'

'Is that a castle, sir?' Stryker asked as he peered over the southern end.

'Aye,' Crane said. 'It dominates the south wall. Also protected by a ditch which is filled with water from the river.'

'The bastions look strong.' Stryker caught the glint of weak sunlight on black iron. 'They have gun batteries at regular intervals.' He looked at the prince and then at Crane. 'Do we know how they prepare within the walls?'

Crane nodded. 'Spies say the streets are barricaded. Many have palisades and even cannon. The entire perimeter of the wall is lined on the inner face with wool-packs to dampen any bombardment we care to give.'

'And will we bombard?'

Now the prince turned, glowering. 'Of course we will bombard them, Stryker, if they do not surrender! And then we will storm them! And then we will slaughter them!'

This, Stryker thought, was why he had been dragged up to this rain-soaked hill to face an angry prince. 'Am I to assume I have a part to play, Highness?'

'You will command a body of men,' Rupert said, 'should we embark upon an escalade.'

'Your service at Newark did you great credit, Stryker,' Crane added.

Or great harm, thought Stryker. He bowed nonetheless. 'You honour me, Highness.'

Prince Rupert turned away with a deep scowl. 'I will send another herald on the morrow. Pray God they accept my terms and open the damned gates,' he said darkly, 'for I would not wish to have another Bolton on my hands.'

# CHAPTER 9

### St Anthony's Hall, York, 8 June 1644

The men lay in rows on the flagstones because beds were in short supply. Their groans formed a baleful orchestra, reverberating around the stone walls and up into the sweeping rafters. Women tended the wounds, skirts bustling as they swept up and down between the pitiful lines, reacting with tired eyes and crimson hands to the barks of the chirurgeon who was sovereign in this empire of weeping men and rotting flesh.

The casualties from the fight at the Mount had been brought here. The women – gentlefolk turned by siege to chirurgeon's apprentices – brought up sheets and boiled water; they ferried jars of maggots to and from the patients with longer term, festering wounds, and held men down as the chirurgeon plied his saw.

'This place has been a hospital,' the tall, slim man said as he walked through the busy hall, voice muffled by the nosegay pushed to his face to mask the stink of putrefaction, 'a workhouse, a house of correction and detention, and a knitting school for poor girls. Now it is turned full circle, and is a hospital once more.'

'Though 'tis a prison too,' the man at his side said. 'We have a score of Roundheads locked in the cellars.'

'Quite so, Jamie,' the first replied. He had an elegant gait, made more elegant still by the exquisite cut of a scarlet suit trimmed in lace. 'A building of versatility.'

Jamie laughed politely. He was dressed more soberly in black and white, with a sharp chin and carefully trimmed hair, moustache and beard, all of which were silver now but showed signs of a formerly reddish hue. 'How is your wound, Captain?'

Lancelot Forrester, walking slightly behind, stared in awe at both of them. The taller, clad in red, was the most powerful man in all of northern England. William Cavendish, Marquis of Newcastle, was unfathomably wealthy, possessed of vast swathes of land and one of the best armies in all three kingdoms of the British Isles, and was a personal friend of King Charles. His companion, the man who had once had hair the colour of copper, was James King, Lord Eythin, a Scottish soldier of great repute and military adviser to the marquis. Forrester could barely believe that he had been graced by their presence, let alone in this dank, stinking hole that masqueraded as a hospital. He touched a finger to the patched cut at his temple, exchanging a baffled glance with Elias Croak, who walked at his side. 'A scratch, my lord.' His mouth was suddenly dry. 'Nothing more.'

'Good,' Eythin said. 'Praise God.'

'I suspect,' Newcastle broke in, halting in the middle of the hall, and lowering the nosegay reluctantly, 'you ponder as to my visit, Captain.'

'The question had crossed my mind, my lord, aye.'

Newcastle offered a white-toothed smile of easy warmth. 'I would see you, sir, to award you this.' He nodded at Eythin, who produced a ball of silk and handed it to him. Newcastle unfurled it, revealing two strips of material – one blue, one red – sewn together in the shape of a cross. He held it out. 'The enemy pamphleteers dub it a popish sign, but it is nothing of the sort. A matter of honour, only.'

'I have seen them worn by others, my lord,' Forrester said, taking the cross. 'On the right sleeve.'

'Its bearer has shown great valour in my service.'

He paused as a commotion struck up at the corner of the hall. A man was screaming. Two women struggled to fasten a tourniquet above his knee. Almost at once the noise faded. So too did the patient.

The marquis seemed to shudder. 'A hard fight was had, yes?'

'Aye, my lord, exceeding hard,' Forrester said. 'The Scots make able soldiers.' He considered the truth of the statement, comparing the men in blue bonnets to the raw Londoners of Waller's new army he had encountered at Basing House the previous autumn. The difference was stark and frightening. 'More than able.'

The marquis looked at Lord Eythin. 'Do they not, Jamie? If only all your countrymen marched for their rightful king, eh?'

'Quite so, my lord,' Eythin said sourly.

The marquis patted Eythin's shoulder. 'I chide you, sir, but it is not only the Scottish foe who endangers this fair city. Yorkshire rebels under Fairfax, East Anglian rebels under Manchester. Yorkshire is a crab bucket, my friends. Each army snapping at the other to feast on the carcass. Sad times, indeed.' He suddenly seemed to notice Elias Croak, and shed his sullen reverie with a brilliant smile. 'Captain! One of my own men! You are commended, sir. And your wounds heal?'

'They do, my lord,' Croak croaked, 'that they do.'

The marquis handed the young officer another one of the silken crosses. 'For recognition of your valour, sirrah.'

The chirurgeon, a rotund man in a hideously stained apron, bustled past, bowing as he went. 'My apologies, my lords. I must administer this poultice. 'Tis for the blood flow.'

'Does not William Harvey write of the blood,' Forrester asked, 'that it moves about the body in circuit? Pushed by exertion of the heart.'

The chirurgeon halted, twisted back, his face exasperated. 'Harvey?' He almost spat the word. 'I employ his treatise to wipe my arse, sir, if you'll forgive the base reply, for that is its proper use. Galen is our tutor in this. Galen, good sir, tells us that blood passes by means of invisible spores.'

'I stand corrected, sir,' Forrester said.

'You are aware,' the marquis cut in, 'our other sconces were taken?'

'A dire day,' Forrester answered. 'They are but a spitting distance from our hearths.'

'All the more reason to celebrate the Mount's salvation,' responded Lord Eythin.

He was seconded by the marquis: 'Quite so. It is our only protection in the south. The enemy creeps, insidious and ruthless. They have built a battery opposite the Walmgate. On a hill. Dismantled a windmill for it, would you believe? A breach is already made in Clifford's Tower.'

'And the Walmgate barbican suffers terribly,' Eythin added morosely. 'The Northern Association has taken the suburbs thereabouts.'

William Cavendish, Marquis of Newcastle, swallowed hard. 'The siege is too close, pressed with too much vigour. I need Rupert's help.'

'He will not come,' Eythin scoffed. 'He will look to his own skin.'

'I will write to him, nonetheless, though God only knows if such word may get through.' He lifted the nosegay as he continued to walk. 'If they breach our wall, then all will be lost.'


## Liverpool, Lancashire, 8 June 1644

The herald rode out from the Royalist lines just after dawn. The sky was purple, suffusing steadily with blazing orange in the east, and it lit the rider's spurs so that they winked as if passing some clandestine message to the king's nephew, who stood and watched from up on the ridge. The herald had been sent to parley with Colonel Moore, the rebel governor, and order his immediate surrender. Now he approached one of the gates set into the earthen rampart, and every member of the Royalist army waited with baited breath as his mount high-stepped through the barren no-man's-land.

Stryker was with Rupert, Crane and a dozen other senior officers. He had spent an uneasy night down in the copse, wondering whether the girl's worries possessed firmer foundation than he'd thought. But as the stars began to fade and the night softened to a hoary grey, he had let Vos take him up to the ridge so that he might see the terms delivered with his own eye. Now he watched in grim silence.

Down in the valley, the herald sat on his horse, as proud as a peacock, resplendent in silk and satin, a wide hat adorned with colourful feathers, a blooming scarf swathing his torso, the jewels in the hilt of his sword twinkling as the sun lit up the sea beyond. He waved to the Parliamentarian sentries as he approached the town, glancing back briefly, acutely aware that all eyes were trained upon him.

A puff of smoke cascaded over the palisade near the gate, followed in a heartbeat by the crack of the shot. Before the echo died in the hills, the herald's horse was down. It was a chestnut thoroughbred, huge and powerful, draped in a silver-threaded saddle cloth, with white streaks slashing both flanks. A magnificent beast, costly and superbly trained, yet all that was wiped away by the single musket-ball of a Roundhead marksman. The beast thrashed as it hit the mud, turning a half-circle on its side as its hooves ploughed great furrows in the earth, its braided tail smacking wetly in the sticky soil, the scarlet ribbon, so expertly interwoven, coming loose to wriggle like a giant worm. The herald was bellowing, trapped beneath the screaming animal, his beautiful slashed doublet daubed in grime, while up on the rampart came the sound of cheering.

'By Christ,' Prince Rupert of the Rhine said softly. 'By Christ.'

All else was silent on the ridge, as if time itself had frozen. Stryker watched, dumbstruck, as the herald finally freed his pinned leg from the stirrup and somehow squirmed clear, taking a kick or two from the wounded horse as he rolled out of range. The defenders looking down upon him jeered, they capered along the wall as though a fiddler played a jaunty reel, and waved the rebel flags that were set at intervals along the rampart. With a final shriek the horse expired, juddering violently and falling utterly still. Its master ran, all dignity punctured as he skidded and stumbled through the quagmire, clutching his ribs.

'By Christ,' the prince muttered again. He blinked rapidly,

swallowed hard, and spun on his heels, glaring at the slack-jawed faces of his subordinates. 'By Jesu!' he bellowed, thumping a gloved fist into the palm of the other. 'The knave! The bastardly gullion!' He thrust out an arm, jabbing the air in the direction of Liverpool with an accusatory finger. 'This is a paltry parcel of traitors and cowards! I tell you, gentlemen, that we will dine under their roofs in short order! It is nothing but a nest of crows that a party of boys might take!'

Huzzahs rang out, though Stryker wondered how many of the voices were inflected with trepidation, for they all knew what was to come.

Just then a cry went up from the men near the top of the slope, and everyone twisted round towards the lookouts on the beacon. Activity had been spotted to the south. Stryker clambered into Vos's saddle and galloped with the rest to the ridge's summit. They reined in, a great line of warriors squinting southward, hands shielding their eyes against the sun. In the distance was the road that ran all the way back to Bolton, and on that mired thoroughfare, as far as the eye could see, came a cavalcade of soldiers, horses and oxen, of wagons big and small, of coopers, smiths and men paid pretty sums for their knowledge of black powder. It was the Royalist artillery train, lumbering a day behind the rest, and at the very rear, hauled by doughty ponies and escorted by musketeers and dragoons, came the unmistakable forms of the big guns, trundling like captured beasts on their great carriages.

Prince Rupert emerged from Stryker's blind left side, standing in his stirrups as his black stallion turned a tight circle. The king's nephew, so young yet so formidable, drew his sword. It sang its metallic tune. The prince made the stallion skitter sideways with a deft touch, steered him about so that he faced the port below, and levelled the blade, peering down its length as if he could shoot bolts of lightning on to the rebel stronghold from its tip. 'Break them,' he said, quietly at first, but then louder. 'Break through their walls and push them out. We will drown the treacherous curs in the Mersey.' He looked up, skewering a group of officers in his raptor's gaze. 'Prepare the heavy guns immediately.'

The Royalist army worked like bees at a hive. Prince Rupert resolved against a crossing of the protective river inlet, for Colonel Moore had astutely set trenches, mounts and guns at all the approaches to that south-eastern sector. Equally, the castle on the southernmost portion of the wall was extremely well fortified. Therefore it was to the north-east that the prince turned his furious gaze, from the point where the river spur petered out, all the way round to the main bank of the Mersey. Across this arc of land the first trenches were to be carved from the cloying mud. Often a besieging army would establish lines of circumvallation, a complete circle of fortified trenches running all the way around the place they wished to reduce, but here that option was negated both by the river and by Rupert's impatience. He wanted to bring Colonel Moore's garrison to heel, and that meant punching a hole right through Liverpool's wall and injecting infantry to do the rest. So in the certain knowledge that he could not entirely cut off the town, his army laid down their muskets and exchanged them for shovels. They dug in shifts, scooping away the sodden soil with buckets, bottoming out the waterlogged gutters with timber and lining the inner face with stakes, and on a plateau below Everton Heights they threw up three gun batteries, from where they might bombard the port's fortifications.

Stryker found himself overseeing the construction of one of the batteries. Fortunately, though the ground remained soft and sapping, the rain held off, and his surly team worked hard to erect the earthen banks. Men found branches thin enough to be woven into large baskets, and soon these baskets, known as gabions, were filled with spoil from the works and then lined like sentries in defence of the half-dozen siege-guns that were gradually hauled into position.

Teams of horses pulled the pieces, braying in exertion as they were whipped raw by their masters. The heaviest guns were demi-cannon, huge hulks of black iron set upon creaking carriages of oak and elm, and though their wheels were shod in iron, sharp strakes adding grip, they slid and stuck so that the crews had to manhandle them on to the wooden platform set upon the battery. But the task, for all its difficulty, was achieved in good time, with a small powder magazine set close by, alongside the supply of iron round-shot that would be hurled at the enemy positions.

'They lie around like dogs, sir!' exclaimed the lieutenant-colonel who came to take command of Stryker's completed battery around noon. He was a fat man – broad as a mortar and almost as short – with cheeks speckled black by powder burns and jowls that quivered when he spoke, and he waddled on to the timber platform as if Prince Rupert himself owed him fealty.

Stryker, mounted on Vos below the biggest cannon muzzle, was lighting his pipe, and he nodded courteously as the irate man peered down at him through the gap between two gabions. 'They have earned a rest, Colonel Wheatley.'

Wheatley shook his head, the saggy skin of his face swinging like a pendulum. 'They are artillery crew, are they not?' He vanished briefly, evidently inspecting the men who sat around the inside of the battery, their aching backs slumped against the baskets as they quenched their thirst on flagons of good beer that Stryker had ordered up. He returned, red-faced and spluttering. 'Are they not, sir? Crew, sprawled about in my presence! It will not do, sir! No, sir, it will not! I'll have 'em in chains, you mark my words!'

'No, sir,' Stryker said, puffing on the pipe and staring up through the smoke. Behind him the battlements of Liverpool opened up, but their aim so far had given him no cause for concern.

Wheatley balked. 'No, sir?'

'They are local labourers, brought here under duress. They have worked well to give you your battery, sir.'

That silenced Wheatley, who eventually waddled down to

ground level. 'Hang the buggers high till death, sir,' he muttered angrily. 'That's the only road to discipline.'

'I find such a road all too often leads to mutiny, Colonel.'

Wheatley thrust chubby palms on to his ample waist, taking a wide stance like a sea captain on a storm-ravaged deck. 'Then how, pray, would you resolve the plague of indiscipline, Stryker?'

'Coin, Colonel.'

'Coin?'

'Pay. A man does not consider mutiny with ease, sir. He understands he will be ordered to march long and hard, to fight, to kill, to die, mayhap. In my experience, even the most craven man will do all these things with a stout heart, if he receives pay enough to keep himself fed and warm.' He pointed with his pipe stem at the battery. 'These men are not soldiers, so I pay them in drink, but the principle remains.'

'Pigswill!' Lieutenant-Colonel Wheatley guffawed. 'A womanly whimsy, Stryker. Thought better of you than that. No, sir. Hang the mutinous curs high and let 'em dangle for the crows, I say. That'll frighten some obedience into the rest.' He clapped his hands suddenly, eyes twinkling as he stared up at the stone and earth walls before them. 'Now, Major. I believe it is time we got to work!'

The bombardment began and never seemed to cease, so many smoking muzzles were in play. For though the prince had three chief batteries, sixteen guns in all, his opponents within the town had many more. They were mounted all the way along the wall, and out on the approaches to the river-cum-moat, and amongst the earthworks to the north and on the castle to the south. Moreover, the ships of Parliament's powerful navy, anchored out in the estuary, belched fire and iron from their inland-facing broadsides, sending their whining shot over the rooftops of Liverpool and out into the encroaching siege-lines. It was a conversation – a violent one – that could find neither conclusion nor compromise, reply after raging reply filling the air with stinking mist. The round-shot flung by the Parliamentarian guns smashed into the land, driving up great clods of earth and making the sappers and engineers shy away as they worked tirelessly to carve their trenches ever closer to the walls. All the while the Royalist guns boomed fire and threat, the heaviest sending cannon balls weighing sixty pounds apiece to smash relentlessly at the fortifications, and taking an almost immediate toll. The guns roared, flamed, smoked and recoiled by turns, their steaming barrels methodically scoured of soot and ember by sheepskin sponges after every salvo. and the bombardment did not let up. They quickly found the weaker places, those where timber and mud peeled away from the stone foundations like sun-parched daub to crumble into the ditch below, and it was there that the fire was concentrated in the hope that a significant fissure would soon be carved. And all the while, up high at the beacon, Prince Rupert made his plans.

### Near Linton-on-Ouse, Yorkshire, 8 June 1644

More than a hundred miles to the north-east of Liverpool a lone rider made his way towards another great siege. He was a short man, skinny as a reed, features gaunt below a grubby Montero cap, the scabs infesting his cheeks whipped sore by the wind. The horse, a bay mare with docile temperament, had been a blessing, though the going had been slow in the marshland that passed for roads, and the rider whispered encouragement as she gamely struggled on. He took the reins in one hand and tugged down the Montero's woollen flaps with the other, cursing the cold that made his ears leak pus that stank and dried crusty on his neck. At least it had stopped raining, he thought ruefully, glancing up at the pregnant clouds. Thank the Holy Mother for that.

The journey had not been as perilous as Devlin Greer had feared. Crossing the hills around Wetherby had taken time, although he had been forced to evade enemy units only twice during the arduous ride. But on this day, the third with his new horse, all was changed. Now the Roundheads were everywhere.

Squadrons of mounted killers galloped in dense lines, fanning out to guard the approaches to York. They swirled around the roads and hedgerows, a sweeping cordon of menace, quick to attack and slow to question. Devlin Greer had ridden close enough to see the revealing glint of sunlight against a trooper's helm, but could not risk anything more ambitious. As an Irishman, capture would mean a swift beating, like as not, followed by an airborne jig from a high, creaking bough. Best to keep his distance and employ a measure of guile.

Now he was close to the gushing river, one of two that cut a course into the city. He brought the mare to a standstill at the thick scrub that tangled the water's edge, and slid down on to the soft earth, cursing the ache in his thighs. Greer stared at the southern horizon, eyeing the thick grey funnels that spilled skyward from York's chimneys. There seemed to be more than he remembered, and he realized that the smoke must be coming from fires outside the city. The Parliamentarians had evidently managed to swing round and plug the northern gap that had been his means of entry and exit. 'What, in God's name, has come to pass?' he muttered.

'There's a siege, sir.'

Greer spun on his heels, pulling a short, hooked knife from his saddle. 'Who are you?'

The man before him was old and stooped, a fishing rod in one hand, an empty pail in the other. 'For—forgive me, sir!' He dropped both items and raised both hands. 'I did not mean to startle you! My name is Richard Weeks.'

Greer kept the knife raised. 'Where've you come from?'

Richard Weeks jerked his bald head rearwards, indicating the river. 'Yon Ouse, sir. Hunting supper, was I.'

'My apologies,' Greer said, lowering the little blade. 'I am on edge, as you can see.' He pointed towards the city. 'You mentioned the siege.'

'Aye, sir. 'Tis in its third month, if you can believe that.'

'I know, friend,' Greer replied, not bothering to conceal his accent, for he guessed the fellow would not know an Irishman from a Dutchman. 'But I wondered how it is that the rebels do stretch their reach all the way up here, to the north of the city. When I was last here, they had not the manpower.'

'Ah,' the fisherman beamed, 'that'll be the lord Manchester. He's brought with him an army from Lincoln.'

Richard Weeks, it transpired, lived in the nearby village of Linton but spent a great deal of his time in a modest shack on the edge of the river on account of a nagging wife, five squawking daughters and half a dozen Scottish musketeers. 'I swear they do drive me deaf, sir,' he exclaimed as he showed Devlin Greer into the tumbledown pile of timber.

'The soldiers?' Greer said, taking the low stool offered by his host.

Weeks shook his head. 'The bloody girls. I'd have married 'em off before now, 'cept they look too much like their mother. No bugger'll have them.'

Greer laughed. 'I can see this place would be a haven. A pleasant bolt-hole, if ever I saw one. But are you not a trifle near the armies? Do they not cause you bother?'

Weeks shook his head. 'They come by, from time to time, but they leave me be, for they know I'm no bother to 'owt but the fish. Besides, I'm sheltering and feeding six o' their surly fedaries, so I'm doing m' bit.'

Greer leaned forwards, propping his elbows on his knees. 'Forgive my rudeness, Master Weeks, but you appear to know plenty about the siege, so you do.'

Weeks pulled a grim face. 'The Parliament has three armies camped outside the walls o' York, sir. Every household has the honour of providing the men shelter. My lot are good enough lads, though Goody Weeks claims they've brought us lice.'

They'll probably bring you the pox to-boot, thought Greer wryly. 'And you say the city is surrounded?'

'Now that Manchester's rabble are here, sir, aye. The Cavaliers could get in and out till the new lot came, but now 'tis truly bottled up tight.'

Devlin Greer swore softly. Then a thought struck him. 'The river flows south, yes?'

Weeks nodded. 'Through York, then on to Selby.'

'You have a boat?'

'A small thing, aye. Few holes,' he chuckled, 'but nowt a bucket and some hard graft won't cure.'

Greer drew his knife slowly. 'Is it nearby, good Master Weeks?'

Richard Weeks said that it was, and Devlin Greer went to commit murder.

The boat was rot-eaten and mouldy, with a full inch of stinking bilge slopping around Devlin Greer's feet as he perched on the edge of the single, rickety bench. But with York surrounded, he had no choice. The River Ouse was always powerful, but now, swollen by rain, it had a malicious streak that snagged the boat as it bobbed out into the deeper reaches, hurling it along with the current so that he barely needed to use the paddle. For the most part, he was content to let the Ouse do its work, concentrating instead on baling out the encroaching water.

Southward he was borne, ever vigilant for prying eyes on the banks, but he saw no one. The land reminded him of his wartorn homeland, and he found himself recalling the hours he had spent on the Boyne, knotting rope to high branches overhanging the crystal clear water so that he and his brothers could swing out, dropping into the chill depths on warm summer's days. He had made love for the first time on those grassy banks, and he smiled as he remembered the lithe body of Molly Peirce and the slow hiss of a swan's wings as it had flown close above them. Well, Molly was gone now, her family slain by the heretics. He felt his heart ache at the memory. The flames and the screams.

The uprising had been glorious in the beginning. A God-given revolt for the defence and liberty of the native Irish. The insurgency was not intended to harm the king, nor any of his subjects, except that matters had tumbled out of control, and Protestants had been massacred. It had never been meant to happen that way, but the die had been cast, Catholics had been slaughtered in reprisal, and before anyone knew different there was a full-scale war. Greer had become involved after Molly's death. He had been with Rory O'More at Drogheda, and the victory had promised so much. But then England and Scotland had sent more troops to defend the Protestant settlers, and defeat had followed defeat. Ireland was in flames, its people destroyed by plague and famine. There were victories, of course, but not enough. And always there was death and destruction, and Devlin Greer had realized that the only way to save Ireland was to defeat the rebellion in England. Because, though the insurgency fought against King Charles, everyone knew he secretly sympathized with the plight of the Catholic majority. How could he not, when he was married to the staunchly Catholic Henrietta Maria? Indeed, it was said that, even now, he was making peace with the Confederates. But the English parliament was driven by Puritan zeal. Westminster – and London itself – was the very bedrock of everything that the native Irish despised, and if ever they secured victory in England, Ireland would be next.

Ahead of him, just beyond the river's rising east bank, he saw a man seated on a large horse. The man wore a helmet with three bars attached to a visor, caging a face that was grim and hard, and his body was encased in armour. He was a cavalryman. Worse still, he wore the tawny scarf of the Parliament, which made him an English cavalryman. Running into a Scot would have been bad enough, Greer knew, but the English Roundheads posed the most danger. The English hated foreigners, but they hated Catholics more. As an Irishman, Greer was both. He grinned, offering a cheery, confident wave.

The cavalryman watched. He cocked his head to the side, examining the boat and its passenger in the way a cat might eye a mouse. With a squeeze of his thighs the horse turned, walking south, increasing its speed to keep pace with the boat. Greer stared up at the horseman, feeling as though he might vomit. He had been an intelligencer for many masters, both in Ireland and England, and knew his business well. Here he was a sitting duck to be pistol-pocked if the Roundhead so wished.

'Where go you, friend?' the horseman called suddenly.

Greer forced the rising bile back down his throat. 'York,' he called back, dry-mouthed. 'That is to say, the Godly army now laying siege to York.'

'Whence d'you hail?' the horseman demanded. 'You've an unusual voice.'

'Wales, sir,' Greer replied, thinking of the most exotic location he could muster. 'Came to England seeking work.'

'What kind?'

'I am a cordwainer, sir.' Greer's bowels churned. 'A good one.'

The Roundhead smiled behind his visor. 'There are plenty o' latchets need mending.'

'That was my hope, sir,' Greer called, twisting as the boat moved further ahead so that he sat athwart the bench. 'Thousands of feet mean thousands of shoes.'

The horse slowed. 'Good fortune, then!' its rider called as the boat slipped further downstream. 'But you'll have to walk, my friend, for we have built a new bridge down at Poppleton! You'll not get through!'

Devlin Greer shouted his thanks, waited for the boat to meander round the next bend, and vomited into the River Ouse.

# CHAPTER 10

*Liverpool, Lancashire, 10 June 1644*

The rain had come again, barely ceasing for two full days. It came from the west, from the sea, and it was a cold, hard, relentless torrent that turned the besieging encampment to a muddy morass. Men waded between the tents, horses were so plastered in grime that one could no longer tell the shade of their pelts, and the mood of Prince Rupert's itinerant city was sombre at best. In the trenches, the engineers and sappers had been forced to delay work on their zig-zagging gullies, for they were knee-deep in brown water that seemed impossible to drain, and so there was no chance of bringing the works close enough to the battlements to begin laying a mine. Yet still the heavy guns fired, spewing their fury from the Royalist batteries, from the Parliamentarian walls, and from the ships anchored on the coast, so that a stinking pall of smog writhed like the devil's own cloud above the sodden hills. The rebel fire achieved little, for Rupert's forces were out of range and his cannon emplacements well protected, but the Royalist gun captains had found their mark with aplomb. In the first frantic hours of bombardment they had sprayed the town rampart, picking at it in various places, always gauging any damage inflicted. With every passing salvo they took stock, exchanged notes, agreed upon the best places to concentrate their efforts, and gradually the vulnerable sections of wall became apparent, gradually the noose tightened. It was mid-morning when the first light could be seen through the high wall, patches of tiles and thatch showing through from the buildings beyond, and the gunners knew that their efforts were coming to fruition. They kept up the barrage, focussed on the cracks, even as Rupert's infantry officers drew their men into battle order, and just before noon the wall caved in.

Perhaps it was the weight and frequency of the iron shot alone, or perhaps the timber-faced sods that buttressed the ancient wall had become too heavy with rainwater. What mattered was that a breach had been made, and the debris from that wide fissure had slithered like a great avalanche into the outer ditch, filling it almost to its brim, so that a bridge of rubble now presented itself. Then the rain stopped, the Royalists cheered divine intervention, and the prince ordered the escalade he had promised.

Stryker commanded almost a hundred men. They were drawn from reformado officers and conscripts and had been cobbled together to form a full company of foot. All three of his regular subordinates were officially part of the storming party, though he excused Hood and Barkworth on the pretence of mild fever so that they could remain behind to watch over Faith. Her presence, he privately admitted, was beginning to take a real toll on their collective ability to discharge their duties, and her situation would require resolution very soon: after Liverpool had fallen, he told himself as he splashed through the most advanced sap, snaking his way towards the town, the breach gaping above. Once the port was under Crown control, they would be able to take stock and consider how best to see her safely back to Sussex.

First there was the matter of the assault. His column stretched back beyond a sharp turn so that he could not see its tail, but he knew his motley band of musketeers were all there, for William Skellen picked up the rear, and even now he could hear the fearsome sergeant's snarls. They did not disguise their approach, for Liverpool's defenders would have seen them muster beneath Everton Heights, and the thrum of drums sounded back at the camp, a resonant, ominous call to war that drove his every step forward. Artillery pieces belched rage up on the rampart, flame coming first, then smoke, and the ear-splitting crack a moment later. Stryker flinched, as did his nervous charges, but still he waded on, his feet dry in good boots but rapidly numbing within the chill slop.

The storming party reached the extent of the sap, still sixty yards shy of the ditch. There they were joined by more attackers, the greencoats of Tillier's regiment, jostling along two parallel trenches. Muskets crackled now. The Parliamentarians had watched them come, waited until they were within range, and decided to patter the mud with lead in the hope of dissuading the attackers from the final charge.

Stryker looked back, cupped hands to his mouth. 'On my word!' he called, voice carrying easily down the half-tunnel. 'My word! Steady now, lads!'

'Godspeed, sir.'

Stryker looked to his blind left flank, where a young officer in a finely slashed doublet of green and yellow waited for a reply. He nodded. 'And you, Captain. I am sure you will fight well.'

The captain seemed to find fortitude in the words, for he set his jaw and stood a little straighter. He touched fingertips to a band of delicate lace knotted at his wrist. 'I fight for a lady's favour, sir.'

'Then you're a fool.'

The captain's face fell. 'She said she'd give me her hand if I proved my courage.'

'And she'll wish you do not return,' Stryker said harshly. He immediately regretted the words, for the young man looked utterly crest-fallen. 'I jest,' he added. 'She will think you brave, sirrah, of course. You will be verily dragged to her marriage bed.'

A smile flickered at the corners of the captain's white-lipped mouth. 'I do hope so, sir.'

Stryker watched as the officer drew a beautifully crafted pistol from his belt. 'It'll shoot high, like as not, so aim low.'

'Low,' the young captain echoed.

'Aim for his head and you'll hit the rampart. Aim for his stones and you'll hit his throat.'

'Yes, sir. Thank you, sir.'

'And remember,' he said, pointing up at the figures taking up position on the battlements. 'They are more scared than you. It is your job to prove they are right to be.'

Stryker did not need to give the order to attack, for one of the other parties had erupted from a trench perhaps thirty paces to the right of his position. They screamed, pouring out on to the open ground like a stream of demons, white-eyed and shrieking. The defending fire grew thick, the sporadic pot-shots of before suddenly building to a wave that was deafening in its concentration. Mud spattered in all directions, kicked up by boots and bullets, and swords glimmered in the feeble sunlight. Stryker bellowed for his men to attack, and then he was up on the cloying terrain, leaping ruts made by cannon balls and scrambling past debris. He screamed as every other man screamed, in the hope that it would frighten the enemy, and because it gave vent to his terror. A musket-ball whipped past his face, for he felt the kick of scythed air, and he ducked as he ran, crouching low like a tortoise in its shell. Around him men slipped in the filth, scrabbled as they tripped on their own scabbards, or wheeled sharply round, punched by bullets into waterlogged graves.

The ordnance fell silent, and he thanked God for that, because it meant that they were inside the range of the bigger guns, but then the breach vanished in racing cloud and the report of a smaller gun shook the ground beneath his feet. He threw himself into the mud; like as not, case shot had been deployed. He sprawled flat, his mouth and nose clogging with foul soil, and then he was twisting, lurching up as men fell all around him. Case shot – small bullets, or even scrap metal, loaded into a canister – was used at close range. The soldiers called it murdering shot, because the canister split open pouring its bounty in a wide arc that could enfilade a dense unit of men, and it had done its duty now, cutting a swathe of slaughter across the storming party's advanced ranks, and some of them, the rawest recruits, had stopped, desperate to be anywhere but this hell-on-earth. Stryker hauled himself to his feet, aware that he must have seemed like a ghoul from beneath the soil, such was his mud-plastered appearance, drew his sword and screamed for the men to press on. Further along the line, out of the case shot's murderous arc, Tillier's greencoats were bearing down on the ditch, and they leapt on to the accidental bridge, scrambling over the rubble that had collapsed from the hurriedly patched wall. Stryker called for his unit to follow their example.

He ran again, joining the greencoats even as the musketry rattled above them. He heard Skellen's familiar battle-cry somewhere nearby, then he was on the stones and the timber spars and the piles of soil that rose out of the ditch like vast ant hills, jumping from one rickety stepping-stone to the next, always fearing he might fall but dreading the enemy muskets more.

He reached the wall. A pistol ball bounced off his sword-hilt, eliciting a savage curse. One of the defenders ran at him, and he found himself chopping wildly at the man, their blades clanging, jarring all the way up from fingers to neck, but he was too strong and he pushed the man back so that he toppled rearward down the slope that had formed like a stone glacier on the inner face of the wall. Now the fight was engaged across the ruined section, from the ditch to the rampart and down into the town where the vanguard of greencoats had bravely striven, but the defenders were many, and they were joined by civilians and by hard-faced men whose leathery complexions spoke of lives lived at sea, and for the first time Stryker realized that Rupert might have underestimated his opponent. The garrison here was stronger than the one they encountered at Bolton; it was better equipped, better trained and more experienced. He moved along the rubble-strewn breach, cleaving at opponents and screaming for the men to keep up the fight, but all the while knowing that it was already lost. Skellen had instinctively moved to his vulnerable left, and he nodded his thanks. The big man was black-eyed as he swept his halberd in crushing half-circles so that none would come too close. Most of the shots had been spent on both sides, and the fight was too furious for any man to stop and reload, so steel became king, and muskets smashed down, used now as bludgeoning clubs, and dirks were pulled to slice and gut when a man was close enough to smell his breath.

A rat-faced corporal stepped into Stryker's way as he picked a path along the precarious crest. Stryker spat in his eyes. The man flinched by instinct and fell by steel. The greencoats were further ahead, just inside the line of the wall, slashing and stabbing their way down the glacis of caved rubble. Stryker made to follow them, but out of the corner of his eye he spotted a small-calibre gun, set on a platform on the inner face of the rampart to the side of the breach. Its crew had been lucky not to have been swept away in the initial rupture, but they had turned their perilous position to supreme advantage, for the gun was now trained on the ditch immediately below. This was the weapon that had delivered the round of screaming case shot, and he saw that its crew were frantically making the piece ready again, but this time they had swivelled it round to fire down on the inner slope to eviscerate the greencoats from behind.

He rammed his sword into its scabbard and climbed. The existing wall was jagged where the stone and soil had fallen away, leaving plenty of footholds by which he could haul himself up, and no man shouted alarm or shot at him from above or below. In less than a minute he was on the platform and his sword was naked again. There were three men tending the gun, packing charge and ball and wadding into the muzzle. They did not see him at first, so the man nearest him died, neck cut right through, and the second man turned in alarm to receive a kick to his stones that folded him double. Stryker smashed the heavy pommel of his sword down on the back of the gunner's skull, feeling a wet crunch as the bone cracked and depressed, and then the third was spinning on his heels, searching desperately for a way off the platform. But he was trapped, for the stairs that had led to this high place had fallen away with the stony avalanche, and so the Roundhead could only heft the long wooden shaft that he gripped, a burning match coiled at its iron head. He swung it at Stryker, who ducked beneath the glowing tip and lurched forwards, driving his sword deep into the gunner's midriff, ripping it up and out so that the man's belly gaped like a slit snapsack, entrails spilling down his legs. The man wailed and dropped the staff, hurriedly gathering up his guts as though they were a tumbled basket of apples. Stryker picked up the staff; it was a linstock, the tool used to ignite a gun's charge.

Down below, the escalade had failed and the greencoats were in retreat. They fell back to join Stryker's company, and together the men retired on to the fallen section of wall, shifting carefully over the outer glacis and on to the filled ditch. All the while more and more of Liverpool's garrison were streaming out from the streets to support the furious defence. Soon they would have enough muskets to destroy the retiring Royalists. Even now, orders rose up, bellowing for the garrison to form ranks to give a dense volley at the green-coated backs.

Stryker touched the linstock to the powder train. It fizzed for a second.

He found himself on his back, staring up at the churning cloud that spewed from the muzzle. Down below he heard cries, sobs, moans of desperation. He sat up, ears chiming like church bells, and peered through the seething fog. The field piece had been loaded with case shot. It had been aimed at the place where the Royalists had gathered, but they had been chased away and now it was Parliament men who were raked by the packed shot, the canister spitting its rage along a wide front so that the formation of musketeers bore a hideous toll. Stryker did not wait for the garrison to recover, rolling instead to the spiked edge of the platform. Outside the wall, the rest of the storming party were picking their way across the ditch, too desperate to comprehend what had saved them. They only knew that the attack had been a failure. With screams of agony and indignation ringing at his back, Stryker followed.

### Near York, 10 June 1644

Devlin Greer crept down to the riverbank. He eased through the rushes, planting his feet carefully. The water, just a couple of yards away, raced past, a bubbling band of pale coldness in the deep night.

He had hidden the boat in the shadow of a weeping willow the previous day, having taken it as far south as he dared after the warning he had received from the trooper. Then he had walked down through the fields until he had come close to the crossing point thrown over the Ouse by the armies encircling York. Poppleton Bridge was not a real bridge. There were no abutments, no keystones, and no arches to pass under. It was made of boats, which had been lashed side by side and planked over the top so that men and horses could pass from one bank to the other. He had watched it from the safety of a patch of spiky scrub, noting the pacing sentries and clattering patrols, and knew that a wide berth would be required. Thus he had waited till nightfall, taken a circuitous route along animal tracks and ancient hedgerows, and bypassed the bridge altogether. And next he had waited, past dawn and throughout the following day, biding his time until the setting sun bled crimson over the west.

Now it was dark again, and he had returned to the river, because it remained the best – the only – way into York. The city itself would not be far away, beyond one or two more reed-fringed bends, and he had resolved that tonight was its time to receive him.

He moved to the edge, paused, senses keen to the sounds of chattering pickets, but nothing spoke, nothing stirred. He dropped, sliding into the inky abyss with a stifled gasp. The water numbed his limbs, froze his heart so that he thought he would plummet to the riverbed without even the strength to cry out. But somehow he kept moving, and all the while he stayed afloat, carried by the swollen currents, gulping down air and forcing his eyes open just enough to see shapes in the darkness. Something brushed his knee, down in the murk, and images of man-eating monsters assailed him, giant eels and ravenous pike ascending from the depths for a frenzied feast. He prayed as he swam, pushing past sludge and weeds and floating debris.

It felt like hours, like a sentence in purgatory. The world was pitch black; the water and the banks and the sky, all gone, all swallowed by the darkness. But there was a sliver of moon. He knew it because of the pale ghost that loomed up ahead, glimpses of its rising bulk snatched with every stolen lungful of air. The ghost was York, or rather its battlements, a vast beacon to give hope to the spluttering Irishman who thanked God for his deliverance. He kicked harder, pulled faster with his arms, and swam to York.

### Liverpool, Lancashire, 11 June 1644

Liverpool was crumbling. Though the escalade had failed, the bombardment had continued with renewed vengeance and fresh targets, so that the gaping fissure in the wall only became wider and the rooftops jutting above the girdle of stone and mud began to show visible signs of destruction. Smoke trails rose from the town and churches began to look dilapidated, as though giants had taken great bites from their soaring steeples. But the majority of the wall remained, the spur of river still ran fast and rain-swollen to protect a large swathe of the defences, and the castle still stood guard to the south like a grey sentinel.

The Royalist sappers kept digging. They knew now that, despite Prince Rupert's claim that the port could be taken by schoolboys, Liverpool was more akin to a lion's den. Thus, more trenches would be clawed from the sticky mud, winding a circuitous route ever onwards towards the enemy ditch. More gun batteries would be constructed, and the process of under-mining the walls could begin. It would be laborious, time-consuming work, and no one had the stomach for it, especially as the rain was never far away. But they had lost almost a hundred men in the assault, killed and captured, and even Rupert knew that he could not attempt another potential bloodbath so soon.

'Put your backs into it, lads,' Stryker called as he paced the sap under his command, thankful for the rough timbers his team had cut to line the base. It was less than an hour after dawn, the eastern sky as vibrantly orange as the west was smoke-blackened by the morose pall lingering above town and river and sea. The trench itself was five feet deep, with spoil piled on the town side to add a parapet of another two feet, so that he was shielded from the sporadic shots taken from the walls. Occasionally, one of Liverpool's larger guns would bark from the rampart or the ships in the river mouth, and he would duck down with the rest of the men, bracing for the inevitable smack of iron and spray of mud, but those were desultory offerings, the defenders content to conserve ammunition and powder while no imminent threat came from their besiegers.

'Couple of other things I'd rather be putting m' back to, sir,' one of the filth-spattered men called from his place on the digging line.

'The latrines need deepening, Toppy,' Stryker replied. 'Why don't you lend a hand, seeing as you're so keen?'

Toppy's grin vanished. 'Weren't what I meant, sir.'

Stryker feigned a look of incredulity and the men laughed.

'I fell in a shit-pit once,' Skellen's laconic voice droned from the far end of the sap. His rank meant that he was not required to dig, but he seemed as dirty as the rest. 'Over in Antwerp.'

'The stink has'nae left you,' Simeon Barkworth croaked as he drove his spade deep to scrape away a sucking gobbet of earth.

Skellen ignored him. 'Blind drunk, I was. Grovelled around in the dung for a good while, trying to find my feet. And you know what? Came up with a gold chain snagged on the end of my shoe.'

'A golden turd,' Barkworth said with a cackle.

'Worth a swim in a latrine, Master Skellen!' Stryker called down the line.

'How much did you get for it, Sergeant?' another man asked.

'Get for it?' Skellen repeated the question as if it were uttered by a madman. 'I'd have been accused of thievery and dancing the hangman's jig before sundown!'

'Then what did you do with it?'

'I made a gift of it, lad.' He closed his eyes in reverence of the memory. 'To Sybylla Henkes, the finest whore in all Christendom. Couldn't understand a word she said, but, by God, she could suck like a bilge pump.'

The men brayed again as talk turned to their own favourite women. Stryker thought of Lisette. He had not seen hide nor hair of the queen's spy since the previous November. He thought of Faith Helly too. Hoped she was safe and well under Lieutenant Hood's watchful eye. Kendrick's company were down in the southern sector, digging towards the castle, which at least allowed him to relax. He absently felt the hilt of his sword, pushing the tip of his finger into the dent made by the pistol ball during the assault. The damage annoyed him, for the weapon had been a gift from Queen Henrietta Maria herself and would be too costly to repair, but immediately he chided himself. It had probably saved his life.

He stared up at the enemy soldiers. There were fewer than usual, just a handful of silhouettes shifting over the patchwork rampart. A dozen colours flew, stubborn and proud from their staked poles, defying the Cavaliers and their Royal commander.

A loud whinny broke his thoughts. He turned to see a horseman rein in on the landward face of the sap, soil cascading on to the timber walkway.

'Major Stryker?' the rider called down as the men stopped work to watch.

Stryker nodded, displeased. 'You are?'

The rider was young and splendidly attired, with a wide, open face that would have been perfectly round had it not been sharpened at the chin by the waxed point of a golden beard. He doffed a yellowish hat, cursing as one of the feathers fell out. 'Lieutenant Brownell. Compliments of His Highness, sir, and you're to abandon this work forthwith.'

'Abandon?'

Brownell leaned to the side of his saddle, eyeing the errant feather as it came to rest on the lip of the trench. 'Take your men to the north, sir, 'neath the beacon. You will be allocated your command upon arrival.'

'Command?' Stryker echoed in exasperation. 'Speak plain, man. What is the Prince's intent?'

'Why, Major Stryker, we are to attack!' Brownell beamed. 'Or, rather, General Tillier's regiment will attack, and you will provide support.'

'Jesu,' Skellen grumbled, not quite quietly enough, 'he's gone mad, sir.'

Brownell's pale eyes swivelled along the line. 'I suggest your creature curbs his tongue.'

'Shut your mouth, Sergeant,' Stryker growled, 'and look to your manners.' He had not taken his gaze from Brownell. 'Make matters clear for me, Lieutenant. His Highness will surely not storm the breach so soon?'

'The breach and many more places besides, sir,' Brownell said, flicking the reins deftly so that his mount loped away. 'For there are none left to repel us. The Roundheads have gone!'

They had not all gone.

A rear-guard remained, out of bravery or duress, but most of Liverpool's garrison had been evacuated during the shroud of night. Major-General Henry Tillier commanded the northern-most section of the siegeworks, those nearest the wide channel where River Mersey became Irish Sea, and his lookouts had been greeted with the rising sun by a view of boats streaming back and forth between the riverside wharfs and the ships anchored at deep water. Despite the heroic defence of the breach, Colonel Moore, the Parliamentarian governor, had evidently decided that drawn-out resistance would not be tenable. The twelve colours snapping in the wind were just a decoy, while the Roundheads were sneaking away.

Stryker took command of a new detachment as they swarmed through an unguarded gate set within the northern run of the wall. Tillier's green-clad fighters formed the spearhead, with Tyldesley's and Pelham's in the rear, and the general himself watched them through the gaping gateway from atop a dappled grey.

'To victory, Stryker!' Tillier bellowed happily. He fiddled with his shoulder-length brown hair and fastidiously trimmed whiskers with a gloved hand, as if the queen herself waited in Liverpool to greet them. 'Flush 'em out, sir!'

Stryker swept his hat low as he went past, pleased to be with Tillier's regiment. They were hard men, veterans of the war in Ireland, the Englishmen branded Catholic by rebel news-books and pamphlets in their desperation to paint King Charles as a secret Papist. And though they had been repulsed the day before, he knew the greencoats were as sturdy a force as any under Prince Rupert's command. He had fought with them at Newark, seen them outmanoeuvre and outfight Sir John Meldrum's larger army outside that pivotal Royalist strong-hold, and knew they would deal swiftly with any resistance here.

'Lieutenant-Colonel Caryl Molyneux is your guide, sirrah!' Tillier was bellowing at his back. 'A local fellow, but knows his business. You're in good hands!'

Stryker did not see Molyneux, who led from the front, instructing the vanguard into various streets, buildings and pas-sageways. Instead he went south, along a wide thoroughfare lined with the premises of clothiers, butchers and glovers, fishmongers, boat builders and net makers. Occasionally a shot rang out from an alley or rooftop, but they were few and far between. His men put windows through with the butts of their muskets, peering into houses to ensure there were none home but frightened townsfolk, and every fifth or sixth building had its door kicked in and its rooms searched. Further out, over the roofs and beyond the streets, more fierce confrontations played out, especially near the river where units of Parliament men still clamoured for their makeshift ferries, but here, in the southern quarter, the territory fell in short order.

It was only when Stryker reached the castle that matters altered. A substantial body of men had fallen back on its sheer walls. Perhaps they had resolved to hold it with bloody-minded purpose, or their route of escape was simply cut off. Either way it did not matter; the loopholes bristled with their muskets, lit match-tips danced in the shadows behind.

The colour draped from the battlements was not one of England's rebellion, and that gave Stryker cause to stall. He held up a hand to stay his troops, and they fanned out into the shade of the buildings fringing the open ground that ran in an arc around the thick medieval wall. Firearms were scoured, loaded and wadded. Some men knelt, others leaned into the pock-marked timber frames as they blew on hot matches and gauged the range of these fresh targets.

'Scotch,' Skellen muttered at Stryker's side, spinning the halberd shaft as he spoke, its base jammed into the mud, light dancing off the triple-puposed head.

Stryker nodded, still eyeing the banner. It was blue, a huge cross stretching to all four corners, yellow inscriptions sewn into each of the segments between the cross's limbs. This was one of the Scots regiments that had invaded during winter, detached from York to counter the Royalist surge through Lancashire. They would be good troops, had probably refused to flee with Colonel Moore's garrison, and now they had found a bolt-hole to defend. He swore savagely, dragged a gust of gritty air into his lungs, and went to give the order to attack. It was only then that he saw the huge black stallion.

Rupert, Count Palatine of the Rhine, supreme commander of His Majesty's forces in Lancashire, glowered from up in the saddle as his fiery-eyed mount clattered on to the open ground. There were shouts from within the castle, the Scots defenders no doubt discussing the merits of shooting the prince there and then, but none took the chance. Instead they waited, as Stryker's men waited, as the tall man with the flowing black locks and predatory stare wheeled his horse in a tight, high-stepping circle beneath the collective gaze of his enemy. Screams drifted on the wind, the smell of burning thatch mingled with the egg-stink of powder smoke, and they all knew that Liverpool was being sacked. But Prince Rupert did not flinch, sparing only a glance down at his beloved dog, Boye, who came to sit, tongue lolling, at the horse's side. Rupert was straight-backed and unruffled, a lone island in a sea of violence. He wore a dark green hat, matching the cloth of his coat, and plucked it free, holding it high for the Scots to witness.

'Enough!' he bellowed.

'No surrender!' shouted the reply. All Royalist eyes went up to the crenellated rampart cresting the fortress like a cockerel's comb. There were perhaps a dozen men on that high place, all – except one – dressed in the ubiquitous Hodden grey of Scottish regiments, blue bonnets capping their heads. The figure who alone wore civilian garb, made martial by a sword held aloft and a heavy-looking gorget at his throat, was evidently the officer in command of this defiant last stand. 'Dash yourse'n against our walls, sir!'

Prince Rupert replaced his hat and pursed his lips. He turned the snorting but compliant stallion again, this time reviewing his own strength. On the second tight circle he caught Stryker's eye and held the beast still without so much as a touch to rein or stirrup. 'What say you, Sergeant-Major?'

Stryker bowed low. 'Highness?'

'Have you the stomach for another fight?'

'We will fight, Highness.'

Rupert's handsome face creased, thin lips peeling back in a grin that revealed brilliantly white teeth. 'But do you yearn for Scots blood, sirrah?'

'Nay, Highness,' Stryker replied, looking up at the forbidding castle. He had no idea how they would find a way over those walls without first enduring a hail of lead. 'I do not.'

Rupert nodded and turned back to address the enemy officer. 'Terms, sirrah! Free quarter to you and your men, should you have the wisdom to offer me your sword!'

'And if not?' the man called from his soaring vantage.

'Then you will not live to regret your foolishness!'

The men on the rampart vanished. There was a lull. Prince Rupert, Stryker and the others waited in the cold dawn. And then, even as musketry and pistol shots crackled through the roads and alleyways of the walled port, the gates of its ancient castle groaned open.

Liverpool had fallen.

# CHAPTER 11

*York, 14 June 1644*

'Four shillings. Not a penny more.'

The butcher wrinkled his nose as he leaned out from the hatch. It was a timber platform, hanging on strained hinges, over which was draped a relatively clean cloth and various cuts of meat. He sucked at his wiry moustache as if mulling over the offer. 'Five.'

The customer, a chubby soldier in a red coat and wide-brimmed hat, rested one hand on the hilt of his sword and jangled his leather purse in the other. 'Five, then. You will require the extra shilling for physic.'

The butcher frowned. 'I do not need phy—' he began, but his wife, plucking a scrawny bird on one of the tables in the main shop behind him, cleared her throat. The butcher glanced over his shoulder, then at the customer, his face draining of colour. 'Four it is.'

Captain Lancelot Forrester offered his sweetest smile as he handed over the coins. 'Pleasure.'

'The making of a deal with menaces,' Forrester's companion muttered as the captain picked up the limp carcass of the chicken he had purchased, 'is hardly Christlike.'

Forrester shrugged. 'The only menace was that blackguard's greed. The common rate is four shillings for a hen, and he damned well knows it.'

Seek Wisdom and Fear the Lord Gardner spat into the mud as they paced down the road. 'I suppose it matters not, boy, for soon we will have none such trouble.'

'They have us well strangled,' Forrester agreed. 'Still, we have supplies for the time being, and negotiations continue.'

'Do you hear this fool, Lord?' Gardner screeched at the grubby-looking sky. 'He believes our grandees negotiate!'

Indeed, Forrester had suspected a tentative conversation had been conducted for several days now, for the furious activity of the Allied gunners had diminished markedly. He suspected, though official hostility continued, that offer and counter-offer had somehow been conveyed between the opposing lines, culminating in the official ceasefire that had been initiated earlier in the day. The guns had been silent for several hours now, precipitating the bustling market that had sprung up, seemingly out of nowhere.

'The parley is not scheduled until eight of the clock,' Forrester said. 'We will know more after that hour.'

'Parley,' Gardner scoffed. 'It is pomp and lies. Piss and wind. Dung and dishonour.'

'The commissioners are out there this very moment,' Forrester retorted in exasperation, waving the flaccid hen in the vague direction of Micklegate Bar. 'A tent has been erected for the sole purpose of agreeing terms.'

'Newcastle dallies,' Gardner replied derisively, 'in the hope of divine intervention. The devil's alliance discuss terms while they dig their cursed tunnels. Duplicity on all sides.'

'I suppose God has told you this?'

'Common sense tells me this, you bloody beef-witted Cavalier.' The priest ferreted in his filthy coat, finding a hunk of bread that looked dubious at best. He tore into it, offering half to Forrester. 'It'll all come to nothing.'

The bread looked to have more grit than grain, but Forrester took it with thanks. 'Mother would make paste of apricot,' he said, suddenly wistful. 'We'd spread lashings of the stuff on a fresh crust.'

'Apricot?' Gardner whistled. 'And broke your fast on griddled swan and roasted crocodile, I shouldn't wonder.'

Forrester ignored him. 'Pear, if no apricots could be found. It was delicious.'

They walked on in the direction of the bar, its towers looming over the market. On its battlements, and along the walls to either side, soldiers waited, staring out at the siegeworks and the tent that hosted the meeting.

Gardner wiggled a bony finger in his face. 'Your mind should be full of the Lord's word, yet it is full of your belly's demands. I shall preach on the subject.'

'Not to me, Father,' Forrester said as they skirted a particularly malodorous pile of horse manure. 'I must attend the Minster on Sunday.'

Gardner cackled, patting Forrester's right shoulder. 'Aye, you're his grace's lapdog now, I forget!'

'It is an honour to be noticed,' Forrest replied dutifully. He looked down at the cross of red and blue that he had paid a seamstress to sew in place. It looked slightly out of kilter against the red of his coat, but he was proud nonetheless.

'Remember, boy,' the priest continued. 'The Minster's a grand enough pile o' stone, but no man ever reached heaven by praying to gilt candlesticks and gaudy murals.'

'If the way to heaven is to dress like a madman and rant at the clouds, I question whether it is there that I wish to go upon my demise.'

'You blaspheme, you decadent English arsehole.'

'And you stink, you mad Welsh—'

Gardner had reached out to grip Forrester's elbow. He nodded towards the gate. 'What d'you make of that, boy?' Micklegate Bar had opened just enough for seven finely robed courtiers to push through. At their backs came a stream of blank-faced musketeers. 'Parley's over, by the looks o' them.'

'Jesu,' Forrester muttered. He had no business asking anything directly of the marquis's delegates, but, as soon as they had stormed past, he waylaid the captain commanding the honour guard of musketeers. 'Well?'

'The rebel commissioners demanded too much,' the officer said, happy to be the source of news. 'Our commissioners raged out of the tent without so much as receiving the enemy's propositions.'

Forrester exchanged a glance with Gardner. 'Then there will be no agreement.'

The officer shook his head. 'And no surrender.'

## Middlethorpe, near York, 15 June 1644

'I understand their commissioners flounced home empty-handed, but a drummer was sent into the city with our propositions, was he not?'

The speaker was Sir Henry Vane; Harry to most, for his father went by the same name. He was a large man, powerfully built, with the same fierce eyes and bushy brows as Sir Henry the Elder. His face was lean, spare and without whisker or beard, so that he looked younger than his thirty-one years, yet his bearing was proud and his jaw angled prominently to give him a face that his wife often bemoaned was as belligerent as a bulldog with a bone. He liked the description, knew other men were intimidated by him, and thanked God daily, for life, faith and war had led him along a path that required such qualities in abundance. Providence had seen him shift from courtier to New World power-broker and back to the mother country, and now, as he clambered out of his father's long shadow, he had found himself seated at a table with three of the greatest lords in the disputed realm.

Across from Vane sat Alexander Leslie, Earl of Leven. The Scottish warlord smoothed down his sandy-grey moustache and leaned back in his creaking chair. He plucked the creased square of vellum from the ever-cluttered table in the centre of his campaign room, and handed it to an aide. 'He has returned with this reply.'

The aide scuttled around the table's perimeter, passing David Leslie, then both Fairfaxes, father and son, the Earl of Manchester and General Cromwell, eventually bowing and giving the letter to Vane, who unfolded it slowly.

'Considering the way in which the negotiations crumbled,'

Vane said, 'I will not hold my breath in expectation of capitulation.'

Leven gave a rueful snort. 'Wise, Sir Harry.'

Vane cast his eye over the spidery black scrawl. '*I have perused the conditions and demands your lordship sent,*' he read aloud, then scanned the next few lines until he reached the nub of the matter. '*I cannot suppose that your lordships do imagine that persons of honour can possibly condescend to any of these propositions.*' He looked up. The moonlight streaming through the arched window made the paper appear translucent in his big hand. He was not a lord, nor a grand military leader, but that did not diminish his standing in such lofty company. Indeed, he was at ease with the half-dozen generals, confident in his mandate from Parliament and potent in his role as the mouthpiece of the Committee for Both Kingdoms. He had been sent here on behalf of the latter institution, the new body that represented the interests of Scots and English alike, and that wielded complete power over the alliance that converged against York. Vane's task had been to report on the progress of the siege, and, as news of the destruction of Lancashire reached Westminster, the Committee had ordered him to persuade Leven, Manchester and Fairfax of the need to release troops from York to intercept Prince Rupert. But the generals had convinced him that such a course would be wrong, and that York's capture was the greater mission. Now, with the parley finished and rumours rife of a possible relief force gathering on the far side of the Fells, he wondered whether they had committed a grave mistake. He stared at each man in turn. 'The negotiations are truly done, gentlemen. The ceasefire is at an end.'

A vigorous rap on the door startled the room.

Leven looked round. 'Come!'

A junior officer shuffled nervously in. 'The malignants have lit a fire, my lord. Up on the Minster.'

Leven glanced around the table. 'A signal?'

The messenger cleared his throat. 'It is answered distantly, my lord.'

'Answered?'

'To the south-west.'

Leven caught the eye of the younger Fairfax. 'What say you?'

'Pontefract Castle,' Sir Thomas answered. 'Held for the King.'

'A mark of solidarity,' the Earl of Manchester ventured.

Sir Henry Vane leaned in, placing his thick elbows on the polished walnut surface. 'Or a message that Prince Robber is on the move.'

Sir Thomas's father, the elderly Lord Fairfax of Cameron, had brought a small pouch with him, and now he opened it on the table to reveal a nest of sugar plums. 'He remains at Liverpool,' he said dismissively as he popped one into the corner of his mouth.

His son seemed to wince. 'It is dangerous to underestimate the Prince, Father.'

'Tish and pish,' Lord Fairfax muttered, stuffing more of the treats past cracked lips.

Vane stifled a wry smile. He could see why men at Westminster whispered of an ineffectual general in the north, holding his rank and dignity by right of birth while leaning heavily on his son's skill at arms. 'Do you believe he will move against us?'

Sir Thomas nodded. 'I fear it, Sir Harry, aye.'

Leven folded his arms. 'Our spies say nothing of the sort. Pray God he consolidates only.'

'But he may make a play for York,' Sir Thomas argued. 'His army is strong, and after Liverpool their morale will be high.'

Vane interjected before the others could respond. 'The Committee writes thus ...' He glanced down at a scroll unfurled beneath his nose, pinned at top and bottom by small weights. 'That the Earl of Denbigh is to muster his forces and rendezvous with Sir John Meldrum at Manchester.'

'The same Sir John Meldrum,' came a derisive voice from beside the Earl of Manchester, 'so utterly outwitted by Prince Robber at Newark?'

Vane looked at Lieutenant-General Cromwell, holding his cool gaze with difficulty. 'The same.'

'He is a good man,' Leven said, louder now, in an apparent effort to regain his authority. 'A Scot. He will do well, I've no doubt. Additionally, I understand that Colonel Hutchinson, the governor of Nottingham, has been ordered to join forces with Lord Denbigh. Together they will stop the Bohemian viper slithering o'er the Fells.' He raked his pale gaze around the table. 'For our part, I say we continue our efforts here. Rupert will not come.'

'He will come.'

Leven's eyes darted back to Oliver Cromwell. 'General?'

'He will come, my lord,' Cromwell replied with measured calm. 'Because he is clever, and because he is brave, and because he is driven by the devil.'

Leven shook his head. 'I will not break off this siege, sirrah.'

'And nor should you, my lord,' Cromwell said. 'But mark me well, for God hath granted me a dream so vivid I thought it as real as this very meeting. The Cavaliers will come for us, my lords, and we will scourge the earth of their vile turpitude.'

A silence followed, each lord and his second keeping private council. Vane studied their faces, marvelling at how such different men could work for the same goal. After a minute or two, he stood. 'If you'll excuse me, my lords, I should make my report to the Committee.' He looked at Leven, the man who believed, at least, that he held overall command. 'What is your next move, my lord?'

Leven stood too, the others following suit. 'A coordinated attack, Sir Harry.'

'Your mines are ready?' Vane asked.

'They flood daily,' Leven said, then let his gaze slide towards the Fairfaxes.

Sir Thomas swept a hand through his black hair. 'I need more time. It will be ready to spring within the week, my lord.'

'My charges,' the Earl of Manchester interrupted, his voice smug, 'are in place.'

Vane looked pointedly at him. 'Where, my lord?'

'The Manor. Originally the abbey abutting the city walls to

the north-west. It was built in the abbey grounds following the Suppression. We have a mine dug beneath the corner tower, St Mary's, and our battery has made a breach in the wall adjacent.'

'Impressive,' Vane mused.

Leven nodded. 'But we must wait for Sir Thomas's mine to reach conclusion. Spring them together, attack the walls at as many points as possible. They will be so alarmed by the twin explosions that our storming parties will be up their ladders before Newcastle knows what has become of his grand fortress.'

Vane studied their faces. Fairfax seemed happy, but Manchester was clearly disgruntled. He stepped back from the table before an argument could erupt. 'Thank you again, my lords. I shall leave you to dig your mines, and will make the Committee aware of your plans. Pray God you will break the city soon, for storm clouds gather in the west.'

Edward Montagu, whose proper title was Second Earl of Godmanchester, had taken leave of the campaign room and now stooped below the lintel of Middlethorpe Manor and stepped out into the night. The air was crisp, the clouds thin. He stretched, worked his jaw until it cracked, and planted his hat atop his head. He looked due north, towards the battered city. The glow from the Minster was impossibly bright against the black cloth of night. It emanated from up on the highest tower, alive with tremulous flame, and he wondered exactly what game the Marquis of Newcastle was playing. He turned away to stare along the cinder path that stretched from the main doors to watch Sir Henry Vane dissolving into the night. 'We shall lend a juicy morsel to your Committee's report, Vane,' he muttered to the big man's retreating back.

'My lord?'

Manchester – name shortened to avoid blasphemy – did not look round. He knew the voice well enough; had expected it. 'The vain Master Vane,' he said softly, 'writes to the Committee. I say we give him a tale worthy of the telling, General Crawford.'

Out of the gloom stepped a man swathed in a long cassock, silver buttons glimmering at chest and sleeves. 'The men are ready,' he said, his accent coloured by Lowland Scots. 'I have six hundred itching for the assault.'

Manchester felt his cheek twitch gently. 'The breach is practicable?'

Major-General Lawrence Crawford nodded enthusiastically, blue eyes sparkling in his thin, cleanly shaven face. 'The malignants have barricaded it with soil and dung, and Lord knows what else, but once the tower's been blown they'll forget the breach is even there.'

Manchester looked back at the manor house, making sure there were no prying eyes at the windows. 'Do what you must.'

Lawrence Crawford grinned excitedly. He was forty-three years old, but his demeanour was akin to that of a schoolboy. 'Does Cromwell know?'

Manchester shook his head. 'You do not like him, do you?'

Crawford screwed up his face in disgust. 'He's nought but a country ploughman. A turnip tugger. I should be at Council, not he.'

'If it comforts you, I do not hold with Independents in high places. It breeds mutiny amongst the men. I trust you, Lawrence, because you are as staunch a Presbyterian as I.' In truth he knew he should chastise the ambitious Crawford, but Manchester was well accustomed to such feelings himself. It was he, as senior Englishman in the York alliance, who should wield overall command. Everyone knew it. But the doddery old Fairfax cared more for sweet treats and sweeter young girls than he did for the etiquette of warfare, and Leven – dour and decrepit and barely literate – possessed the most powerful of the three armies in situ. There was nothing Manchester could do.

'Thank you, my lord.'

'But,' Manchester went on, 'Cromwell is a natural soldier. Keeps a level head under fire and commands the respect of his men. His moral austerity makes for perhaps the best troops I have seen. They do not steal, do not swear, do not terrorize the common folk.'

'He has served nowhere,' Lawrence protested bitterly. 'He is a novice. Claims he was commanded to war by God Himself.'

'Were we not all of us commanded by God?' Manchester patted Crawford on the shoulder. 'I do not hold with Cromwell's burgeoning power, so perhaps on the morrow you will give the Committee reason to supplant him with a man more suitable?'

Crawford's head bobbed in the moonlight. 'I will, my lord.'

'And Lawrence?'

'My lord?'

Manchester turned away, boots crunching loudly. 'Breathe a word of this conversation to another soul and it will be the last breath you draw.'

# CHAPTER 12

*Liverpool, Lancashire, 15 June 1644*

The Royalist army took respite at Liverpool. It had been a frenetic and dangerous few weeks as they had fought their way across Lancashire, and the capitulation of Colonel Moore's garrison marked a logical moment for Prince Rupert to take stock. The men still talked of York, but they talked, too, of joining the Oxford army – the king's main field army – and combining to destroy threats further south. None knew what was to come. It was their duty simply to wait and wonder as to the machinations of their Bohemian chieftain, who galloped in and out of the shattered town on matters of high business, flanked always by grim members of his Lifeguard. The fighting column had suffered heavy casualties at Liverpool, and expended vast quantities of powder and ammunition, which meant they had to wait for more to come up from the magazines at Bristol and Worcester. Moreover, there were new recruits to be enlisted and trained, more horses to be purchased and supplies to be hoarded. In the meantime, the men revelled in their rest, savoured the stability of steady billets with dry roofs and hot hearths. They played Queenes and Hazard, bragged of the spoils they had plundered and toasted their success. With the exception of the stoutly held town of Manchester, all of Lancashire was now under Royalist control, and with the conquest of Liverpool, the king's men had secured a crucial landing place for the expected troops from Ireland. Reinforcements that would soon sail across the sea to counterbalance the unholy alliance of Scotland and Westminster.

Stryker paced through the battered town. It was Saturday, market day, but no vendors lined the streets with their wares. Almost four hundred soldiers and citizens had died in the final attack. Though the garrison had fled on to the waiting vessels with most of their valuables, the victorious Royalists had been intent upon wreaking revenge for the days of toil. Some Parliamentarians had been killed in small groups, stubbornly defending positions that conscience would not allow them to vacate, while a few of the Scots had failed to reach the safety of the castle in time, finding themselves overtaken and over-whelmed. Most of the death, however, had been wrought by wanton violence. It had not been as bad as Bolton, but buildings were still burned, homes still robbed, men slain and women raped. Aldermen had banded together beneath a white rag and begged the conquerors to cease, and Rupert had theoretically agreed, but still the destruction had continued in unseen alleys, attics and cellars. Now only a few ventured on to the streets; haggard, stooped wraiths working in gaunt-faced silence, loading waxy, bloated bodies on to creaking wagons.

Stryker skirted round one such team as they dragged a pair of stripped, mottled-blue cadavers from the doorway of a house. One was a male, his throat gaping open from ear to ear, the bloodless flesh flapping like the mouth of a fish. The second was that of a woman, her neck horribly blackened, the bruises shaped like fingers. He looked at the corpses, feeling a pang of guilt, but shook it off. This was war.

A hundred yards on and he reached the bakehouse that was his temporary home. He paused outside, checked he had not been followed, and knocked on the heavy, studded door. It opened to reveal Simeon Barkworth's yellow eyes. Stryker stepped over the threshold. It was gloomy inside, despite the bright day, and not for the first time he felt a stab of discomfort for bringing Faith Helly to a place full of ovens, given what had come to pass at Bolton. But the girl had taken it in her stride, and he could hear her light, almost musical voice chattering from the next room.

'There is no infallible interpreter,' she was saying. 'Not Pope in Rome, nor Archbishop in Canterbury.'

Stryker weaved his way past an upended worktop, his boots leaving prints in the layer of flour that dusted the stone floor. He tossed his hat at a hook set into the wall, and nodded a greeting to the faces that turned to him. Skellen loomed in the shadows, methodically running a whetstone along the cutting edges of his halberd, while Hood sat opposite Faith, staring intently.

Faith was as usual clutching her Bible. She smiled at Stryker, before returning her gaze to the lieutenant. 'You see, Thomas,' she continued, 'no church, no priest or saint, can be interposed between the soul and God. There is no ordained pathway to Grace. The only interpreter of God's Word is the individual. You or I.'

Hood frowned. 'How would I know that what I interpreted was right?'

'You pray,' she said, as though it were the most obvious answer imaginable. 'Pray that you are guided by the Holy Spirit. Read the Word.' She tapped her fingertips on the small book's leather cover. 'And follow your inner voice. Your conscience. Why should a robed bishop tell you how to listen to God's wisdom? How does that man – an imperfect, sinful son of Adam – have the right to style your belief?'

'He is educated.'

'You are educated.'

'He prays.'

'And that,' she said, 'is why you must pray. Then you will be no weaker than he, in the ways of Scripture.'

Barkworth appeared behind Stryker, and both sat down on dusty chairs. 'Dangerous talk,' Stryker said.

'Thomas is keen to learn,' Faith said, 'and I believe God is keen for me to speak.'

'Lieutenant Hood,' Stryker replied, 'should be keen to keep his neck at its current length. Turning Banbury-man is not wise when it is just such men we have so recently fought.'

Hood rose to his feet with an apologetic smile to the girl, and moved away. Faith Helly turned in her seat to face Stryker. Flour speckled the red strands of hair that strayed beyond the coif's edge. 'You wish to be rid of me.'

'I said we would come to a decision once we captured Liverpool. Here we are.'

She set her jaw determinedly. 'I will not go to the women.'

'So you have repeatedly stated. Yet I cannot very well stroll down to Sussex with you, and nor will I send you alone.'

'Then?'

'Then it is to the Prince you will go. He can decide your future.'

She held his gaze for a second, her knuckles blanching as they gripped the Bible tighter. 'No.'

'No?'

'He is a Papist in all but name.'

'He is my general. He is the king's nephew.' Stryker stood. 'He will treat you fairly and honourably.'

Faith did not move. 'He will hand me to the Vulture.'

Stryker pressed a palm into his eye, rubbing hard as if it would cleanse his exasperation. 'For the last time, Mistress Helly,' he muttered through gritted teeth, 'the Vulture does not want you. He toys with your fear for his own amusement. And besides, why would the Prince give you to him?'

She grunted a derisive chuckle. 'Prince Rupert is a murderer. He commanded at Bolton.' She waved the Bible in the direction of one of the half-shuttered windows. 'Look around you, Major. Liverpool is a dead place. Your general does Beelzebub's work, and I will not go to him.'

'Sir,' Hood cut in suddenly. 'I would ask that she stay.'

Stryker turned to glare at the young officer. 'You would ask, would you?'

'She has helped me these last days,' Hood persisted, though his voice trembled.

'Helped?' Stryker echoed incredulously.

Now Faith stood, moving to stand between the two men. 'The Book of Proverbs warns us against strong drink, Major

Stryker.' She closed her eyes as she recited, 'In the end, thereof, it will bite like a serpent, and hurt like a cockatrice.'

'She has helped me, sir,' Hood said. 'Truly. I owe her a great deal. I will stay with her.' He offered a bashful smile. 'Be her very own lifeguard.'

'And when we march?' Stryker asked, hearing heat inflect his words. 'When we are ordered on some mission? What then? You'll simply disobey? Refuse the Prince? Refuse me?'

'I—' Hood began, but tailed off, cowed by his commander's voice.

Stryker spun on his heels and walked out. When he was outside, he realized Barkworth and Skellen had followed. He glowered. 'Spit it out!'

Skellen grimaced. 'He means well, sir.'

'He is young and stupid,' Stryker snarled.

'He lost two sisters to the bloody flux,' Barkworth said. 'It haunts him still.'

'And?'

Barkworth thrust a tiny hand towards the open doorway. 'And now he has a new sister to protect.'

Skellen nodded. 'And she preaches at him.'

'I've noticed,' Stryker said sourly.

'It reassures him, sir,' Barkworth said. 'He is happier.'

'He don't shake no more,' Skellen said.

And Stryker realized that his sergeant was right. Hood did seem calmer. He blew out his cheeks. 'Then we keep her? Our very own hot-gospelling Puritan, to keep Thomas Hood from drowning in wine?' The others offered nothing but shrugs. 'Christ,' Stryker muttered. He waved them away. 'Begone. Sergeant, find us kindling for the fire. Simeon, fetch vittels for this evening.'

Barkworth's lips parted in a wolfish grin. 'Vaughn's have a good store o' salted fish.'

'I do not care who you rob, Master Barkworth, just see that you are not caught.' He felt the cool pricks of raindrops on his head. 'Jesu, I have left my hat inside.'

⋆　　⋆　　⋆

He sensed something was amiss as soon as he re-entered the bakery. He slunk behind a thick post and hurriedly primed and loaded his pistol. Softly, he eased the hammer to half-cock, wincing at the click that suddenly seemed a hundred times louder than usual. Then he was moving, slowly, carefully, grateful for the flour dust that muffled each step. Up ahead, Faith and Hood were standing against the conical form of the biggest bread oven. They were closely flanked by two men brandishing swords. Stryker hung back, concealed by the gloom.

The sergeant he remembered first; that strong, proud face, with hard eyes and a hedge of russet moustache. Stryker had seen him at Bolton, at Lathom House and again in the copse below the Everton ridge. On the other side was a man who was near featureless; he had no hair, no brow, no eyelashes, and some ravenous disease had eaten away most of his nose so that it was little more than a gaping maw out of which foul liquid appeared to seep. Both wore long, blue coats and clutched curved sabres, with which they herded their quarry together so that they could not ignore a third man as he spoke.

'Where is it, whore?'

'I am no whore!' Faith Helly protested, pressing into Lieutenant Hood's side.

'Well?' Captain John Kendrick continued. He faced away from Stryker, but there was no mistaking him. 'Where is it? Tell me now, Sydall whelp, or you will be fucked and then you will be flayed.'

Hood made to move towards the interrogator, but a snarl from the two Hungarians froze him in his tracks.

Faith's arms were folded tight over her Bible. 'I do not understand, sir,' she answered, voice pleading. 'I know nothing of what you ask.'

The Vulture tilted back his head, casting his eyes up to the roof in exasperated dismay. 'The golden flagon,' he said slowly, as if entreating a halfwit to repeat a simple phrase. In a flash his knife, the broad cinquedea, was free and he jabbed the space between himself and his captives. 'The cipher, damn you, you God-bothering bitch!'

'You speak in riddles, sir!' she cried back.

'Do not dissemble with me, girl.' He twirled the cinquedea deftly between his fingers. 'The cipher is hidden in a golden flagon, my dear. Give it to me. That is all I want.'

'Cipher? What is a cipher, sir?'

'We searched the house,' Kendrick went on as though she had not spoken, 'and it was not there. Someone took it. Someone has it. Hate-Evil Sydall would never have been so desperate to perish had he not first brought his whelps into the greedy scheme. Give me the flagon.'

'But I am not Master Sydall's daugh—' Faith began. She was abruptly cut off by a backhanded slap to her cheek.

Kendrick watched as she dabbed cool fingers against the hot skin. 'I'd be happy to cause you pain, my lovely,' he said eventually.

Stryker stepped out, drew the pistol to full cock, and aimed it at the back of Kendrick's head. 'And I'd be happy to scatter your brains over that oven.'

For a heartbeat no one moved. The Hungarians growled, but they could do nothing without Kendrick's word. He turned, observed Stryker as the latter approached, and slid his knife back into the sheath at his belt. 'She is a rebel spy, Stryker, do not be a fool.'

'Then why do you sneak into my quarters like common thieves, Captain?' Stryker said. 'Why not bring half the army to capture this notorious agent?'

'I applaud your bravado, Major, though I question your intelligence. There are three of us. You will pull that trigger and be cut to ribbons.'

Stryker smiled. 'But you will be dead.'

Kendrick canted his head to the side, weighing up his choices. He evidently decided they were limited, for he glanced back suddenly at his two men. 'Turn them loose, Sergeant Janik.'

Stryker was now skirting the group, arm still rigid, level with

Kendrick's face. He walked sideways like a crab, feeling his route through the debris with shuffling feet and an outstretched left hand. He reached a side door, pushing it open with his rump as Hood and Faith slid behind him. It was raining harder now, and their boots splashed as they backed out into the bakehouse's small yard. Their own horses were stabled in a chapel with the thoroughbreds of the Lifeguard, but the absent baker had kept a sturdy little pony, and the tatty-coated beast twitched nervously as they approached. Hood unfastened its tether, slipping the reins from an iron ring set into a patchy wall, and Stryker ordered him to run. For a moment he hesitated, but then he scurried away, sliding every few strides, holding his balance enough to vanish under an arch and out on to the main road. Stryker handed the pistol to Faith, leapt up on to the pony, and took the weapon back. He trained it on the doorway for a heartbeat, ensuring there were no curved sabres at their backs, then uncocked the hammer, propped it between his thighs, and bent low so that he could hook his hands under Faith's armpits. She yelped as he threw her over the saddle, belly down, like a sack of grain.

Kendrick's hajduks were at the doorway when he looked up. Sergeant Janik was in the lead, sword in hand, and Stryker knew there was no time to snatch up the pistol. Instead, he kicked him in the face.

Janik brayed like a gelded hog as he reeled back, dropping the blade and landing with a wet smack in the mud.

'Spit out your teeth,' Stryker commanded as the bald man and Kendrick burst from the doorway. Janik did as he was told, a fountain of blood and bits of broken tooth spilling into his lap as he mewed in pain. Stryker had the pistol now, and he yanked back the hammer. 'Try it again, and it'll be your guts spewing on the mud.'

'Major Stryker!' Kendrick called up to him. His furious face shone luminous in the rain. 'Do not be a fool!'

Stryker raked his spurs along the pony's flanks. The beast screamed, jolted forwards, and they were on their way.

*     *     *

'You did not believe me.'

The clouds were gathered over Liverpool, forming a pall that turned day to dusk as the roads became rivers. Thunder rumbled as though cannon fire had returned to the defeated town, and lightning lit up the castle and the river and the hills. Stryker and Faith had galloped as fast as the squat beast's matted hooves would allow, only easing when the girl spotted Hood loitering in the doorway of an abandoned house. They walked after that, sending the horse on its way, and found themselves outside the old fish market. The lieutenant was dispatched to find Skellen and Barkworth, and after less than an hour he had returned with both men and a raft of questions.

'He mentioned a golden flagon,' Stryker said, sitting on a pile of empty sacks and threadbare netting. 'A cipher.'

'You did not believe me, Major,' Faith Helly repeated herself, more loudly this time.

She was slumped against one of the cold pillars opposite him, and Stryker met her angry stare. 'A matter of regret, Mistress, truly. You were right about Kendrick. He does have designs upon you, but not in the way you imagined. He does not wish you dead. He wants this cipher.' He saw the bafflement in her eyes. 'A secret way of writing. A way to keep things hidden.'

'It is how spies communicate,' Thomas Hood added pointedly.

'I know nothing of any secret writing,' she said, her voice muffled under the hammering of rain on the roof above. She removed her coif, shaking free her hair. It made her look much younger. 'Nor any golden goblet.'

'He believes you are a Sydall,' Hood said.

'But I am not.'

'Kendrick does not know that,' said Stryker. 'He stumbled across you at Bolton, and that was by chance. But it was no accident that led him to Master Sydall's house in the first place. He wanted something that Sydall possessed. He thought – he *thinks* – you know of its whereabouts.'

She shook her head and sniffed against the onset of tears. 'Why?'

. 'Because he believes you are Hate-Evil Sydall's daughter.'

Hood glanced left and right, checking that Skellen still guarded one side of the market and Barkworth the other. 'We could tell him he is mistaken. Tell him Mistress Helly's story.'

Stryker stifled a laugh. 'You think he would believe such a tale?'

'Then he will try again,' Faith said, as colour dyed Hood's cheeks.

Stryker nodded. 'Aye, this is certain.'

'Then we must alert the Prince,' Hood said. 'Call upon his protection.'

'Protection,' Stryker said harshly, 'from one of his most able officers? A man hunting a Puritan in our midst? A Puritan he will claim to be a spy?'

'I am no spy, sir,' retorted Faith hotly.

'But Kendrick will say otherwise. I do not imagine Prince Rupert will provide any more protection than we, and perhaps a deal less.' They fell silent as a cart trundled past on Skellen's side of the building, thick brown spray flinging out from its wheels. The driver's bellows echoed about the colonnaded expanse like worship through a cloister. Stryker plucked the gloves from his hands and pulled the twine band from his soaking hair. It fell freely over his shoulders, and he ruffled it, then bunched it in a fist at the nape of his neck. 'Jesu,' he hissed, as water cascaded over his fingers. 'I found that hat on a German battlefield. It has brought me luck.'

'Superstition is sin,' Faith chided, as Skellen raised a hand to indicate safety.

Stryker retied his hair. 'Then I am a sinner. Now, what of this cipher?'

Faith bit her lower lip. 'I cannot say. I knew nothing of any scheme Master Sydall might have involved himself in.' She peered at Stryker, eyes wide. 'Nothing at all. I was a visitor. A guest.' She drew her knees up to her chest, clamping the Bible between them and resting her freckled chin on its spine. 'It is all so hard to fathom. As for a golden flagon … He did not allow a drop of strong drink beyond his lips, sir. The only flagon in his house was the Word of God. The vessel that held wisdom and guidance.'

Stryker's eye slid down from her face to her knees and the book pinned between. 'Give me that.'

Faith frowned. 'I will not, sir.' She lifted her head, taking the Bible in hand as she leaned back and cradled it like a new-born. ''Tis my only comfort.'

Stryker's heart was rattling now, his throat tight. 'You took it from the house.' He recalled the day when Bolton had burned. 'Is it yours? Do not dissemble now, Mistress, does it belong to you?'

She shook her head. 'I saw it on the floor as you led me from that awful place. God told me to take it.' She gripped it tighter against her chest. 'Thy word is a lantern unto my feet, and a light unto my paths.'

Stryker reached out for it. She squealed, pulled back, but he was too strong and prised the Bible from her grasp.

'Be still, girl!' he snarled. He clambered to his feet. His boots scraped loudly on the flagstones as he opened the leather-bound book and flicked through the pages with a thumb. The print was tiny, but bold and clear, expertly set by masters in London or Cambridge, and he squinted as he scanned the black lines, searching for something out of kilter in the uniform leafs. In the end it was his nail that betrayed the buried prize, for it snagged on a single page that did not reach the width of the rest. The difference was minute, imperceptible to the naked eye, but the inky blur ceased abruptly. Stryker looked up. 'Here. A cuckoo in the nest.'

Faith peered at the open page. 'Numbers?'

'This is a cipher, Mistress Helly,' Stryker said, planting his index finger on the centre of the well-thumbed leaf. It was a grid, laid out by a meticulous hand, each square populated by a single or double digit number. Immediately beneath was another grid, the corresponding squares inked with the letters of the alphabet. The page had been crammed into the centre of the book, wedged between others of genuine printed text so that a cursory glance would trick the eye, but there was no mistaking its purpose. Stryker shook the Bible in triumph. 'The Word of God, a spiritual flagon, brim-full of wisdom and guidance.'

Thomas Hood whistled softly. 'Brim-full of secrets, too.'

Stryker handed the Bible back to Faith. She stared at it as if it were a lit grenado. 'This is secret correspondence?'

'No,' Stryker said. 'This is the key to reading such correspondence. There are many kinds of cipher, and their complexities are varying. Simple ones will substitute a number for a character, but there are many more difficult kinds. There appears to be no sequence to this. It is complexity derived from indiscriminate placement. One would need this Bible to decipher any message.'

'Thus it is useless to us,' Hood said, crest-fallen, 'with no messages to unravel.'

Faith looked up, blinking. 'No messages, sir. But there are more numbers.'

They left the fish market as soon as the rain eased, walking through the streets until they found a taphouse at the northern end of town. It was nestled amongst a row of ramshackle tenements, with a broom hung from a dripping eave to advertise its business. The place was busy, housing a score of pikemen who lounged like engorged cats after a feast, uninterested in the newcomers. Here, Stryker decided, was a good place to lie low.

'So what 'ave we found?' William Skellen echoed Stryker's swirling thoughts as they retired to the snug at the rear of the taproom. Faith was with them. In a town full of soldiers and their plunder, another frightened young girl dragged into the shadows was not a strange sight.

Stryker lit his pipe and took a long, lingering drag at the tooth-worn stem, letting the smoke out slowly through his nose. 'It is a cipher, Sergeant.'

'For spies.'

Stryker nodded. 'The middle page contains the key. Letters and their substitutes. There is also a list on the back page, arranged in two parallel columns, one containing three-digit numbers, the other a series of words.'

'Places?' Skellen asked, reaching for a bowl of seeded bread hunks. 'Names?'

Stryker drank the smoke again, blowing hard to increase the pall that roiled around them like a shroud. 'Animals: eagle, otter, stoat, cony and the like.'

'A symbol for each intelligencer.'

'Aye, but no use to us. All we know is that Kendrick wanted the book.'

Skellen frowned. 'Then why did he murder Master Sydall?'

'Because he knew Sydall would never give it up,' Stryker said, 'and because he had already seen Mistress Helly curled in the oven. He presumed she knew where it would be, for she was better hidden than the rest, and that she would be altogether easier to coerce.'

'Then why this furtiveness?' Skellen demanded. 'A girl with knowledge of Crop-head spies marches with the king's army and Kendrick sneaks around trying to snaffle her from under our noses. Why not simply take her? Tell the Prince and he'd give that fuckin' Vulture a hundred men for the task.' He glanced, embarrassed, at Faith. 'Beg pardon, Miss.'

'Unless it is not a rebel cipher,' Stryker said.

'One of ours?' Simeon Barkworth said. He leaned in on his elbows, eyes like golden nuggets in the fug. 'Imagine Sydall is a turncoat. An agent of the Crown.'

Faith shook her head determinedly. 'Never.'

'But even so,' Barkworth persisted. 'The same would apply. There'd be no creeping about like a fox in a hen-house. The Vulture would have simply walked into Bolton and asked for the book.'

Lieutenant Hood had been staring at the little book, but now he looked up. 'You saw the Vulture whispering in the dark, sir.'

Stryker threw his mind back to the village of Standish in the days after the massacre and the private rendezvous he had witnessed between John Kendrick and a lone stranger. 'I did.'

Hood shrugged. 'Perhaps that is relevant.'

'Perhaps,' Skellen's drone reverberated around the snug, 'Sydall *was* a Parliament man, and perhaps the Vulture is too.'

'Then why would Kendrick slaughter Sydall?' Barkworth scoffed. 'Makes no bloody sense.'

Stryker rubbed a hand over his face. 'There is more to this.' He looked first at the Bible, then at Faith. 'Keep that troublesome book close, Mistress. It is key to all.'

## York, 16 June 1644

'Let us beseech Almighty God to be near to us in this, our great calamity.'

There was a downside to everything, as far as Captain Lancelot Forrester was concerned. To a grand feast, there was the inevitable tightening of a man's coat round his belly; to a victory in battle, there were the comrades left behind; and to becoming a confidant of the greatest man in northern England, there was the expectation that Forrester would attend the infamously turgid sermons in York Minster. He girded his loins and dipped his head.

'We pray blessings upon his Excellency, William, Marquis of Newcastle, Lord General of His Majesty's forces in these northern parts,' the priest in flowing robes boomed from the pulpit, 'and many other counties of this blessed kingdom.'

'Archbishop Williams,' a low voice rasped into Forrester's right ear, 'high-tailed it back to his native north Wales at the first rattle of scabbards.'

The pungent odour of lavender overwhelmed Forrester. 'Master Killigrew,' he whispered. He glanced at the ratlike intelligencer, who squeezed his ample rump in next to Forrester. 'You are well?'

Killigrew's grin betrayed his relish. 'And poor Bishop Bramhall, here, finds himself in the pulpit.'

'He is Bishop of Derry, is he not?'

'Aye. Exiled when the Ulster Presbyterians ran amok. Though he is a Yorkshire man by birth, so it is no great hardship.'

'We pray,' Bramhall was saying, 'that the torrid seas of base rebellion will be navigated by our great leader.'

Seated in front of them, Newcastle muttered thanks and amens, echoed by at least a dozen obsequiously bobbing adherents. Forrester chimed in as required, while the bishop continued. It was Trinity Sunday, the first Sunday after Pentecost, and the Minster was packed full. Forrester was near the front, but he occasionally stole a glance over his shoulder to witness row upon row of officers and their wives and children, eyes clamped shut as they joined the opening prayers. They were dressed in their very best finery, of course. Feathers and lace, silks and satins, silver gorgets and voluminous skirts, ruby-red scarves and bucket-top boots folded fashionably low. And yet the strain was beginning to tell. Outside, even as dozens of smaller services played out amongst the various units in Newcastle's army, the guns grumbled relentlessly. Musket fire yapped at the walls like a vast pack of dogs on the hunt, while orders shouted by foul-mouthed sergeants drifted through the lancet windows lining both transepts to pierce the bishop's droning exhortations. Soon, at least, the congregation would sing, and the singing would drown the noise of war, but as they prayed for God to intervene in their plight, the atmosphere was tense.

'That his hands may be strong, his heart bold, and his wisdom overflowing with divine assistance,' Bramhall continued. 'We pray that we shall live to see contented days, and peace upon Israel.'

'Amen,' Forrester muttered. Contented days. It was almost beyond imagination, so long had he been at war. There would be no contentment for the people of York, he felt certain. They believed in their walls and their ditches, their batteries and their white-coated heroes, but he had seen bigger, stronger cities fall, and he had seen the vengeance meted out upon inhabitants. That chaotic blood-letting had mercifully not infected this new war in the first months, but a note of heightened acrimony played its sad tune as the conflict drew on. And they had all heard the tales coming out of Bolton. Newcastle and his officers had scoffed at such talk, but Forrester knew that war was a plunging spiral that led only one way.

'You saw the beacons?' Killigrew whispered. He paused for Forrester's nod. 'Let us pray the Parliament men did not see the bluff for what it was.'

Forrester kept his eyes on the preacher. 'There is no relief force en route?'

Killigrew snorted derisively. 'It would be amusing if it were not so tragic.'

Now Forrester looked at him. 'You believe we are lost?'

'You do not?' Killigrew wrinkled his sharp nose. 'The King is timid, God preserve him. He would have his nephew come to York, but only when he believes his army is strong enough to engage the alliance we presently face. It will take time that we do not have.'

'The sconce at the Mount remains in our hands.'

'But they press us hard elsewhere. The battery opposite the Walmgate takes a fearful toll, and they will eventually slip a mine under our feet before we can flood it.'

Someone hissed irritably for silence nearby, and they bowed their heads.

'And, Lord, we beseech thee,' Bramhall went on. 'Preserve us from the violence of the wicked.'

'Preserve us,' Forrester said.

'Preserve us,' Killigrew echoed.

And in that moment the world erupted.

Forrester pushed his way along the nave as the Minster's very foundations shook. He burst out into daylight smudged by gritty miasma, at its thickest to the north and west, where the Manor compound abutted the main city wall. It projected precariously into the siege-lines of the Eastern Association, and it hardly surprised him that the area was under attack once more. But this was different. The Manor sat in the shadow of York Minster, and even from the cathedral's grounds he could see that St Mary's Tower, the proud sentinel marking the north-eastern corner of the compound, was now little more than a pile of jumbled stone.

Musket fire, furious and thick, erupted from the direction of the Manor. Forrester ran, clamping down his hat with one hand and drawing his pistol with the other. He weaved through the tide of terrified folk as they fled towards the safety of the Minster. He reached one of the gates leading through the main wall into the Manor and paused, loading the pistol with fumbling fingers. When it was done, he shouldered the gate open, wincing in expectation of a hail of lead, but none came. The fight was to the north, along the wall. The Manor grounds formed, he guessed, all of ten acres, walled entirely except for the western flank, which was protected by the river as it entered the city. That side had been shielded from marksmen by an earthen rampart, and he could see garrison men crouching on the muddy palisade as they gave fire across the water. On the compound's right flank, beyond its own wall, was Bootham Bar, one of York's great gates, and he imagined no serious threat was posed to so sturdy a barbican. But up ahead, over the open terrain of bowling green and orchard, was the long stretch of wall that ended with the crumbling remains of St Mary's Tower, and there Parliamentarian soldiers streamed over the battlements almost unopposed.

'Christ,' Forrester hissed. He thumbed back his pistol's hammer. The enemy had already made a breach in the battered wall, between the tower and what remained of a cannon-smashed church, but the garrison had plugged the gap with rubble and sods. Yet now, with the tower sliding into the abyss on the outer face of the defences, the Parliament men were climbing unopposed to drop on to the inner face of the Manor grounds.

Forrester swore again. The smoke was clearing. He could see more men hauling themselves over the wall on either side of the breach, and knew that this was a well-planned assault.

Nearby, at the old abbott's residence, the Manor House, doors flew open. Men ran out on to the gardens. They wore white coats and they brandished muskets and blades, halberds and axes. Forrester ran to them, noting the red scarf at the waist of one grey-whiskered officer. 'Captain Forrester,' he panted, 'Mowbray's Foot.'

The officer offered a curt nod. 'Where is your unit?'

'I was at worship, sir.'

'Then you'll have to do.' The officer was tall and elegant. His coat was white like that of his men, but trimmed with exquisite lace and slashed at the sleeves to reveal a lining of red silk. 'Sir Phillip Byron,' he added, 'colonel in this sector. Rogues have sprung a mine under St Mary's. They're coming in.' He drew a swept-hilt rapier, kissed the blade tenderly, and pointed it at the tower. 'I mean to stop them.'

With that, Byron broke into a charge. His men, numbering no more than fifty, jostled past Forrester, who followed them through the gardens and the orchard. They reached the bowling green quickly, and there they ran into four times their number.

The Parliamentarian troops had been massing on the neatly trimmed green. They were not ready to repel a concerted counter-attack, which is what saved Forrester and most of Byron's men, for the majority were engaged in loading and priming their muskets before the next phase of the assault. The Royalists ran headlong into the enemy's foremost lines, discharging their weapons and then flipping them over to present their heavy wooden stocks. But there were simply too many to fight, and by the time Forrester reached the fray they were already overwhelmed, falling back across the green beneath the crushing blows of the butt ends of muskets. All the while more and more Roundhead troops swarmed through the breach, over the undefended wall and up through the ragged fissure that had been the corner tower.

Sir Phillip Byron – yet another member of the great dynasty so entwined with the King's cause – held his elegant rapier high, slashed it down at a tawny-scarfed officer with purple lips and a milky eye, and sneered as his blow was barely parried. Then he was down. Forrester was behind him, shouting at Byron to get up, but he saw the rapier lying in the grass, saw the colonel's hands clutching at his belly, gut-shot by some unseen assassin. The milky-eyed Parliamentarian needed no encouragement. His blade went hard and deep, crunching up through the colonel's neck until it jarred on bone. Forrester screamed the retreat, and in seconds the Royalists were bolting across the open ground towards the Manor House.

A huge cheer went up. Forrester swore viciously, wondering how they could possibly mount an effective defence with so few men. It was only when the cheer was repeated that he realized it had come from behind rather than in front. He looked back towards the gate leading through the city wall. Hundreds of men in suits of white were flooding into the compound. They were grim-faced, chanting war-cries, a huge red banner swaying on its pole at their head, cutting through the smoke like the prow of a ship.

Beneath that banner was a man dressed in blue and silver, his chest encased in iron, his hat adorned with huge, white feathers. William Cavendish, Marquis of Newcastle, general of Royalist forces north of the River Trent, looked like a man possessed. His teeth shone white as he screamed encouragement to his white-coated men, his Lambs, eyes blazing through the powder cloud.

'On me! On me!' Newcastle was bellowing. 'I am with you, my lads! And God is with me!'

Forrester ran to him as the veteran units of Newcastle's army fanned out across the orchard. 'Where else do they threaten, my lord?'

Newcastle seemed nonplussed for a heartbeat. 'Nowhere, Captain, thank the Lord. I bring two thousand brave men. I mean to purge the Manor clean of rebel stink!'

Forrester could hardly believe his ears. 'Nowhere, my lord?' It was almost beyond comprehension that the escalade would be attempted at a single point, given the formidable garrison available to repel it. 'They will surely stretch us, will they not?'

'Satan gives them arrogance,' Newcastle said. 'They will learn.'

Forrester glanced back at the breach, at the foot of which the massed ranks of the storming party were edging forth, firing by volley across the bowling green. Bullets whined and whistled over his head. One of the marquis's officers went down, shot through the face. Forrester made to leave, but the marquis grasped his elbow with an angry glare.

'You mean to run, sir?'

'I mean to trap them, sir!' Forrester replied. 'I must get out of the city!'

'Out?' Newcastle was bewildered. He shook his head. 'Bootham Bar is barricaded.'

'A postern then?'

Newcastle glanced at an aide, who stepped forwards with a nod. 'Private sally port on t'other side of Bootham, sir.'

Forrester took Sir Phillip Byron's men. He had around thirty in all, for the unit had abandoned several dead and wounded on the overgrown lawn. They went out of the Manor complex, beyond Bootham Bar, and through the tiny door set into the thick city wall nearby. They were outside in moments, exposed to the fury of the Army of Both Kingdoms, the huge barbican immediately on their left, with the carcass of St Mary's Tower teetering above. Forrester ran towards the sound of musketry and clanging steel, a din growing more furious with each passing second as the whitecoats advanced behind their blood-red colour.

He prayed aloud as he ran, begging God to cloak them from enemy sharpshooters, and wondering how on earth they would be able to skirt the outer face of the wall without being cut to shreds. The Manor wall was not covered by an outer ditch, but it was surrounded by siegeworks, and they leapt, one by one, into the first trench they reached. They scuttled along it, fetid brown water splashing all around, keeping their heads down until they reached a dead end. They clambered up and out, rolling over the lip of the trench and scrambling in amongst a nest of gabions for protection. Forrester risked a peek over the top of one of the large baskets. Nothing stirred in the lines. He looked out over the network of excavations. The besiegers had burrowed right around the city so that the entire circuit of walls was edged by a warren of gun emplacements and zig-zagging saps, and he knew that if he led his troop north, away from the battle, he would eventually stumble into the Eastern Association's main army. He took his time, scanning each gully until he found the right one, the most advanced trench the Earl of Manchester's sappers had dug: it was a passageway, five-feet deep, that ran flush with the Manor wall. Calling for the sally party to follow, he jumped in.

On they went, working their way around the corner of the compound. Forrester poked his head above the edge of the trench to see what was left of St Mary's Tower. Half of it had collapsed into the ground around Bootham Bar, and a vast crater had cored the earth at its foot. Above them, smoke-wreathed and jagged, was the breach. They waited, scanned the terrain on all sides, but no soldiers lined the siegeworks, no engineers waded through the filth in their heavy iron suits, no artillery pieces were being hauled up to play upon other sections of the wall. It was as if every man available for the escalade had already hurled himself over the ladder or through the breach. Did the rest of the army even know what transpired? Forrester laughed. He was terrified. His guts turned like a mill wheel and he could feel his breakfast inching its way up towards his mouth, and yet he laughed, because there was no one to stop him. So he climbed.

The sally party scrambled up the slope of rubble and soil in Forrester's wake. There was a crude palisade of stakes and wicker baskets at the top, and his men pushed through until they were on the inner face. Now shots rang out behind, for someone in the siege-lines had noticed their action, but it was all too late. Forrester turned his heels outwards, sliding on the filthy glacis until he was halfway down and well out of sight of anyone outside the city. There he halted, planting his feet hard so that there would be no slippage, and barked orders for his men to prepare their weapons as he drew his own blade.

He stared down into the compound. Immediately below, the Roundheads were in trouble. Plenty had come to the attack, perhaps as many as six hundred, but with no additional explosions, no extra breaches, nor even feinted assaults at other places on the wall, the Marquis of Newcastle had a large proportion of his garrison to spare. Now Forrester reckoned there were as many as two thousand Royalists in the Manor grounds, advancing by well-timed volley fire against a far inferior force. The Parliamentarians had captured the Manor for a matter of minutes, but now it had been violently wrested back into Cavalier hands.

Forrester waited until the first of the enemy officers called a full-scale retreat before he snapped the order for his men to present their muskets. The muzzles came down as one, a complete cordon stretching across the breach. There followed a terrible moment, for the Roundheads had seen them now, and they knew they would have to fight their way through, so that Forrester feared his thin line would be punctured by desperate fugitives. But they veered away in their fear, making instead for the chasm beside the collapsed tower. Scores made it through, but many were shot in their flight, and eventually that escape route was blocked too, so that they had nowhere to go. They threw down their arms, the swords of their officers clattering at the feet of Newcastle's senior men, and the Royalists cheered. It was over. York was safe.

# CHAPTER 13

## Outside York, 18 June 1644

The dappled grey gelding heaved its filth-spattered legs up the gentle incline, each hoof sucking as it was plucked from the mire. Its rider called encouragement into a flattened ear as he clung on against the rolling motion, knuckles white where they gripped the reins. Up ahead, a wagon was being loaded with what looked to be heavy sacks. The air suddenly carried the tang of putrefaction. He looked round at the man mounted on a big bay just behind. 'We brought everything on this cursed expedition, Davey. Everything but a supply of pomanders.'

David Leslie, Lieutenant-General of the Scots in England, did not look up into the seething rain. 'There's always somethin'!' he called.

Leven held a gloved knuckle to his nose as they skirted the wagon. He could feel the eyes of the local labourers, forced to collect the corpses under duress, bore into him, and refused to meet their collective gaze. He wondered how bountiful today's bitter harvest had been.

The Army of the Solemn League and Covenant had begun to die two days before the attack on the Manor. It started with a gunner, then a wheelwright and his family, their faeces turned the colour and consistency of the water in the siege trenches. Within two days the sickness was devouring a regiment of dragoons and rumours were circulating of sweating, vomiting musketeers in the ranks of Lord Fairfax's Northern Association. It was all forgotten with the breach and the explosion and the assault. Eyes and minds went to that exposed corner of York, where flame and smoke pulsed, and where the din of battle smothered all. But that had gone now, replaced by lethargy, sickness and an insidious foreboding. Two days on from the abortive attack, and the pestis seemed once more to be in the ascendancy. All the while the carts piled with lime-sprinkled corpses trundled out to the burial pits, and everyone knew that disease would finish the grand alliance as sure as any army.

Leven kicked at the struggling grey as the slope became steeper. The horse grumbled but quickened its step a touch, snapping big teeth at a mangy dog that scuttled too close, a dubious looking scrap of flesh lolling from its mouth. 'There they are, Davey.'

Leslie peered up from beneath his hat. 'Black Tom looks ready to blow.'

Leven allowed himself a chuckle, though he barely felt the ghost of mirth. 'That he does. A shame his mine does not.'

Up ahead, on the crest of rising land beside the River Ouse, Sir Thomas Fairfax's slender figure craned over the neck of his horse as he jabbed a finger at the man forced to stand before him.

'Crawford's ears'll be ringing till dusk,' Leslie said.

Leven nodded. 'So they should.'

'Thirty-five dead,' Fairfax was saying as they reached the meeting point, the river rushing on their left as they overlooked the smoke-wreathed battlements of York. 'One hundred wounded, and twice that captured.'

Major-General Lawrence Crawford's face was tight. 'The mine was flooding!' the standing man protested. 'I had to blow it lest all our efforts go to waste.'

'And flood so quickly, did it,' Fairfax retorted caustically, 'that there was no time to warn the rest of us?' He shook his head in unconcealed frustration. 'We might have attacked, sirrah. Sent thousands of men against the walls all around the city while you took the Manor.'

Leven gazed down at Crawford. 'It was an ill-conceived and

uncoordinated venture, General. Destined for failure from first shot to last.'

'There was no time,' Crawford argued. He was flanked by his immediate superiors, Manchester and Cromwell, and he twisted to cast the former a plaintive look.

'Hubris,' Fairfax scoffed, ignoring the line of dragoons that clattered over the bridge of boats fifty yards at his back. 'Arrogance. You meant to steal the glory for yourself, General Crawford, and now your precipitation has ruined us. The failure so destroys morale that the men are not keen to attack again.'

That was the crux of the matter, thought Leven. What had begun with the undermining of a tower, had ended with the undermining of the entire Parliamentarian enterprise. Heralds had gone into York as the smoke had cleared. They had pleaded with the Marquis of Newcastle to see sense. Why fight the inevitable, they argued? Why put more lives at risk by this unnecessary stubbornness? The attack on the Manor might have failed, but it was merely a taste of things to come. There would be more assaults, more bombardments, more powder-filled tunnels sunk deep beneath the walls. They reminded the Royalists that their besiegers were not one army, but three, numbering thirty thousand or more, and when they cleaved a way into the city there would be no satisfying their hunger for destruction. Every man, the heralds claimed, had heard rumour of Prince Rupert's action at Bolton-le-Moors, and every man thirsted for revenge. But Newcastle and his arrogant Cavaliers had not given an inch, so the forces of Lord Leven, Lord Manchester and Lord Fairfax had had to set about digging new saps, raising new batteries and planning new mines, and all the while the men on York's walls, on its gates and towers and barbicans, fought back with musketry and cannon fire. The rain fought too, and because it was the Parliamentarians who toiled in the boggy ground, it felt as though God had sided with the king. More men fell sick, some died, so that new burial pits were dug alongside the works overseen by engineers, and always there were rumours of a relief force massing on the far side of the mountains.

'And where is your own contribution?' the Earl of Manchester said turning to Fairfax, finally coming to the aid of his man. 'Must the army of the Eastern Association do all the real work?'

Fairfax bridled. 'The Walmgate mine is flooded, my lord. Always flooded. It will take days to bring to bear. The rain is an implacable foe.'

'As is Prince Robber.' It was Cromwell who spoke. He was wrapped in his usual trappings of leather and metal. 'You are beset with fever, Sir Thomas?'

'It ravages my regiments as greedily as any other.'

'Then we must look to the west.' Cromwell continued: 'If we cannot break York, we must break camp. When the Papists arrive, we cannot face them so ruined with pestilence.'

'We have time, gentlemen,' Leven said placatingly. 'Have faith.' He looked deliberately at Cromwell. 'And Rupert may yet go south.'

Cromwell shook his head. 'He will come, my lord, and he will fight.'

### York, 18 June 1644

Though forty-eight hours had slipped by since the skirmish at the Manor, Lancelot Forrester's entire body still ached. He was in the south of York, west of the Ouse as it snaked its way through the streets, the heavily guarded Skelders Gate straight ahead. Here, in the sector directly opposing the Scots army, Sir Edmund Mowbray's Regiment of Foot had been billeted, and it was to the home of a lawyer – driven out for his rebel sympathies – that Forrester had been summoned.

He wore a heavy woollen cassock against the rain, and he pulled it tighter across his chest. The gutter running along the centre of the road was swollen to breaking, a torrent of putrid effluent rushing away towards the riverbank, and he leapt it as he approached the house where the meeting of senior officers was due to convene. It would be dull, he knew. A discussion of supplies and casualties, of sentry duty and of ammunition audits; but that was regimental life. He passed a doorway that was wide open to the elements, and ducked under the lintel for a cursory glance. Inside, a man was screaming. He was down to his shirt-sleeves – his green coat hooked on the wall behind – a pulpy-faced whitecoat standing at his back with hands clamped firmly at his trembling shoulders. The chirurgeon leaned across the seated fellow, squinting through wire-rimmed spectacles as he probed underneath his patient's collarbone with a metal instrument. On the floor, between the wounded man's shuffling feet, was a bowlful of crimson water and a neatly placed sheet laid out with three saws of varying size, a couple of chisel-like tools and a large pair of darkly congealed scissors. The chirurgeon gave another speculative jab at the wound, the seated man brayed to the rafters, and Forrester shuddered. He understood why the door was open, for the whole place stank. Suddenly his own aches seemed to fade.

'Beg pardon,' he muttered when the chirurgeon noticed him. He ducked out of the building, but a voice hailed him from within the makeshift infirmary.

The chirurgeon was standing straight now, while two assistants bound the injured soldier's chest. In his hand were long tweezers, their tapered jaws clamped around the half-flattened disc that had been a musket-ball. 'Will you deliver a message for me, sir?'

'I am expected by my colonel, sir.'

''Tis only upstairs, sir,' the chirurgeon said. 'I am exhausted.' He looked down at his heavily stained apron. 'And not dressed for polite interview.'

Forrester nodded. 'Very well. Be quick about it, sir.'

The chirurgeon held up the bloody bullet. 'With Chirurgeon Turner's compliments, sir, would you let Master Killigrew know that this man will live?'

'Dear Lancelot.' Ezra Killigrew was standing at the only window in the small chamber, staring down at the street through diamond panes of glass. 'To what do I owe this pleasure?'

Forrester bounded up the stairs two at a time. He took a few paces into the room, noting a shelf full of scrolls on the wall and a table neatly stacked with sheets of paper in one corner. 'I have a message to deliver, sir. Master Turner's compliments.'

Killigrew turned. 'Well? What has our dear chirurgeon to say?'

'The wounded man, sir. The greencoat.'

'Ah yes,' Killigrew nodded. 'One of Manchester's Roundheads. Found in the Marygate rubble, bleeding like a stuck pig.'

Forrester opened his mouth to speak, but paused when he saw shadows move under a door set into the far wall. Someone waited in the adjacent room.

Killigrew cleared his throat. 'I dare say you are eager to attend upon Sir Edmund.'

Forrester blinked hard as he pushed the strange shadow from his mind. 'I am to tell you that he will live, sir.'

'Good,' Killigrew said. 'He will be able to answer some questions, then. Is that all?'

'That is all, sir,' Forrester replied, realizing that the building was designated for interrogation rather than recuperation.

'Then you are free to go.' Killigrew curled his upper lip. 'Do enjoy Sir Edmund's council, Lancelot. And try to stay awake, there's a good chap.'

Forrester knew that loitering in the inner sanctum of Killigrew's nest of spies was an invitation to trouble, yet here he was, back pressed against the panelled wall abutting the closed door through which he had walked only moments before. The shadow had been there, too close for anything but an eavesdropper, and Forrester wanted to see who the hidden listener had been. Killigrew had been too keen to be rid of him.

'Dog.' A stranger's voice sounded from within the chamber. 'That'd be right, so it would.' Forrester slid as close as he could to the door hinges, breath held tight, ear pressed to the meagre chink.

'Have a care, man,' Killigrew was saying. 'Do not speak of such things here.'

'But dog?'

'Suffer it, sirrah, or find another employer.'

'We're among friends in this fair city, are we not, sorr?' the first man replied. He was an Irishman.

'York is for the King, aye, but nowhere is safe. Now, to business. You are recovered?'

'Well enough, sorr. Was a bastard of a swim. Still coughing up weed. But you got m' report?'

No answer. Killigrew must have nodded, for he said: 'And you say he searched Sydall's house?'

'Top to bottom, sorr, so he claims.'

'Then he is right.' There was a pause. Forrester heard the scrape of a cup as Killigrew lifted it. 'The flagon is with this whelp. You say he knows where the bitch is?'

'Aye, sorr,' the Irishman said, 'so he claims. Reckoned she was with an officer. Protected by him. Probably ploughin' her fresh wee cunny, so he was, the lucky bastard. Still, he'll be a dead'un by now. The girl will have squealed her secrets too. That's all I was to convey to you, Master Killigrew.'

'Christ, but this is a rare mess,' Killigrew's voice rasped, muffled, perhaps, by a knuckle pressed to his mouth.

'You're telling me, sorr.'

'Yours is not to make sense of it, Devlin. I am the hammer. You and Kendrick are the nails. Understood?'

'Understood. This particular nail is now without a horse, seeing as I'm not likely to get out o' this goddamned hole in time to fetch it.'

'You'll be recompensed,' Killigrew said, 'have no fear. Now out of my sight. I have other matters to address.'

### Everton Heights, Liverpool, Lancashire, 19 June 1644

There were dray carts loaded with coils of match-cord parked on the village green, a trio of small boys racing between them as they kicked a ball amid shrieks of delight. A group of harquebusiers cantered along the main street, helmets bright, scarves a livid red in the noonday sun. Stryker nodded to their leader as Vos stepped past, receiving a knuckled visor in reply, and let the big stallion climb the hill. When he reached the brick-built house he handed Vos's reins to a welt-chinned ostler and bounded up the flight of steps to the large, red door, knocking hard and turning to look out over Liverpool. It seemed so tranquil from up on the ridge, the damage to its walls almost imperceptible.

The door opened to reveal a fresh-faced lieutenant who looked as though the angel of death had personally come for his soul. 'Y—yes?'

Stryker smiled widely, knowing the gesture would only tug gruesomely at the mottled scars across his left cheek and eye socket. 'Major Stryker to see His Highness.'

The lieutenant swallowed thickly. 'Welcome, sir. I'll show you through.'

Stryker blinked hard as his eye adjusted to the dim light of candles. The corridor smelt of rosewater and fresh flowers. He removed the hat he had fetched from the bakery by cover of darkness, tapping it against his palm lest any traces of flour remained.

At the end of a long passageway another door opened and the young lieutenant stepped out of Stryker's path, ushering him inside. It was brighter in the room, bathed as it was in the daylight of three broad windows with vertical mullions and painted sills. Stryker stared at the faces before him. There were many he did not recognise, but plenty he could guess. Sir Richard Crane was present, and he offered Stryker a brisk bow, but there were others too. Lieutenant-General Goring, the famed leader of the Northern Horse, and Lord John Byron, Rupert's second in command, with Lucas and Langdale standing close. Grandees of Foot, such as the unflappable Henry Tillier, the earnest Tyldesley and the elegant Napier, were gathered too, each one listening intently to the man who was seated in an ornately carved chair studying a small sheet of paper that lay, with dozens of others, on a large, untidy table.

'*Nephew,*' Prince Rupert of the Rhine read aloud as a large dog with tightly curled fur ambled to his side. It slumped beside the chair, watching the prince's foot as it tapped rapidly. '*First I must congratulate with you for your good successes, assuring you that the things themselves are no more welcome to me than that you are the means. I know the importance of the supplying you with powder, for which I have taken all possible ways, having sent both to Ireland and Bristol.*' He looked up, spearing a clerk sitting at the far end of the table with his rapier stare. 'Dated the 14th. Should expect a consignment any day, roads permitting.'

The black-fingered clerk was hunched over his own stack of paperwork. He nodded mutely, scratching something with a long quill as the prince scanned through the next few lines.

It was the first time Stryker had been summoned to army headquarters since their arrival. He suspected that the rumours of imminent action, whispered on the barren streets and in the bawdy taverns, were not coincidental. Now, as he stood stock still in the opulent drawing-room, he could hear his own pulse rush in his ears as his general shared with them a dispatch from a monarch.

'*But now I must give you the true state of my affairs,*' Rupert continued, '*which if their condition be such as enforces me to give you more peremptory commands than I would willingly do, you must not take it ill.*' The prince paused. He stood up and walked to a window. All eyes followed. Rupert glanced down at the letter once more. '*If York be lost I shall esteem my crown little less; unless supported by your sudden march to me; and a miraculous conquest in the south, before the effects of their northern power can be found here. But if York be relieved, and you beat the rebels' army of both kingdoms which are before it; then — but not otherwise — I may make a shift, upon the defensive, to spin out time until you come to assist me.*'

'Spin out time?'

'That,' Rupert replied, jabbing a long forefinger at the text, 'is what he says, Sir Richard.'

Crane, commander of Rupert's Lifeguard of Horse, picked with his nails at the wide, puckered scar that gave him his forever-grin. He frowned. 'Forgive me, Highness. He says that, should you relieve York, and beat the devil's alliance in the field, he can hold out against Essex and Waller until we march south to his aid?'

'That seems to be the crux of it,' Rupert said.

'Thus, it is a command for you to engage the Allies?'

The prince found his place half way down the handwritten sheet. '*Wherefore I command and conjure you, by the duty and affection which I know you bear me, that all new enterprises laid aside, you immediately march, according to your first intention, with all your force to the relief of York.*'

The men in the room exchanged glances. Crane nodded. 'Then we have our orders.'

'*But,*' Rupert said sharply, reading on as if Crane had not spoken, '*if that be either lost, or have freed themselves from the besiegers, or that, from want of powder, you cannot undertake that work, that you immediately march with your whole strength, directly to Worcester, to assist me and my army.*'

One of the others, a gruff, silver-whiskered commander from one of the infantry regiments, cleared his throat. 'We lack powder,' he said pointedly, 'and men. And the city will surely be lost before long. Thus, His Majesty orders we march to Worcester.'

'*Without which, or you having relieved York by beating the Scots, all the successes you can afterwards have must infallibly be useless unto me. You may believe that nothing but an extreme necessity could make me write thus unto you; wherefore, in this case, I can no ways doubt of your punctual compliance with. Your loving and most faithful friend, Charles R.*'

Prince Rupert of the Rhine walked back to the table and placed the letter upon a stack of other correspondence. 'He makes no disguise as to York's import. And he freely admits that in order to relieve that poor city, we must fight the Scotch.'

'We have not the strength to fight them,' said a tall man with intelligent brown eyes, light brown hair, and a brown suit of expensive material that shimmered in the light's beams. Stryker knew him to be James Stanley, Earl of Derby, master of Lathom

House and leading Royalist in Lancashire. His sharply waxed beard and moustache twitched as he spoke. 'This is not an order, Highness, but news and advice. His Majesty, God preserve him, would not have you dash your army in so raw a state at so formidable a foe. He gives you leave to avoid a pitched confrontation if you are not in a position to emerge the victor.'

Men murmured agreement. Others grunted repudiation.

Rupert gnawed his bottom lip. He picked up the letter again. '*Immediately march, according to your first intention, with all your force to the relief of York.*' He sucked in a lungful of air, blasting it out through his long nose, and fixed each man in turn with that baleful glower. 'It is a command, gentlemen. Not only to relieve York, but also to fight the Scots and Roundheads that lay siege to it.'

Derby shifted his weight from one foot to the other. 'It is ambiguous at best, Highness.'

'It is a sovereign directive, my lord,' Rupert said scathingly.

'You have conquered Lancashire,' Derby responded tightly, 'is that not enough?'

'It will never be enough. Not until the last beat of the last rebel heart.'

Derby's face was pained, contorted by fear of a prince, and a prince's intent. 'To face the Allies in the field is to invite only ruin and death. Is that what you want, Highness?'

'What *I* want, my lord, is not worth a groat.' Rupert held the paper aloft, waving it as though it were a flag. 'What the King wants, however, is victory. And I mean to give it to him.'

The ostler returned Vos, accepted a clipped silver coin for his trouble, and slipped back to the stable. Stryker breathed in the air that seemed so much cleaner up on the ridge and poked his toes through the first stirrup. Some of the other officers, joined by waiting aides and subordinates, came down the steps, fielding the inevitable questions as they awaited their own mounts. It was then that Stryker saw Kendrick standing alone in the centre of the village green. Stryker had not yet pushed up on to the saddle, and for a heartbeat he froze, half dangling, for he could barely believe that the Vulture would strut across his path so openly after their last encounter. But there he was, swathed in his bear-skin pelt, face pale as milk, eyes black as coal pebbles.

People were filling the road now, eager to discover the army's next move, and Stryker knew it was folly to threaten Kendrick publicly. And yet he took a fistful of Vos's reins and stalked over to the green.

'Ah, Major Stryker.' Kendrick flashed his dagger grin. 'A joy to see you again.'

'You are up to no good, Vulture.'

'I have as much right to be here as any, *sir*,' Kendrick answered, spitting the final word out. 'I report to Colonel Chisenall for the time being, and he, as you will know, has been at audience with young Longshanks. Though, I confess, it is apt to meet you here. I have been meaning to ask: what is your name? It has been bothering me.'

'Stryker.'

Kendrick's thin brow shot up. 'You were christened, Sergeant-Major? Curious.'

Stryker would not take the bait. 'You are brazen, sirrah. You attack my men in broad daylight and expect no consequence.'

'I attacked a rebel spy that you see fit to shield.'

Stryker looped the reins about his grip, putting his free hand to his sword-hilt. 'If you touch the girl again, I will pull those fangs out through your nose.'

Kendrick licked his lips. 'Know her way around a privy member, does she, sir?'

'I am warning you, Kendrick.'

'I want—no—' Kendrick paused, glancing at the grey clouds as he searched for the right words. 'I *need* the girl.'

'You will not have her.'

'Trust that it is for the good of the Crown, Major.'

'If it were for the good of the Crown, you would have informed the authorities. Whatever your design, it is not for the Prince's ears.'

Kendrick sighed. 'Then consider this, Major Stryker. If you do not hand her to me, I *will* tell the Prince. I shall tell him that you harbour a Puritan polecat who lets you swive her in return for information.' He thrust a finger in Stryker's face. 'He'll not be best pleased.'

'You will not tell the Prince,' Stryker said, sure that Kendrick would already have taken such a tack had it been in his interest. 'You think she possesses something. This golden flagon. You should know that she does not.'

'You lie,' Kendrick said contemptuously. 'And you cannot trumpet her presence either, can you? She would be ejected from this army, at best, and left to my tender mercies. Thus we reach an impasse. You will try to protect her, and I will take her from you.'

'You,' Stryker said, 'will stay away from the girl!' He pulled his sword halfway out of the scabbard.

Kendrick retreated hastily over the lawn. Stryker dropped Vos's reins and pursued him, freeing the rest of the blade so that sunlight danced along its length.

'Gentlemen!'

Stryker halted. Kendrick did too. The voice was sharp and clear and terrifying. Stryker slid the sword into its scabbard as quickly as it had come free, turning with slow dread. On the top step of the grand house stood Prince Rupert. The lip-chewing, foot-tapping tension that had marked the Council of War had been washed away as if by a deluge. Now he was the warrior-prince again, almost six and a half feet of handsome, fearsome, menacing soldier, and he filled the door-frame, a head higher than the lintel behind, big hands on his hips, jaw set firmly as he surveyed the officers and men gathered at the foot of the steps. Stryker breathed a sigh of relief, realizing that the prince had not addressed him and Kendrick, but the crowd at large.

'Friends!' Rupert bellowed as if he hawked pies at a country fayre. 'I have been ordered by His Majesty, King Charles, to march upon York and destroy those who would take it from the royal bosom! To that end, the Scots lion must be tamed! Who is with me?'

A great huzzah roared up from the throng that was growing with every moment, soldiers and common folk swelling the nucleus of generals. Rupert raised a clenched fist, as though the very decision signified an end to the war, and cheers rose to a deafening crescendo.

John Kendrick appeared at Stryker's side. 'The German hawk will tame the Scots lion,' he said, just loudly enough for Stryker alone to hear, 'and the Vulture will skin the one-eyed wolf.' People were filling the green, moving between them, jostling for a view of the triumphal prince. Kendrick had walked backwards before Stryker could reply, melding into the mass of bodies. Just as he disappeared, he clamped shut an eye in grinning mockery. 'Watch for me, Major! Watch for me!'

# CHAPTER 14

## Lancashire, 22–26 June 1644

The Royalist army was fifteen thousand strong when it marched out of Liverpool. It was eleven days after the port had fallen. Prince Rupert left a substantial garrison, for the route needed to be kept open to convoys from Ireland, but the majority formed a vast column that stretched for the better part of five miles.

They went north, reaching Preston by nightfall, and, as a weak light tinged a rain-lashed dawn, pushed forth into the great fells that ran like a spine through England's core. The Northern Horse, under Goring and Lucas, peeled away after Preston, taking a more northerly route that would protect Rupert's flank and take them via the potential recruiting grounds of Hornby and Settle, while the rest tramped into the rising sun as the hills became steep and the horizon jagged.

It was an ambitious gambit, to say the least, for Rupert, invigorated by the urgency in the king's order, risked fatal exposure in the hills and mountains. The Army of Both Kingdoms loomed to the east like a ravenous beast, disturbing the dreams of even the hardiest campaigner, and the almost endless rain turned roads to streams, streams to rivers, and rivers to torrents. But spirits were high for all that. The army had prised their way into Stockport and Bolton and then Liverpool, albeit to great cost, and now they felt as though they had earned their freedom from smoke-shrouded trenches and corpse-strewn streets. They could fool themselves, just for a short time, that no enemy lay in wait.

Stryker's party was somewhere towards the middle of the column, at the rear of the remaining cavalry but ahead of the laboriously slogging infantry, artillery and baggage. It suited him, for it meant that they no longer needed to conceal Faith Helly. The High Command were a long way to the front, and Kendrick's Company of Foot languished far behind.

Heathcliff Brownell – the grinning, fair-haired youngster who had brought the news of Liverpool's capitulation – commanded the unit to which, for the ease of the quartermaster, they were temporarily attached. 'Prince Robert,' the young lieutenant had chimed as his chestnut horse struggled gainfully through a swollen brook, 'speaks highly of you, sir.'

'It gladdens me to hear,' Stryker replied. He doubted the prince knew this chirpy stripling referred to him by the name coined by his inner circle of friends, but he smiled nevertheless.

'Says you have spilt blood in every European nation!' Brownell exclaimed.

'I have had my own blood spilt in every European nation,' Stryker said as Vos sloshed over the brook's shifting pebbles. Faith was pressed behind him, twig-thin arms wrapped tight around his midriff, though every so often a hand would snake away to pat the saddlebag in which Sydall's Bible had been stowed. 'Not quite the same.'

Brownell seemed crest-fallen, and then beamed. 'You jest, sir!' He slapped a hand across his thigh. 'By Jesu! Major Stryker jests with Heathcliff Brownell. I shall write to Papa at once!'

All that dreary Sunday they marched, pausing briefly for rapid sermons delivered by harassed clergymen, moving east and north along the foot of a large escarpment known as Longridge Fell. It was marked by a sharp drop, they were told, at its northern edge, so they should feel grateful that the prince was leading them along that gentler southern slope. Except that further south, running parallel with their course, the River Ribble smashed its roaring way back towards the Irish Sea, and that river had broken its banks, flooding field, forest and road. The army, then, were funnelled like penned sheep between the dark hill and the silver water, and it took them all day to cleave a way to the rendezvous at a place called Ribchester.

'It is Roman, sir,' Brownell had announced as his troop had filed into the village. Many of the houses were flooded, and much of the army was being sent out to seek billets in the surrounding farmsteads.

'You have made a study of the place, Lieutenant?' Stryker asked while a surly quartermaster bellowed orders for them to locate a hamlet named locally as Stydd.

'I am intrigued by matters of antiquity, Major,' Brownell explained, his fifty horsemen jangling behind in double file. 'It is a disease, Mama says. Ribchester was an important place, once. Long ago, mind, but they yet discover great stones carved with ancient symbols, and coins with faces long forgotten.' He sighed. 'Now it is a place for cotton weaving, more's the pity.'

Stydd lay to the north of Ribchester. It was a modest collection of single-storey hovels, all of which were built in the same sandstone rubble that could be seen along the river valley. At its centre was a sparse chapel, St Saviour's, and it was there that Brownell and Stryker chose for the night's quartering. It was a simple affair of porch, nave and sanctuary, laid out in a rectangle with straw on the floor beneath a slate roof. There was no seating of any kind, which suited them, for the horses could be brought in from the rain, and as darkness descended so the heat from the many bodies warmed the interior and steamed the glazed windows. Faith had seen enough of the world to be wary of a night spent in a single chamber with more than fifty men, but Stryker warned the others off, and they had kept their distance.

'You do not tell folk your name,' Faith said as she lay on her side when the salt pork had gone and the tall tales were exhausted. Skellen and Hood were already asleep, and Barkworth was on watch.

'Innocent,' Stryker said. 'That is my name.'

She sat up, gaping. 'You jest.'

'I do not.'

'One of the Godly,' Faith whispered. 'You have a Puritan's name.'

'My father had a notion of spiritual austerity, though he was not an austere man.' He smiled ruefully: 'Nor was he godly.'

Faith was still staring up at him. 'You are godly.'

He shook his head. 'I have done things, Mistress Helly, that would condemn me a thousand times over.'

'I will never condemn you, sir,' she said, easing back as she shut her eyes. 'Not ever.'

The morning was dry and the air crisp. Stryker took Faith into the encampment that had sprung up around the chapel during the night as the slower elements of the vast army had trickled into Ribchester and its surrounds. Awnings had sprouted like toadstools, clustered in patches as far as the eye could see, and, after questioning a farrier, a dragoon and a provost, Stryker had learnt that a sutler and his family had made camp on the edge of a small wood just outside Stydd.

There was a thin mist rolling off the river as they reached the treeline and saw the two carts laden with goods, their spokes daubed blue as the provost had told him. A large tent had been erected at the rear of one of the vehicles, and a white-haired woman wearing a leather camisole, red apron and woollen cap stood at the entrance hanging a tiny doll in the wooden frame above.

'A charm against witchcraft,' Stryker said as they approached. 'The men say the hills hereabouts are home to demons.'

'Master Sydall hated witchcraft.'

'I'd wager he hated a great many things, Mistress,' Stryker chided.

Faith laughed at that. 'Portraits, curled hair, painted faces,' she counted each item on her fingers, 'dancing, long hair on men, short hair on women, stage plays, health drinking, bonfires, music, excessive laughter …'

'He and I would not have been friends, I fear,' Stryker said.

The sutleress performed an awkward curtsy and began to list

her wares. She had food, spirits, tinderboxes, various rags, tobacco, whetstones, pewter buttons, wooden bowls, some moth-eaten shirts, two pairs of child's shoes, several bandoliers – though none with a powder box – and coils of twine, ribbon and match. Stryker shook his head. 'I want a blade.'

'We do not carry weapons, sir,' the sutleress said. 'We have not the permission.'

Her husband, a stout, short, ruddy-faced man appeared from the side of the tent. 'Captain Stryker, I do declare!'

Stryker lifted his hat. 'Major, now, Jed.'

'Major,' the sutler echoed, 'well, bless me.'

'A knife, sir,' Stryker said. 'A good one.'

'To cut an apple?' Jed asked tentatively.

'To cut a throat.'

'As I thought, sir,' Jed said, and he beckoned them to the front of the wagon. He lifted a box packed full of sotweed. Underneath was another, similar container. He glanced around before levering it open with grimy fingernails.

Stryker and Faith peered into the box. Inside were several large, sheathed daggers. Stryker chose one with a bone handle, easing back the leather sheath and turning the steel slowly. The blade was six inches long, double-edged, and he tested it with his thumb. 'This will do.'

Faith shook her head rapidly. 'I do not want it.'

'We will soon do battle. I cannot protect you then. Take this. Use it if necessary.'

She shook her head again, but her hand went out to take the dagger. Stryker dropped a stack of coins into the sutler's waiting palm. Jed's fat fingers curled around the money; then he went again to the wagon. He lifted out what looked like a bowl, but it was metal on the outside and soft within. Stryker frowned. 'A secrete?'

The sutler winked. 'A good one. Red velvet lining, as you can see.'

'Where did you get this?'

'A great many things are found after battle, Major.'

'What is it?' Faith asked.

'A steel cap,' Stryker said, taking the object. He removed his hat and placed the secrete on his head. 'Worn underneath a hat, it protects the skull.'

'A perfect fit,' Jed exclaimed. 'As though it were made just for you, Master Stryker.'

Stryker took it off, holding it out to the sutler. 'A frippery.'

'Buy it,' Faith said.

He turned to her. 'If I wanted a helmet, I would wear one.'

'But you will not wear a helmet,' Faith replied, 'so you should wear a secrete.'

The sutler licked his lips. 'I'll give you a wonderful price, Major.'

Drummers hammered out the march as Prince Rupert's army left Ribchester. Banners flew ahead of every unit in every colour imaginable. The infantrymen sang as they paced, their combined voices echoing up and down Ribble Valley. They were quickly forced to veer north of the road, for the flood waters had risen further despite the break in the rain, and climbed into the lower slopes of Longridge Fell, filing through a sleepy place called Hurst Green.

'Bastard mud,' Skellen snarled as his stumbling mount almost threw him.

'We are fortunate, in a way,' Stryker called back. 'An army on the move in late June is often marked out by a dust cloud. Wet roads mean no dust.'

'I'd take the dust any day, sir.'

'My wee granny,' Simeon Barkworth said, 'used to put dust in goat's milk. Chalk and charcoal too. Drink that, she'd say, and you'll live to a hundred!'

'And?' Lieutenant Hood prompted.

'The old biddy died o' rotten guts!'

After several hours they reached another powerful waterway, the River Hodder, which made a fork with the Ribble further south.

'Perhaps he will not fight,' Faith said as they clattered across a stone bridge. 'Perhaps it is a ruse.'

'I was present when he reached his decision,' Stryker said. 'He will fight.'

'The men say you will lose.'

Stryker shrugged. 'Rupert is not accustomed to defeat. He tends to find a way through the most pungent swamp and clambers to dry land smelling of rose petals. But it will be a very deep swamp this time, for certain. If I do not return, you must find a way to the Parliament lines. They will protect you from Kendrick.'

'You will return,' she said firmly. 'Your head is protected now, leastwise.'

They regained the main highway as it turned sharply north, pushing on so that with the arrival of dusk they could see the town of Clitheroe on the horizon. They could also see the huge, sloping plateau of Pendle Hill to the east. Local conscripts whispered of witchcraft on that vast crest, and prayers were hissed long into the night as they quartered in the shadow of Clitheroe Castle.

The next day took them to Gisburne, and the day after that they mustered before dawn with renewed vigour. They had reached the border. By nightfall they would be in Yorkshire, where a city was under siege, and where an enemy waited.

### Middlethorpe, near York, 26 June 1644

Alexander Leslie, Earl of Leven, and Sir Henry Vane were enjoying a repast of fresh bread and boiled duck eggs when the messenger was shown in.

'The Prince is at Skipton Castle, my lord,' the messenger said without prompt. His face was sweaty and his long buff-coat and tall riding boots were caked with mud. 'There he makes rendezvous with Newcastle's cavalry.'

Leven had been holding an egg between thumb and

forefinger, and he set it slowly down on his plate. He looked at Vane. 'The Northern Horse, under General Goring.'

Vane furiously chewed, swallowing down the last of his mouthful. 'Goring is a drunk and a wastrel.'

'Goring is a born soldier. Together, he and the Prince are formidable.' Leven waved the messenger away, waiting until the door was firmly shut. 'We pursue our objective.'

'Skipton?' Vane asked. 'Is that not rather close?'

'Forty miles, or thereabouts. But he must yet pass through the hills.' Leven pushed back his chair and went to the campaign table and the map spread across its surface. 'The most direct route is the southern road, taking him through Wetherby.'

'He is nothing if not direct.'

'Aye.' Leven jabbed the map with his forefinger and went back to his meal. He clapped his hands loudly before he regained his seat, and the door creaked open, the sheepish face of an aide poking through. 'Summon Lieutenant-General Leslie.' The aide vanished, and Leven looked at Vane. 'That is the route he will take, I've no doubt. I will order Davey to get his riders out to block the southern approach. Cromwell will do the same.'

Vane smiled slyly. 'If Manchester agrees.'

'The Committee for Both Kingdoms will support the directive, will it not?'

Vane nodded. 'Aye, my lord, I believe it will.'

'Then Manchester will agree.' Leven picked up his egg again, rolling and squeezing the soft white flesh in his fingers. 'We will block Prince Robber and his wee army in the hills. And then, Sir Harry, we shall devour him.' He pushed the egg into his mouth and chewed.

*Skipton, Yorkshire, 28–29 June 1644*

John Kendrick scraped the iron file back and forth between his front teeth as he watched the horse dealer with interest. The noise grated in his skull, but he was used to it. To his satisfaction, the horse dealer looked positively nauseous.

'You see, Andor,' Kendrick said, licking the file and slipping it back inside the folds of his cloak, 'you must observe the animal in all situations. In the stable, when tethered or fed or mucked out. While grooming, of course, and during time with other mounts. All these aspects of a horse's life are crucial, and a man must take care to witness each one before parting with his tin.'

They were in a barn, the high noonday sun shining through owl holes set amongst the rafters. The floor was paved in brick to allow carts to trundle in and out, while the corners were roped off to form makeshift stabling. The horse they had come to see was a black mare with a white spot on her face and three white fetlocks. The dealer – a short, wiry Dutchman with huge hands and eyes that were never still – dipped under the rope to pat the beast. 'I can assure you, gen'men, this horse is the best I've to offer. She is, she is.'

Kendrick swung his legs over the rope. As he did so, he brandished his broadest smile, exposing as many sharpened teeth as he could. 'It had better be.' He stroked the mare, who pushed her neck into his hand willingly. 'We must be alert to the subduing of the creature,' he said to Sergeant Janik, who remained outside the ring. 'It is not uncommon for an unscrupulous tradesman to pacify a naturally flighty disposition by the administration of potions, or simply to run the poor devil into the ground.'

'You'll find none o' that, sir,' the dealer said hurriedly. He ducked to indicate the beast's undercarriage. 'No sweat under there, has she, has she?'

Kendrick took a cursory glance. 'What say you, Andor?'

The big Hungarian pursed lividly bruised lips so that his moustache smothered his nose. 'I hate horses.'

Kendrick laughed. He looked at the dealer again. 'Be sure in this, sir. I will slice off your stones should your word prove false. And you shall eat them, one by one.'

The diminutive Dutchman swallowed hard. 'She a good horse, sir. She is, she is, she is. We have thousand new cavalry here.'

Kendrick glanced at Janik. 'Goring brings them from Cumberland and Westmoreland.'

The horse dealer nodded earnestly. 'And you ask them. You ask, you ask. I do excellent price for many of their comrades. And I shoe their mounts, and groom. Never a complaint. Never, never.'

'Then we shall do business,' Kendrick said. He winked, holding out a tight fist.

The horse dealer extended a hand. 'You are dragooners, sir?' he said, as his customer's fingers uncoiled to loose a trickle of coins that dropped like a waterfall into his waiting palm. 'Your men, I notice, carry muskets.'

'No, sir, we are foot,' replied Kendrick. 'But duty compels us north, into the hills, and I'll be damned before I walk. I purchase a new mount for the expedition, and two more for my best men.'

The dealer's eyes lit up. 'I have plenty more.'

'Three will do.'

'When do you depart? I can have them ready within the hour.'

'An hour it is.' Kendrick turned to his sergeant. 'Prepare the men.'

'Then God preserve you, sir,' the dealer said as he watched Andor Janik stalk from the barn. The coins vanished about his person. 'And God save the King.'

Prince Rupert's army had arrived at Skipton two days earlier in order to rendezvous with Lord Newcastle's Northern Horse. The place itself was small, a market town hedged by woodland and moor, the shadow of the Dales looming to the north. It was a modest, sleepy place, with more sheep on its verdant hills than people on its streets. But it was a high point in the pass through the hills, and it had a castle – a strong, ancient, thick-walled structure surrounded by an outer curtain wall and protected by a formidable entrance of gatehouse and two stout drum towers. The main building was not large, by the standards of most medieval fortresses, but it boasted six more drum towers fringed with sturdy battlements, and these were topped with cannon and pierced by loopholes. It was the ideal place, then, for Rupert to defend, should the need arise, and Rupert had ordered his newly bolstered ranks to rest awhile as they set camp both within and without the town. Rest, because word had spread of the king's orders. All knew that they were en route to relieve the city of York, and all knew that such an act would provoke the Allied rebels to battle.

Lieutenant Heathcliff Brownell's Troop of Horse was quartered in an imposing two-storeyed tavern in the shadow of the castle. It was a comfortable enough billet. Indeed, given the size of the army and the scarcity of rooms within the town, Stryker had been astonished that such a place might be allocated to them, until Brownell had jangled a full purse with an impish wink.

'Grease the wheels,' he said as they sat beside one another on a long bench between a crude table and a wall hung with shepherds' crooks and scythes. 'Papa always said so.' Brownell was in his element. He had invited Stryker and his men to join him and his troopers, and clicked his fingers as he noticed their pots nearing empty. A woman, no older than his own eighteen years, sidled over. She wore a tight coif and her face was plain, but her apron and skirts did nothing to conceal the swing of her hips. 'More ale, if you please.'

She smiled, leaning over the table to upend a blackjack into each of the cups.

Brownell beamed. 'And have you wine? No cheap muck, understand, but a good drop.'

'We have a passable claret, sir,' the girl answered.

He ordered she bring a jug up, then slid the ale pots to Barkworth, Skellen and Hood. 'Your health, gentlemen.'

Stryker glanced through the window as he took his own drink. It was dark outside, but the air was dry for once, and the shutters had been thrown open to release some of the smoke. On the far side of the street he could see a couple rutting against a wall, the man's lily-white buttocks thrusting in and out of the shadows, his companion's face appearing intermittently over his shoulder. She opened her eyes, caught Stryker's stare and winked. Stryker laughed and took a long draught of ale.

Brownell belched and wiped his golden whiskers with a sleeve. 'This is the life, eh? Where is your niece, sir? The red-headed preacher? Will she not join us?'

Stryker shook his head. 'She will not enter the taproom.'

Barkworth cackled and glanced at the blackened ceiling beams. 'She prays above us this very second, sir.'

'How long have you served, sir?' Thomas Hood asked.

'Six months,' Brownell said without a shred of embarrassment. 'Papa was proud as a bloody peacock, and no mistake. Mama less so.'

'She did not approve?'

Brownell shook his head. 'She lost a daughter to plague, a son to a Spanish war-hammer at Rheinfelden.' He shrugged. 'I could hardly begrudge her caution.' He paused as the serving girl set a large earthenware flagon of claret on the table. 'Still, all is well. I have my own troop, until a new captain can be found to replace the old, leastwise.'

Skellen sniffed. 'He died, sir?'

'Stabbed in the rump, of all things,' Brownell said. 'Stepped over a corpse. Well, he thought it was a corpse.' He lifted the flagon of wine and took a lingering swig.

'Wager it were a corpse,' Barkworth said, 'a moment later, sir.'

Brownell's chuckle was rueful. 'But not before the sly bastard had jabbed a dirk into poor Captain Roberts' arse. Looked innocuous enough, but it went bad.' He wrinkled his nose. 'Stank to the heavens. Christ, but that stink'll never leave me.'

'You inherited his troop?' asked Stryker.

The young lieutenant nodded. 'I am captain of forty-seven men, in all but title, and I intend to relish it.' He drank more claret directly from the large vessel. 'And I fight alongside the famous Major Stryker!' Now he lowered the flagon and poured a large measure into his pot where the ale had been. He poured some for Hood, whose own cup had been drained, and pushed it across the table to him. 'She keeps dogs, you know. Tiny ones. They yap so. Shit too. Jesu, but Papa is oftentimes hoarse with raging at the little demons.' Brownell's eyes were glassy. 'I miss them.'

'Your mother and father?' Stryker said.

'The dogs,' Brownell replied. 'Foolish, is it not?' He put the pot to his lips and drank the wine in a single gulp. 'Will we win, sir?'

'For certain.'

Brownell's gaze narrowed. 'You lie, sir. It is said they have near thirty thousand. We have fifteen, or thereabouts.'

'If we join with Newcastle's army, we'll have twenty,' Stryker said.

'And the rebels are shittin' water, so they say,' Barkworth said. 'The pestis robs them of a good many men.'

'And we have Rupert,' Hood added, raising the wine to his lips.

'To Prince Rupert!' Heathcliff Brownell exclaimed. He raised the pot high above his head. 'God save the King! And a pox on Parliament!'

The whole tavern echoed the toast, and then Brownell slid sideways off the bench.

Stryker had seen plenty of hardened men collapse when in their cups, had been victim himself more times than he cared to admit, yet this was too quick. He ducked while the others laughed, pushing his head under the table top to get a look at Brownell, who lay on the floor, curled like a foetus. What he saw made his guts convulse.

Brownell shook. It was violent, juddering, his boots kicking at Stryker's shins as his legs jerked uncontrollably. Stryker shot out from under the table and slapped the pot of claret clean out of Thomas Hood's hand. Then he went back down, half turning Brownell to see his face. The lieutenant stared wildly back at Stryker, unblinking, pupils huge like black moons. Saliva frothed at his lips, jaw working maniacally, and then there was blood in the bubbling spittle, his tongue cleaved open by gnashing teeth.

Brownell spasmed, his spine arching with such ferocity that Stryker felt sure it would snap. He made a hideous choking sound, then gasped once, a colossal gulp that would befit a man set to drown, and slumped back as if his very lungs had burst. Pink froth slid down both sides of Brownell's chin, glistening like jewels in his triangle of beard and staining his collar. His eyes stared intently, but they saw no more.

Fight the Good Fight of Faith Helly stood as she heard the commotion. It rumbled up through the rickety floorboards as though the very earth shook the tavern's foundations. She had been reading Master Sydall's Bible, studying Leviticus, and she tossed it on to the bed behind her and walked quickly to the door. It burst open before she had reached for the handle. Two men strode in without word. They wore dark cloaks, but immediately threw them off to reveal blue, knee-length coats fastened with yellow string. Their breeches were tight, their boots low and their shoulders draped in thick animal skins. Their heads were covered with felt caps, decorated with goose feathers, and there were curved sabres at their waists.

Faith stumbled backwards into the room. She recognized their strange clothing from Bolton and Liverpool, but might not have felt the old, stomach-churning terror had she not recognized one of the faces. He was bald, without a hair even on his face, and his disease-ravaged nose possessed just a single, gaping, oozing nostril. She made to scream, but the second assailant – a thick-set, grey-haired bullock of a man – leapt with surprising agility to grasp her around waist and mouth.

The diseased man drew his sword and levelled it below her chin. 'Hush now,' he whispered, words heavily accented. He pressed a finger to his lips. 'Window.'

Downstairs a woman was screaming. Faith's arms were free, and she beat at her stocky captor, receiving only a chuckle for reward. In a moment she was being dragged backwards, her heels scraping the boards. She tried to bite the hand at her face but it pressed too firmly. Then they were at the window. The bald man skirted round her to the ledge, calling something in his native tongue, and moved back with sudden speed to catch the end of a rope that flew past Faith's ear. She tried in vain to cry out. The bald man tied the rope to one of the rafters, then nodded. His accomplice released Faith for a moment, she drew breath, gasping air, then she was on the floor. Hands were on her, lifting, turning, and she found herself in the air, staring down at the unusual boots of the men. She was on the stocky soldier's back. The floor turned beneath her. Cool air rushed around her face. They must be at the window ledge, preparing to descend. She heard the creak of the rope. A voice called from the road below.

She stabbed the man twice before he dropped her on the floor. She flopped on to her back. Stryker's knife was still in her hand, blood coursing back down the handle to run slick and warm between her fingers. The two blue-coated men were standing over her, backs to the window. The bald one was snarling in a language she did not understand, his friend, bent over, was sobbing as he pawed at the wounds in his shoulder.

They exchanged a frantic stream of words, the grey-haired man shaking his head and whimpering like a whipped hound. The bald man spat at him, shook his head angrily, and stooped, tearing the dagger from Faith's sticky grip and tossing it across the room. Then he grabbed her by the hair, hauling her upright, dragging her to the window and the waiting rope. His comrade was already outside, shuffling gingerly down the creaking cord, every movement accompanied by yelps of pain.

Suddenly a shout came from the doorway. Faith rotated her torso, her scalp searing as her hair was wrenched by its roots. Finally she found voice and strength enough to scream as she fell forwards, her knees cracking on the boards. The wind whipped at her back, and she lifted her head to see the man in the doorway. And then she wept.

They buried Heathcliff Brownell at dawn.

His troop, all forty-seven of them, were dismissed after the short service, for the order had come down from on high that the army was to leave Skipton as soon as was practicable. Stryker and his three men remained at the graveside as the hole was filled and Faith read from her Bible. Once she had finished, they moved away, one by one, and Stryker turned to see Sir Richard Crane, the colonel of Prince Rupert's Lifeguard of Horse.

'A good lad,' Crane said, removing his hat.

'Aye, sir.'

'To be snuffed so cruelly from the face of the earth.' Crane shook his head. 'They say his heart gave out.'

'No common malady worked here, sir. He was poisoned.'

Crane's jaw tightened. He stepped forwards, lowering his voice. 'Proof?'

'I have seen such deaths before,' Stryker said. He would not be enlightening the colonel as to the other element in the night's drama. Crane would assume the girl was just another camp follower, and that suited Stryker well. 'It was the Vulture.'

'Kendrick?' Crane frowned. He paused as new recruits, hastily armed and given a standard issue shirt, coat, sword and snapsack, were driven like cattle out on the road, their sergeant's bellows ripping through the cemetery's peace. 'Now hold your reins tight, my friend,' he continued when they had gone, 'for so serious a charge requires better provenance than mere enmity.'

Stryker pictured the tavern. The frothing, writhing Brownell had died the way a poisoned man dies. And only he had imbibed a significant amount of wine. Hood had had enough only to sicken his guts for the night. Someone had put an evil substance into the claret jug, he felt certain. He had quizzed the tapster, physically shaking him to a tearful, quivering mess, and the pot-boys and serving wenches, but he had discovered nothing. There was also the kidnap attempt that had played out immediately above their heads. He did not for one moment believe the two events were coincidental. 'It was the Vulture, Sir Richard.'

Crane shook his head. 'Kendrick has gone north.'

'North? You are certain?'

'I gave the order myself. His company patrol the high ground. They watch for wolves among the sheep. It was not Kendrick,

Stryker, and you must let go this antipathy towards him. He is brutal, aye. Cruel, even. But he is feared by the enemy, and we need him, now more than ever.'

Stryker had seen the kidnappers as they slid down their rope and into the night, and he had recognized them as Kendrick's Hungarian mercenaries. He opened his mouth to speak, realizing that only a full explanation could prove his point.

'You have Brownell's,' Crane cut him off abruptly.

Stryker was taken aback. 'I am no cavalry officer, sir.'

'You are a reformado, sir,' Crane said, his face unyielding. 'You will go wherever the Prince demands, and he demands you take charge of Brownell's headless troop. When battle comes, they will be brigaded with others. You will not require knowledge of their particular evolutions. But for now, they need a leader, and you are it.' He put his hat back on. 'Keep 'em busy. Take their minds off this unfortunate business.'

An hour later, under a brooding sky, Stryker, Faith and his fifty men rode east.

# CHAPTER 15

*Knaresborough, Yorkshire, 30 June 1644*

Stryker's troop cantered over the bridge spanning the Nidd and followed the road to the right, flush against the swirling river's north bank, as woodland gave way to civilization. He led the way on Vos, Faith clinging firmly at his back and Brownell's cornet following, the small, fluttering flag of green and white held proudly aloft. They nodded and waved to the folk who peered from their homes, some tossing flowers, most cheering, and pushed up the side of the gorge at a spry canter.

Knaresborough, like Skipton, was a prosperous market town, staunchly Royalist, and possessed of a strong castle around which Rupert's army could gather, and already there were units that had arrived during the dusk hours, with many more lagging over the miles behind.

In the hours after Brownell's funeral the Royalist army had formed its marching column and striven further into the wartorn county, taking the road down from the highest climbs to enable a swifter journey. Denton Hall, near Ilkley, was their billet for the night, and the men, Stryker imagined, must have laughed around their camp fires at the irony of mustering at the home of the arch Parliamentarian, Lord Fairfax. For his part, he had kept Brownell's sullen troopers on the move, roving the tight hills and always watching the distant terrain for signs of the enemy.

Those signs had come quickly enough. Less than an hour after leaving the sanctuary of Skipton, the telltale gleam of a horseman's pot had winked from a wooded rise perhaps a mile or so to the south of the road. Stryker had waited and watched. He had led his riders on to a rocky bluff above a silver stream, and from there they studied the hazy line where emerald land met granite sky. Soon the glinting metal of many more helms had been pinpointed by a treacherous sun.

Stryker had sent back a gentleman trooper with the news that would come as no surprise. The Army of Both Kingdoms was tracking their movements and gauging their strength. They would already be sending parties out to strip the land of forage, to fortify the passes and destroy every bridge. They would be ready for Prince Rupert, Stryker reported. Indeed, it would be no surprise at all should an army appear on the southern road to engage the Royalists while they were yet stretched and frayed between the hills.

At dawn the next day Rupert had ordered his army north. The message reached the scouting bands, Stryker's included, by noon, and they joined the huge column as it laboured back up into the higher, less hospitable terrain. The baggage train and ordnance had been grimly problematic, but the prince, sustained by renewed excitement at the prospect of outwitting his foe, had ridden up and down the column, hollering encouragement and ordering even his closest aides to dismount and help in dragging the guns and wagons over the rocky slopes.

By dusk, a miracle had been granted. Knaresborough, just fourteen miles west of York, had opened its gates to receive the conquering prince, and an army had begun to trundle over the bridge and on to the north bank of the river, spreading into the surrounding forest to set camp within a day's march of the rebel position. They fortified the bridge so that the deep water protected their backs, and then they rested. They had out-flanked the Parliamentarian cavalry Stryker had seen haunting the southern passes, and now, as thunder rolled deep on the foreboding hilltops, they were in position to make a play for York.

In the enfolding darkness, Stryker's troop gathered around a dozen small fires that struggled gainfully against a thin rain permeating the forest canopy. The flames hissed as they flickered, and men turned the carcasses of spitted chickens taken from a lonely steading earlier in the day. The smell of roasting flesh wafted deliciously over the itinerant township.

Faith was sitting cross-legged on a spare saddle cloth and staring into the fire, Hood, Barkworth and Skellen seated protectively round her. Stryker took off his cloak and wrapped it around her narrow frame, and she hauled it in, overlapping the heavy material so that she was entirely cocooned within, only her head exposed. Then he left them, to walk into Knaresborough itself.

The rain was harder by the time he reached the jagged battlements of the curtain wall. He felt no chill, for his woollen coat was warm and the doublet of buff hide swathing his torso had been oiled to imperviousness, but still he hunched low, tilting his hat over his face to let the water sluice off the brim. He reached the gate, which was opened by sentries who recognized him in the hissing glow of torches, and passed under the portcullis, its vicious iron teeth hanging ominously above. The castle comprised two walled baileys set one behind the other, and he crossed the outer ward without hindrance, the stables, workshops, kitchens and forges silent under the wretched shower. More guards protected the doors to the inner ward, and he was delayed for a few moments as credentials were verified, but soon he was free to roam the castle's core, the vast five-sided keep soaring over all, its flame-lit windows radiant in the darkness, like the blazing eyes of some mythical beast.

The inner ward also contained a series of domestic buildings, but it was the large, relatively modern complex known as the Courthouse that interested him.

'Sergeant-Major Stryker,' he said to the sentry. 'I would see the chief clerk.'

The soldier's eyes sparked recognition. 'If you will follow me, sir.'

The room was panelled, hung with tapestries and stiflingly hot. 'Gone?' Stryker said, untangling the leather ties of his buff-coat. 'What do you mean, gone?'

The clerk paused. He laid down the quill and made a steeple of ink-stained fingers, resting his chin upon them. His eyes were rheumy, strained to destruction by hours of scribing by candle-light, and he squinted at Stryker as though he were far distant. 'It is not my responsibility to indulge the idle curiosity of soldiers.'

Stryker gritted his teeth. 'Indulge me.'

The clerk sighed and picked up the quill, glancing back down at his work. 'Captain Kendrick has not returned. Nor has any man under his command. They were expected here, for the general muster, but here they are not.'

'Lost?' Stryker asked, imagining the slashing blades of Parliamentarian cavalry in the isolated ranges of the Dales. 'Come, man, tell me! Tell me, lest you wish to pluck that goose feather out of your backside.'

He had ridden out of Skipton consumed with revenge. The poison had been intended for him and his men. Indeed, it had very nearly taken Lieutenant Hood, but for Brownell's insatiable thirst. An assassination of enemies and a diversion for the purpose of kidnapping Faith Helly. Stryker had consoled himself that at Knaresborough he would find the infantryman's billet and deal with the Vulture once and for all. Except that the Vulture had flown the nest.

Eventually the clerk looked up, gnawing his lower lip. 'This must go no further. It is not the kind of thing His Highness wishes bandied about.'

'Well?'

'Scouts report spying his colour far to the north-east, around Tollerton.'

Stryker took a step back. Tollerton was too close to the Allied lines for a patrol to venture, especially one on foot. 'He has turned his coat?'

'I cannot say, but—'

'He has turned his coat,' Stryker cut in. 'Jesu,' he whispered, and turned away.

### *Rufforth, near York, 30 June 1644*

It was the bitterest summer night anyone could remember. The deepest hours fast approached, lightning flared among the star-shrouding clouds, and men in the half-flooded siege-lines hunkered low in their cloaks like snails in shells. Yet it was into this tumultuous darkness that the grandest men of the Army of Both Kingdoms galloped, summoned by the Earl of Leven, the most senior of the various Allied generals. He knew it would not be a welcome gesture, but he had issued the order regardless.

'Prince Rupert is at Knaresborough,' a trooper told Leven as soon as the generals swept into the sodden farmstead that was the agreed meeting place.

'How?'

'We have been watching the southern passes, my lord. He . . .' The trooper tailed off.

'He?' Leven demanded.

The trooper winced. 'He swung to the north, my lord.'

Leven felt suddenly nauseous. His sleep each night had been granted due in large part to the belief that the Royalist relief force could be bottled like flies in the hills. 'And you did not anticipate this?'

'We did not, my lord.' The trooper swallowed hard. 'We considered the terrain insurmountable. And the speed with which he made his move, sir.' He shook his head. 'It was—remarkable.'

'What is more remarkable,' Lieutenant-General Cromwell's blunt tone rang from somewhere at Leven's back, 'is that he is not on our doorstep already.'

Cromwell's commander, the Earl of Manchester, spurred forwards. 'Can our outriders engage his rear? Surprise him?'

Leven shifted his rump. He caught sight of both Fairfaxes, but addressed the younger. 'What say you?'

Sir Thomas shook his head. 'Our forces are on the south bank of the River Nidd. Knaresborough is set high on the north bank. The water shields Rupert utterly.'

David Leslie, Leven's second, spoke the words all the others were thinking: 'Then he has outfoxed us. We can no longer block his passage eastward.'

Leven nodded. 'He may march on York at will.'

'Can he fight us?' Lord Fairfax looked to his son for reassurance.

Sir Thomas thought for a moment. 'He is too weak, Father. He has half our number.'

Cromwell leaned forwards to stroke his black horse's neck. 'But the Marquis has another four thousand inside the city. Prince Robber will look to free them and join the two armies together before he faces us.'

'May I?' the trooper ventured nervously. He looked across the sea of faces like a man thrown to lions. 'We have seen his vanguard ride hither, my lords.'

'Then,' Cromwell said, 'he is already on the move.'

'But we cannot divide our force to maintain the siege while we deal with him,' Manchester argued.

'Agreed,' Leven said. 'We lift the siege.'

There was a moment of silence as the assembly considered the implication. Eventually Lord Fairfax broke the stalemate. 'After all the blood and sweat and—'

'Fever ravages our lines, Ferdinando,' Leven replied. 'There is benefit to be gained in freeing the men from their fetters.'

'We cannot divide our forces,' Cromwell added, 'and we dare not sit before York in the hope that the enemy will not come. What is there left to do but lift the siege and march west? We must block the main road from Knaresborough. Force the Prince to do battle before he can relieve York, before he can ally himself with Newcastle's garrison.'

'Aye,' Leven agreed. 'We crush the malignants in detail. First

Rupert's field army, then turn about, renew the siege and destroy Newcastle's garrison.' He gathered up his reins. 'God is with us, gentlemen. Let us see His will be done.'

## Near Knaresborough, Yorkshire, 1 July 1644

A murky dawn was shading the east hills, the direction in which Stryker was squinting. He was seated atop Vos, but while the valley was low and flat between soaring escarpments on both sides, still he wished he had brought a perspective glass. The lone horseman was the better part of a mile away. He had dismounted several minutes before, taking a knee to inspect his horse's front fetlocks. The beast, Stryker guessed, was lame, but its rider, blissfully unaware of the arrival of Heathcliff Brownell's Troop of Horse, seemed only concerned with his victuals as he sat on a storm-felled log to take his ease. Stryker watched him, ensuring that this was no trap. He wished Barkworth had come, for his skills in stalking quarry were second to none, but the Scot had volunteered to stay back and watch Faith.

Stryker silently indicated for his men, under Hood and Skellen, to slide down from their saddles. He sent them up into the wooded slopes, a team on either side, with the order to overlap and encircle their ignorant prey.

The horseman continued to rest and eat. Stryker waited, giving his flanking men as much time as he could risk, and then, with a high-pitched whooping cry, he raked Vos's flesh with his spurs and bolted forth. The lone man fell backwards off his perch, limbs flailing in the long grass, and then he was up, running back to his mount and kicking hard in the opposite direction. The animal struggled, its damaged leg slowing it, but still it hacked on. Stryker gave chase, the remaining twenty men at his back, and he thought for a moment that the quarry would vanish into the gloom. Then the gap was closing with astonishing speed, and Stryker realised the lone horseman had drawn up abruptly, great clods of wet earth flinging from hooves scrabbling for purchase. And on the far side, at the end of the valley, a line of dismounted troopers screened the road, each with a pistol or carbine in hand. The hunters had their prey, and he knew it, for he spat a curse and slid from the saddle, unsheathing his sword and tossing it away in resignation.

Stryker had been angry following the exchange with the clerk. Furious, in fact. Kendrick may no longer have posed a constant threat to himself and Faith, but he wanted revenge for Heathcliff Brownell. Thus, his newly inherited troop of horse had thundered east behind their green banner in the night's smallest hours, risking collision with Roundhead or Scots detachments, to scour the road for Kendrick's force. It was a vain hope, and they had found nothing but this lone rider whose lame mount had condemned him to an audience with a one-eyed Royalist hankering for a fight.

Stryker dismounted and stalked over to the captive. 'Full candour, sir, if it please you.'

The prisoner, a Parliamentary officer by his tawny hat-band, was panting heavily. 'And if not?'

Stryker's black mood quashed any respect for the man's bravado. He kicked the prisoner in the crotch. The man crumpled to his knees, forehead thudding into the hoof-whisked soil. His hat rolled off, and Stryker kicked it away. 'Then I shall lever off your fingernails with my dirk.'

The man looked up, mud plastered down to the bridge of his nose. 'What do you wish to know?'

'Strength.'

'Twenty-five thousand. Perhaps nearer thirty.'

'Shite,' Skellen's deep voice intoned from the ring of onlookers.

'Field pieces?' Stryker went on.

'A great many.'

'Do they lie before York or do they sally forth?'

'Sally.'

Stryker glanced at Hood and Skellen in turn. 'Where?'

The Parliamentarian looked as though he might fasten shut his lips. Stryker drew his sword and stabbed the man's arm. His victim fell back, a hand clamped to a sleeve dyed bright red and steaming.

Stryker wiped the blade on the man's breeches. 'Where?'

'A moor,' the Parliamentarian whimpered. 'Beside the Knaresborough road. 'Tis masked by a ridge. You will cross the Nidd and they will attack your flank.'

Stryker sheathed the sword. In that moment he forgot John Kendrick. He had lost one enemy, but fate had handed him another. They stripped the Roundhead scout, sharing his belongings and leaving him breeches, boots and a lame horse, and then they galloped west, to find Rupert of the Rhine.

### Shipton by Beningbrough, Yorkshire, 1 July 1644

'It is a trick.'

Captain John Kendrick bowed low. Lower, even, than he would for the peacock prince. 'No trick, good sirs. We offer our swords, our very hearts, to the Parliament.'

The harquebusier glowered down from his white-eyed bay, the single nasal bar of his Dutch-style pot splitting a face that betrayed nothing. 'Were you at Bolton?'

Lightning rent the sky behind the horsemen, arrayed as they were in a long line across the road. 'No,' Kendrick lied.

'When did you join?' another of the troopers asked.

'After Liverpool. We had defended that fine place with Colonel Moore.'

'Then?'

'Then it was stretched necks or turned coats,' Kendrick explained smoothly, 'and we chose the latter. We are sell-swords, after all. Our business is the fight.'

The lead horseman, the one with the Dutch-made helmet, spat at Kendrick's feet. 'The army of the Eastern Association would have only righteous men in its ranks, for it is righteousness and prayer that wins battles.'

'Come now, sir,' Kendrick said, stifling his disgust. 'At times such as these, it is surely better to have experienced fighters in your ranks, whatever their relationship with the Lord. Besides, we are sober, God-fearing men, though our chosen profession may belie the claim.'

'You are spies,' the Parliamentarian said.

'We are deserters,' Kendrick retorted quickly. 'We have been desperate to turn our coats since Liverpool.'

The idea of turning his coat had never once appeared attractive during his time with the king's army, for the self-righteous prigs of a Puritan Parliament were not his kind of people. But things had changed and his plan had gone awry. They had been watching Stryker for days, shadowing his group, seeking a chink in the bastard's armour. He could not attack the one-eyed major directly, and, though he threatened to expose the Sydall whelp as a rebel spy, he knew he could never risk such an accusation because Prince Rupert could never know of the Sydall cipher, or of his golden flagon. So they had lurked in Stryker's wake; witnessed him join with Brownell, watched them settle into the tavern in Skipton, and made their plans. The arrogance of the man still astonished Kendrick. To assume, even after his warning, that the Sydall bitch was safe, was insulting.

They had gone to work as soon as the moment was right, paying off the serving girl with the equivalent of a year's wage. She, by all accounts, had fulfilled her task admirably, and a man at the right table had expired. But he had been the wrong man, and Kendrick had not been able to snaffle the red-headed little slattern and drag her back to Bolton, there to be deflowered and defiled after leading him to the elusive prize. So Kendrick had run away, lest the girl damn him with her testimony. He had gone east, over the hills, beyond the range of Rupert's hounds, then south, straight towards York and the first Roundhead patrol he could find. Maybe, just maybe, his chance would come again. There would be battle soon, and the Vulture would cut a swathe through Prince Rupert's ranks to swoop upon his quarry.

'We offer our services to the Army of Both Kingdoms,' he said solemnly. 'You have need of men? We will fight for my lord

Fairfax or my lord Manchester or my lord Leven. We care not which, so long as the chance to slaughter malignants is opportune.'

'You are in Lord Manchester's sector, Captain.'

'Then he is my new lord and master.'

The trooper turned his horse south, York Minster's towers splitting the rain-lashed distance like cliffs. 'This way. The army musters.'

# CHAPTER 16

*The ridge, near Long Marston, Yorkshire, 1 July 1644*

First light illuminated the craggy hump that rose between the Knaresborough road and the village of Long Marston. Today shouts and drums and trumpets and the thunder of hooves had shattered its usual calm; three armies had come.

'He cannot reach York without marching below us,' Alexander Leslie, Earl of Leven, announced as his fellow generals reined in. They were on the summit of the ridge and had been joined by several cavalry units, the main brigades of foot drawn up on the moor below. 'We take him in the flank. The river blocks his line of retreat.'

The River Nidd flowed south from Knaresborough and then curved back in a gigantic U-shape before joining the Ouse north-west of York. The main road to York cut across that sweeping arc, covering much of its distance to the besieged city on the Nidd's north bank, and then crossing it by a wide stone bridge and continuing on to York. It meant that any traveller taking that road would be forced to use the crossing, and any army would be funnelled and stretched over its great arches. From here they had a good view of the surrounding terrain, all the way back to the bridge, and from here, as Rupert attempted his crossing, they could launch their vast force into his exposed column.

'And if the Marquis sallies forth from the city,' Edward Montagu, Earl of Manchester, said as he unfastened a drinking flask from a hook on his saddle, 'we will fall on him in like fashion.'

Leven nodded. 'A good perch, if ever there was one.'

Ferdinando, Lord Fairfax, blew a smoke ring. He waved his pipe as he spoke. 'Scots eagles and English hawks.'

Manchester laughed. 'Newcastle's lambs were never more aptly named.'

An aide galloped up the ridge.

'Large body of horse heading right for us, my lords,' he said, breathing hard.

'How large?' Leven asked.

'In the hundreds, my lord.'

Manchester and Fairfax exchanged a meaningful look. 'The vanguard, you suppose?' Fairfax suggested.

'Let us perch awhile, then,' Leven said as he gazed down and to his left at the bridge that would bring him a prince. Already he could see the first banners of enemy cavalry appear on the road. 'Rupert will cross the river, and we will give him slaughter.'

## North-west of York, 1 July 1644

Prince Rupert did cross a river, but it was not the Nidd.

Stryker, at the head of Heathcliff Brownell's troop, had bolted back to Knaresborough with the news that the Army of Both Kingdoms was in the process of lifting their siege and lying in wait. They were drawing up on a moor beside the road, he told the prince in the hastily convened council of war, in the expectation of a Royalist advance.

'Then we shall give them what they expect,' the king's nephew had said, his dark eyes twinkling. He had looked at his second in command, Lord John Byron. 'Send them a sizeable body of horse, John. Advance along the road as far as the bridge, and, for all our sakes, make it appear authentic. Pomp and bluster, John. Pomp and bluster. Make them believe we come for battle.'

The Royalist army had marched north-eastwards at a whirl-wind pace. Acutely aware of the need to cover the distance before his cavalry's feint was discovered, Rupert himself, as he had on the march from Denton, raced along the extended line, calling encouragement wherever it was needed. He placed horse in the van, in the rear and on both flanks to provide cover against any intercepting force, and extra men, taken from the ranks of pike and musket, were transferred to the artillery train in order to lend muscle to the back-breaking task of shifting the great guns.

The first river to traverse was a branch of the Ouse called the River Ure. They reached it by mid-morning, finding the bridge sturdy and wide enough to get a reasonable flow of traffic over its great stones, and on they hurried, curving eastwards in a race to the second waterway, the Swale. Rupert had hoped to ford it without a search for a permanent crossing, but the rainwaters had rendered such an attempt impossible, and they had been forced to continue to the village of Thornton Bridge, where surprised locals lined the roads to wave at the unlikely spectacle. Mercifully, the bridge there had again been in good repair. Moreover, the awestruck folk informed them that all had been quiet in recent days. There were no Parliamentarian or Scots armies abroad. Not even a patrol. By late afternoon, Rupert's fifteen thousand men had performed a sharp right turn, marching due south along the east bank of the River Ouse to approach York from the north.

'You are God's own lions!' Rupert had bellowed as the army mustered at the edge of the vast Forest of Galtres, which smudged the land north of York. He waited for the cheers to ebb. 'We have placed the River Ouse between us and the enemy!' He paused again as the ranks huzzahed, raising hands to quell the furore. 'But I am to understand that the rebels have constructed a bridge of boats on the far side of the wood. Should they become aware of our thrust, they may yet sally from their position to cut off our march. We must fly with all speed, my friends! Are you with me?'

They surged on, drums beating the pace, even as drizzle turned the evening chill and oppressive. Spirits remained high, sustained by the knowledge that they had achieved the impossible already, and that the three armies of the alliance had not foreseen their gambit. But always there was the bridge of boats spanning the Ouse at a place called Poppleton, and, as the army broke ranks, filtering through the thick stands of Galtres's trees, a formidable body of cavalry was detached and sent south to clear the way.

Stryker lit a fire as he watched them go. Brownell's troop – *his* troop now – had tied their weary mounts to the lowest branches of oak and beech and ash, and they had foraged for anything remotely edible and collected the driest kindling they could find. The fires around about them, warming so many other troops and companies in the cold dark, smoked thickly, but the canopy gave just enough cover to keep the hissing flames at the dance.

A preacher snaked through the trees nearby. 'For the Lord thy God walketh in the midst of thy camp to deliver thee!' he called to whoever would listen. 'And to give thee thine enemies before thee!'

'There will be battle,' Faith Helly said as she sat on a damp patch of leaf-mould beside Stryker.

He nodded, staring at the fire. 'The morrow, aye.'

'Would you like to run away?'

He looked across at her with a wry smile. 'No man wishes death.'

'You think you will die?'

'We are outnumbered.'

'Death's part of life,' William Skellen intoned as he prodded the glowing twigs with a gnarled branch. 'But a puzzle serves to quicken the soul. We need to figure about that bloody book.'

Faith frowned. Stryker laughed. 'Not the Bible, Mistress; the cipher.'

'It hardly seems important now, Major.' She placed the Bible carefully down, as if setting the mystery to one side, and gathered up the cloak Stryker had given her, balling it up tightly. 'Would it anger you,' she asked in barely a whisper, 'if I said I wished you defeat?'

'It would surprise me if you claimed to wish us victory,' Stryker said.

She placed the cloak on the ground, patting it into the shape she wanted. 'But I do not wish you harm. Any of you. I pray God keeps you safe.'

'Thank you,' Stryker said, amused to share what could be his last night on earth with an ardent rebel. 'When we stand to arms, you must get away. Take my horse. Ride far. Hide yourself.'

'I am from Sussex, Major,' she said simply. 'I would know not where to go. I will wait with the baggage. With the women.'

'In York? That is surely where they will go.'

She screwed up her face to show her distaste at the prospect. 'The supply wagons, then. The Parliament men will not harm us, should the day go ill for your prince.' She delved under the cloak, producing the dagger Stryker had purchased for her. 'And I have this, sir. It has saved me once already.'

She lay on her side, easing her head on to the makeshift pillow. Stryker stayed upright, drawing his knees to his chest and propping his chin upon them. He shut his eye, though no sleep would come. For sunrise, he knew, would bring slaughter.

## Near Long Marston, Yorkshire, 1 July 1644

'Is it true what they say?' The Earl of Leven, astride his dappled grey mare, screwed up his face against a spiteful wind that gnawed his leathery cheeks. He tugged the black cassock up higher, feeling the cold of the silver buttons through his sandy and silver whiskers. 'That you have a man paid for the defacement of churches?'

The Earl of Manchester shared the collective gaze as all three generals stared down at the flat ground on the far side of the River Nidd. 'My Provost-Marshal, William Dowsing. A more Godly man was never created, save our Lord Jesus Christ. Dowsing is commissioner for the destruction of monuments of idolatry and superstition. A most crucial task, I'm sure you'd both agree.'

Leven grunted his assent, though he secretly despised the idea. His had been a past immersed in the violence of European conflict, and he knew well the destructive, divisive harvest to be reaped when zealots and iconoclasts were given free rein to vent their sectarian spleens. He simply wished to know if the rumour was true. It informed his opinion of the man, if nothing else.

'And did not,' Manchester was saying, 'the Parliamentary Ordinance of last summer state that all monuments of superstition and idolatry be removed? Were they not to be abolished? Fixed altars, rails, chancel steps,' he counted aloud: 'crucifixes, crosses, images of the Virgin Mary and pictures of saints or superstitious inscriptions.' He took a long breath. 'Angels, rood lofts, holy water stoups, and any image, in stone, wood, glass or on plate.'

'Thorough,' was all Leven found to say. He looked back towards the river and forgot about Manchester. The Royalist cavalry had not come back. They had ridden in a bright, snorting, trumpeting column towards the Nidd, assembled amid much fanfare and rattling of swords. Some had fired pistols over the water in direct challenge to the men watching from the ridge, but Leven had ordered that no member of the alliance, Parliamentarian or Covenanter, was to engage pre-emptively. They would wait, he had decreed, until a meaningful number of Rupert's army had streamed over the water. Then, and only then, would he issue the command to advance from the moor. Except that the Royalists had not crossed the bridge. Not even their noisy advance party. They had mustered on the far side, in full view of the Army of Both Kingdoms, practising evolutions, yelling insults and generally loitering with menaces. And then, as night fell, they had vanished. At first Leven presumed they had fallen back to join the main column, perhaps to replenish supplies or seek shelter from the rain, but they had not returned. Now he felt a rising dread, and he did not know why.

The answer came on the back of a pony, mud covering it from hoof to belly. It was wounded, a gaping slash at its rump and a narrow, blood-weeping hole in its flank. It carried a dragoon who looked ghostly pale in the darkness as he bellowed for safe passage up to the crest. 'My lords! My lords!'

Leven turned his horse. The dragoon had not come from the west, where the enemy were concentrated, but from the east. 'Speak.'

'He has come!' The stench of vomit was on him, potent despite the wind and rain. It was the true scent of fear.

'Come?'

'The bridge!'

Leven glanced instinctively at the Nidd crossing, still ominously empty.

'No, my lord!' The dragoon shook his head as though his skull were aflame. 'The boats!'

'Blast your tied tongue, sirrah!' Manchester snarled suddenly, kicking his own mount closer. 'Of what boats do you speak?'

Leven held out a staying hand so that Manchester turned to him. 'Prince Rupert has outwitted us again,' he said quietly. 'You refer to the bridge of boats at Poppleton, do you not?'

'I do, my lord!' the dragoon gasped. 'My company were guards there. Malignant horse smashed from the north. We lost many in the fight. We were overwhelmed.'

'The north?' Manchester echoed incredulously. 'His mind is befuddled.'

'No,' Leven said. 'This,' he waved at the silvered band that was the Nidd, 'was a feint. A hoax. He went north. By God, he went north. And now he controls the crossing of the Ouse.'

Manchester's face fell. 'Then he may strut into York at his pleasure.'

'Aye,' Leven nodded. 'We stand out here in the cursed rain, while the wolf strolls through our door.'

# PART 3

# AS STUBBLE
# TO OUR SWORDS

# CHAPTER 17

## York, 2 July 1644

'We are to march!' Captain Lancelot Forrester bellowed, hands cupped at his mouth. 'Drummers! See to your drill!'

The beat struck up, softly at first, ragged and out of time, then building as the drummers found their rhythm. It became a crescendo that reverberated around the towering Micklegate Bar, joined with every passing second by the thrum from other companies as each unit practised the various calls that would articulate and spread orders while on the march or on the field of battle.

'Eager, boy,' Seek Wisdom and Fear the Lord Gardner muttered as Forrester came to stand at his side.

'The men must hear the drums, Father, for it stirs the spirit.'

Gardner nodded. 'Aye, it does. But there's plenty o' time to spare.'

'Colonel Mowbray says the order was quite clear,' Forrester said, straining to keep his voice calm amid rising frustration. 'His Highness demanded we march at four of the clock.'

'Yet here we all are, boy. Taking the air, such as it is, and pissin' into the wind. Do you see any urgency from the high and mighty, hereabouts? I've seen no man with rank of colonel, let alone the likes of our esteemed leader.'

Forrester looked again at the gatehouse. It was open, its earth and rubble barricades torn away for the first time in weeks. He knew the army of Prince Rupert lay on the other side, mustering even now on a moor down on the Tockwith road, and he yearned to be with them. Instead the army of the Marquis of Newcastle was caged as it had ever been, this time by the inertia of its own leaders.

The city of York had been formally relieved the previous evening. George Goring, General of the Northern Horse, had been give the honour of leading his cavalrymen down from Rupert's forest encampment and through Bootham Bar, to be greeted by a chorus of cheers. The beleaguered defenders had seen the empty trenches, abandoned and silent, and they had crept out to plunder what they could from the three Allied leaguers. But Goring's was the official liberation, and the folk of York had turned out in their droves to welcome him.

Goring had given Newcastle a message from Rupert. The prince was to hunt the Army of Both Kingdoms. To that end, he would break camp before dawn, cross the bridge of boats at Poppleton, and push south and west to where the scouts reported a concentration of the three rebel armies. Goring brought with him the expectation that Newcastle's four thousand men would sally forth at the same time, combining their strength before the sun had fully risen, yet here they were, formed into marching order, drums beating, weapons shouldered, and already the day was slipping by.

'Christ,' Forrester hissed through gritted teeth, 'it is almost nine o'clock. We must move soon. What game does he play?'

'Lord Eythin will not march,' a new voice broke in at Forrester's back, 'until he is certain of his strength.'

Forrester spun on his heels. 'I did not mean to gripe, Sir Edmund.'

Sir Edmund Mowbray was short, auburn-haired and fastidiously groomed. He wore a beautiful crimson coat to match – if only in colour – those worn by his regiment, with a large, silver gorget at his throat and lace at his sleeves. He tipped his feathered hat at Gardner. 'Father.'

The preacher gave a mad-eyed grin. 'The Lord tells me General King wishes to drop his dung on Prince Rupert's shoes! Say it is not so Colonel!'

Mowbray struggled to keep his shrewish face taut. 'Lord Eythin, to use his proper title, is not a friend of the Prince, that is no secret. But I'll not have rumour of deliberate sabotage bandied around the ranks, Father, understood?'

Gardner affected an expression of hurt. 'I merely relay what the Almighty whispers in my dreams, Colonel.'

Mowbray looked at Forrester. 'Lord Newcastle has taken his new guardsmen to Long Marston, there to meet with the Prince. The Foot, under Eythin, will follow up behind.' He patted Forrester's shoulder. 'It will not be long now. There has been some delay in rooting some of the troops from the empty siege-lines. One man came across almost five thousand pairs of shoes, would you believe?'

Forrester ran a hand over tired eyes. 'We have four thousand men here, sir. Good men. The whitecoats too. The Prince needs us if he is to fight.'

'Hold firm,' Mowbray said, 'and keep the men ready. The order will come. We will march. Of that, you have my word.'

### Near Tadcaster, Yorkshire, 2 July 1644

'Pray God they watch our backs,' the Earl of Leven said as his grey mare splashed through the glittering stream.

'The Horse are well fed and well led,' a gruff tone sounded in reply.

Leven twisted in his saddle to regard the Earl of Manchester. 'This campaign has taught us nothing if not the foolishness of complacency.'

The Army of Both Kingdoms had stood to arms all night beneath a sky grumbling with portent. On the ridge above Long Marston, the three generals discussed their next turn, aware that they had been utterly outmanoeuvred. At a single stroke Rupert

253

had both liberated York and rendered the Allied position worthless. There was no point remaining on the ridge, but where should they go next? They suspected Rupert's army to be much smaller than their own, but rumours were rife that he had somehow collected enough waifs and strays en route from Liverpool to bolster his force such that he could ably give battle. Moreover, his army was now free to amalgamate with that of the Marquis of Newcastle, the latter possessing some notoriously hardy fighters, chief of which were Newcastle's personal regiment, his Lambs. But of utmost concern was the possibility that the prince would cut straight through York and appear on the road south, which was why, throughout the damp morning, the vast rebel horde had slipped away from the ridge. They would produce their own sleight of hand.

'If we can hold Tadcaster,' Leven said, gripping his wet saddle with aching thighs, 'all will be well.'

The Scots Foot were in the van, Manchester's in the rear, and the rest formed a bristling column that stretched all the way from Long Marston to Tadcaster. Leven had left three thousand horsemen on the ridge, made up of elements of all three armies, Oliver Cromwell, Sir Thomas Fairfax and David Leslie taking command. Those horsemen would provide a screen against any advance by the malignants, while the main bulk of the force would make haste to the rendezvous.

'Hold?' Ferdinando, Lord Fairfax, echoed from out in front. 'The Prince may not approach it at all.'

'He has York,' Leven said, 'and its bridges. If I were the Prince, I would cross the Ouse and march directly south.'

'But you are not the Prince,' Manchester answered wryly.

Leven ignored him. 'The town is a crossroads. If he blocks us there, he will hem my army between Tadcaster and York, he will prevent your army retiring to East Anglia, and he will sever us from our reinforcements coming up from Cheshire.'

A rider interrupted them, careening through the stream and hitting the south bank at such pace that his mount overshot their position by some yards. The rider wrenched the animal back and brought her to a halt in front of the three generals. 'My lords,' he panted, without pause for pleasantry. 'You are required at Long Marston.'

Manchester raised an eyebrow. 'Required?'

'Generals Leslie, Cromwell and Fairfax send for you. All of you.'

'Well?' Leven snapped. 'What are they about, man?'

'The enemy marches.'

Leven glanced back at Manchester. 'What did I tell you? He makes for Tadcaster.'

'No, my lord,' the rider blurted. 'He draws over a great number to the moor below the ridge. His whole force, mayhap. I am told to request you recall the armies in their entirety. Prince Robber marches not upon Tadcaster, my lord. He seeks battle.'

## Marston Moor, five miles west of York, 2 July 1644

'Christ knows where the rest of the bastards have scuttled off to.' Sir Richard Crane, commander of Prince Rupert's Lifeguard of Horse, scanned the high ridge through the tin tube. 'What d'you make of it?'

'Retreat?' Stryker said hopefully, taking the perspective glass from the colonel. He drew it slowly, left to right, letting the detail of hedge and crop blur across his vision. He rested the glass at the western limit of the crest, the right-hand end as he looked at it. There were blocks of horsemen drawn up on the fields, bright cornets hanging limp in the thin drizzle. It was a strong body, perhaps as many as two or three thousand, but still a small fraction of the whole.

'I doubt it,' Crane said, holding out a hand for the return of the instrument. 'They have twice our number. How to explain such craven behaviour to the Committee? They'll come back, you mark my words. Their horse hold the ridge. Would have run by now if they had no intention of keeping it, which means they'll fight. And why would they fight without the rest of their army?'

Stryker had no idea as to the whereabouts of the rebel foot and ordnance, but he supposed it mattered little. As Crane asserted, the horsemen on the ridge harboured apparently no intention of hightailing it away, which meant that blood would run. And that, he reflected, was precisely what Prince Rupert wanted. He had his order, the one he had read out in Liverpool, the one that demanded he engage the Scots and Parliamentarians if at all possible. Since then he had looked for battle in every move he had made. From wrong-footing the enemy at Denton and Knaresborough, to resisting the calls for his army to enter York, he had expedited the journey to this field; this moor. It had all been for this.

Now the Royalist army was gradually forming up in battle order in the expectation that, wherever they were, the Army of Both Kingdoms would soon return. Stryker had attached his troop to that of Crane, for no better reason than proximity of their respective camps, and Crane took up position in the rear-most line, his elite force of a hundred and fifty troopers forming the right wing of the reserve, Sir Edward Widdrington's brigade completing the left. Now they waited as the opposing units stared at one other, Vos nuzzling Crane's black mare as the beasts tore up the grass.

Stryker handed back the glass, observing the regiments of foot that shuffled before them into position. The battle-hardened units brought back from Ireland were there, moving to the centre around Tillier's greencoats, while a brigade made up of Rupert's own bluecoats and some men behind the red banner of Colonel Robert Bryon edged forwards to form a pike-fringed promontory at the very front. More were coming all the time, trudging on to the moor to the steady hammer of drums, the cries of sergeants and junior officers ringing out to mould them into order.

Prince Rupert stood in his stallion's bright stirrups as he rode back and forth, issuing orders to whomever might catch his eye.

He was ready for the fight, the bucket-shaped tops of his boots pulled back to his groin, his lean torso wrapped in buff hide and encased in black enamelled plate at spine and breast. He had foregone the typically flamboyant hat, choosing instead a lobster-tailed *Zischägge* helmet that was plain, practical and musket-proof. Rupert's dog, Boye, ran at the stallion's hooves, black eyes like coal pebbles against its matted white coat as it stared up at its master.

'Talk of missing rebels,' Crane was saying, 'has me wondering about our own prodigal comrades.'

'The Northern Foot,' Stryker said, thinking the same. Newcastle's cavalry, under Goring, were already to be seen at the moor's edge, having ridden out after their triumphal liberation of the city, but the infantry, though summoned with the rest of the army, were conspicuous by their absence. 'They will come, will they not?'

Crane laughed. 'There will be some explanation required should they disappoint.'

If they disappoint, Stryker privately thought, there will be none left to hear the explanation. 'Aye, sir.'

'Which reminds me,' Crane went on. 'Are you willing to explain *your*self, Sergeant-Major?'

Stryker stared at him. 'Sir?'

'That filly you have riding with you. She is no ordinary camp follower, and I'd guess she is too young to be warming your bed at night.'

'My niece, Sir Richard.'

Crane sighed. 'If we survive the day, Major Stryker, you will try again, and you will keep your lies for one more dull-witted than I. Are we understood?'

'Sir.' Stryker twisted back, eyeing his troop, which was drawn up behind the Lifeguard. 'If you'll excuse me, Sir Richard.'

He rode back slowly, unwilling to strain Vos so early in the day. The ground was already churned and sapping. He nodded to the flanking troopers and slipped round the back to find his three men and their young charge. 'You are warm enough?' he asked when he reached Faith Helly.

Faith was perched atop one of the ponies captured from the dragoons at Poppleton. She patted its neck as she spoke. 'I verily boil, my heart races so.'

The army had set out from the Forest of Galtres at four in the morning, winding its way down to the bridge of boats. It had taken a long time to cross the Ouse, for it was no easy task to filter so many men and horses over so narrow a structure, especially one that moved with the currents beneath. Mercifully, a practicable ford had been scouted during the crossing, and the artillery train of sixteen field pieces was able to avoid the precariously bobbing bridge. Now the entire Royalist army and baggage train found themselves traipsing on to the fallow moorland west of York, staring up at an arable ridge that swarmed with tawny-scarfed horsemen.

'If matters go ill for us,' Stryker said, 'you must make for York.' He looked at Hood, Skellen and Barkworth in turn. 'You hear? Get her to safety.'

Each nodded. Faith shook her head. 'If matters go ill for your prince, I will make my own arrangement with your enemies.'

'Kendrick will be with them.'

She hesitated for a moment. 'Master Sydall was a devout man and a staunch Parliamentarian, and there will be many Parliament men who lament his death. My chances of finding such friends in so vast a host are greater than running into a single enemy. Besides, how would I fare in York if you are no longer there?'

Stryker knew she was right. 'The supply wagons will retire to the woods, there.' He pointed to the trees several hundred yards to the rear. 'You will be with them when shots fly.'

'Sir!' Skellen's hard voice barked suddenly.

Skellen was pointing over the heads of the forming infantry, to the rightmost edge of the ridge. A large body of horsemen was cantering down from the undulating crest in a broad swathe. Musket shots rattled at the same moment, and more horsemen filled that end of the ridge, except that these surged up from the lower ground, and their scarves were red against the slate-grey morning. Rupert, it seemed, had dispatched his horse to take the high ground away from the rebels. The day's first killing had begun.

# CHAPTER 18

William Cavendish, Marquis of Newcastle and commander of the king's northern army, reached Marston Moor as the fight swirled on the lower slope of the ridge. He arrived in a coach drawn by four white horses draped in the same red and white livery as the driver. Almost every gaze turned to the vehicle as it bounced off the road and on to the moor, chains jangling above the hideous creak of strained axle-trees, a muscular destrier in the same livery tethered at the rear. The coach was escorted by a bodyguard of gentlemen troopers, who wore their own civilian clothing beneath various pieces of armour, and Stryker, spurring out from Brownell's former unit, supposed they had been raised for just this occasion, recruited from the finest men York had to offer.

'What a day to strap on your grandpapa's sword, eh?' Crane muttered as Stryker reined in beside him. 'I suppose Rupert has pulled their ballocks from the flames, so it is only right that they lend their vigour to our cause.'

'They shan't do any fighting, Colonel,' Stryker replied, aware of the bitterness in his tone.

Crane snorted. 'Dare say you're in the right of it.' He glanced behind. 'Men ready?'

'Aye, sir.'

'Come to stick your ugly nose into the business of generals?'

'Aye, sir.'

Crane's scar tissue puckered as his mouth turned upwards. 'Then observe, Major.'

Prince Rupert of the Rhine cantered past them at that moment and intercepted Newcastle's coach. The proud sentinels of his bodyguard parted like the Red Sea to let the king's nephew through, and he dismounted as the coach door clunked open.

Newcastle, resplendent in a green and silver cassock and huge felt hat, stepped briskly on to the squelching grass and returned Rupert's bow. 'At last we meet Your Highness.' He glanced up at the ridge. 'The fight begins?'

'We clear their horse from that corn hill. I would take the high ground while time is on my side.' Rupert's face was tight, his lips pressed firmly in a pale line. 'My lord, I wish you had come sooner with your forces, but I hope we shall yet have a glorious day.'

Newcastle frowned. 'My men have lately suffered much privation, Highness. They plunder the enemy siege-lines. It takes time to gather them together.' He paused as a great shout rolled and built from the trampled crops of the slope. The song of swords rang out, echoing down to the woods at the Royalist rear, as the opposing bodies of cavalry clashed. 'I urge you, Highness, do not attempt this thing rashly. I have good word, *reliable* word, that there is much discontent within the alliance. They are resolved to divide themselves imminently. We have given them many wounds, these last weeks, and their leaguers ooze with disease. They are likely to march away, should the moment be opportune.'

'March away?' Rupert repeated the words as though they were uttered by a Bedlamite. 'Divide? No, my lord, I would face them here, now, while they are one, so that I may destroy them as a whole.'

Newcastle swallowed thickly. 'This is folly.'

'This' – the prince raised his voice, more heads turning towards them – 'is His Majesty's wish. I possess a letter, in my uncle's own hand. It tells a tale of woe. Of the Oxford Army's imminent annihilation if help does not reach them soon. His Majesty commands me to relieve York, to defeat the Scots and Roundheads, and then to march south with all haste, to lend him my strength. I have achieved one of those aims. Now, together, we will see to the second. You have four thousand foot, yes?'

Newcastle grimaced. 'The siege whittled us without mercy. It is nearer three.'

'Three thousand,' Rupert said, turning the figures in his mind. 'We will come to twelve thousand foot when all is joined. And over six thousand horse. How many do the enemy bring to bear?'

'Fever struck them, this we know, for we perceived their digging of grave pits. But I know not what toll it took.'

'Then?'

Newcastle blew out his cheeks. 'Not a great deal fewer than thirty thousand.'

Trumpet calls captured the attention of both Royalist leaders at once. Prince and marquis turned together, squinting into the drab morning to witness the rout of their cavalry. The Parliament horse had swept down from the crest in numbers, first hitting the Royalist party, then enveloping it, so that they pressed too closely for the supporting musketeers to fire. In a matter of minutes the skirmish was over, king's men crashing pell-mell down towards the safety of the moor.

'Christ's bleeding wounds!' Prince Rupert bellowed, thumping fist into palm. 'Who are those horsemen?' He jabbed a finger towards the summit. 'Who?'

An aide let his mount take a stride forwards. 'Eastern Association, Highness.'

'Bible thumpers to a man,' Rupert hissed scornfully. 'Make for good fighters, more's the pity. Commanded by?'

'Lieutenant-General Cromwell, Highness.'

'God damn farmer!' Rupert raged again. 'Send more men up that bastard hill and take it.'

Even as the aide nodded acquiescence, another rider on a mud-caked gelding slewed to an arcing stop beside the young general. 'Highness! Body o' foot climbing the ridge, thither.'

Rupert followed his outstretched arm. 'How many?'

'This one? A thousand.'

'This one?' Rupert repeated. 'How many bodies of foot are there?'

'All of them, Highness,' the rider replied. 'The Scotch army and all the English. They return as one.'

Rupert swore viciously, turning to Newcastle. 'We are in dire need of your regiments, my lord. Where are they?'

'Lord Eythin brings them forthwith.'

'Eythin?' Rupert spat. 'I no longer wonder as to their tardiness, my lord, for James King is a knave and a scoundrel.'

Newcastle scowled at the insult to his adviser. 'I understand you two have your differences, Highness, but you have my word that he will bring my men to the field soon.'

The tall prince rubbed his lean, cleanly shaven chin as he regarded the ridge. 'I've a mind to take that hill with my full force and scatter the enemy to the wind.'

'Wait, Highness,' Newcastle urged. 'My lads are as good foot as are in the world. Lord Eythin will come.'

'He had better, my lord Newcastle,' Rupert said, still staring at the ridge, 'for delay will be our undoing.'

Alexander Leslie, Earl of Leven and senior commander of Allied forces about York, ascended the ridge at noon. The journey back from Tadcaster had been fraught, riven by waking nightmares of a horde of red-scarved wolves marauding over his uncoordinated and confused brigades. But now, as he finally arrived to resume the position he had maintained during the previous day, he gave thanks to God, for miraculously the Army of Both Kingdoms still held the high ground and the wolves remained on the moor.

Leven kicked his whinnying grey up to the highest point towards the eastern end of the ridge. When he had been here previously, the moor had been secondary to the River Nidd in his mind. He had used the vantage – a view unsullied all the way from that shimmering river in the west to the walls of York in the east – to warn him of Prince Rupert's approach. Now, though, his eye was attuned to the terrain itself, for this time his enemy had not played him false. This time, the only viable Royalist army in the entire north of England mustered on the flat plain below. The infantry were manoeuvring into position at the very centre of the formation, while huge bodies of cavalry formed both wings; the Northern Horse on their left, while the rest, under Lord John Byron to judge by the colours, took the opposite flank. Leven was pleased with all this, because he had the advantage of the terrain. Had Rupert's earlier play for Bilton Bream proved successful, the reverse would be true, but Cromwell, that dour, blunt-speaking cudgel of a man, had led a fine action in defence of the position, beating Byron's horse clean away, and Leven knew that it might well have won him the day already.

Because Marston Moor was a killing field.

Leven had been through the hellfire of conflict many times, and one thing he had gleaned was that battlefields were not perfect. They were not usually like the wards of a castle, where engineers designed and delineated fiendishly clever zones into which men might be coerced and slain. Yet what he saw before him now was exactly that. The moor *was* delineated, by God, if not by engineers. The ridge on which he stood, climbing high above all, marked the southern boundary. Villages – Tockwith and Long Marston – provided clear limits to the west and east respectively, while a dense forest, Wilstrop Wood, shrouded the land to the north. Immediately below Leven's position, the ground fell steeply away, easing into a gentle slope as it met with the moor at its foot. Away to his right, around Long Marston, the terrain was rough, broken by hedgerows and ditches, while to his left, at Bilton Bream, pioneers with picks and shovels were already setting to the task of clearing a large cony warren so that Cromwell's horse could move unhindered.

Immediately before the ridge ran a track connecting the two villages, while beyond the track, a ditch – intermittently hedged – curved through the plain, marking both the extent of the cultivated land and the extent of the enemy forces. He watched that hedge. It was difficult to see exactly what awaited anyone brave enough to assault it, but it seemed obvious that the prince would have men lying in wait.

'He has fewer than we feared.'

Leven looked to his left to see the lords Manchester and Fairfax approach. 'I see no colours belonging to Newcastle's foot. When they arrive it will bolster him markedly.'

Manchester stroked his horse's ears and stared at the enemy lines. 'My guess is we look upon fewer than fourteen thousand. With the Northern Foot, he'll have eighteen at a pinch.' He shrugged. 'We have thirty thousand in reply.'

'Twenty-eight,' Leven corrected. 'So many did the fever take.'

Fairfax laughed as though he were out for a Sunday hack. 'It is enough, my lord. Look at them! They are magnificent!'

Leven could do nothing but agree. Like the Royalists down on the moor, their flanks were formed of horsemen. On the far right, facing Goring's Northern Horse, were the cavalry and dragoons of Fairfax's Northern Association commanded by the lord's son, Sir Thomas, who rode in the front line, which, in turn, was comprised of five bodies of horse interspersed with units of musketeers. There was a line behind, of equal strength, and a third line of Scots horse in reserve. Over on the left, at the already bloodstained Bilton Bream, the cavalry were commanded by Manchester's second, Oliver Cromwell. He too had a trio of deep lines, leading the first in person, with the second commanded by Colonel Vermuyden. The third was again made up of Scottish cavalry, to be led by David Leslie. The centre of the army was dominated by foot, and that was where Leven's proud Covenanters brought their strength to bear. Fairfax had taken three thousand foot to the gates of York, while Manchester had supplied twice that number. In contrast, Leven's army had fourteen thousand pikemen and musketeers, and now they marched past him in huge, snaking columns to take up position on the ruined fields of corn. The Army of Both Kingdoms had suffered much during their abortive siege, with cannon, musket and plague pecking at them without remorse, but still, after all that, Leven could gaze upon a burgeoning battle line that would, within an hour or two, boast the better part of twenty thousand infantry. More, indeed, than the entire Royalist army combined.

Eventually he looked at Fairfax and nodded. 'Pray God you are right, my lord.'

Stryker stared up at the ridge. They had stood to arms the entire morning and watched, with unease and then horror, as the escarpment had filled with soldiers. The cornfields had gone, replaced by metallic killers on red-eyed destriers, by phalanxes of musket and pike, by dragoons with long-arms slung across their backs, by gun crews and their black-muzzled murderers. There were so many banners on that hill. Reds and blues and yellows and blacks. They swirled high, every blurring smear of colour a marker for each individual unit, though he could not count them all. He had not seen an army so vast since the Low Countries. It spread over the ridge and down part of the steep slope like a swarm of bees, vastly outnumbering his own army. A vague memory of Bolton-le-Moors swirled through his head, and he found himself wondering if this day was God's revenge.

He took some salted trout from his snapsack, tearing off strips and handing them to the others. Skellen and Barkworth were behind him, their mounts flanking Faith's hirsute pony.

'The unholy trinity,' Thomas Hood said. He was saddled at Stryker's right side, chewing as he spoke. 'I see the Fairfax Foot hold the centre. Thank the Lord, for I'd rather our lads face them than the blue bonnets.'

Stryker saw Lord Fairfax's banner in the middle of the Allied infantry. The front row, from what he could see at so low a perspective, was made up of ten regiments. They were brigaded into five divisions, two regiments apiece, and on the right, as Stryker saw it, were the red and green coats of the Earl of Manchester's army, while on the far side were the grey Scots in their blue hats and plaid shawls. Between them they accounted for all but one of the brigades, and that, in the very centre, was the one that had taken Hood's eye. It seemed strange that Lord Fairfax's men – those who had suffered many defeats to Newcastle's grizzled whitecoats – would be entrusted to hold the very epicentre of the Allied line, the fulcrum around which the rest of the foot brigades would turn. 'They hurried back,' he said, considering what had prompted the deployment. 'They are not drawn into their separate armies, but mixed and spread. The Yorkshiremen probably reached the field first.' A thought struck him as he glanced at Hood. 'The banners are not easy to make out. You are sober?'

'The men have drained the sutler dry,' Hood said with mock chagrin.

Stryker laughed. 'I need your wits, Thomas.'

'You have them, sharp and clear.' He twisted to see the girl. 'I have Miss Helly to thank.'

'Do not turn hot-gospeller on me, Lieutenant,' Stryker said as Faith blushed, 'for I plan to get blind drunk in York this night.'

Hood nodded. 'I look forward to it, sir.'

'Amen to that,' Skellen muttered.

Faith opened her mouth, but her words were drowned as they crossed her lips. The volley had come from a line of heavy guns up on the ridge, its thunderclap reverberating across the moor. Vos edged to the left, and Stryker had to grip hard to keep him steady. One man, a dragoon away to the right, was thrown, his mount rearing in terror. A mighty flock of birds rose from the forest at their backs, speckling the sky amid a crescendo of flapping wings and shrieking caws.

'Steady!' a voice was bellowing out in front, from somewhere within the dense rows of the prince's foot brigades. 'Steady my good men!'

The guns flashed orange again, tongues licking the crest of the ridge. Smoke billowed, obscured the black muzzles in bitter cloud, and then the rumble shook the earth. The half-dozen lumps of iron whined over their heads, crashing into the forest canopy. A nervous murmur rippled through the ranks.

'Saker, sir,' Skellen said. 'Tickles my back teeth.'

'Did'nae think you had back teeth,' Barkworth replied.

'With the Major's leave, you shall have no front teeth,' Skellen growled.

The tall Gosport man and the tiny, yellow-eyed Scot glared at one another and then they were all laughing as the first of the Royalist artillery pieces rent the damp afternoon. Skeins of smog threaded back through the brigades into the woodland. Faith caught her breath, smothering her face with her sleeve. For Stryker, it was as though an apothecary waved a pungent potion to his nostrils, livening his senses and churning his bowels.

Skellen's voice turned to a whisper. 'There's a lot of fuckin' rebels up there.' He glanced at Faith. 'Beg pardon.'

'Like fleas on a dog's back,' Barkworth reflected.

'Only one dog I'm interested in,' Skellen said, and Stryker looked back to see Boye, the large white poodle that had seen more battle than most, barking madly as Prince Rupert cantered out to the left wing with a group of aides.

'You believe him Satan's creature?' Faith asked dubiously.

Skellen wrinkled his nose. 'He can't win a fight, lass, but he'll lose one right enough.'

Stryker tore his gaze away from the party around which the dog sauntered. 'The men believe, Mistress. The simple folk, dragged from their ploughs to spill the blood of their neighbours for kings and nobles they will never meet and principles they can never understand. Remember the sutler's charm?' He paused for her to nod. 'They pray to God, right enough, but also to the faeries in the forest and the wraiths in the rivers. Those men believe Boye brings us luck. If he is harmed, they will believe the magic brook runs dry.'

'And then, Miss,' Skellen said, 'we really are in trouble.'

The bombardment was feeble. The great guns on both sides shredded the afternoon, Scottish crews spewing fire and venom from atop the ridge, king's men replying by turns, but the rain had persisted, and the ground had turned to bog. The mattrosses worked tirelessly with scourer and sponge, rammer and priming iron, but the damp powder fizzed meekly and the soil beneath the huge wheels shifted and collapsed with each recoil so that every new shot required a different elevation than the last. And all the while the targets moved as brigades on both sides were cajoled into amended positions to accommodate new arrivals.

It was around five o'clock when the singing began. The cannon duel had petered to nothing, and the big sakers and demi-culverins seeped smoke from silent muzzles, their barrels hissing as the unrelenting rain pattered. Some of the smaller pieces engaged in their own duel, the higher-pitched spitting of drake minions and falconets continuing where their monstrous cousins had ceased. But in the main there was quiet, and out of that quiet came voices.

'The enemy don white paper in their hats,' a haughty messenger with russeted armour and hair in glossy ringlets called down to Stryker as he cantered past.

'Paper?'

'Or handkerchiefs.' The horse continued by so that he had to twist hard to keep hold of the conversation. 'We, therefore, shall wear none!'

Stryker knuckled the edge of his hat. 'Field word?'

'*God and the King!*'

As Stryker turned to pass on the order, a wave of sound rolled down from the slopes and flooded the moor, deep in tone but temperate, pleasant even. The Royalist army seemed collectively to hold its breath.

'Psalms,' Lieutenant Hood said.

Faith nudged her pony forwards. 'It is beautiful.'

'Aye,' Stryker said. All across the ridge, the armies of Parliament and Scotland sang together, voices rising and falling in unison. It was jarring in so martial a scene, yet he could not deny the strange, raw beauty of it.

'They sing psalms!' a man's voice, risen to a childlike pitch, ripped through the chorus. 'I knew it! We stand here, fearful and silent while the righteous worship on high!' He was dressed in the leather and steel of a harquebusier, but he had dismounted, staggering across the open ground between the foot brigades that made up the second line of Rupert's infantry and the cavalry reserve commanded by Crane, Widdrington and Stryker. He reeled away from his horse, turning a full circle and staring up at the sullen sky, raindrops soaking his face. 'Oh, Jesu, we are lost! All is lost!'

'Shut him up, for Christ's sake!' Crane's voice bellowed from further along the line.

An officer with a silver-capped blackthorn cane spurred his white mount from one of the nearby horse brigades. 'Smith!' he called. 'Get back to your saddle, sir, this instant!'

Smith laughed a crazed, manic cackle. 'Doom and damnation is all we may find on this cursed moor!'

The officer bore down on the ranting trooper, hitting him hard with the blackthorn. 'To your saddle, man!'

Smith seemed not to notice. 'Do you not hear them, my lord? They do sing their psalms, for they know they are Godly and they know they will carry this day.' The officer caned him again and this time the moon-eyed harquebusier stumbled to his horse. 'God is on their side, my brothers!' he called as he clambered into the saddle. 'He is on their side! We shall be routed! Do you hear me? Routed, and scattered and slaughtered like hogs!'

A brace of drakes spluttered into life from halfway up the hillside, their bounty screaming over the heads of the foot brigades, dipping as they raced between Stryker's troop and Crane's. The woodland crackled behind as branches severed and fell.

Smith laughed again as his horse walked back to his own section. 'I will be slain!' he yelled. 'Jesu, help me, I will be slain this day!' His officer, shepherding his return, snapped a rebuke. Smith lurched to the side and vomited. 'God damn me!' he spluttered as a stream of greenish bile soaked his thigh. The drakes barked again. 'God sink me!'

The blood came before the vomit ceased. The drake bullet, all five careening pounds of it, took Smith in the stomach. He folded in half, dropping the reins and clawing helplessly as his guts spilled down his horse's flank. Then he was off, toppling face first in the grass. His mount went back to its meal. The Royalist ranks stared, and the Allies sang. A drummer played a solitary rhythm that might almost have been a lament, except that a trumpet call joined in, and then a shouted order and another drum, and Stryker looked to his left, past the Lifeguard and the long line of troopers under Colonel Widdrington. From the direction of the city, entering the field behind banners of distinct red and white, at long last, came the Northern Foot.

# CHAPTER 19

'Move those guns!' Prince Rupert of the Rhine shouted at the cowering gun captain. He pointed to a hummock of rising ground that blemished the flat moor close to the ditch. 'The hump, there. It will be more advantageous.'

The gun captain, commanding a battery of four small field pieces that had been playing upon the horse of the Allied left wing to virtually no effect, scrunched up the shiny skin of his powder-burned face. 'It is closer to them, Highness.'

'It will be better drained.' Rupert glanced pointedly at the half-buried wheels of a smoking robinet. 'You will not sink.'

'Very well, Highness.' The gunner doffed his cap.

Prince Rupert steered his stallion away, cursing his subordinates as roundly as his warbling enemy. His only prayer was that the Roundheads would attempt an advance upon the ditch that was shielded by thorny hedge and lined with muskets. He kicked hard when he saw the red flag of the Marquis of Newcastle bobbing above the densely packed bodies filling the moor, because it was not a small cornet, rippling on the breeze at the head of horsemen, but the huge square of taffeta carried by an ensign of foot.

'It has been a long wait,' he said bluntly as the leading man, riding before the colour on a sleek charger, took off a yellow-feathered hat to let his tightly curled red hair flow free.

James King, first Lord Eythin, set his sharp chin. 'I have had to drag the men from the enemy camp.'

'So I understand,' Rupert said, bending slightly at the waist as the Marquis of Newcastle reined in beside him on the liveried warhorse that had been brought with his coach. He looked again at the marquis's military adviser. 'Saps lined with treacle, were they, General King?'

'It is Lord Eythin now, sir,' the Scot replied coldly.

'And it is Highness, as it ever was, General King.' Rupert appraised the broad column of pikemen and musketeers that trudged on to the field. Each banner denoted a new company. He was privately so relieved that his insides churned, for there were thousands, and a large proportion wore the white of Newcastle's highly regarded regiment. 'Your tardiness has thrown away the opportunity to attack while they were in disarray.'

Eythin bridled. 'And your eagerness to dash men against a superior foe does you no credit.'

Newcastle raised his hands for calm. 'Let us dispense with this foolishness, gentlemen. It is undignified in front of the men.'

Rupert nodded grudgingly and took a sheet of paper from the neckline of his breastplate. He handed it to Eythin. 'I have marshalled the army thusly. What say you?'

Eythin scanned the sketch, shaking his head before he had even looked up. 'I do not approve, sir, for it is drawn too near the enemy, and set at heinous disadvantage.'

Rupert glowered. 'The Roundheads are compelled to cross the ditch, yonder.'

'While we are compelled to advance up a steep hill.'

The prince sucked at his upper lip, then sighed. 'I will consider withdrawing to a distance deemed safer, if that please you gentlemen?'

'No, sir,' Eythin replied before his patron could open his mouth. 'It is almost six of the clock. Too late in the day for battle. We must look to rest the men before nightfall.'

'I would fight yet,' Rupert said.

The Scot fixed him with a stare few risked. 'Sir, your forwardness lost us the day in Germany, where yourself was taken prisoner.'

'I was took prisoner, General,' Rupert's retort was caustic, 'on account of a cavalry charge which would certainly have succeeded had it been properly supported by your own troops.'

'Gentlemen,' Newcastle cut in plaintively, 'this brings us nothing but consternation. What say you, Your Highness? Will you consider an action upon the morrow?'

There followed a period of silence as prince, marquis and lord eyed one another. The singing on the ridge had ceased, as if the entire Allied army awaited their decision. 'Move your foot to the right of the formation, General King,' Rupert commanded eventually. The robinets he had relocated opened up a new barrage to break the spell. 'I would have them in place should matters take a turn. But send men to bring provisions out of York. We will make camp here for the night and see what the morrow brings.'

Lieutenant-General Oliver Cromwell thanked the pioneers as they finished their work. The warren, installed at Bilton Bream to feed the villagers of Tockwith, had long since broken its man-made limits, and burrows infected the slope like syphilis in flesh. But the team of surly Scots, wielding shovels with calloused hands and brawny shoulders, had done their job well, and a smooth causeway split the pitted terrain so that the soil would not prove hazardous for his beloved harquebusiers. Moreover, the wall and hedge perimeter had been cut through, leaving nothing but a clear run down which any attack could be launched.

'Will you allow me, Uncle?'

Cromwell bit his lip as he curbed his huge destrier, Blackjack, the beast grumbling as the robinets down on the moor opened up on their position. 'Nay, Valentine, I will not.'

'Uncle—' said the boy to his right, who was mounted on an admirably docile mare.

Cromwell stared at the modest hillock beside the ditch that was shrouded now in thick cloud and where the crews worked furiously. 'Nay, Captain Walton,' he repeated, the official title a rebuke in itself, 'and calm your temper before the men. Leven has command.' He pointed behind, up at the crest near the knoll on the far side that marked the highest point. 'The battery there will give a salvo to mark the advance.'

Valentine Walton grimaced but decided to relent. 'The ditch will not be easy to negotiate. They have shot therein, I am certain.'

'Undoubtedly.'

The Royalist guns at their new position erupted again. This time the trajectory was good, and their shot flew devilishly close, roaring between the troopers on both sides. The horses made their fears known, skittering sideways with shaken heads and restless hooves. Cromwell called for calm, and his men reformed.

'Perhaps we will not attack,' his nephew said. 'The Northern Foot has arrived. Impetus is lost.'

'Aye, perhaps,' Cromwell said. 'Remember the Book of Acts, nephew: *To do whatsoever thine hand, and thy council had determined before to be done.*' He pointed skyward. 'The Lord has determined all. There is no impetus, no opportunity, without He who has determined it. We must pray, and allow events to fall into their rightful places.'

It was then that the last of the guns, having misfired during the full salvo, finally loosed its charge. The ball whined as it traced the slope, only halting when it shattered Walton's kneecap.

Stryker gave the order to stand down.

As the duel between the opposing gun crews had reignited, the foremost sections of the Allied army had moved a short way down the slope in the hopes of drawing the Royalists across the protective ditch, but Rupert had evidently not been swayed. Indeed, the directive to rest had come almost immediately. They were to keep formation, remain all night in line of battle to block the enemy's route to York, but save their strength for the morning. The men complained, of course, for the moor was rapidly deteriorating into a morass, and the rain kept falling, but supplies were promised from York and their bellies would soon be full.

The Marquis of Newcastle had retired to his coach to dine, and his personal cavalry unit had escorted it from the field, returning, Stryker assumed, to the comforts of York. Prince Rupert had declined to accompany the marquis, preferring to remain with his army, but he had taken his Lifeguard, under Sir Richard Crane, to the north, seeking privacy from the rabble of his common soldiers and the fury of the cannon.

The rest of the cavalry reserve, Stryker's men among them, dismounted and walked their horses to the trees a short distance to the north. Some tethered the animals to the outermost trunks while others went to collect kindling from the drier depths within the forest, but most watched as the Northern Foot made their way on to the moor.

Field command of Newcastle's pikemen and musketeers devolved to Sir Francis Mackworth as the units began to take their places within the main infantry body. It would be time-consuming, for there were several thousand, but no full engagement was expected. Time was something they had in abundance.

As they came through behind their great, swaying banners, Stryker was able to see the pattern, hitherto known only to the High Command, gradually resolve. The regiment of Colonel Cheater and the smaller detachment of Derbyshire foot were forced to move over to the left to accommodate the latecomers, in order that the men released from York could take up position on the right-hand side of the infantry formation.

With Newcastle's forces, the foot brigades would be deployed in three lines across the centre of the open moor. Each body – or battaile – in mirror of their counterparts on the rising ground, placed their pikes in a dense block, flanked on both sides by parties of musketeers. The hardened veterans of the Irish wars, under the unflappable Henry Tillier, had long since held the front row, and they would remain in position. The second row was comprised of seven bodies, which had been deliberately arranged to cover the gaps between the units in front, and it looked to Stryker as though four – from Cheater's, Chisenall's and the Derbyshire men – had been joined by three of Newcastle's. The third line, forming up immediately in front of his own horsemen, contained the last of the Northern Foot, Newcastle's whitecoats, supported by a brigade of horse.

Mercifully, the rain ebbed. Someone sang. It was no hymn,

but a bawdy ditty from a dockyard or tavern, and the men laughed and bellowed along, revelling in the contrast with the men on the high ground. A wagon came up – the first, they hoped, of many – and its hogsheads of ale were broken open and distributed as the genesis of a hundred small fires flickered into life and the musty depths of snapsacks were plumbed for food.

Yet all the while they took their beer and bread, the gun batteries played out a private contest. Over on the left – the enemy right – the muzzles flashed to little effect, but to the right, up at the place of decrepit cony warrens where the first of the day's blood had been shed, the hitherto tight-knit lines of Eastern Association cavalry were in disarray as a single nest of Royalist guns caused havoc from a raised scrap of moorland. Stryker had stayed to watch as volleys barked back and forth, but now he turned Vos towards the wood as his own stomach gave complaint.

'The Prince sees sense, Lord!' a familiar voice hooted at his back. 'You told me he would, and he did!'

Stryker froze. He wheeled Vos round. It was just after seven o'clock, still daytime for July, but the malevolent skies brought on a dusky veil that made him squint at the face before him. 'Seek Wisdom?'

A grin of rotten gums opened like a black slash across the white-bearded face. 'The Lord told me, boy.' The old man, cloaked and hooded, jerked a gnarled thumb over his shoulder to indicate the successful battery. 'That prince, the Lord said, will put his bloody guns where they won't sink! And Hallelujah for that! 'Tis Cromwell up there, did you know? His bastards are the best horse they got, boy. Need to kill 'em first!' He tapped his nose with a finger. 'They're good troops, boy. Godly, pious.'

'Piety does not make a man swift with steel, Father,' Stryker chided.

'They're Puritans, boy! Is your mind full of mould? You listen to us, boy; me and the good Lord above. Those bastard horsemen are deeply religious. Not in a wise, thoughtful way like myself, you understand, but hard-nosed and unswerving. Their dogma is one of Predestination. You know what that is?'

'That all things are fated by God. Man can change nothing.'

The craggy face creased deeply. 'A creed which tends to make its adherents fear nothing. Nothing! It makes 'em brave, boy, and it makes 'em ruthless, and it makes 'em mad as rabid badgers. You'll not break those bastards, boy, for they do not fear death!'

'Keep yourself hushed, Father,' Stryker warned, 'lest you wish to frighten the men.'

Seek Wisdom and Fear the Lord Gardner winked, twirled about like an acrobat, and cupped palms at his mouth as he bellowed at the nearest of Brownell's troopers. 'Worry not, boys, for we will win this fight! The ugliest man in Christendom doth fight the foe!' He pointed at Stryker. 'They'll ignore your blades and run from him!'

Stryker slid down from the saddle, boots squelching. 'It is good to see you.'

'Likewise, boy,' the priest said, shaking the soldier's proffered hand. He let his ice-blue eyes drift over Stryker's shoulder. 'Sergeant Skellen. Mister Barkworth.'

Barkworth and Skellen had walked out of the wood edge, Faith a little way behind, and both greeted him warmly.

''Tis a melancholy sort of eve,' Gardner went on. 'Thus, the Lord demands I provide some amusement, do you not, Lord?' He turned with a wink. 'So feast your eyes on this!'

'Cap'n Forrester, sir!' Skellen exclaimed on seeing the officer stride from a group who had been in deep conversation.

Forrester offered an ostentatious bow, plucking off his hat. 'Well met, my friends. Damn me, but you are well met indeed.'

Stryker shook his hand. Forrester's sandy hair was thinner than he remembered, and the corners of his eyes bore new lines. 'A hard few months, Forry.' He threw a soft punch at the captain's shoulder, where a blue and red cross had been stitched over the red wool of his regimental coat. 'And what is this?'

Forrester blushed immediately. 'An award from the Marquis.'

'Valour, boy!' Father Gardner cackled, shifting his weight from foot to foot. 'Did I not pledge to amuse? Bloody valour!'

'They recognize it here,' Forrester said stiffly.

'Pah!' Gardner scoffed. He began to walk away. 'My prayers are needed with the regiment, Stryker, but the good captain will regale you, I'm certain!'

'You must regale us,' said Stryker, fixing Forrester with a wry smile. 'Come.'

The guns kept firing as they went over to the trees and the skeleton encampment. 'You are well, sir?'

Forrester nodded as he took bread from Thomas Hood. The group gathered under a thickly leafed bough that kept the rain at bay. 'As can be expected. In truth,' he added, looking out towards the moor, 'I had thought to be lying dead by now.'

'Should have been fighting hours ago,' Hood agreed.

'But it seems my lord Eythin fancied a stroll from York, rather than a march. I swear he did it to irk His Highness.'

Stryker had wondered the same during their day stood to arms. 'Eythin blames Rupert for the defeat at Vlotho, back in thirty-eight.'

'You fought there, did you not, sir?' Hood asked.

'I was captured with the Prince, Tom, aye. Shared a dungeon with him. Rupert was barely a man back then, but he was just as you see him now.'

'All glare and fury.'

Stryker laughed. 'Aye.'

'Was it his fault?'

'Vlotho? Nay, I do not think so. But his action did not help matters.'

'Thus, our delay eats up the light,' Forrester said. 'Marquis and prince do retire to York for the night, but the rest of us must sit in the rain and watch the Roundheads.' He glanced sideways at Faith Helly. 'Though, perhaps your companion would be better served within the city walls? The guns will continue, I've no doubt. The danger will not pass with darkness.'

'I remain, sir,' Faith answered firmly.

'I present to you,' Stryker cut in, reading Forrester's baffled face, 'Mistress Fight the Good Fight of Faith Helly.' He looked at Faith. 'Mistress, this is Captain Lancelot Forrester. A rake and a wastrel and a fine Cavalier. You will detest him.'

Forrester bowed low. 'Your servant.'

She eyed him coolly. 'Captain.'

'You fire a musket?' The corner of Forrester's mouth twitched as she shook her head. 'Then—?'

Stryker said, 'We met at Bolton, Forry.'

'Bolton?' Forrester's brow furrowed; then his eyes widened. 'We heard tell of a terrible massacre there.'

'Aye.'

'Major Stryker rescued me,' Faith said. 'Saved me from the Vulture.'

'A man named John Kendrick,' Stryker explained.

Skellen spat. 'Bad apple, if ever there was one.'

'Kendrick?' Lancelot Forrester said. 'I have heard the name.'

Stryker nodded. 'He has repute. Fought the savages in the New World, though his own savagery garnered the reputation.'

'No, old man,' Forrester replied, staring at the damp ground as though he could dig some long lost memory from beneath the leaf mulch. He looked up sharply. 'He was spoken of in York. By Ezra Killigrew.'


'And I commend Captain Valentine Walton, my beloved sister's beloved son, to You, oh Lord. That You settle exquisite peace upon him, peace that passeth all understanding, as he fights for his life. Grant him healing, Lord, for You do not test a man with more than he may bear. If, however, his passing is ordained by Your almighty hand, then take him swift and sure and painless unto Your house.'

Oliver Cromwell opened his eyes. The drake's shot had mangled the mid-section of his nephew's leg, almost severing it at the joint, and the lad, bleeding profusely, had been dragged back to Long Marston where saw-wielding chirurgeons would doubtless finish the job. Cromwell silently mulled the difficult letter he would soon have to write as he watched the troublesome Royalist gun emplacement explode in flame once more.

'Major-General Crawford!' he shouted when the noise had faded.

Crawford, the Earl of Manchester's chief of infantry, had ridden up to review the disposition of his men nearest the flank, and Cromwell, on seeing his colour, had demanded an audience. Now Crawford was at Bilton Bream, watching stony-faced as the grim harquebusiers fought to keep their snorting mounts calm under the heavy fire. 'General?'

'This heat is too much to bear,' Cromwell called. 'Get a battery of guns in place at the bottom of the slope.'

'The bottom?' Crawford balked.

'Do you have wool packed into your ears, sirrah?'

'No, General.' Crawford stared at the moor. Was it his responsibility to protect Cromwell's treasured troopers? They were both generals, after all. 'They have musketeers in the ditch.'

'Then send your own body o' shot,' Cromwell snarled. 'Two field pieces, with two regiments to protect them. Let our guns dispose of that wretched position. I will not have my riders threatened so.'

'General Cromwell, I—'

'General Crawford!' Cromwell ripped across his protest. 'It was your folly disgraced the Eastern Association before York! God offers you an honourable counterbalance. Take it, sir. Our field word will be *God with us*!'

Crawford swallowed hard. 'Sir.'

Cromwell nodded. 'Does not Ephesians tell us to redeem the time in these evil days? Redeem the time, General Crawford. Redeem the time for the honour of the Eastern Association and the glory of God.'

On Marston Moor, Stryker explained their journey with Faith from Bolton's carnage to the walls of York by way of the kidnap attempts by the Vulture's men. 'Kendrick is dangerous. Takes pleasure in the pain of others.'

'And now he has vanished?' Forrester asked. 'Good riddance to him.'

'Tell me again,' Stryker said. 'You heard Killigrew speak of him?'

'I eavesdropped upon a conversation. The name Kendrick was uttered, I'm certain of it.'

'And who was it Killigrew addressed?'

Forrester shrugged. 'One whose voice I did not recognise and whose face I did not see. An Irishman.'

'What was said? On what hook was the Vulture's name dangled?'

'Killigrew referred to himself as the hammer,' Forrester said. 'Kendrick is his nail. Kendrick was supposed to locate something for him. A flagon, I believe he said.'

'The golden flagon,' Stryker mused. 'He has been searching for it ever since.'

'And he was hunting you, Mistress?' Forrester asked, looking at Faith. 'You have this flagon?'

Faith was holding her Bible. She held it up. 'This was Master Sydall's golden flagon, though I did not know it until recently.'

'Look in the centre pages,' Stryker said. 'And there is more in the back.'

Forrester took the book and leafed through it. 'It is the means to decipher disguised text.' He looked sharply at Faith. 'A spy, madam?'

'No, sir.'

'Then how came you by this?'.

'Bolton-le-Moors,' Faith explained. 'Master Sydall owned the book. I took it, seeking nothing but Scripture within.'

Forrester looked at Stryker. 'Sydall was a spy, then?'

'Evidently.'

'One of theirs, or ours?'

'Not yours,' Faith interrupted hotly. 'Never yours.'

'He was a strong Puritan,' Stryker said.

Forrester's mouth turned down at the corners. 'Stranger things have happened.'

'He hated the King, sir,' Faith insisted. 'He would rather die than help your cause.'

'Charmed, young madam, I'm sure,' Forrester replied. He turned back to Stryker. 'But do we not have our explanation? Sydall, a rebel spy, has a cipher hidden in his Bible; *this* Bible. Killigrew hears of it, given his own line of work, and decides he wants it, so he sends his creature to fetch.'

'Ezra Killigrew wanted the cipher,' Simeon Barkworth muttered, a breathless whisper below the musket crackle that suddenly flared near the ditch. 'Bloody hell.' He put his head in his hands. 'Bloody hell. And we've been hiding it.' He looked up, pinning Stryker with his glowing stare. 'We're in for trouble now.'

There followed a pause as each man regarded the other. Out on the moor, the spiteful scrap grew hotter by the moment as the Parliamentarian escort came under heavy fire from the Royalist musketeers lining the ditch. The opposing gun emplacements, a matter of yards apart now, billowed smoke and fury at intervals, the ground shaking in reply.

Hood broke the deadlock. 'But why such effort? Why not simply kill the spy?'

'The cipher is more important than the life,' Forrester replied. He blew out his cheeks in exasperation and regarded the Bible in his hand. He thumbed it open, flicking through the pages.

Stryker shook his head. 'Then why not send the entire army against him? Why just one man and his company? I challenged Kendrick at Liverpool. Dared him to go to the Prince with what he knew.'

'And?'

Stryker shrugged. 'He tried to poison me instead. Tried to take Mistress Helly. Fled when he failed.'

Forrester looked up. His blue eyes round. 'King Jesus and all his wounds.'

'What is it?'

Forrester had reached the end of the Bible. 'You have a list of animals here.'

'Aye, denoting some command or place or name, I know not which.'

'I do,' Forrester said. 'They're names.'

Stryker glanced at the others. 'How can you possibly know?'

'Because the Irishman referred to himself as *dog*. He was not best pleased with the name, but Killigrew would entertain no complaint.' He stabbed the page with his finger. 'There you have it. *Dog*. Dog is the Irishman.' His face was taut with excitement as he stared at Stryker. 'Suffer it, that's what Killigrew told him. Suffer it, or find alternative employment. It is reasonable to assume, then, that Killigrew is one of these other creatures.'

Skellen peered over the page, scanning the list. 'My groat's on *eagle*.'

'Ezra Killigrew,' Stryker whispered the name. 'By Jesu.'

Faith Helly's eyes had been darting from one face to the next, trying to follow. Now she placed a hand on Stryker's arm. 'Ezra Killigrew?'

'A spymaster; for the King.'

She paused as the implication settled, then said: 'And for the Parliament?'

Stryker nodded. 'He did not receive intelligence of the existence of this cipher. He knew all along, because he is part of it. He knew Sydall was a spy, because they worked with one another.'

'This is a dangerous path to tread,' Forrester muttered quietly. 'Killigrew is a turncoat. A double agent.' He swallowed thickly, breathed deeply, and swore viciously. 'Then why suddenly turn on Sydall? They are not enemies, but colleagues. Why take the cipher? Why murder him?'

'Because he feared what we would find,' Stryker replied. The pieces were falling into place even as he uttered the words. 'He knew we advanced upon Bolton, did he not?'

'Undoubtedly,' Forrester affirmed. 'York was not cut off until the Eastern Association arrived. Until that point we had information freely.'

'He hears Prince Rupert plans to assault Bolton,' Stryker went on, mind racing, 'fears that Sydall will be taken. Fears Sydall will give him up to save his own hide. So he plots to have Sydall killed in the assault, and to take the cipher – the golden flagon, as he knows it – for good measure, lest his own name appear therein.'

'But does the cipher damn him?' Faith asked.

'We cannot know of their secret discourse without their correspondence,' Stryker said. 'But the presence of his name in a rebel cipher itself is damnation enough. Killigrew is likely the eagle, our Irishman the dog, and Kendrick will be some other creature.'

'We cannot prove it,' Forrester warned.

'Not without a corresponding message,' Stryker agreed, 'but one such as Killigrew would kill a hundred men to avoid the risk.'

'Surprised that Irisher would work for the Banbury-men, sir,' Skellen mused.

'He does not necessarily know he is, Sergeant. He – and Kendrick, for that matter – are loyal to Killigrew. They do as they're told, and no more. They probably knew nothing of Killigrew's duplicity. Sydall was a Parliamentarian through and through. The Irishman is probably Royalist through and through, and Kendrick cares not for which side his colours fly. He follows coin and nought else. The only true traitor in this is Ezra Killigrew.' A thought struck him then, one that stole the breath from his chest. He remembered the gold he had been sent to recover from the island of Tresco the previous autumn, and the rebel agent who had so nearly foiled him. 'Tainton.'

Forrester frowned. 'Roger Tainton? What of him?'

'How did he know where to find the Cade treasure?'

'Never discovered that particular nugget of information, did we?' Forrester stopped suddenly. 'Killigrew?'

'I asked him. I asked Tainton, before I killed him.' Stryker's mind returned to the fortress of Basing House. 'He laughed at me.'

'And now we know why, old friend. Now we know why.'

'*To arms!*'

Stryker looked round. A brightly dressed herald galloped between the trees.

'To arms!' the herald shouted again, weaving deeper into the undergrowth. 'All men to arms!'

The musketry was thick now, crashing over the whole moor from the westernmost end of the ditch. Drums boomed; events were moving fast. Stryker led Vos out on to the open ground, his group immediately behind, clambering into the saddle to improve his line of sight. Forrester had handed back the Bible and was already running towards the red and white banners of Sir Edmund Mowbray's Regiment of Foot.

Over on the right of the Royalist front line, large sections of infantry were moving. Drums gave the order to advance, and from Stryker's position, behind the centre, he could see a huge square of black and white taffeta swirl in a figure of eight through the hedges of pikes that rose like a steel-tipped forest. The colour was marked with black piles streaking over a white field, with black amulets set diagonally across the centre like the eyes of peacock feathers. 'Rupert's bluecoats are on the move.'

Lieutenant Hood reined in at his side. 'And Bryon's lads.'

On the Royalist right wing, immediately in front of Lord Bryon's two and a half thousand cavalry, was a single brigade of foot formed in three bodies. They were advancing towards the hedged ditch to bolster the musketeers who poured heavy fire into the Allied infantry escorting their guns. The whole area was wreathed in dirty smog.

Stryker twisted round. 'You must go,' he said to Faith.

'You said there would be no battle. That it was too late.'

'Momentum,' he said, pointing to the fight at the ditch. 'No order for battle has been given, and yet men are sucked into the fray. What wagons remain are deeper into the wood. Find them.'

She kissed the Bible and then waved it at him. 'You will need this, Major.'

'I had thought—'

'That you would have to rip it from my fingers?' she said with a wry smile. 'You need God's Word now more than I. And you will need this,' she added, tossing it to Stryker, 'to catch your traitor.'

He caught the book. 'But you have a rebel heart, Mistress. Killigrew is no traitor to you.'

'He is the man who ordered a good family slain,' she said. 'I want you to snare him for me, Major Stryker. I want justice. The Bible is your proof.'

Stryker nodded, slipping the Bible into his saddlebag and shooed the girl away. And then, from up on the ridge, a massive barrage of Parliamentarian guns shattered the dusk.

The Earl of Leven had watched as the Royalist troops prepared to settle down for the night, turning his next move over in his mind. And then events had slipped out of his grip, because out on the left flank, Oliver Cromwell had attacked the ditch.

'Give the signal,' he had said, quietly at first, but then louder.

The Earl of Manchester was waiting nearby, and he had ridden immediately to Leven's side. 'It is too late in the day, my lord. Far too late. Night draws swift.'

Leven had rounded on him. 'Open your eyes, sirrah!' He indicated the long ditch, fringed with hedges, that divided the opposing armies. At the western extremity it was almost completely obscured by smoke, only the flashes of muzzles glimmering through the miasma. 'Your own lieutenant-general has begun matters in spite of our timidity. We must follow his example.'

The volley exploded from the mouths of the biggest field pieces and the whole hillock seemed to shudder under the force; up above it was as though God Himself gave His blessing, for the heavens gave like reply, splitting open in a bolt of lightning and a clap of thunder that rumbled for miles in all directions. The drums – each unit's beating heart – began, and the shrill cries of a hundred trumpets joined the cacophony as the entire Allied army surged down the slope. Out on the wings, thousands upon thousands of horsemen kicked their mounts to the gallop, while in the centre, as Leven screamed them on, the foot regiments – brigaded in pairs and clustered in their pike-hearted battailes – made for the flat ground and the deadly ditch. In the first line of foot, Lawrence Crawford had soldiers from both English armies, while the Scots were commanded by Major-General William Baillie. The second line was constructed entirely of Scottish Covenanters, Leven's granite fulcrum, while Lord Fairfax and the Earl of Manchester took personal command of their brigades in the third line. Leven, remaining with a reserve of his doughty Scots, held the crest and watched the Army of Both Kingdoms march to war.

'Our moment is opportune,' he whispered as his vast horde, one of the largest ever assembled in the kingdoms of Britain, trampled the rich Yorkshire corn. 'If God be with us, who can be against us?'

The battle of Marston Moor had begun.

# CHAPTER 19

The Royalist army had not been ready. The majority were resting, if not asleep then seated cross-legged and unsuspecting, weapons thrown to the grass and matches snuffed cold. The desperate cries to arms had been repeated by officers from the ditch to the wood, from Tockwith to Long Marston, and yet still, as the vast Allied line swarmed like Moses' locusts towards them, they struggled to rouse themselves. The Northern Foot were not fully deployed; many of the horse, especially the reserve nearest Wilstrop Wood, had slipped into the trees. Regardless of the cannon duel that had raged for most of the evening, they had simply not expected to fight. Moreover, the supreme commanders of both their armies, Rupert and Newcastle, had apparently left the field, and were nowhere to be found.

As Stryker stood tall in his stirrups to look across the field, he saw only an army stricken with inertia. And down the slope, at a running march, came the enemy. He turned away as the first shots rang out from the front-most Royalist ranks, plumes of bitter smoke rising to mark the unseen musketeers, and galloped across the face of his inherited troop, urging calm. Something hard knocked against his knee. He glanced down, noticing the curve of the secrete, purchased from the sutler in Ribchester. A half-smile crossed his lips as he delved inside to retrieve the steel cap. He removed his hat and planted the felt-lined secrete flush against his skull. Then he clamped the hat over the top, pressing it down hard. It felt strange, unwieldy, yet, staring out at the surging tide of Roundheads and Scots, he did not feel inclined to remove it.

He drew up at his troop's right flank, loading both pistols and packing them tight with wadding before returning them to their holsters. He slid his sword in and out of its scabbard, knowing it would not stick but checking anyway, and then he looked round. Skellen, Hood and Barkworth were behind him, mounted and ready.

'God and the King,' he said.

'God and the King,' Lieutenant Hood echoed. His face was pale and strained, but he would fight with a clarity of mind he had not possessed for far too long, and the sight encouraged Stryker more than the young man would ever know. 'And God preserve us.'

'We'll drink King Charlie's health after,' Barkworth said, eyes like orbs of molten gold in the storm-darkened murk.

Skellen hawked up a gobbet of phlegm, spitting it to the hoof-mashed soil. 'God and the King, sir,' he droned, 'and a pox on the Parliament.' His halberd, knotted with twine at each end of its shaft, was lashed across his spine, and he adjusted it before drawing his sword. 'Now let us go to war.'

Sir Thomas Fairfax cantered down the ridge at the head of the Allied right-wing horse. '*God with us!*' he screamed. 'God with us!'

He had no clue as to what had transpired. They had stood all day on the ridge, braving weather and fatigue, only for a scrap to flare out to the west. Then all of a sudden, like a pipe's tiny dripping fracture splitting to become a deluge under the sheer weight of water, it had all happened. More and more men had come into contact with the enemy guarding the ditch, and Leven had evidently decided that it was simpler to attack than perform a dangerous withdrawal. Ultimately, the whys and wherefores did not matter. The signal had been given. Now Black Tom held his breath.

Ahead, where the slope petered into flat moorland, the smoke slewed sideways a yard or two from the ground to betray the beginnings of Royalist defensive fire. It marked, too, the line of the hedged ditch that ran from east to west through the moor.

The ditch was the dividing line between the men of the Crown and those of Parliament, the obstacle his horsemen would be forced to cross. To his left, further behind as the advance opened up, the Allied infantry marched to the deep clamour of their drums, and further still, though he could not see through the impenetrable thickets of pikes, he knew the left-wing horse under Cromwell would be keeping pace with his own. He prayed loudly. He was not a man to show his devotions so publicly, but if he did not, he knew he would be physically sick.

He spurred on, gripping the reins tightly. Up ahead, the terrain was treacherous, for the land immediately to the right was made impassable by the beginnings of Long Marston village, its outbuildings and enclosures cluttering the landscape and clogging any flanking manoeuvre. It meant that he would have to cross the smoking ditch by way of a narrow passage their maps referred to as Atterwith Lane. To the left of the lane, the ditch was deep and artificially banked to make it steep, while to the right it was fringed with thick hedging. He knew they would be hard-pressed to force a way through, so he kicked forth, plumping for speed over caution.

They reached the lane in three broad lines. Sir Thomas took personal command of the first, Colonel John Lambert the second, and the Covenanter, Lord Eglinton, the third. They reached a gallop at the last moment, Sir Thomas's front line funnelling into the lane in order to smash its way through. The rest could not hope to follow the same route, so they jumped the ditch, some clearing it, others not, and smashed straight into the hedge, trying to cleave ragged fissures with blades and hooves.

The musketeers opened fire.

George Goring commanded the opposing wing of horse, but it was his supporting infantry that showed themselves first. They were beyond the ditch, crouching, lying, and now firing in a huge, juddering volley that rippled all the way across Sir Thomas's line. He shrank down in the saddle, galloping into the lane, as men screamed around about him. He saw a young cornet punched into mid-air, flag twirling, by a leaden ball that shattered his ribs. Somewhere behind, a shriek and whinny announced the tumble of a horse.

Smoke shrouded everything as he raked spurs into his horse's flesh and drew his sword. His men were riding four abreast now, so narrow was the lane, and the rain made their hooves slip alarmingly in the clinging mud. A gust of wind shifted the bitter fog to reveal more musketeers some fifty paces up ahead. They fired. Sir Thomas gritted his teeth until he tasted blood, and clenched his buttocks to keep from voiding his bowels. More men died, but they were building their speed, and he knew they would hit the infantrymen before they could reload.

The line of Royalist musketeers splintered like dry wood as Sir Thomas's first troopers burst through. He bellowed a war-cry as the hedge line began to fray, revealing space where before there had been only obstruction. He veered left, off the lane and through one of the gaps to the open moor. The Royalist infantry seemed to be everywhere, their shots sporadic now as formation disintegrated, and he saw that his three thousand horsemen were surging at all quarters in a wide, ragged wave. They had forced their way over the ditch bravely, but the price to pay had been disorder. It was too late to put that to rights, for the enemy could be afforded no time to regroup. He raked his spurs, feeling the upwelling of power, and roared for the charge to continue at all costs.

And then he saw the enemy cavalry. Goring had apparently decided to let his musketeers take the brunt of the attack, for his red-scarved horsemen were in good order, spanning the field in two lines, knee to knee, broken only where bodies of musketeers waited between them to give supporting fire. Sir Thomas wrenched around, looking back at his force, which was in dis-array. Three or four hundred men had traversed the lane at his back, and they were close enough to follow his lead. The rest, too spread out to advance with any cohesion, would have to fend for themselves. He dipped his head and angled his mount to bear down on the rightmost corner of the Cavalier front line. The enemy musketeers, arrayed amongst their horse, put down a tirade of musketry that rebounded across the moor, and then vanished behind the bodies of the snorting animals as the troopers came on, kicking into a canter with cornets bobbing and blades held aloft.

Sir Thomas Fairfax prayed, and he cursed, and he challenged death. And then he slammed into the Royalist line.

Immediately his horse faltered. They had run into a wall of horsemen, squeezed on both sides by grimacing Cavaliers who hacked and slashed at man and horse. Sir Thomas was tangled, his thighs crushed against those of his enemies, and he found himself parrying heavy blades on both sides, one with his sword, the other with his gauntleted forearm. One of the blows made it through and clanged against his breastplate, rocking him back so that his groin screamed in anguish as he gripped to stay in the saddle. He was vaguely aware of his own men, pushing in from behind, and he knew he could no longer retreat, even if he had a mind to. The opponent on his left hit him again, this time slipping past the gauntlet, and the cutting edge bounced off the crest of his pot. Sir Thomas saw the sword come down on his other side, parried it desperately, and instinctively cringed in expectation of the first man's follow-up thrust. But his helmet had sent the weapon glancing away with such a jolt that the hilt had slipped from his enemy's grip. The Cavalier's lips worked furiously behind steel bars as his empty hand fumbled at his saddle holster. Sir Thomas blocked another swipe on his right, then drew his own pistol, cocking it in one motion. Both men fired at once. The Royalist's arm was low, and Sir Thomas felt a judder ripple through his horse as the pistol ball thumped into its hindquarters. His own bullet had taken his would-be killer in the throat, and the man was already wilting sideways. Sir Thomas remembered the foe on his right, twisted round too late, and took a jabbing sword thrust to his own face, the point passing between the protective bars to jar against his cheekbone. It seared like a glowing brand, blinding him for a moment, and he braced for the final cut. The man screamed. Sir Thomas forced open his eyes to see his personal cornet, a dark-blue acanthus pattern over a blue field, jabbing time and again at the Cavalier's face. His standard-bearer was at his side, kicking his horse into the cacophonous press and using his banner as a lance.

Then they were through. The fight was raging away to Sir Thomas's left as the rest of his fragmented wing fell upon Goring's solid line, but the few hundred who had come along the lane with their general had carved a channel through the extreme edge, and those Royalists were peeling away, turning tail to bolt back in the direction of York. Sir Thomas bellowed for his men to leave them, to rein in their natural urge to pursue in order to turn the Royalist flank and surround the enemy. But they ignored him, too drunk with bloodlust to heed his cries, spurring into a whooping gallop to chase Goring's routing troopers. So Black Tom went too, praying that Colonel Lambert would have the same success against what remained of the Royalist left wing.

Whilst the Parliamentarian and Covenanter horsemen were crossing the ditch to the east, the Allied left wing was coming down from Bilton Bream at the walk. Opposite, on the Royalist right flank, John, Lord Byron, tugged at his freshly trimmed beard. His part of the moor was already veiled in smoke, but he could see enough glimpses of tawny scarves and the scraps of white paper tied to wrists or thrust into helmet visors to know that Cromwell's daunting horde was on the move.

Byron checked his pistols. His bodyguard, a burly Irishman who had been a wrestler and champion at the prize play, swung a loaded carbine across his back and nodded. Byron swallowed. It hurt, his mouth parched and sticky. He took a last look at the men under his command. In the front line were eleven hundred harquebusiers; the sum of Byron's own regiment, and those of Urry, Vaughn and Trevor, veterans all. On the extreme right, set slightly back in a protective stance, were two hundred more under Samuel Tuke, then a second full line, comprising the regiments of Molyneux, Tyldesley and Leveson, with the formidable sight of Rupert's own cavalry forming their left flank. Byron had two thousand, six hundred horse in all, and, though he reckoned they were outnumbered by the enemy horsemen, he had absolute faith in their ability. And that was why he was considering an attack.

He had been ordered to remain in position, to stand his ground, relying upon the ditch to disrupt any enemy attack. He had musketeers there too, both in the channel and on his side of the ditch, so that any advance by the Eastern Association would be met with heavy fire. And yet his cavalrymen were eager. Byron was eager. He looked at the big Irishman. 'Shall we give 'em a hiding, d'you think, O'Reilly?'

Oliver Cromwell, Lieutenant-General of Horse, thanked God for the gift of this sector, for it posed few of the questions being asked of his compatriot on the far side. There was still the gully, of course, defended by musketeers, but Tockwith's enclosures did not encroach upon the battlefield like those near Long Marston, nor were there any lanes or mature hedgerows to add complication. He could see the Royalist horse waiting for him on the far side of the obstacle. Moreover, the first throws of the fight had begun on this flank, and the enemy muskets were already entrenched within their own brawl, occupied by the tussle with Crawford's foot regiments that had earlier descended to support the cannon. As it was, Cromwell felt confident. He commanded his line to halt, then lifted his helmet's visor. 'Fraser!'

The extreme left of Cromwell's formation was made up of a regiment of Scottish dragoons, and their colonel, receiving the summons by a chain of shouts, peeled his mount away from his men and kicked it to Cromwell's side. 'General.'

Cromwell stole a brief glance at the ditch. 'As things stand, we must fight through those malignants.' He looked back at Fraser, the rain wetting his cheeks and stinging his eyes. 'And then, when disordered on the far side, we will be charged by Byron's horse.'

The Scot, a wiry man with a sharp, red nose and watery eyes, nodded. 'Aye, sir, that's the sum of it.'

'I would have your men ride down there, Colonel Fraser, and purge the ditch.'

Fraser's thin mouth pressed into a line. 'Purge, sir?'

Cromwell touched a hand to his chest. 'Beneath this cold steel,' he said, patting the plate, 'buttoned beside my heart, there is a pamphlet. A soldier's Bible. Sixteen pages containing nought but the word of God. They give fortitude to those who would fight the enemies of King Jesus.' He closed his eyes. 'Deuteronomy, chapter twenty, verse four: *For the Lord your God goeth with you, to fight for you against your enemies, and to save you.*' He fixed the dragoon colonel with an unflinching stare. 'God goeth with us, Fraser. We cannot lose. Now get your men down there and purge the ditch.'

The Scottish dragoons poured down the slope as Cromwell's plate-clad harquebusiers resumed their steady walk. Dragoons were mounted infantry and, as such, they carried muskets. Their function was speed and mobility. Their horses, though not as swift or powerful as those used by full cavalry, were able to move them around a battlefield with a swiftness traditional foot regiments could never match, and, as Cromwell looked on, he knew he had made the right decision. The dragoons slid free of their saddles within musket shot of the ditch, all the while drawing heavy fire, and immediately shrank behind the bodies of their horses for shelter. Then they were shooting back, protected by their shields of leather and flesh, and their concentrated volleys were far more effective than the desultory barks snapping up from the smoke-capped trench in response.

It was a matter of moments before the Royalist defenders were overwhelmed, and they fell back, scrambling up the north bank of the channel and running for their own lines, while the dragoons edged forth to secure their prize.

Cromwell lowered his visor, looking at Fraser. 'A fine job, Colonel. Your men did well. God grants them victory.'

Fraser dipped his face 'Thank you, General. May God grant you success also.'

Cromwell shook his head. 'God has preordained all. Pray for nought but His will.' He reached for his sword-hilt and bellowed: 'We ride out right away, good fellows, and fear no earthly enemy! King Jesus has brought victory to the righteous! We must simply give thanks, draw swords, and receive His bounty!' The long, heavy, single-edged blade was pulled free. 'God and Parliament!'

'God and Parliament!' the men echoed.

Cromwell spurred Blackjack into a gallop while praying to reach the ditch before his malignant counterpart could respond. A heavy jolt punched his hip, but God had given him a mind to don tassets this day, and leg armour beneath his buff-coat skirts, and one of those thick pieces mercifully deflected the ball. Then they moved, the Royalists, lurching forward in two deep lines. They were quickly at full speed, and their blades came loose, shimmering like a shoal of trout under the hoary clouds. Then they were leaping the ditch, whooping and laughing as though they rode to hounds. They were dashing and valiant, the flower of the king's court, mounted on expensive destriers shipped from France and waging war dressed in silk and feathers. At their head was Lord Byron's banner, flapping like the tongue of a vast serpent.

Oliver Cromwell could not believe what he was seeing. It was a miracle, and he praised God for it, because he did not have to cross the ditch. Instead he gave the signal for his wing to slow their advance and wait for the courageous enemy horsemen to come to them. For Lord Byron was very brave. And he was also, Cromwell realised, fatally foolish.

John, Lord Byron, knew he had made a mistake as soon as his dun-coloured gelding crossed the ditch. His men had been straining at their invisible leash and he had yearned to release them. And then the Scots dragoons had swept away his screen of musketeers, leaving a clear path for the waiting harquebusiers, and Byron had decided to seize the initiative before the Eastern Association cavalry had the chance to gather momentum.

By crossing the obstacle, Byron knew he had thrown away any advantage he had. His men in the ditch might have been scoured from their positions, but he yet had a strong body in reserve, and, had he been thinking clearly, he might have moved them up to pelt the advancing cavalry with a hail of lead. Now his front line of eleven hundred was further advanced than that reserve, blocking their line of sight, nullifying any muskets they might bring to bear. But more importantly, he had risked a crossing of the one barrier that would throw Cromwell on to the back foot by interrupting his neat formation. Now, Byron knew, it was his own men who would enter the fray confused and disordered.

He looked left and right, reassuring himself that his troopers had, at least, made it across with him. Of course they had, because they were the cream of his battle-forged killers. Men who had been at Edgehill, Burford and Cirencester, at Roundway Down and Newbury. Men who knew how to fight. But they were no longer set in their snug lines; they were being riven, splintered into small groups, gaps appearing all across what should have been a horse-flesh breastwork. And then the enemy were at the charge, and he felt his guts flip as their snarling faces bore down, lips pared back and eyes wide.

The first body of rebel horse hit them like a surging tide. Bryon saw steel and teeth. He had sword in hand, and he cleaved the air, aiming at nothing and everything at once. His gelding could not move. He reached for his pistol, clicked back its dog lock, fired into the mass, but already his ragged line was shunting backwards, pushed inexorably towards the ditch behind.

Byron called for his men to hold firm, to push back, and for a heartbeat hope soared within him as the momentum was wrested back, but then another body of Parliamentarian horse careened in behind the first, and their weight tipped the scales again. Byron caught a vague glimpse of a trooper squeezing his black stallion between two comrades to come face to face with him. His bodyguard, O'Reilly, was there immediately, and the trooper vanished as the big Irishman levelled his carbine and shot him square in the chest, but the stallion, frightened now, began to snap its grass-stained teeth at Byron's gelding. He found himself high up as his mount reared, jerked aloft as though he rode the crest of a wave. It took every ounce of his horsemanship to keep control. And in this moment he knew that the fight was lost, for his briefly raised vantage showed him a line of Royalist cavalry that was bowed and fragmented, and on the brink of collapse.

From his position on the right side of Rupert's cavalry reserve, Stryker watched the disintegration of Byron's first line with mounting horror. They had advanced, inexplicably, and it had cost them dearly.

He kicked hard, letting Vos take him across the face of his fifty harquebusiers, finding Sir Edward Widdrington out in front of his brigade. 'Where is the Prince?' he called. 'Where in hell's name is Rupert?'

Widdrington, an austere man in his early fifties, offered a meek shrug as he tugged his mare round to receive Stryker. 'We cannot find him. I have riders at the search.'

'Christ,' Stryker hissed. He pointed back in the direction of the Royalist right flank, where the cavalry battle raged beyond the ditch. 'Will you come, Sir Edward?'

'I will not, Sergeant-Major,' Widdrington snapped. 'By God, I will not. We are the reserve. Byron must attend to his own misfortune.'

'If Byron loses that wing, Colonel, we are undone.'

Widdrington shook his head dismissively. 'He has a second line, Rupert's own horse among them.'

Stryker turned to glance at that second body of horsemen, who waited in position on the Royalist side of the ditch. Widdrington was right, of course. Byron's backup had some of the most experienced fighters in the entire army. 'But Byron cannot lose them too. If his first line fails, he will be forced to commit his second. Sir Edward, we must support him, if only to keep the second line in place.'

Widdrington considered the idea for a second, then shrugged again. 'Be my guest, Stryker.'

Stryker left Widdrington's four-hundred-strong brigade where they stood and galloped to the rightmost flank of his small unit. The nearest trooper, an older man judging by the grey bristles on his upper lip, was clambering into the saddle, having voided his bowels on the grass. His face was green and his hands were shaking as they fastened his helm. 'Our turn, Major,' he managed to say.

Stryker nodded, guilty that he failed to recall the fellow's name. 'You have seen any action?'

The trooper smiled sadly. 'Enlisted to protect my son just five weeks back. We did not wish him to fight, but he would not heed our voices. My goodwife insisted I follow him.'

'He is with us?' Stryker asked, looking along the line.

The trooper shook his head. 'He caught a fever. Now he is dead and I am here.'

Stryker stared at the cacophonous melee playing out on the far side of the ditch. 'Keep together. If we hold our form, we will stay strong.'

The trooper forced a stoic smile. 'We have drilled daily, sir.'

'One cannot practise fear,' Stryker said. He edged Vos forward. 'Godspeed!'

Then he kicked hard. Behind him, with a howl of terror and rage, Heathcliff Brownell's Troop of Horse rushed out to battle.

Vos's fore-hooves thudded on to the clinging mud on the south bank of the ditch. Stryker drew a pistol, emptied it in the direction of a group of rebels, then plunged it back into the holster. He drew his sword, the beloved weapon forged by a master and gifted by a queen, and then he was yards from Byron's splintering line. A large number of Royalist horsemen had already turned tail, Byron's personal standard bobbing amongst them, and they were flooding past Stryker's men, making for the ditch and the safety of the main army. It was a complete rout, endangering the whole wing if the bleed was not staunched. The few remaining Royalists were grouped in pockets, clustered in threes and fours as their Roundhead persecutors slashed and hacked a way through, desperate to draw the rest of Byron's wing into contact.

Brownell's Troop of Horse slammed into the melee. Stryker let Vos push him between two Royalists, then ducked beneath the swiping back-sword of a Parliamentarian. He brought his own blade close to his body, stiffening his wrist, and jabbed upwards, slipping below the face bars of his opponent's pot and crunching through the sinews of the throat. He wrenched it out, fighting the sucking flesh, and a fountain of hot blood sprayed his rain-soaked face, souring his tongue. He spat, brought the sword up, then whipped it round in a horizontal arc to batter the shoulder of another rider, and, though it failed to penetrate the quarter-inch leather, the man yelped and steered instinctively out of range.

Stryker saw clear space. The line had opened up before him as horses parted, and he slashed at Vos with the reins. The sorrel stallion whinnied, shook its head in complaint, but went anyway, and Stryker was through, the melee behind him, another party of enemy riders ten yards in front. He screamed, hoarse and unintelligible, and dipped his head. He bore down on the advancing group, drawing his second pistol and firing it into their tight formation. Then the first enemy riders came at him, and his sword was high, coming down in a crushing blow that snapped the steel of one man and dented the breastplate of another.

It was only then, as the riders wheeled out of his way, that he realized where he was. He had never before encountered Oliver Cromwell, but he knew the man as if he were kin. Cromwell was the Earl of Manchester's second, his Lieutenant-General of Horse, and as such he was conspicuous by his plain white cornet, held by a rider on his left, and by the screen of harquebusiers riding close at hand that Stryker was smashing to pieces. Cromwell was mounted on a muscular black warhorse, a bilious tawny scarf brightening his chest above russeted plate, hemmed with tassets to shield his thighs, and a full-length buff-coat that was elegantly embroidered at elbow and cuff in golden thread.

This was the great man, the famous leader of the most feared cavalry Parliament possessed. Stryker went straight for him.

Oliver Cromwell was scanning the battle, hoping Byron's second line would be tempted over the ditch so that his own reserve, Leslie's Scots, could be blooded in short order. Then they would turn the flank, arcing inward to invade the unprotected Royalist foot brigades. He was counting men and flags, and reading the terrain. Half an eye was on the movement of infantry over to the right as the Allied centre advanced to the ditch to engage their malignant counterparts, and at first the lone assailant registered as nothing more than a distraction. Except that the man was coming ever closer.

What he saw was a demon. He had known all along, since the very moment the treacherous king had raised his standard in a Nottingham squall, that the struggle for England would be contested on a spiritual as well as a physical plane. Now he had his proof. The man – the creature – that cleaved a path through the barricade of steel and hide was fearsome in the extreme. His face was torn in half, the left side ruined and melted, while his remaining eye was a feral silvery grey. His skin and coat were spattered in blood, his lips peeled back in a rictus grin as he smashed down with his huge, double-edged sword with its heavy pommel from which a red garnet winked. He rode a flame-red stallion, its teeth bared and its eyes white. The beasts were sent from hell's fires, Cromwell knew, and he believed they were coming for his soul.

'To me!' he bellowed. A pair of his best troopers immediately shielded him at left and right. Another went out in front to intercept the demon. He had a long cavalry sword with a single cutting edge, but his crushing swing was parried easily, turned deftly, and the demon lurched past, his mount mud-spattered and gnashing. The men at Cromwell's flanks shrank away, and the lieutenant-general saw that the waters of their faith did not run as deep as they had professed. He brayed a prayer, kicked on, and surged towards the demon. They clashed, blades meeting high as the stallions crossed, thudding flanks together and crushing the riders' thighs in an agonizing embrace. Then they were apart, each slashing backwards at the other's head. Cromwell gritted his teeth, because he felt nothing but thin air on the end of his sword. And because the demon's sword had struck home. Immediately he felt the warmth of new blood on his neck.

Stryker believed Cromwell would die. The tip of his Toledo steel had found the chink in the general's helm, between riveted lobster-tail and studded ear-piece, and, though the blow was weak as it flailed, he had felt the connection sturdily enough. Cromwell was wheeling away, the black horse kicking up clods as it scrabbled for purchase on the slick turf, and his guards had closed rank around him. Stryker made to pursue.

The shrill cry of a trumpet pierced his battle-rage. It called the retreat. He ignored it at first, but then Simeon Barkworth's piercing eyes were on him, the croaking voice working to rise above the gunfire and screams. Skellen was there too, his shovel-like hands waving from his own saddle, beckoning Stryker back to his men.

'Sir!' Thomas Hood's voice broke through the blur. 'Major Stryker, sir! Do not abandon your men!'

He found he was staring at the carnage beside the ditch. Oliver Cromwell was retreating, galloping at full speed up the ridge, a hand planted firmly to the side of his neck, but he was the only member of the Eastern Association to have turned his back.

'Major!' Hood was screaming again. 'We must retire!'

Byron's first line had been utterly defeated. The men had never recovered from their disorderly attack, and the close-knit, disciplined Roundheads had dissolved the Royalist formation like water on salt. Now the tatters of Urry's regiment, of

Vaughn's and of Byron's straggled back over the ditch in complete disarray, all the while pressed by the Eastern Association men, who kept faith with their battle-order, despite the obvious temptation to give chase. Stryker's troopers performed admirably, lining the southern bank of the ditch to cover the retreat, but their stoic fifty could be no match for the inexorable advance of the Parliament men. He rode back to their line, called for courage, and ordered his men to cross over to the north side of the moor.

Another trumpet called, just as they were traversing the ditch, but it was not the retreat. Stryker looked back. The Roundheads were slowing. The trumpet shrieked again, and he realized that it came from the Royalist side. Byron's second line, led by Lord Molyneux, was shuffling forwards. It was in good order and, significantly, it possessed the harquebusiers of Rupert's own regiment of horse, and he immediately understood why the enemy riders were caught in two minds. But the Parliamentarian second and third lines were coming up, even as their leaderless prow listed, and in moments they were surging on.

Stryker retreated. His meagre group would be scattered like dust, so he led them through the gaps between the bodies of horse, there to reform, recover wits and tally the butcher's bill. Just as his riders formed up, Lord Molyneux, astride a brilliant white palfrey on the Royalist extreme right, whipped his hat in a blurred halo, and his division went to the gallop. The Parliament men – Scots banners of blue and white swirling now as the third line joined its English comrades – jumped the ditch and crashed into Molyneux's force, but not before the latter had fired pistols and carbines in a flaming current that coursed all the way along the line. The Allied horse were well equipped, and most wore plate that was impervious to anything smaller than musket shot, but oiled hide could not stop a ball, and limbs were clipped and mounts felled. It was their turn to fray, theirs to stretch and tatter and lose momentum.

The lines met in a heart-rending thud and clang. Horses

pressed, arms locked and swords tangled. They stood, shoving and jabbing and slashing, like a pair of vast, steel-scaled leviathans, contesting the wing at point of sword, able to smell the stench of their enemies' rasping breaths. It was a hard fight wreathed in the foul haze of mud, blood, sweat and smoke, and for a time Stryker did not know if his paltry force would be called to support a faltering Molyneux, but then there were more shrill notes of brass, more bellowed orders, and the lines broke apart. This time, to his palpable relief, it was the Parliamentarians and their Scots allies who were in retreat.

The exhausted remnant of Lord Byron's wing removed itself from the ditch line to ensure the infantry, away to their left, was amply protected. Byron himself was nowhere to be seen, but Molyneux cantered over to greet Stryker.

'Saw you challenge Cromwell,' Sir Richard, Lord Molyneux, shouted above the din.

Stryker looked over to where those huge brigades were becoming locked in bitter exchanges, but the place was so heavily obscured in smoke it was almost impossible to discern the beginning of one army and the end of another. He nodded to the young commander. 'He was in front, my lord. I could not ignore him.'

'Quite,' Molyneux beamed. 'Killed him, d'you think?'

Stryker shrugged. 'Nicked his neck. Such a thing can heal swiftly or kill just as well. It is a matter of time.'

'And of God. Let us pray He snuffs the bugger out, eh? Cromwell's troopers are the best we've seen.' Molyneux wound the red strand of an ear-string about his little finger as he eyed the Eastern Association horsemen who milled at the foot of the ridge, reorganizing themselves into their original two lines, with the body of Covenanters behind. A unit of lancers appeared to join them. 'We must be prepared for their next move. Still, we have maintained the right flank, praise God.' He twisted, looking back at the tree line. 'But where in Christ's holy name is the Prince?'

*　　*　　*

Prince Rupert of the Rhine was seated on a felled oak eating manchet when the huge volley had burst from the ridge top.

Having decided that no battle would be joined this day, and still smarting from the spat with Lord Eythin, he had rejected Newcastle's invitation to dine in York, preferring to take refreshment with the unswervingly loyal men of his Lifeguard of Horse. Rupert and Sir Richard Crane had taken their one hundred and fifty elite troopers along a narrow track bisecting Wilstrop Wood, travelling far to the north to find some peace. The volley and the subsequent flurry of musket fire took them by complete surprise. The prince had ordered they make themselves ready to move as sounds of fighting floated through the lush canopy, but still they had remained, unwilling to panic over what must surely have been a false alarm. But then the messenger had thrashed through the forest to find them.

'Tell me again!' Rupert barked at the wild-eyed trooper, who did not even bother to dismount, such was his anxiety. The prince was already pulling on his coat and breastplate, checking pistols, slinging his baldric and tying his scarf. 'And make it quick!'

'Colonel Widdrington's compliments,' the rider panted, 'and you're to come to the battle forthwith.'

Rupert went to his horse, taking the reins from the waiting aide. 'Battle?' He stooped to pat Boye's shaggy pelt. 'You say battle, sir?'

'I do, Highness, for it is battle we have.'

'Where?'

The messenger wrinkled his nose. 'Everywhere, Highness. The enemy advances across the entire front.'

'And?'

'We have success in most quarters, Highness.'

'But?'

'Lord Byron suffers.' He visibly winced. 'He crossed the ditch and received a dire beating.'

Rupert glanced at Crane, who was settling into his own saddle. 'Crossed? I told him to keep behind it.'

Crane nudged his mount forwards. 'He thought different.'

Rupert crammed on his *Zischägge*. 'I fear we have missed the day, Sir Richard.'

Crane pursed his lips. 'At the gallop, Highness?'

# CHAPTER 20

The Allied infantry had advanced through the centre of the battlefield as the cavalry attacked the flanks.

Their front line, commanded by Major-General Crawford, was formed of ten bodies, representing all three armies. On the left, four regiments of the Earl of Manchester's Eastern Association were already engaged along the line of the ditch, having been drawn into contact by General Cromwell's insistence that the enemy gun emplacements be neutralized. Next in line were two regiments of Yorkshire Foot, and then four from the Army of the Covenant. Together the forward brigades enfiladed the Royalists lining the ditch. Their numbers were superior, and their momentum, coming off the steep slope, allowed them to strive close to the obstacle before the defenders could gather their wits and properly load their weapons.

The fire-fight flared right the way across the curved line as battle raged between the opposing horsemen on either flank. The storm overhead hampered all, turning powder damp and matches soggy, but enough shots were loosed to make the trench a glimpse of hell on earth. The Parliamentarians and Scots pressed hard, pikemen ready to launch across the barrier as their screening bodies of musketeers rippled with crackling volley fire. Men fell on both sides, punched back by lead, their places filled by those waiting behind. Field pieces, the smaller kind that could be manhandled by teams of men, coughed and recoiled, sending their missiles into the closely formed targets of flesh and metal.

In the Allied front line, Captain John Kendrick sucked hard at his pipe and closed his eyes for just a moment, remembering the wonders of New England and of Esme DeHaan in particular.

'Stupid bitch,' he heard himself say.

'Sir?' Sergeant Andor Janik was standing right next to his captain.

Kendrick drew on the pipe again. A dense pulse of musketry rattled from the far side of the thorny hedge, but he did not flinch. 'Miss DeHaan,' he repeated. 'You recall?'

Janik noticed one of the hajduks on his right shift backwards a pace, and he reached behind with his halberd, hooking the frightened Hungarian back into line. 'How could I forget, sir? Her fault we end up in this shit-stinking country.'

Kendrick had fled the Colonies because of Esme's murder, and it irked him still. 'Stupid bloody bitch,' he said again. Then he looked along the line. Crawford was there, mounted and waving his sword this way and that like a mad beast. He looked at Janik. 'Make ready the men.'

Kendrick's company had been absorbed into the army of the Eastern Association and placed out on the left flank of the Allied front line, under Major-General Crawford. From here they had witnessed the near destruction of the Royalist right-wing horse, cheering as the reckless Cavaliers had crossed the ditch to their own demise. But then Crawford had taken his infantry to the blood-drenched gully, the musket duel had erupted all around them, and the field had been consumed in acrid fog and bright flame, obscuring all but the few yards in front.

Kendrick took a final lungful of fragrant smoke, letting it meander through the gaps in his filed teeth, then drew a breath that was dirtier. 'Test your matches!'

Pan covers were closed, protecting the black powder within, and each man carefully worked his trigger to pivot the serpent, checking that the match would fall in the centre of the pan when the time came to fire. A couple required adjustment, most did not, and Kendrick emptied his pipe, thrusting it into his fur-trimmed cloak as he bellowed: 'Blow off your coals!'

Muskets were lifted to chins, lips pursed, and every man blew gently on the lit end of his match, still dangling limp in the serpent, to ensure that it glowed brightly in spite of the rain. Kendrick took a last look at them, his fine company of swash-and-buckler men. Though the failure at Skipton smarted like a livid wound, they had followed him, turned their coats as he had turned his, and he was proud of every single one.

'Present your piece!'

The company – an amalgam of English cutthroats and Hungarian sell-swords, of French footpads and Swiss thieves – shifted forwards, extending the left leg to turn bodies in profile as they lifted the long-arms into position, nestling wooden stocks against shoulders and training the barrels at points along the defended hedge line.

John Kendrick pulled his cloak tighter against his neck and cheeks, finding comfort in the thick bear pelt. He drew his sword with his gloved hand, pulled free his broad cinquedea with the metallic fingers of the other, and hauled air into his chest. 'Give fire!'

The volley tore across their first two ranks. It was joined by that of the rest of Crawford's left flank, creating a vast torrent of lead shot, which sprayed forth over the ditch, splintering and fraying the hedgerow. A lull in return fire told Kendrick that a heavy toll had been paid by the defenders. Crawford emerged from the smoke, screaming orders that none could hear, but the drums repeated them in a deep, reverberating thrum that shook boots and ribs, and the Allied brigades shunted forwards. They faced a formidable foe. On the far side of the hedge were the regiments of Rupert's army. Many, beneath the banners of Broughton and Tillier, were fresh from the war in Ireland; sturdy fighters turned ruthless and cruel, skills barbed and poisoned by sectarian hatred. But they were outnumbered, overwhelmed, and they could not return fire with the weight mustered by the Army of Both Kingdoms; they would surely be falling back under so great a pressure.

'I am a *hard-man*!' Kendrick shouted to his followers. 'I have supped of the conjurer's brew, and cannot be killed! With me, my lads! Let us play butcher for the day!'

The Royalist centre, like that of their enemies, was made up of infantrymen. They had around ten thousand pikemen and musketeers, but it was only roughly half the Allied number, and Lancelot Forrester, standing beneath his red banner adorned with two white diamonds and the cross of Saint George, expected to die.

As part of the York garrison, Sir Edmund Mowbray's Regiment of Foot were positioned in the Royalist core, at the middle of the second infantry line and brigaded together with a regiment of Northern Foot. It was from this position that Forrester witnessed the disintegration of the front line under Tillier. It all happened so quickly. The respective armies engaged across the ditch and hedge, the whole area marked in seconds by rising pillars of smoke that billowed outward, melded together and smothered the moor like a vast, grit-flecked blanket. Then out of that shroud came the Allied foot, too numerous for Tillier's veterans to turn back. The Earl of Manchester's crossed first, for their section of ditch was shallowest, and immediately they wheeled to their right, giving flanking fire that enfiladed the Royalist musketeers, forcing them to a steady retreat. And all the while, Lord Fairfax's regiments at the very centre came on to the Royalist side of the moor, and the Scots under their swirling saltires joined them to the east, and then they were all across.

''S'precious blood,' Forrester hissed through gritted teeth. 'This will be a hard pull.'

'Trevor's gone.'

Forrester looked up to see that Sir Edmund Mowbray had reined in beside him. 'Dead, sir?'

Mowbray smoothed down his russet moustache, as was his way when anxiety pulled taut. 'Engaged on the right. Caught up with Byron.'

'Jesu,' Forrester muttered. Colonel Marcus Trevor's Regiment of Horse were supposed to be held in support of the infantry. 'Then we have no succour?'

Trumpets and drums played out, shrill cries sharpening the beating thrust. It was the order he had expected. 'Old Oak! Get that colour up, if you please!'

Michael Oakley, sixty years of age and, so he claimed, all of twenty stones of pure muscle, hefted Forrester's ensign into the wet air. It was a gesture rather than a tactical move, for the company had been absorbed into the huge battaile of men and weaponry, but he felt a swell of pride all the same as the staff creaked like a mast, the taffeta banner sweeping back and forth as the other regimental colours began to churn in unison.

Forrester drew his sword and stepped out of line, nerves jangling uncontrollably. The drumbeats quickened as the men paced forward by a half-dozen long strides, settling where a green-cheeked lieutenant waved a partisan horizontally at waist height, indicating the extent of the formation. When they were arranged, the brigade adjacent to the others of the second line, a preacher strode out in front, shrieking damnation upon the advancing enemy. Two small field pieces coughed from the ditch. One took the preacher's head clean off, the other careened through an entire file of Mowbray's pikemen. The great ash staves tumbled, rattling on those behind, and a groan of horror rippled through the formation.

'God and the King!' Sir Edmund shouted from high up in the saddle. 'God and the King!'

Most echoed the cry, though their efforts were muted.

Forrester suddenly needed to urinate, so he went there and then, the hot liquid strange in breeches made so cold by the rain. The guns fired again, one missing, the other taking a sergeant at knee-height only yards from where Forrester stood. The Allied army cheered, and to his ears it sounded like the gates of hell called to him. He swallowed back a rush of bile that seared his throat and soured his tongue.

'We move up to support General Tillier!' Mowbray was calling.

Forrester looked along the line. There were whitecoats to the left and right. They were formed up tightly, swaying forests of pike in each battaile's centre, with thick blocks of shot on either side. Dotted around, from company to company, were the red banners of the Marquis of Newcastle, white crosses, like Mowbray's diamonds, denoting the status of each company commander. Forrester slipped a hand to his own shoulder, touching the fabric of the silken cross the marquis had awarded him. Now that he was in line with the whitecoats, it somehow mattered.

He twisted back, finding Mowbray. 'In case I am slain, sir.'

Mowbray stared over his nose at the captain. 'Well?'

'Killigrew is a traitor.'

That threw the colonel. He blinked rapidly. 'Ezra Killigrew? The spymaster?'

'He masters spies for the Parliament as well as for the King.'

Mowbray laughed wildly, as if the revelation sat logically on so terrible a day. He unsheathed his sword as the next set of drumbeats sounded the advance. 'Well I'll be damned. You did well to tell me, Lancelot.' The musket-ball took Mowbray square in the face, erasing his features in a single moment. His head snapped back, then his body fell.

Forrester felt a new dampness on his cheeks as his colonel's blood sprayed forth, mingling with the raindrops. 'Christ,' was all he could murmur, but then the whole Royalist second line was in motion, lurching forwards to fill the space left by the routed first, and he was forced to forget Mowbray and move on.

There were no more than thirty paces between Royalist and Parliamentarian now. The powder smoke was heavy, filthy, and Forrester's gums seemed fouled with grit, but the shifting murk was not opaque. He squinted as they surged forwards, pushing through the gaps between what was left of the first line. Ahead was a sea of men, of morion pots, pike staves, Monmouth caps and banners, rolling like an incoming tide.

The fear vanished, as it always did. Forrester knew he would die, and the terror that had been twisting his innards to knots only moments before dissolved. Now all he felt was a serene detachment, as if he floated above the killing field. He cocked his pistol without thinking. The enemy were close now, a matter of two-dozen yards, and they fired their dense volleys. Mowbray's regiment shivered with the impact, but it kept going, pace by bloody pace, and the musketeers on either flank fired their own weapons en masse, causing the Parliament men to falter.

'Rear half-file!' someone bellowed from within the block. 'Port your pikes!' The rearmost rows of pikes tilted forwards as one, like a stand of willows harried by a gale, so that their leaf-shaped tips fell from vertical to diagonal, hovering above the heads of the men in front.

'Front half-file!' the same voice, parched to breaking by the smoke, called again. 'Charge your fackin' pikes, lads!' There were just a few paces separating the two advancing bands of foot, and the front three ranks of pikes came down to head-height, the very front row thrust out to meet the oncoming enemy, the shafts behind laced between their helmets so that a great wall of steel would greet the Parliament brigades.

Forrester fell back with the reloading musketeers just as the push of pike slammed home. The opposing blades crossed in mid-air, the shafts threading like a tangled lattice of ash, and then the first men fell. A few died there and then, their gurgling cries strangled as the lances crushed chests and windpipes, but most were simply shoved off their feet, curling like foetuses against the trampling feet of their comrades. Forrester had used his own pikemen as a human battering ram in the past to smash a foe into rout by speed and shock alone, but here, where a gap in the line could expose the entire Royalist centre to surprise cavalry attack, he was obliged to keep pace with the rest. Thus, the field was alive with a sonorous, visceral snarl as the slow press played out. The men shoaled together, shoulders as closely squeezed as possible, and they heaved on, grinding shoes into the sodden turf and investing every ounce of power into the propulsion of a tapered length of razor-tipped ash. Far to his left, Cheater's brigade were locked in deadly embrace with the distinct grey and blue ranks of the Scots, while to the right, another body of Newcastle's Foot faced men in the green and red worn by the

Earl of Manchester's army. Immediately in front, Forrester saw that his own men had collided with a brigade less uniformly attired than the rest, and he realized they had crashed into the Yorkshire infantry of Lord Fairfax.

The difference was an inch or two. Tillier's front line had been part of Rupert's army – men who had marched over the hills and valleys that formed England's formidable spine in order to relieve York. They had had nights of privation, with scarce supplies and kindling too saturated to catch a light. They would almost certainly have trimmed their spears in those darkest hours, shaving the butt ends down to feed the flames. And they had paid the price, for their pikes were shorter than those of the enemy, a disparity that had seen them toppled back and routed. But the Northern Foot had been sheltered by York's ancient stone, their hands warmed by its hearths, and they stood strong and bold against the brigades of Manchester, Fairfax and Leven.

The musketeers were ready. They shunted forwards as the pikes pressed hard, eyes and teeth glowing like ghoulish sparks behind their staves in the gathering gloom. Forrester went too, and he saw that the opposing brigade, scraps of white tied on wrists and helms, were not yet ready. Some of their number gave fire, but these shots were desultory and disorganized, unity temporarily thrown by their initial success against Tillier's men. They scrabbled with their weapons, dropped matches and fumbled with scouring sticks, their officers shrieking for haste. And the Royalist musketeers presented their pieces with the practised efficiency that had made the white-coated companies famous in the north. Forrester did not hear the order to fire, but he levelled his pistol and squeezed the trigger as the entire Royalist line opened up. The Fairfax pike push disintegrated, so many close-knit bodies at such close range providing a target that even the rawest recruit could not fail to miss. And the Allied fulcrum began to fold in on itself as the men in the front fell, while those behind dropped their pikes and ran.

More trumpets cried out. The noise and the smoke and the screams deafened Forrester so that he knew nothing but that which was in front; yet he knew a cavalry call when he heard one, and braced for the worst. Then the horsemen struck. They came from the rear, over on the Royalist left flank, their cornets bursting through the mist, colourful and bright against the onset of stormy dusk, and some of the infantry officers began to call for their units to perform defensive manoeuvres, charging pikes to screen the vulnerable musketeers. The field word came then, carrying to Forrester through the busy fug, and it was the song of seraphim in his ears. '*God and the king*!' the riders cried, surging from the north, angling their attack to weave between the blocks of Royalist foot, arcing round to the east and bowling headlong into the Parliamentarian flank.

'Blakiston's!' Old Oak was bawling nearby as he waved Forrester's colour as though it were a rag on a twig. 'It's Blakiston's boys, sir!'

Sure enough, Forrester saw Sir William Blakiston's personal cornet sweep past in a blur of green and black, and he realized that, even though they had lost the support of Trevor on the right, Blakiston had identified the danger on the opposite side.

'Prepare your pieces!' Forrester shouted. 'Make 'em ready!'

The horsemen kept going, sweeping across the face of their huddled prey like wolves herding sheep, picking out the weakest specimens against which to set slashing steel or crushing hoof. They found success in the very centre, where Yorkshire banners flew in dense thickets, and there they lingered, working at the line like miners at a rich seam, chipping parts away to weaken the whole. The infantry began to shift in response, staggering out of the exposed line to form a hedgehog, pikes ringing the outside, muskets protected within. It was a slow, cumbersome manoeuvre, a wounded bear struggling to stand amid a pack of snapping mastiffs, but eventually they had enough pike shafts charged to convince Blakiston to disengage.

The Royalist battailes – made up of the Northern Foot, Mowbray's and Cheater's – opened fire, and a crescendo of mus-ketry ripped forth. A large section of the Allied front line broke. The brigade opposite Forrester, Lord Fairfax's Foot, bore the brunt. Unsure whether to remain in a hedgehog to fend off another cavalry charge, or to deploy in line to engage the foot, they hesitated and took heavy casualties from musketeers who could not miss. In moments their beleaguered ranks caved, tossing away weapons in their desperation to be away. The panic spread to the adjacent Scots brigades and those in the Allied second line, and before Blakiston's harquebusiers had even gathered for a second charge, the majority of the front row was collapsing. The Royalists advanced.

The infantry of the Earl of Manchester's army, the Eastern Association Foot, held firm and watched the horror unfold to their right. They did not break, because theirs were strong brigades, experienced and well drilled, and Major-General Crawford – mounted at the very front – inspired loyalty from the sheer peril of his position. But, more importantly, they did not have to face cavalry. The destruction of Byron on the Royalist right had been the catalyst, for any horsemen who might have endangered the Allied left were fully engaged in the salvage of that wing and the repulse of Cromwell's troopers. Thus, the Eastern Association front line – made up of four regiments in two brigades – held its ground, even as the rot from Lord Fairfax's defeat was spreading to the Scots. They edged forwards behind their general, loading and firing, rank by rank, the pikes ever ready to deploy should Blakiston alter the focus of his attack, and all the while their nervous eyes darted to the east, where the regiments of Rae and Hamilton, two of the four Covenanter regiments in the front line, had also broken. Immediately behind them, in the second line, the Scots of Buccleuch and Loudon were routing too, and it was all Crawford could do to keep his men's minds on the task at hand. He stood in the saddle, screaming, seemingly oblivious to the musket-balls racing by at every angle.

John Kendrick looked for Stryker in the chaos. The Allied infantry were drawn up in the Swedish style, with three squadrons, five hundred men in each, clustered into an arrowhead formation around the central pike block. Kendrick's company was attached to a squadron of Manchester's shot, formed six ranks deep on the right flank of the pikemen, and he squinted through the filthy air, hoping to catch a glimpse of the man he hated. He knew it would be almost impossible to find a lone figure in this ocean of carnage, but he looked all the same.

'I just want to kill him, Andor,' he muttered as a section of Northern Foot, one of Lord Newcastle's regiments, shunted rearwards, beaten back by Crawford's relentless advance. 'Just kill him.'

Sergeant Janik was using his halberd as a crook through the morass. He frowned deeply. 'We want girl, no?'

That was true, he supposed, for she remained his only realistic chance of locating the golden flagon. His desertion to the Roundheads had ended any direct association with his erstwhile master, Killigrew, but that did not mean he must abandon all ambition. If he could yet present the flagon to the Parliamentary High Command, his determination and resourcefulness would be proven.

In this moment, however, all that was left was simple vengeance. Here, on this blood-slick scrap of moorland, all he wanted was to slay the man who had ruined his plans, almost snuffed his star before it had risen; gut the man who had forced him to leave the king's army and enlist with this judgemental gaggle of preachers, prayer-prattlers and psalm-warblers. It was worse than purgatory, but all Kendrick knew was war, all he could do was fight, and the murder of one Lieutenant Brownell had rendered fighting for the Crown impossible. So he would fight for men he despised, because there was nothing left, and he would search for the man he hated. After that, after Stryker had died, he would forge a new path. He pointed at the Royalist lines and looked at his moustachioed sergeant. 'We want Stryker.'

The Northern Foot had retired out of musket range, regrouping after Crawford's stinging riposte. Kendrick risked a step out of line to look back at the rest of the Allied foot. The second and third lines were still generally in good order, save the routed Scots in the centre, who had been swept up by the panic of Fairfax's men immediately to their front. But they had shuddered to a halt, unwilling to advance and probably tempted to full-blown retreat. He hoped they would hold firm. The horsemen who had turned the tide of the infantry exchange were wheeling away now, breaking formation to pursue the fugitives back over the ditch towards the ridge, and they would be easy pickings.

'Better to stay in formation, lads!' he shouted to any who might hear. 'You run, you're dead!'

Drumbeats carried fresh orders, but the battle-din drowned everything to an indistinct hum. Kendrick looked for Crawford, who appeared to be ignoring a livid stripe of fresh blood beneath one eye, and saw too that the general had three brightly dressed heralds with him. The heralds nodded vociferously and hauled their mounts about in unison, spurring to different parts of the two surviving Allied brigades. One of the riders reached the lieutenant-colonel in command of Kendrick's, and the orders were passed from officer to officer.

'Wheel right!' Kendrick echoed the directive when it reached him. The manoeuvre was far from seamless, for the brigades were blinded, deafened and forced to trample over a sea of mud, but, sure enough, the huge bodies of men clunked and juddered to their right hand, facing along the line where once their comrades had been. That front line had gone now, the other brigades collapsed and broken, and in their place were the advancing blocks of Royalists whose counter-attack threatened to overwhelm the Allied centre.

Kendrick drew an acrid breath. 'Double the files! Double the files, God rot your pox'n pizzles!' His experience had been in detached warfare. From the mountains of eastern Europe to the maple forests of New England, he had led men in small groups, ambushing, burning and torturing his way behind enemy lines, always keeping away from the massed blundering of organised battle. Yet he knew enough to relish this moment as his rearmost ranks of musketeers moved up to fill the gaps between the trio of front ranks, transforming the six-rank formation into a bristling three. The front rank proceeded to kneel, the second rank crouched behind and the third rank stood, so that every available muzzle was trained on the flank of the advancing Royalist line.

Crawford's drums fell silent. The shot commanders gave the order to fire, and all three double-sized ranks exploded in flame and smoke. The sudden doubling of firepower delivered a devastating blow, enfilading the Royalists, cleaving deep, ragged holes in their flank and stopping their advance in its tracks.

'Reload your pieces!' John Kendrick snarled, but already the enemy were retreating, leaving their horsemen to hunt the routed Scots and Parliamentarians alone. If the tide had not been turned, it had at least met a formidable reef.

'General Cromwell is wounded, my lord.'

The Earl of Leven, watching the evening unfold from up on the knoll, scowled at his fresh-faced aide. 'How wounded?'

The young man made a chopping motion with a flattened hand. 'Sabred about the neck.'

'Dead?'

'He is tended at Tockwith village, my lord. By all accounts he means to return to the field forthwith.'

'Pray God he does. We need such men now.'

Gauging the battle had proven difficult, partly due to the speed of events, and partly because of the smoke. Where it moved, Leven could see a troop wheeling, a gun juddering upon a waterlogged rut, a company of shot adjusting match or thumbing powder boxes. He could read the battle, albeit in stolen glimpses, and he knew he was losing. Cromwell and Leslie, notwithstanding the former's wound, had stalled their progress on the left, while on the right, the dark mass of Black Tom Fairfax's horse had been scattered by terrain and circumstance so that it was unclear what exactly transpired. And in the centre, destruction was imminent. Crawford seemed like a man possessed, atoning for his foolishness at the Marygate mine by cleaving a bloody swathe into the opposing foot, while his Scottish counterparts on the extreme right, a pair of regiments brigaded together under the Earl of Crawford-Lindsay, also held position against heavy fire from the Royalist infantry units. But the rest of that front line, the very centre, had disintegrated, and already large parties of fleeing soldiers could be seen scrambling over ditch and road in the direction of the ridge. The Royalist second line, having saved those in front, was now coming up in pursuit, supported by the cavalry whose charge had caused so much destruction. Manchester's men, under General Crawford, had done much to stem the flow by a fearsome flanking volley, but still the situation was dire. The rebel cause teetered on the brink.

'It is the horse,' Leven said.

'Lord?'

Leven stared hard at the chaos around the ditch. 'They fold not for push of pike, but for the intervention of those damnable horsemen. We must counter the threat.'

The aide looked left, towards Bilton Bream, then down at the plain below, where the Eastern Association cavalry, backed by Covenanter horse, were reforming for their next attack. 'Should I send for Lieutenant-General Leslie, my lord? He commands in General Cromwell's absence, and can spare the men.'

Leven shook his head. 'Let him await Cromwell. I would have them finish their business against Byron.' He turned his horse. 'I'll find Sir Thomas myself.'

'You, my lord?'

Leven rounded on the astonished youth. 'I was at war while you suckled your mammy's tits, lad. Call up a squadron from the reserve. Now, damn your eyes! We must fan our flame now, or see it extinguished for good.'

Leven went towards the right wing of his combined army at the gallop. With him he took a hundred Scots dragoons, and they made for the lane bisecting the ditch without stopping, the infantry battle raging furiously away to their left. He could immediately see what trouble Fairfax the younger must have had in deploying here, for, unlike the rest of Marston Moor, the ditch at its easterly extremity was at its deepest and the area all around was broken by hedges. When Leven led his men across the barrier unopposed, he felt a stab of elation, for surely Sir Thomas had succeeded in sweeping all before him to such an extent that not a single malignant haunted the trees. Only corpses lingered here, torn and limp, curled amongst the foliage like so many macabre puppets. Leven whooped, feeling the old delight invigorate his veins. He rounded an eviscerated horse, leapt a pair of musketeers who stared sightlessly at the stormy sky, and looked for signs of Sir Thomas Fairfax's blue banner.

In that moment the lane a little distance to the north filled with horsemen. They came from the left, through a gap in the hedge, and Leven saw that they were his cavalry, or, more specifically, those of Lord Fairfax commanded by his son and sent to smash the Northern Horse under Goring, for the rags of white in their hat bands seemed abnormally iridescent in the gathering dusk. He hailed them with a wave of his hat.

It was only when they came within fifty yards that he understood these were not men enthused by victory, for they came at the gallop and did not slow. They did not even acknowledge him.

The musket fire was muffled by the trees, but still Faith Helly trembled.

Most of the Royalist baggage and the army's huge camp following had retired behind the walls of York, but some wagons, ammunition mostly, remained, and it was with them that Faith would wait. They were at the northern end of Wilstrop Wood, an itinerant hamlet of vehicles arrayed among the oaken boughs and guarded by a score of anxious recruits armed with firelocks. None spoke; instead they waited, sitting on their carts or on damp logs, listening to the sounds of a battle they could not see. The deepest rumbles had ceased, for the big field pieces had been silenced by the coming together of the armies, but muskets discharged in dense formations made their own kind of clamour, like the snarl of a vast pack of wolfhounds, and that was enough to make the blood run chill.

Faith hated Royalists, despised the king and knew that God

was on the side of the Parliament. But she could not simply stroll into the Parliamentarian camp, for the Vulture was there, somewhere, and his black pelt, his broad knife and his fangs were the ever-presents of her nightmares. Stryker had saved her, kept her alive on the long march from Bolton, and it was to him, an enemy, she entrusted her life.

So now she must wait and wonder and beg the true sovereign, King Jesus, for understanding as she prayed. Because, though she asked Him for an Allied victory, she prayed, too, for the life of a one-eyed malignant and his men.

At the tree line of Wilstrop Wood, Colonel Sir Edward Widdrington received his commander-in-chief with a bow from the saddle. 'Highness.'

Prince Rupert of the Rhine curbed his black stallion in a torrent of muddy clods, his face thunderous. 'With me, Sir Edward. Your reserve and my Lifeguard as one body, under my personal command.'

Widdrington looked beyond the prince, regarding the long line of elite harquebusiers that galloped up in his wake. 'Where do we ride, Highness?'

The prince pointed west as his large poodle sauntered to stand below his stirrup, white coat matted with mud. 'Byron's position.'

'Lord Molyneux commands now, Highness. Byron is swept away in the rout.'

'But Molyneux holds yet?'

Widdrington nodded. 'He does, Highness. Rumour has it that General Cromwell was wounded in the scrap. General Leslie consolidates for another assault.'

Prince Rupert raked his spurs across his mount's heaving flanks. 'Then let us go and stop him!'

'Speak quickly, boy! What has happened?'

The Earl of Leven had almost been trampled by his own cavalrymen. The Allied right wing, hitherto commanded by Sir

Thomas Fairfax, had been defeated. They raced south, fleeing as the infantry in the centre fled, desperate to be away from the deadly moor. Leven had managed to wrench his snorting grey into the tangled scrub at the side of the lane as dozens of horses thundered past, some bearing pallid-faced riders, many carrying nothing but a smear of blood where once a man had been, and for a time he simply watched, stunned, as the troopers stared ahead, panic blinding them to all but escape.

Eventually a pair of horsemen, teenagers with red-rimmed eyes, had been snared by members of Leven's bodyguard.

'We are undone!' one wailed, oblivious to the status of the man he addressed. He threw his head round, as if some invisible terror leered at his shoulder. 'The malignants did charge us! They did shatter us!' Tears pulsed down his cheeks. 'We are undone!' With that, as Leven glanced at his senior dragoons, the boy shook his reins free of the corralling grip and bolted.

'You, man,' Leven said to the second fugitive. 'Where is your general?'

'Sir Thomas is dead.'

'You saw this with your own eyes?'

The fellow nodded rapidly. 'He took his men through their line on't first charge. We ain't seen him since. He never returned. The enemy rallied.' The trooper shuddered, a steaming trickle of vomit cascading over his chin to dye his falling-band collar a luminous yellow. 'They pushed us back,' he blurted through a series of dry heaves. 'Charged us with great vigour. We broke, by Jesu. We broke. They pursue, even now.' The trooper's eyes fixed upon Leven's, drilling into his skull. 'Please, sir, let us be gone from this cursed place. They will be upon us in a trice.'

Sir Thomas Fairfax held a hand to his cheek, hoping to staunch the blood. His helm jangled from the side of the saddle, fastened there by its chin strap so that he might tend to the cut at his face. His vision was distorted, tinged red by the hot, leaking blood smeared from below his right eye, but he could see enough to know that he was in trouble.

He had chased the routed Royalists north, then west, towards York. He guessed around four hundred of his men had broken through Goring's first line in that initial charge, and they had spurred after the men, howling and whooping like so many hounds after a stag, leaping hedges and careening through trees as they bore down on Goring's riders. Except that their quarry had only been a small part of the Royalist left-wing horse. Only when the pursuing mob drew close to York, slashing at the backs of fleeing, isolated Cavaliers, did Sir Thomas realize there were neither enough routed enemy, nor enough pursuing comrades to constitute the full complement of horsemen that had clashed before Long Marston. He had hauled on his reins at this point, wheeled back to face the south where the dread sounds of battle yet rent the sky, and returned to Marston Moor alone, expecting to meet up with his victorious regiments as they looked to press the advantage gained by conquering the right flank.

Now he saw the full extent of his folly. He urged his horse into a trot despite the pistol ball lodged in its rump, and let it carry him into the debris-strewn field. This was the plain on which his disordered charge had careened into Goring's well-formed cavalrymen, and yet he barely recognized it. There were helmets scattered like boulders, blades of steel where blades of grass had been, and bodies, so many bodies, twisted and mangled, the macabre flowers of a blood-streaked meadow.

'Jesu,' he whispered, because he saw, at the southern end of the clearing, several large blocks of horse drawn up in battle formation. Even with his sight so badly compromised, he could tell that none wore the white field sign of the Army of Both Kingdoms. 'What has happened here?'

'Tom?'

Sir Thomas turned in his saddle with a start. Below and to the left, lying on his side with knees drawn up to his chin, was a man he recognized but could not place. He dismounted at once, frowning as he strode across the squelching turf. When his good eye focussed, it filled with tears. 'Charles?' Sir Thomas fell to his knees beside the man who, behind the nasal bar of an ornate Dutch pot, shared the same swarthy, almost Mediterranean complexion as himself. 'Oh, God, Charles. You are hurt.'

The prone man grimaced. 'I was caught by a musket-ball, Brother. I am like to die.'

Sir Thomas found Charles's hand, scooping it up in his own. 'Nay, Brother, you will live yet.'

'I am no child, Tom. Do not treat me so.'

Sir Thomas peered across his younger sibling's bent thighs at the wound they were drawn up to protect. A wide, ragged hole gaped in the steel of his breastplate, just below his diaphragm. 'You are gut-shot, Charles.'

Charles Fairfax rumbled a bleak chuckle. 'The worst death of all.'

Sir Thomas looked up. 'What has happened here? I broke through their line and gave chase ...'

'And God bless you for your valour, Brother,' Charles rasped through teeth gritted against a wave of agony, 'but you were the only man to do it. The rest of us did take a fearful thrashing.' He paused to cough and finally spoke again: 'We routed in a minute or two.'

Sir Thomas thought of the second and third lines who had been galloping in support of his charge. 'What of Colonel Lambert? The Scots?'

'Beaten. Some fight still, but they are few. Most have gone, pursued to the south—' Another wracking cough consumed him. 'The wing is lost either way,' he said at last.

Sir Thomas raised his face so that his brother would not see the grief that must have etched his face. His gaze rested on the horsemen at the far end of the field. They had not noticed him, for their backs were turned, facing westwards towards the centre of the battlefield. 'Which men are they?'

Charles did not move, but he seemed to know his brother's meaning all the same. 'Sir Charles Lucas's.'

'The enemy's second line?'

'Aye. They are well mustered—' Charles spluttered again.

'They were not required against us, Brother, so complete was our trouncing. I fear they prepare to strike against our foot.'

Sir Thomas sat back, his world spinning. 'Oh, Lord, forgive me,' he whispered. A thought lanced him as he stared at the waiting enemy troopers, and he glanced back at his white-faced brother. 'How fares our left?'

'Cromwell? I know not. Better news, pray God.'

Better news. The idea swirled in his mind. He gripped his brother's hand again. 'I must leave you, dear Charles. I will send help, you have my word, but now I must go to General Cromwell.'

'He may have routed too.'

'Aye, he may. Or else he may not.' Sir Thomas shrugged. 'If the latter be true, then there is still a chance to save this fight.'

Charles Fairfax grimaced, a morbid expression of scarlet teeth and swivelling eyes. 'You cannot hope to pass through their entire army unmolested, Brother.'

# CHAPTER 21

Up on the ridge above Marston Moor, the three leaders of the Army of Both Kingdoms convened in a panic-stricken summit.

Alexander Leslie, Earl of Leven, had called them to the knoll on his return from the tattered enclosures around Long Marston village, where he had discovered the fate of his right wing at first hand. He kept a flask of whisky in his saddle and reached for it, his craving suddenly as potent as the liquid itself, but found it already drained, though he barely remembered putting it to his lips.

Ferdinando, Lord Fairfax, was staring hard at him, his face seeming to be more deeply lined than before. 'What of my horse?'

'Routed.'

Fairfax swallowed, his bottom lip quivering a touch. 'My sons?'

'Dead, most likely,' Leven answered, unable to find gentle words in a moment of such horror. He shook his head. 'It is chaos. Carnage.'

The Earl of Manchester had been staring at the cloud-smothered battle, eyes narrowed to slits as he discerned units in the roiling fog. 'My horse hold the left. They reform even now.'

'But Cromwell is wounded,' Leven said. 'His men will not perform as well without him.'

'And the centre is c-crumbling as we speak,' Lord Fairfax stammered. 'The King's horse wheel off the flank to threaten what remains of our foot.' He snatched off his hat to run quivering fingers through lank, snowy hair. 'Jesu, help us. We must flee. For God's sake, my lords, we must flee!'

Muttering voices carried to them like the sudden flutter of wings, and a gaggle of worried-looking aides reined in. They had been at the edge of the ridge, perched above the butchery, and now they alighted to add their voices

Leven waved them away. 'Begone, fellows! This discourse is not for your flapping ears!'

The aides exchanged looks. One let his mount edge out a step. 'But my lord, Leven—'

'Speak quickly.'

'The enemy.' The aide pointed to the eastern fringe of the ridge, a few hundred yards distant. There were horsemen on that high ground, and they wore no white in their hats. Indeed, the few who donned scarves bore material of richest red.

'Jesu,' Lord Fairfax whispered. 'My Jesu, they have reached the summit.'

Leven searched for his bodyguard troop, finding them already spurring to intercept the invaders, and sucked hard at his sandy-grey moustache. 'Goring's horse. They who routed Ferdinando's son.' He glanced at Fairfax. 'We must be away.'

One of his Scottish squires nodded violently. 'To Bradford, my lord, or Leeds.'

'Do not be so craven, man,' Manchester snarled angrily.

Fairfax made a clicking sound with his tongue and his horse moved away. 'I go to Cawood. Write to me there when the mist has cleared.'

Leven sighed, utterly deflated. He looked back at the inter-loping Cavaliers. They were like a shiver of ravenous sharks tearing at the carcass of the greatest army assembled for a century. His troop had waylaid them, for the skirmish raged amongst the gorse thickets furring that section of the crest. 'Let us depart this place before we are taken.'

Manchester's face tightened. 'You cannot—'

'Cromwell is dire hurt on the left,' Leven cut him off tersely. 'Sir Thomas is routed on the right. Goring's horse bear down on our persons even now, his second line close upon our infantry, which looks likely to break at any moment.' He wrenched at the reins, the beast whinnying as its head snapped round. 'All is lost, sirs. We must ride from this place while we have breath in our lungs!'

Manchester looked likely to demur, but then, as he regarded the enemy cavalry so close at hand, his rigid face began to sag. 'My God,' he whispered, 'how have we arrived at this?' He looked again at the battlefield, shrouded in smoke and littered with debris, and Leven saw moisture glisten in his eyes. He wiped them with his sleeve. 'Very well, my lords, let us abandon Marston Moor. Let the Devil have it.'

Sir Thomas Fairfax nodded to the Cavalier horsemen.

He was riding through their massed ranks, leaving the wreckage of his shattered wing behind and passing between the bristling enemy troops that thronged the eastern side of the moor. His poor brother had been right. Sir Charles Lucas, George Goring's second in command, had evidently not been employed during the destruction of the rebel horse, for his men were drawn up in organized lines and ready to enter the fray. Thus, Sir Thomas found himself in the midst of his enemies, his pistol-shot mount loping uneasily under enemy cornets while he sat as confidently as he could in the saddle. His heart raced, his jaw ached with the tension of the moment, but still he carried on. He had replaced his helmet for protection and to hide a face that, despite its grievous wound, may yet prove recognizable, but had removed his tawny scarf and the scrap of paper that marked him as Parliamentarian. That was all. A simple enough thing, but with the field sign gone, he was just another man among thousands.

'God and the King!' he called to a harquebusier who seemed to take more than a passing interest in his presence. 'God and the King!'

The inquisitive rider let his gaze linger for another second, then nodded, turning his snorting mare away, and Sir Thomas let out a breath. And then he was away, the expanse of the moor opening up to his left clouded in thick, scudding smoke and clogged with men and horses, flame and death. Phalanxes of pike met, joined, pushed and retired, leaving their friends behind, skewered and sobbing, while files of musketeers engaged in private duels, pouring hellfire into the packed rows of enemy units, each desperately trying to force a break in the opposite formation. To his right was Wilstrop Wood, the northern limit of the moor. He remembered seeing the Royalist cavalry reserve waiting there, but they were no longer there, and he wondered to what purpose. Did they destroy Cromwell's flank even now?

Behind, to the discordant song of trumpet shrieks and the colourful swirl of circling flags, the Royalist cavalry line, through which Sir Thomas had miraculously slipped, began to move. It swarmed south and west, the crumbling remains of the Allied infantry brigades its inevitable target. But Sir Thomas Fairfax did not care. Not yet. He went instead to find Oliver Cromwell, if the man still lived.

The second line of the Royalist left-wing horse had been forced to wait. The men had watched their comrades – Goring's favourite regiments under Frescheville, Langdale and Eyre – deliver a shattering charge, annihilating the Fairfax horse and opening up the entire flank, and they had felt jealous, impotent, denied the chance for glory on a day that slid inexorably into the Crown's vengeful lap. Yet Goring had led his horde south, over the ditch, over the road and up on to the ridge, the temptation to plunder the rebel baggage train a siren song impossible to ignore, and that had left the field open for their covetous comrades.

Now, as sunlight finally faded from the butchery, they injected their own thunder into the day as they crossed the ditch. In front lay the wide expanse of the moor. On the extreme right of the Allied front line, a brigade of two blue-bonneted regiments held their position. They had retired in good order to the south of the ditch, a feat impressive in itself, and now deployed in broad lines to present a wide front of fire in the face of their advancing Royalist counterparts. They were out on a limb, the adjacent brigades disintegrating around them, and devoid of cavalry support. Easy prey.

Sir Charles Lucas, thirty-year-old hero of Powick Bridge and Padbury, was encased in armour that was enamelled in black, riveted in gold, and scarved in scarlet. He knew that his attire made him conspicuous, and, though it rendered him a target, it would guarantee him fame when the victory was secured. None could mistake who led the decisive charge.

And so he grinned as he raised his sword – an exquisite Milanese artwork with engraved fuller and patterned shell guard – and he laughed when he looked along the line to observe the knee-to-knee formation that would take his fresh division into battle, and he crowed like a demon when he kicked into the gallop.

Lucas knew how to lead a charge, and knew that, above all, success was a matter of form and discipline. To hack pell-mell at a body of foot meant to collide with them in disorder, where gaps meant weakness. Weakness was a disease, insidious and undermining. A good leader of cavalry took his troopers across the battlefield at a canter, loosing the first volley – be it pistol or carbine – when the target was close at hand, and then spurring into the gallop at the very last moment. That way the line would be preserved, the gaps kept firmly shut, and the infantry, facing a solid wall of steel and horse, could do nothing but run. At this point the real killing would begin, for broken infantry were easy pickings, their spines and skulls exposed to swords, and to second pistol shots kept back for just such a moment. Yet now speed was paramount, because he knew that the blue and white banners of the king's northern dominion would soon sway to the beat of a fresh drum. A beat that would call them together, moving them out of line and into a pike-fringed ring, a hedgehog, that would be fiendishly difficult for cavalry to break. The musketeers – hitherto so fatally exposed – would hide behind those great spines, firing from within, and Lucas's riders would be forced to swerve away, all the while cresting a wave of lead that threatened to drown them in their own blood.

That was why Sir Charles Lucas clawed his spurs deep, and

screamed. He filled his lungs with bitter air and shouted at the moody skies, and his men added their voices as they seared over terrain scattered with dented steel and ruined flesh.

They slammed home. A shiver went through the Scots brigade, like a ripple in a pond, and the entire body shunted back a step. The horsemen were amongst them, hacking and slashing, the front hooves of so many powerful warhorses rearing and stamping, teeth huge and white as they snapped at the faces of the outermost musketeers. A groan swept through the ranks, one of fear, pure and unconcealed, and the exposed soldiers shied away, pushing in on the pikemen arrayed at the centre of their human diamond, protection their only concern.

The pikes did their duty. They should not have done, for the great clattering stand of ash staves was surrounded by muskets, the brigade's hard centre covered by a soft shell, and yet Lucas could already see them pushing their way out to the fringes. His horsemen had penetrated the formation, as he had expected, but they had not punched deeply enough. The Scots had not broken, they had failed to run, and the pikemen were coming, filtering out through the press of desperate musketeers to thrust their spiked shafts into the faces of horse and rider alike. Lucas was at the corner of the diamond. He screamed for his men to stay steady, to cleave a way through so that the enemy would finally shatter, but from up in his saddle he could see well enough the inertia that had stricken his charge. They were stuck, clogged amongst the dense Scottish block, unable to tunnel deeper into the files of musketeers for fear of the pikes that had somehow been brought to bear above the heads of the vulnerable outer ranks.

He called the retreat. They were not beaten, but nor could they achieve the rout he desired, at least not at this first attempt, and so they would regroup, catch breath and load pistols, and then they would charge again. Once more, and the Scots would crumble, then the rest of the Allied centre would dissolve, and the day would be won. Just once more.

★    ★    ★

The Earl of Crawford-Lindsay was quite aware that the darkening evening would turn upon him. There had been four Covenanter regiments in the front line, brigaded in pairs and commanded by Lieutenant-General Baillie. But one brigade had gone, and Baillie had been swept up in that disaster, leaving only the Fifeshire and Midlothian regiments to stop the rot. Crawford-Lindsay led the isolated brigade, and he had cowered with the rest as the Cavalier charge had collided with his right flank, but now they were gone, wheeling back to reform, and it was time to show them what the Army of the Covenant could do. His officers moved, in saddle and on foot, amongst the clusters of blue bonnets, their blades exposed, glassy with rain, screaming the order Lindsay did not have to utter. It was the only order they could possibly give.

The brigade charged for horse. It was an astonishing thing to witness, for the shifting of almost fifteen hundred men, blinded by smoke and dusk, into any kind of coherent formation was difficult in the extreme. And all the while they were harassed by enemy fire from the far side of the ditch. Yet the manoeuvre, lumbering and chaotic though it was, came to pass in the time it took for Lucas's cavalry to draw themselves back into a solid line some hundred paces to the east. Lindsay watched in awe as his pikemen – the biggest and strongest members of a regiment – continued their outward momentum, forming up in a wide ring two ranks deep while the rest went to the centre. The outlying pikes were angled up, butt ends wedged into the instep of the bearer's rear foot, while the second rank interlocked behind, plugging the gaps between the men in front to form a solid wall of Hodden grey and plaid, charging their great spears horizontally. The result was a spiny ring, the hedgehog, and he placed himself at the creature's heart, where the banners of two regiments clustered like blue and yellow trees. The earl was a strict Presbyterian, and he did not believe in saints. Yet there were more flags flying the saltire of Saint Andrew than any other, and those proud crosses pricked the haze, their white slashes lurid in the oppressive vapour. He had never felt so proud.

The Royalists surged into a new charge. They must have known, as Lindsay knew, that if they could break the stubborn brigade, the rest of the Allied infantry would be fatally exposed, and so they came at the gallop, slashing madly at their steeds, their war-cries shrill and piercing.

But the Scots were good. The muskets gathered within the hedgehog were deployed behind the pikes, forming a third rank, their weapons trained between the heads of the men in front. The men on the north face, opposite the ditch, fired upon the infantry looking to cross, while those on the eastern side looked to halt the charge. At this distance they aimed low, targeting the horses, which were easier to hit than the men bobbing above, and they poured their rage into the Cavalier line, causing fractures to open as the first enemy riders fell. The musketeers retired to reload, replaced, man for man, by their waiting comrades, but this time they changed their tactic. The Scots knew that a heavy destrier killed at close range would keep going, would stumble and tumble and then slide in the mud, and the sheer momentum of the huge form would take it straight through the outer ranks of the pike ring, holing it as sure as any cannon ball. So the blue-capped musketeers lifted their muzzles as the Royalist horsemen drew closer, picking at the bodies and faces of the riders themselves in the hope that, without the commands, a horse would veer away from the pike points.

The second volley ripped through Lucas's harquebusiers, tearing their line to pieces, but still they came on, just yards from the braced ring. The musketeers revolved again, more coming up to the kill, but this third volley was not commanded to wait. They let loose, firing at will as the Royalist horsemen reached the steel hedge. Faces of men and horses leered through the powder smoke, glowering apparitions looming above the pike points, and the outermost pikemen cringed under the expected impact. But none came. The horses veered away at the last moment, frightened by the crackling shots and unwilling to leap so lethal a fence. The enemy swirled around the flame-lit circle, in and out of the skeining mist, slapping at the pikes with swords and shooting down into the thickly arrayed bodies with their pistols. But the men of Fife and Midlothian did not give way. They took the punishment with challenges of their own, the saltires swept high and defiant in the stinking fog, and the Royalists could find no chink in their armour. Somehow, miraculously, the Allied front line, teetering on the brink of oblivion, managed to cling on.

—⁓—

Oliver Cromwell read his soldiers' pocket Bible as the chirurgeon tied off the dressing. The bandage was thick, winding thrice round his neck, but the pain had ebbed and the bleeding was staunched. The lieutenant-general's survival was nothing short of the will of God.

'You will not be able to fasten your collar,' the chirurgeon said, standing back to admire his work, 'nor hang a gorget at your throat.'

'No matter.' Cromwell closed the pamphlet and kissed the cover, putting it into its pocket beside his heart. He stood and gathered up the rest of his clothes. 'If King Jesus had wanted me dead, it would be so. I am to live, it is ordained.'

The crows-feet at the chirurgeon's eyes deepened. 'You must rest now, sir.' He wiped crimson palms on the crusty apron that stretched tight across his belly. 'The blade cut is deep.'

'Did you not hear me, sirrah?' Cromwell snapped. He looked around the room. They were in Tockwith, in the home of an evicted Royalist. It was a substantial building, with a great parlour in which the floor space had been draped with sheets, and it was on those sheets that the wounded from the fight below Bilton Bream were tended. The lieutenant-general stepped over a prone body and made for the door. He stepped by a large hearth, noticing the kettle and skillet had been thrust aside, their places in the lambent flames taken by a sawbones' tools. He stifled a shudder, thanking God for His deliverance from such torture. 'Where is my horse? My armour?'

'General,' the chirurgeon bleated as he pushed open the door, 'you will reopen that wound if you take no care of it. I must protest.'

The air stank of sulphur. It was not yet dark, but the dusk was gathering apace. He turned back. 'No, fellow, you must not. God preserves my life for His purpose.' He stalked from the house, spotting the huge black destrier waiting across the street. 'Ah, Blackjack, my old friend,' he said, crossing quickly and taking the reins from a trooper. He leaned into the beast's ear. 'We are to fight again this evening. Praise God for your loyalty, old boy, for it is cherished.'

'General Cromwell, sir,' a trooper greeted him. The man had been invalided from the fight by a smashed ankle.

Cromwell nodded. 'My plate, my weapons.'

The trooper pointed at a bulging sack. 'Clean and ready for you, sir.'

'You have my thanks. In what manner will I discover my men?'

'They hold the left flank, sir.'

Cromwell frowned. 'Hold? They have not attacked Byron again?'

The trooper winced. 'All is not well, sir, I regret to report. A large part of foot has routed, the rest under mortal threat. General Leslie maintains his position lest the malignants make play to encircle the infantry.'

'Our right flank? Fairfax?'

'I know not, sir.'

'What says Leven in this?'

'My lord Leven has departed, sir.'

'Expired?'

The trooper scratched his chin awkwardly. 'Fled, sir. As have my lords Fairfax and—' He hesitated, studying his boots: 'and Manchester.'

Cromwell's skin grew cold. 'My own general.' If all three rebel commanders had abandoned the field, then surely the end was near, and yet something nagged in the back of his mind. He had lived, miraculously, and nothing transpired without reason. 'Help me,' he said suddenly, going to retrieve his armour.

'Sir, I—'

Lieutenant-General Oliver Cromwell waved him away, ignoring the pain in his neck as he hefted the sack. He instinctively slid a hand to his heart, feeling the straight edges of the pocket Bible through his buff-coat. One of the section headings branded itself upon his mind, and he closed his eyes as he recited it. '*A Soldier must consider that sometimes God's people have the worst in battle as well as God's enemies.*' He opened his eyes, fixing them on the trooper. 'God's plan is all laid out before us. We have had the worst. Now it is time to have the best.'

---

Stryker watched the battle raging away to his left. The infantry fight that was consuming the centre of Marston Moor ebbed and flowed along the line of the ditch, and it looked as though the king's men had the best of it, but still the two edges of the rebel front line, Manchester's men nearest, Covenanters on the far side, were holding their ground, and it was a rallying cry for the waning spirits of the Army of Both Kingdoms. He wanted to be there, with the Royalist foot, to lend his steel and complete the victory, but knew he could not. His troop needed him, for, though they had repulsed the Parliamentarian cavalry, their wing remained precariously weak. Byron had vanished, caught up in his front line's destruction, so that Lord Molyneux commanded the remnant, but already the opposing force of cavalry, two bodies of Eastern Association horse and a third made up of Scots, were edging across the moor for a renewed assault.

'Keep the line!' Molyneux shouted as he took up position on the rightmost periphery of the horse and steel blockade. Byron's folly had been negated by Goring on the far side, and all that was required was a cool head and a steady nerve. They would be a barricade against the Earl of Manchester's horsemen, who would be naturally reticent after the wounding – perhaps death – of their general, Cromwell, and as long as the flank held firm, the Royalist foot would roll over the fracturing rebel divisions, and the encroaching night would fall upon a great victory.

'Keep the line!' Stryker repeated the call. He was with his men, Brownell's old command, at the centre of the line. On his right were the regiments belonging to Molyneux himself, and those of Tyldesley and Leveson, while on the left, most reassuringly, he saw the banners of Prince Rupert's Regiment of Horse, the most fearsome cavalry in the land. The line was outnumbered by those that now rose to a slow walk towards them, but they were not deterred. 'Keep the line!' Stryker called again. 'Pistols!'

He loaded his own twin flintlocks, then slid his sword in and out of its scabbard to ensure the blood of Cromwell had not glued it fast. He was vaguely aware of more horsemen rumbling a few hundred yards to the rear, tracing the line of Wilstrop Wood, but he put them to the back of his mind. All that mattered was the charge that he knew they would soon face.

The horsemen skirting Wilstrop Wood behind the expectant Royalist line wore no field sign, but they were not Cavaliers. Sir Thomas Fairfax stared straight ahead. His men, the human debris of a collapsed wing of horse, kept their gaze on him, though each of them prayed harder than ever they had before. Sir Thomas had made it through the enemy cavalry, leaving it to attack the Allied foot brigades, knowing that his failure had left those poor infantrymen so exposed. He had ridden hard, passing by the southern edge of the forest, the battle raging to his left, always watchful for enemy units hidden in the trees. There had been troopers haunting those ancient trunks, but they had been the flotsam of his own command, the very men smashed to smithereens by Goring, and they had emerged, little by little, from their hiding places, hoping that he would lead them to safety. Except that Sir Thomas Fairfax was not looking for safety; he was spoiling for a fight.

The fugitive Roundheads, perhaps a hundred out of the original three thousand, formed line behind their general, tearing away their white handkerchiefs and cantering from one side of the blood-streaked moor to the other, crossing the ground immediately behind the Royalist horsemen preparing to face the

Eastern Association riders. Sir Thomas gazed ruefully down at the line of the trench as his mount crossed it without breaking stride. Here the obstacle was barely a feature in the landscape, the depth shallow, the hedges low and sparse. If they only knew how difficult the crossing had been at the far side of the moor. As a lieutenant spurred ahead to explain their presence to the men riding beneath the cornets of the Earl of Manchester, Sir Thomas slumped in the saddle. He was half blind, his eye congealed with the blood from the wound in his cheek, and exhausted.

Out of the blurry near distance cantered a man wrapped in leather and plate. Even through his dizzy reeling, Sir Thomas recognized the prominent nose, the wide mouth and the wart above the right eye. He noticed, too, heavy bandaging at the man's neck. 'You are hurt?'

Lieutenant-General Oliver Cromwell seemed not to hear. 'What news?'

'My flank was routed,' Sir Thomas said. He forced himself to stay in the saddle. 'I am ashamed to report.'

Cromwell looked past him. 'These men you bring?'

'Mine,' Sir Thomas heard himself say. 'Gathered from defeat.'

Cromwell's gaze narrowed. 'And you have ridden here?'

Sir Thomas gave a bark of laughter that hurt his chest. 'All the way through the enemy.'

'How, sir?'

'Guile.'

Cromwell laughed too, a deep, guttural storm. 'God hath truly granted you great favour, Sir Thomas.'

Sir Thomas forced himself upright. The horse, pistol ball still lodged in its rump, skittered sideways a yard. 'You must take the flank, sir. Give our infantry succour, for our fortunes will fall as the moon rises. We are defeated in every quarter, save this.'

Cromwell glanced again at the hundred newcomers. 'That is my intent. And I will use these troopers for His purpose.'

Sir Thomas made to argue, but his face throbbed an acute prompt. 'I fear I am no use, Master Cromwell.'

'No, Sir Thomas,' Cromwell agreed. 'But your gallantry will be forever praised. Give me your men. I will use them well, you have my word.' He looked at a couple of Sir Thomas's troopers. 'Get him from the field.'

As the troopers tugged at his wounded mount's head collar, Fairfax glimpsed the approach of the man who commanded Cromwell's third line of horsemen, Lieutenant-General David Leslie. 'A charge?' the Scot asked.

'My men will tackle them head-on,' Cromwell answered. He gazed back at his line of horsemen. 'At the trot! Keep tight and the fight will be ours!'

Leslie's face grew taut. 'I would use my men, General. They are keen to fight.'

'With respect, General Leslie,' Cromwell said firmly, 'your men may be keen, but your steeds are too small and weak to break the malignant line.'

Leslie bridled. 'I have some of Balgonie's regiment. Their lances are long, Cromwell.' His voice was suddenly caustic: 'Of great range, compared to a Cavalier sword.'

Cromwell's brow furrowed for a second, but then he nodded. 'You take the flank. At the gallop. Use your lances, sir, for God will sharpen their points.'

David Leslie offered a tight bow and turned his mount. 'To work, gentlemen!'

Cromwell bellowed, his voice unwavering: 'To work, I say, for it is upon the left flank that this battle shall turn!'

Stryker only realized that the troops moving at their rear were not friendly when they circled completely round to the front and parleyed with a group of riders below Parliamentarian banners.

The horsemen of the Eastern Association formed two lines and turned their walk into a trot. There was something unnerving about the advance. The core of the king's cavalry were the gentry. Young, brash, arrogant men, born to the saddle, raised to the hunt and instilled with a reckless superiority that made them courageous and skilled. The Parliament men, by contrast, had none of this. They had required teaching, training, and, after too many defeats to count, they had come upon a system of warfare that suited their more pragmatic sensibilities. Where the Cavaliers favoured speed, the Roundheads favoured order, relying on organization and discipline to overcome the dashing opposition. As they crossed the ditch in good order, presenting a slow, measured approach, so the Royalist line, Stryker included, seemed uncertain of how to engage an enemy that seemed to deliberately dawdle.

'*Charge!*' Lord Molyneux screamed, just as Stryker was wondering whether the order would come at all. The Royalist line burst forth straight into the gallop, discharging pistols as they did so. But the enemy did not break, did not even falter, and then their own volley erupted, flashing bright in the encroaching gloom.

Stryker shrank low, straightened when the immediate danger had passed, and dragged his sword free. The first Parliamentarian line struck home.

It was not the melee Stryker had expected. When two forces met at the gallop, they scythed through one another, blades clashing as they crossed, only to wheel immediately about to engage in personal duels, intermingling so that field words and signs were the only way to differentiate friend from foe. But here there was no meld of man and horse, no crossing of the lines, no confusion. The Eastern Association troopers held their line together. Where the more advanced Cavaliers, those with the best steeds, smashed home, the rebel line parted, allowing the eager king's men through in ones and twos, but then they came together once more, closing the gaps as if they had never opened. And the tactic was working precisely because the two forces were not evenly matched. There was a second line, more men from the Earl of Manchester's pious army, and they isolated the overreaching Cavaliers, cutting them down as they crossed through the first line. Then the real fight began, and Stryker was there, his troops around him, slashing at whoever faced him. They were two masses of horsemen, like a pair of pike blocks at the press, each shoving and cleaving at the other, hoping their combined weight would cause the opposite wedge to splinter and collapse. It was a hard fight. A dirty, bloody, bitter fight. Skellen was near, for Stryker could hear the Gosport man's filth-laced war-cry even though he could not see him. Hood would be somewhere in the line too, and Barkworth, and they snarled and smashed and hacked, aware that they were outnumbered but knowing that theirs was the force with the famed, seasoned regiments belonging to Prince Rupert of the Rhine. They would not, could not break, for Rupert's Horse never lost a fight.

Then the trumpets blew.

David Leslie, Lieutenant-General of Horse, gritted his teeth and dipped his head as he steered his line to the right. They went east as soon as they crossed the ditch, peeling around the flank of the Royalist horsemen just as Cromwell led his first two lines directly into the enemy front rank. Leslie had the better part of a thousand men, and most were standard light cavalry, harque-busiers, who would do the work to which he set them without murmur of complaint. But it was the lancers he ordered into the vanguard.

It was a curiosity of war that brought lancers to Yorkshire. The English had no time for them, preferring the heavily armed, brute strength of the harquebusier, but equipping a man in helmet and plate, not to mention the array of weapons a caval-ryman brought to bear, made it necessary to put him on a large, powerful horse. Such creatures were difficult to come by in England, but north of the border it was next to impossible. Lancers, however, required smaller, lighter steeds. Theirs was not the tactic of weight and muscle, but of speed and manoeuvra-bility. That was why the Scottish army had lancers, and now they would show the sneering English how vital their contribution could be.

Leslie tried to shout some encouragement, but found his dry tongue glued firm to his teeth, so he prayed silently, let his bowels open in his breeches, and slowed his horse to watch the lancers go to work.

Stryker felt the blow. It came from his left, where Prince Rupert's Regiment of Horse made up the broad line, and at first he wondered if they had been impacted by a cannon ball. The force made the whole line shiver, like a wave crashing through a gorge, and he glanced in the direction of the left flank as Vos forced a Parliamentarian's horse back a step with a hammering hoof.

The lancers had torn the Royalist flank ragged. He had not even seen them advance, too thick was the smoke from so many discharged pistols, but now he could not miss their horrific toll. The Scots pierced deep into Rupert's prized troops, shredding their cohesion by surprise and by steel. Their long weapons snagged horse-flesh and punctured stomachs, crumpled breast-plates and dented helms, the sheer speed of the charge propelling them into the heart of the Royalist block. And though they might have been driven out by cooler heads, they were met with pure, blind panic.

Stryker, mired in the press with the Earl of Manchester's men, parried a wild sword slash, offered one of his own, and then found himself moving. He had given no command, but Vos was pulled by a tide that was not to be dammed. He braced, thighs burning, clinging for his life, and then, in a heartbeat, the Royalist formation was gone. The packed ranks disintegrated, cracking and scattering, turning their backs in terror, screaming at their own men to move aside so that they might flee. Terror-stricken faces leered at him in the chaos, the faces of king's men, hitherto unbeatable, blanched to ghostly wisps in the smoke. It was a rout of the worst kind, complete and unstoppable, and its tremors shuddered from Molyneux's troopers all the way to Rupert's. Pressed at the front by Cromwell's grim machine, and on the flank by skewering Scots lances, the entire Royalist right wing crumbled and fled. And Major Stryker, carried on the current, fled too.

★　 ★　 ★

Rupert, Count Palatine of the Rhine, Duke of Bavaria, First Duke of Cumberland, First Earl of Holderness, President of Wales and supreme commander of Royalist forces on Marston Moor, rode his mighty black stallion at a furious gallop headlong into the flight of his very best cavalry. He did not realise at first, could not countenance anything but a victory by the cream of his army, but then he saw the red scarves intermingled with the shredded cornets of Lord Molyneux, of Thomas Leveson and of Thomas Tyldesley, and he knew that at least part of his second line had shattered. And then, as he weaved his way through the thundering stream of refugees, he glimpsed his own flag. A small, bullet-holed scrap of blue and black cloth, hanging limp from the staff gripped by an equally shot-through cornet of horse. He drew up hard, positioning himself in the midst of the routing horde, holding palms skyward.

'S'wounds, do you run?' he bellowed. 'Follow me!'

Some reined in when they caught sight of their prince, though most did not so much as spare him a glance. In the eventide murk many would not discern him from any other rider, while most simply heard nothing but a panicked pulse in their ears.

The prince swore savagely, stared at the small group who had reformed with him, and saw a familiar face. It was one of scars, blackened by powder stains, with a single eye that glimmered quicksilver in the failing light.

'Stryker!' the prince snapped, kicking his stallion into the reclaimed party of troopers. 'Speak to me!'

'Manchester's horse attacked, Highness,' Stryker said rapidly. He knew how risible his explanation must be to the prince's ears, and felt himself colour. In the end he simply shrugged. 'The Scots swept our flank.'

Rupert's fierce stare lingered for a second, then he twisted in the saddle, summoning Sir Richard Crane with a quick wave. 'Get your men across this goddamned road, Sir Richard! Block the craven bastards!'

Prince Rupert drew his sword and kicked his black steed to

face southwards. 'Follow me, I say! We will unleash hell's flames upon these upstart Roundheads!'

Stryker's blade was already naked, smeared from hilt to tip in blood that streaked dark on the steel. He let Vos walk to take position a short way behind Rupert. Over the tall general's shoulder he could see thousands of helmets bobbing towards them in a vast swathe, like a string of grey pearls on a black cloth. These were not the broken Royalists, but the victorious Parliamentarians and Scots. They had not been unleashed to seek easy kills and easier plunder, but kept together, disciplined in their original formation, and they came to win a battle.

'With me!' Rupert screamed, holding his blade high. Boye was barking at his stallion's hind legs, as if cajoling the beast to the fight. 'God and the King! God and the King!'

Stryker looked over his shoulder as the cry echoed again and again. He reckoned they had four hundred men, perhaps five; it was not nearly enough. In the gloom he saw Skellen's laconic smile. The sergeant's cap had been knocked away by a blade that had also scalped him, and rivulets of blood drew dark lines round his sepulchral eye-sockets and all the way down to his chin. Lieutenant Hood was at his side, breathing hard, and the feline gaze of Barkworth glowed a short way behind them. Stryker nodded to all three, and Prince Rupert ordered them to charge.

It was not even a fight.

The three tight-knit and slow-moving lines of rebel horsemen, made up of troopers loyal to the earls of Manchester and Leven, had received very few casualties, and they overran the Royalist counter-attack in seconds, their vast, deep line curving around the small body of Cavaliers, enfolding and swallowing them whole like the gaping maw of a ravenous monster.

Stryker was behind Prince Rupert, forming the point of what had become an arrow formation, and they hit the enemy first. He found himself parrying on both sides, offering almost nothing in reply, and streaks of crimson were opening along the line of Vos's neck where steel tips nicked his flesh. There was no way out and no way to win. Stryker knew he would die. Then Simeon Barkworth was with him, forcing his mount to Vos's right, and the two fought side by side, kneecaps thumping, each protecting the flank of the other. The tiny Scot, so strange to behold and so lethal in a fight, screamed his Gaelic war-cry that promised a thousand terrible deaths, and crowed to the dark skies.

It was a carbine ball that killed him. A trooper with a black moustache and a white horse shot him from no range at all, and the bullet caught Barkworth flush in the throat. His head snapped back. The scar tissue swathing his neck, burned there by a German noose, was spattered in blood. His yellow eyes dimmed; then he toppled sideways, gargling, and vanished amongst the churning hooves.

Barkworth's horse bolted. It reared first, thrashing wildly, and Stryker was forced to duck lest his skull be cracked like an egg, but then the riderless creature gave in to its fear and lunged forth, punching a way through the thick mass of Parliament cavalrymen. The passage opened for just a moment, the blink of an eye, but Stryker took the chance with both hands. Vos had seen the gap too, lunging through as Stryker hammered at the intercepting blades that scythed into their path.

'*Highness!*' Stryker bellowed. '*Highness!*'

By the time he let out his breath, he was in clear space. Vos, wounded and heavily panting, had drilled right the way through to the far side of the melee, and Stryker whispered his thanks to Simeon Barkworth. He risked a glance behind. The Royalists had been utterly routed. Many riderless horses skittered around the outskirts of the swirling fight, while a large part of Rupert's cavalry were extricating themselves from the killing field, fighting their way out to gallop pell-mell back in the direction of York. In the darkness, he could see a that handful of horsemen had followed him west. Some were rebels, for he could see the white field signs fastened to their lobster-tailed pots, but three he recognized. He hauled on Vos's reins, turning the sorrel stallion in a wide arc to face his pursuers. Because one was the willowy visage of Sergeant Skellen and another was young Thomas Hood, and his heart leapt to see them alive. But it was the third man that really made him pause: he was tall and lean, billowing scarf ostentatiously knotted at his waist, and his head was encased in an unusual *Zischägge* helm. Running at his mount's hooves, barking wildly, was a large, white dog.

'Good Christ, I had never thought to see the like,' Prince Rupert of the Rhine blurted as he reined in. They had outrun the chasing pack, and now they gathered perhaps five hundred yards to the west of where the brief, bloody fight had taken place. Already they could see that the killing ground had shifted. Those Royalist horsemen who had managed to break clear of the broiling clash had been pursued by a large body of Eastern Association horse to be hunted all the way to the gates of York. The rest of General Cromwell's victorious wing was now reforming in perfect order and wheeling about to observe the infantry conflagration burning along the line of the ditch in the centre of the moor. Rupert watched them, his handsome face utterly forlorn. 'My own troopers beat. What sorcery have they conjured here?'

Stryker thought it best not to note that discipline, bravery and religious zeal was a more potent brew than any witch's broth. Instead he eyed the chasing pack that was closing in quickly. 'What now, Highness?'

Rupert was weeping. He sniffed hard as he cleared his throat. 'To the fight. We'll die here, my friends, for I'll not live in a land where mine own regiment is routed by the likes of Oliver Cromwell and a parcel of Scotch lancers.'

Stryker shook his head. 'You must endure, Highness.' He slammed home his blade. 'You are our champion.'

Skellen, face almost completely masked in congealed blood, wiped his sword on his horse's neck and propped it on his shoulder. 'Wi'out you, General, we're done for. The lads fight in your name.'

The prince shook his head. 'They fight in the name of the King.'

'He is in the right of it, Highness,' Stryker said. 'You are their talisman. You must survive this.' He looked back towards the chimneys of Tockwith. Around the village, he remembered, there were fields of thick crops. 'There. Into the beanstalks, I beg you. Hide away, Highness. Do not let the enemy make sport of your capture. It will damage your uncle's cause most terribly.'

Rupert wiped away tears with his sleeve. 'All is lost.'

'The flank is lost,' Stryker argued, more brusquely than he would ordinarily have risked. 'Not the battle. Not the war. But you cannot fight your way back to our lines. Your person is too conspicuous.' The five enemy riders, four Parliament men and one Scots lancer, were close now, and he watched as Skellen and Hood spurred out to cut them off. 'Go, Highness.'

Prince Rupert of the Rhine, the most formidable warrior in the land, was suddenly, shockingly the boy Stryker had once known, lost and frightened. His face was pale, gaunt and strained in the half-light. His fine clothes were tattered, smeared in dark stains and nicked by blades. His thin mouth flapped open like a net.

'For Christ's sake, Highness, go!' Stryker cried. Rupert blinked.

There was no time left. Stryker kicked Vos hard, felt the animal flinch beneath him, and knew the strength was fast ebbing from his old comrade, but now was not the time for such concerns. Skellen had already killed one of the Parliament men with a well-timed thrust, and Hood was engaged with another. Stryker did not bother with his sword, drawing his flintlocks instead, and kept them low, concealed behind Vos's neck until the last moment. The riders came at him from either side, aiming to slice him like pincers. He let them come as close as his nervous heart would allow, then levelled the pistols. To his rushing relief, neither misfired in the damp, and one of the rebels was snatched clean off his saddle. The other was clipped in the shoulder; it was not a killing blow, but was enough to send him wide with an agonized grimace. He went to assist Hood, but a shrill yowl made him wrench violently round. He expected to see the

349

prince in trouble, but what he saw was a dog impaled on a long lance. The Scots rider was looming above Boye, Rupert's beloved poodle, grinning as he walked his mount past the skewered creature. The Scot laughed as he dismounted to collect his prize, for the death of Boye would be a tantalizing morsel upon which the rebel printing presses would feast. For a moment Stryker thought to butcher the man, but he barely had the strength to fight dangerous foes, let alone a man hefting a dead dog into a saddle, so he chose to go to his prince.

But Prince Rupert of the Rhine had already gone. Stryker caught a glimpse of a shimmering helm at the shadowy edge of Tockwith's bean fields, and then, like a wind-blown candle, it vanished.

Edward Montagu, Second Earl of Manchester, had been swept away in the rout, and now his group were one small part of the detritus of a battle lost. Always they scanned the land to the north, terrified that the next arrival would be a harbinger of Goring's victorious horsemen.

They reached a crossroad a mile to the south where a neatly arrayed body of horsemen had drawn up. They were incongruous amongst the rabble of Manchester's party.

'I gather men, my lord,' the commanding officer replied when questioned by the earl.

Manchester stared hard at the officer, half expecting a Royalist ruse. 'To what end?'

The corners of the officer's mouth turned down in bewilderment. 'To fight, lord.'

Now Manchester was certain of trickery, and he signalled for his bodyguards to be ready. 'The battle is lost.'

'I had thought as much,' the officer replied, 'but I received a rider from General Cromwell.'

'Cromwell?' Manchester shook his head. 'He is wounded.'

'He returned. His wing has destroyed the malignants on that side. Even now they prepare to assist our foot.'

Manchester's heart was beginning to quicken. His mouth was

dry. 'Our foot is beaten,' he persisted, pointing back at the road and the shattered Allied infantry. 'Do you not see these thousands, man?'

'Many are beaten, but not all, my lord. Your own foot, under Crawford, do hold their place on the left, while Lindsay's brigade fight with great valour on the right. That is what General Cromwell's message conveyed. He orders every man back to the field forthwith.'

'Then we return,' the Earl of Manchester said. 'I will take my banner back to the moor.'

One of his advisers urged his horse closer. 'My lord Manchester, I must advise against such a course. It can lead only to ruin.'

'To flee will lead only to humiliation,' Manchester said firmly. 'Did you not hear this man? The day is not lost. Not yet, leastwise.' He cast his gaze across the assembled men, then back at those trailing along the road. 'Do not desert our cause, fellows! God is with us! Follow me!'

# CHAPTER 22

Lieutenant Hood joined Stryker and Skellen as they rode back into the heart of Marston Moor. They were forced to pass between blocks of enemy cavalry, but Skellen had taken a blue bonnet from a wounded Scot, while the officers snatched scraps of paper from some of the myriad corpses littering the field and inserted them into their hats. The victorious rebel horse were not interested in three stragglers bearing the correct field sign when a larger prize called to them.

Hood took off his hat, pushing sweat-matted hair from his eyes as he looked nervously behind. 'They do not give chase.'

Stryker mused: 'They mean to fall upon our exposed flank.' The Royalist foot brigades clustered in the very centre of the moor, their stands of pike swaying like miniature forests as they moved. It was almost dark now, but such was the ferocity of musket fire that banks of flame flared all the way along the disputed ditch, highlighting patches of the battle. What Stryker saw was a bitterly contested brawl. The nearest enemy infantry battaile had crossed to the north side of the ditch, battering their way into the Royalist position inch by bloody inch, but the rest of the rebel front was severely lopsided. The other battailes remained on the south side, their Royalist counterparts pushing right up to the hedgerow fringing the trench. He could see pike blocks judder forwards across the shallow frontier, fall to a swift, thrusting engagement, and retire for their units of shot to light up the smoky gloom. Scores of drummers rumbled a constant beat: it was a sound like thunder not heard since Noah's time. With it mixed the yells of thousands of men clashed in hideous discord.

What was clear, however, was the congestion throughout the

centre of the moor. All three of Rupert's carefully plotted battle lines had effectively converged after the first hectic moments when the front line had been shattered and the second had come to its aid, and now they were bunched into one mass, contesting the part of Marston Moor around which all else pivoted.

'We must warn the foot,' Hood said as he steered his mount past a drake, its wheels splintered, muzzle buried in the mud. 'They have no support.'

'Did not Goring win over there?' Skellen growled, indicating the area to the east where the modest homes of Long Marston would be. 'Where's the bastard got to?'

Stryker squinted at the chaos. There were horsemen in that maelstrom, but there were not enough of them to constitute the full Royalist left-wing horse. Where were they? A knot formed at the pit of his stomach, and he pointed up at the ridge line, a black mass against the slate southern sky. 'Filling saddle bags, like as not.'

'Shite on a shovel,' Skellen intoned. 'Not again.'

Hood spat on the slick turf as his horse trampled a broken halberd into the gory mire. 'Forgive me, sir, but have our Cavaliers learnt nothing?'

Stryker shrugged. It was the ill-gotten reputation of the Royalist horse that allowed Parliamentarian pamphleteers to refer to Rupert as the Duke of Plunderland. Once again it seemed the prince's riders were more interested in treasure than glory, and this time they had left their infantry out on a precarious limb.

Skellen took a bottle from his bags. 'A pox on those arseholes.' He lifted the vessel in a toast. 'To fallen fedaries. Them with more honour in their elbows than Goring's fuckin' magpies.'

Stryker took the bottle and drank. It was small beer, watery and tepid, but it was like elixir on his parched throat. 'To Simeon Barkworth. A better man there never was.'

'Jack Sprat,' Skellen intoned. Stryker thought he saw tears in the big man's eyes.

Hood drank too. And then they rode to the fight.

\*       \*       \*

Over on the rightmost flank of the Allied front line, Sir Charles Lucas galloped to glory. His brave Cavaliers had wheeled, consolidated, and charged for a third time. Crawford-Lindsay's Scots, he knew, would not withstand another attack. They were shaken enough by the rout of the bulk of their front line, but to endure two heavy charges on one flank while taking thick musketry on another was tantamount to suicide. No one could fight on two fronts, and Lucas would prove it.

'Cheer!' he bellowed into the rushing air. 'Cheer, you devils! Let them hear you!'

His blade, the Milanese beauty, whipped a silver circle above his blackened helm, and he felt elation in his veins. A dead horse, its rider mangled beneath, seemed to rear from the turf, and he braced, but his mount flew clean over it, as if it sprouted angels' wings. Then they were close, achingly close, and the pikes were down, presented in a wall of needles that now showed gaps where none had been before. This time the obstinate Scots would break.

The volley crashed across the near flank of the hedgehog. Smoke belched as hundreds of flaming tongues lapped the faces of the men who had pulled triggers in unison. Lucas heard the screams of his Cavaliers, but they knew they had gone too far to pull up. They would smash their way into the formation and slay the musketeers cowering within, and then they would continue on into the heart of the faltering Allied line. The pikes would drop, thrown down by disheartened and exhausted men. Any moment, Lucas thought. Any moment now.

It was only when the charge hit the hedgehog formation that he realized the pikemen had held and the charge would end on their spear-points. The Royalist horsemen swerved away, and it was their mounts, rather than the waiting Scotsmen, who were exhausted, lumbering about impotently to swirl around the edges of the blue-capped brigade. And all the while muskets cracked at them, picking at mount and man indiscriminately, horses tumbling with anguished cries as they snapped legs and crushed their riders.

Lucas slashed in useless rage at the hedge of staves that rattled against his steel, but not even they would snap, for their tips were strengthened with iron cheeks so that the blades could not be severed. He could barely believe his bad fortune as he kicked away from the jeering circle. He had never seen infantry stand for so long under such furious an assault, and he wondered how in the world he would break the Earl of Crawford-Lindsay's resolve.

Lucas was still wondering when his horse collapsed beneath him, a front fetlock shattered by a shot from one of the small field guns operated somewhere within the Allied foot. The animal hit the ground face first, throwing his rider clear of the stirrups. Lucas immediately tasted mud, then blood. Then the world went black.

Oliver Cromwell's harquebusiers had barely suffered a handful of casualties in the final rout of the prince's force, and it took them only moments to reform. Now he led them east in a broad wave, letting the thudding hooves trample the wreckage of the fight as they regarded the bitter struggle for the battle's core.

Cromwell took off his helmet and wiped the powder stains from below his eyes as the rider he had dispatched reined in at his side. 'Well? Who commands?'

'My lord Manchester, sir,' the rider answered hoarsely.

Cromwell shook his head. 'He fled.'

The man shrugged. 'He returns.'

'Praise God,' Cromwell murmured. If Manchester had come back, then the foot would fight all the harder. 'And Rupert?'

'Disappeared.'

'His flank? They rally?'

'They do not.'

'Good,' Cromwell said. 'Disposition of our infantry?'

'The enemy foot has the best of it, but Lucas has been beaten.'

'Beaten? He fell upon our infantry on the far side, did he not?' Cromwell's neck smarted, and he pressed a palm into the layered dressing. 'I heard tell they routed.'

'Many routed. But Lord Lindsay's brigade fought him off, praise God. They have killed his own horse and taken him prisoner. Baillie and Lumsden bring up support even now. The matter is stable.'

'What of Goring? The Northern Horse defeated Fairfax. Where are they?'

'To plunder.'

Cromwell thanked God as he whispered: 'Folly of greed.'

'General?'

'Be under no illusion, sirrah. If Prince Robber's troops coveted less and prayed more, they would be unstoppable. Thank Jesu for their avarice. It has won this battle.' And indeed it had, Cromwell thought. The Royalist right-wing horse had been completely destroyed, and its left wing appeared to be in self-inflicted disarray. George Goring's tidal wave, which had swept through Black Tom's force with such ease, had been the cause of its own destruction. Lucas had shown discipline, but he had been unfortunate enough to run headlong into the most courageous brigade possessed by the Covenanters. But Goring had allowed his men to chase fugitives and sack baggage, and thus they were nowhere to be seen. The Royalist foot were about to suffer a nightmare.

Oliver Cromwell gazed eastwards to where almost two-score regiments cluttered Marston Moor, bunching around the line of the ditch in smoke-clogged battle. He put his helmet back atop his head. 'Send to Lord Manchester with my compliments,' he said eventually. 'I mean to obliterate the enemy infantry from the flank. Make plea for him to press their centre. We will crack their resolve betwixt us.' He closed his eyes. 'Let us finish this.'

The fight in the centre of Marston Moor fulminated at the cusp of the ditch. The Royalists were on the north bank, the Parliamentarians and Scots on the south, save the Earl of Manchester's brigade, under Major-General Crawford, who had striven across the barrier to take the fight to the prince's army. The ditch itself was bare now, its broken hedge line almost entirely shredded to stubble by pike and shot, and its depths had been filled by bodies that lay sightless and knotted in macabre piles along its length.

Captain Lancelot Forrester was part of the Northern Foot in all but name. His regiment, Mowbray's Foot, had been brigaded with one of Newcastle's white-coated units, so that they already acted as one, but now Colonel Mowbray was dead, and the battle was as hot and lurid as anything he had ever experienced, so that barely an order, by voice or drum, could be discerned through the din. Thus, they moved with one mind, the pikemen and musketeers, driven only by instinct and the need to survive.

They had been winning the fight. The middle brigades of the Army of Both Kingdoms had crumpled and fallen, and the Royalists had moved up to secure the kill, but the Englishmen under Crawford had ground out an unlikely advance to Forrester's right, and the Scots under Lindsay had somehow endured an hour of hell over on his left, which meant that the Royalist flanks were exposed to volley fire, and all that had come of their early success was a cruel stalemate. Now the brigades operated independently as they came up against an opposing force, so that both armies were bunched, their cohesion gone as pike blocks advanced and retired by turns, with neither side managing to punch cleanly through.

Forrester's brigade had wheeled to their right to engage the strident men in green and red coats beneath the banners of the Earl of Manchester. The fight pulsated back and forth, the rebel battaile inching north, only to be pushed back at point of pike by its Royalist counterpart. Forrester, on the edge of his redcoats, used his pistol, firing into the dense rebel block with no idea as to where the bullet flew. The fog was thick and choking. The grass was wet with rain, blood and entrails, and he slipped at every pace. Occasionally he would hear a thud as a musket-ball slammed into flesh. He might have vomited with the terror of it, but there was nothing left in his twisted stomach.

A huge volley crashed in smoke and flame from the Parliamentarian position. Forrester shied away, turning his body in profile as though he waded into a strong wind. The files in his battaile bunched together like a folded fan as each man sought shelter behind the man in front. Screams ripped through the perpetual roar, but then they were on the attack again, advancing over the bodies of their friends to put their own lead into the filthy ether. Forrester stepped back to load his pistol. He caught sight of a messenger on horseback, pulling on his reins to gallop free of the front line. Then he saw a familiar face in the crowd; one that was badly blemished and perfectly round. He commanded whitecoats but wore a suit of blue with a blue and red cross stitched on the arm.

'Captain Croak!' Forrester ran to him. 'Heartened to see you alive, my friend!'

Elias Croak, the man who had saved his life at York's Mount sconce, brandished the grin Forrester remembered well. 'We've done it, sir!'

'Done it?'

Croak's cheeks were soot-shaded, his twitch furious. He flinched as the iron ball from a small field piece ripped hot through the air just a few yards away. 'Fairfax's horse were routed in the east, so said the herald. Goring gives chase. There is word that all three of the enemy's generals have abandoned the field!'

Forrester gritted his teeth. 'You kick a man when he's down, you must make sure he dies. Lest he kick you back.'

'But they are in disarray!' Croak blurted. Now he levelled the sword eastward. 'Look, sir, Goring's horse almost have the beating of them.'

Forrester followed his gaze as more musketry bellowed near and far, but all he could see was the tussle between the stubborn Scots and what remained of the Royalist horse. 'They should have penetrated by now. And where are the rest? That is one small part of our left wing, Elias.'

Croak seemed not to care. 'They will join soon enough.'

'And where the devil is our right wing?' Forrester went on. 'Prince Rupert's own regiment is there. They should have swept the enemy clean back to East Anglia by now.' He looked to the rear, where the reserve of horse had been. 'Widdrington's regiment. What happened to them? All is not well. And where is Newcastle?'

'He is here,' Croak chirped, unperturbed. 'He returned with his guard. They fight at all quarters.'

Forrester almost laughed. 'So our generals are nowhere to be found. Prince Rupert has not been seen at all, while the marquis gallops the field as though he were a company captain. If we are a great beast of war, Captain Croak, where in God's name is our head?'

'You worry too much, Captain, truly you do. Look there.' Croak pointed into the west where a body of horsemen walked towards them. 'Here they come. Our brave cavalry, back from the fray. The Prince at their head, I'll wager.'

Forrester looked. 'That is not our cavalry,' he whispered as more and more came into view, tightly arrayed, deep in rank and vast in number. There were thousands. Their banners could not be read in the murk, but he could see the scraps of white glowing from their pots. His guts lurched. 'Oh, Christ Jesus, help us.' As Croak gaped, Forrester cupped hands to his mouth. 'Charge for horse! Charge for horse!'

The cavalry of the Eastern Association were coming, and with them they brought only death.

It was just as well, John Kendrick thought, that he was a hard-man, and therefore unable to be killed, for otherwise he felt sure he would have died a hundred times already this day.

All three of the Allied lines were engaged now, the third ordered up to support the faltering men in front. Things might have been over, Kendrick believed, had the Northern Horse broken Lindsay's brave resistance, but somehow those suicidal Scots had weathered the storm long enough for reinforcements to make their way into the blood-drenched bout, and the worm had well and truly turned.

Kendrick stared up at Lord Manchester as the earl cantered past his unit, braving bullets for the sake of conspicuousness. The effect of Manchester's sudden, unexpected appearance on the field had reinvigorated the tiring troops, and now he hailed his infantrymen despite the danger. 'Generals Cromwell and Leslie have taken the flank!'

The men huzzahed in a deep, rolling chorus.

The earl drew breath. 'Prince Robber is defeated,' he bellowed, 'perhaps dead, pray God!' He paused as the men cheered again, louder than before. 'Their foot have no support! We will hold our position until our cavalry strike, and then we shall advance!'

Kendrick stared westward. Out there, in the gathering gloom, he could see the parading banners of Scots and Eastern Association cavalry emerging on to the moor. Manchester, it seemed, had already made contact with Cromwell, and a plan was in the offing.

Kendrick studied the field, his eyes straining against the shroud of smoke and dusk. The enemy brigades appeared to convulse as they prepared for the rebel horsemen sweeping from the left like the bristles of a vast broom, Royalist stragglers, stranded by their wounds, felled at a stroke and mowed mercilessly down. The cavalry moved slowly, because they were unopposed and because they were expertly led, and Kendrick imagined with relish the dread their steady poise would engender. It was left to the infantry, so embattled and ragged, to maintain the press, keep enemy eyes trained on the threat to the south while their flank would be ripped to shreds. This was a pincer movement that would crack Royalist resistance and snatch glory from the jaws of defeat.

Still Kendrick looked for Stryker. Still he was disappointed. But now, at least, he would be part of a famous victory, and he turned the cinquedea in his iron-clad hand, letting the last light dance on the blade as it slanted through the clouds. He would bide his time, wait for the enemy ranks to shatter, and then he would go to the slaughter.

Stryker had made for Sir Edmund Mowbray's Regiment of Foot, but in the swirling chaos he could find neither the colonel himself nor his huge colour of red and white. Instead he, Hood and Skellen ran upon a brigade of Northern Foot dressed in coats of green and of yellow. One of the many flags was yellow and silver, one he recognized as the standard of Sir Richard Strickland. The regiment had been in the Royalist third line during the day, but it was now in amongst the rest as the whole battle line converged haphazardly, blasting at the rebel line with all it could muster.

He had come to warn them of the enemy cavalry advance, but they could see the Earl of Manchester's horsemen bearing down upon the centre of the moor for themselves, and had shifted into their hackled formation without delay. They were unwilling to part for three unknown riders, so Stryker and his men were forced to linger on the outside. He kept Vos under tight control, holding the jittery animal in sway by granite thighs and fists. He searched for Strickland, could not find him, and shrank low as a fierce volley of shot rent the air all around. The enemy infantry had extra impetus now, for they must have seen their cavalry begin its move, seen too the torpor that would result in their opponents' hunkering into the solid but static hedgehog, and the air seemed suddenly closer, hotter, as the Parliament ranks laid down renewed fire.

'Keep form!' Stryker screamed into the pike forest. 'Keep the shape! They will not charge circle!'

But that all depended upon the circle remaining intact.

Lieutenant-General Oliver Cromwell had begun the day with four thousand horse. Now, with a portion of his cavalry riding into the country to hunt down the routed enemy, he rode at the head of just over two thousand, made up of his own troopers of the Eastern Association and of David Leslie's Scots. The English units thudded gauntleted fists upon shining breastplates, the clang echoing over the hills, while the Scots chanted a war-cry in their exotic tongue. The lancers of Balgonie, on their spry mounts, lofted the long, sharp spears that had already put paid to Prince Rupert's highly experienced regiment. They were a deadly battle line, forged together in the blood of the shattered enemy wing, and now they went towards the fulcrum of the day's encounter.

The English harquebusiers of the front line drew the first of their two firearms, for some a carbine, for others a pistol, and carefully looped the leather reins about the free hand.

Cromwell, out in front, fastened his helm and lowered the face guard. He raised a gloved hand, held it like the sword of Damocles, and waited for a new shiver of pain to trace its way over his injured neck. Then he swept it down, slapping his thigh.

The horses went to the trot. They swept across the moor, splitting line only to skirt the detritus of battle, reforming as soon as they could to present an unbroken front of steel and malevolence. As they rode they chanted psalms, shouted prayers, and felt their hearts hammer against the Bibles that were held fast against their ribs. The rain had gone but the wind was up, and their cornets fluttered and snapped as they bore down on the flank of the enemy infantry, who would be hesitant to form the spiny defensive perimeter because they would be easy prey for the muskets of Crawford's foot brigade.

They were a hundred yards out. The earth shuddered beneath their hooves. They could hear the frightened shouts coming from the Royalist divisions, but knew nothing could stop their assault. They raised their voices, praising God in the highest, but always, always keeping to the steady trot their dour general insisted upon.

'God with us!' Cromwell called, his throat suddenly arid.

They swarmed over the moor, sweeping from west to east in a wave that would roll over the human shore, drowning everything in its path. Infantry could stand against cavalry. Men could huddle behind a breastwork made of ash poles and entrust their survival to a horse's fear of sharpened steel. But they could not achieve such a feat if its other flanks were raked at the same moment by cannon balls and bullets. Lord Lindsay's hard-nosed Covenanters had done it, but they had faced only a small number of Goring's original complement. Now the malignant brigades would shudder under Cromwell's well-ordered wing, and their fortunes would not turn so favourably.

When they were fifty yards out they levelled their firearms. The pikes fell to the charge position, ready to impale any man or beast foolish enough to risk contact.

Thirty yards and still at the trot. They pulled their triggers. Smoke crashed around the riders' heads. The Royalist blocks visibly shivered. They thrust home the flintlocks and drew their swords.

And the first of the enemy ranks fell apart.

Stryker felt Vos shake. At first it was a tremor, as though the creature was cold, but then the great Dutch stallion stumbled. He fell forwards slowly, and Stryker slid on to the horse's granite-hard neck. He felt the blood, slick on his gloves, and knew there was too much. Then Vos was down, slumped on his fore-knees, his breathing a gargled rasp like an iron file on a grate, and Stryker jerked his boots from the stirrups, rolling to his right as the beast collapsed in the opposite direction. He scrambled up, throwing himself over Vos and dropping his sword so that he could cradle the heavy head. The beast's breaths were unfathomably fast and pathetically shallow. Stryker counted five bullet holes in his neck, ragged and black and gleaming.

Vos meant 'fox' in the Dutch – he had named him thus for his red coat – yet that magnificent pelt was now dyed from ear to shoulder in a deeper, darker hue. Stryker held the horse, his companion through so many fights, as the animal gave a final, violent shake and fell still. He dropped the head, muzzle sinking into the gore, and scrambled for the saddle, hands plunging into the bags, ripping the straps, gutting the innards as blood smeared. His pipe came away, dropping into the mud at his knees, and a wooden bowl, a tinder box and a length of match. Skellen was above him, on foot, shouting at him to get up, and Hood was there too, grasping at his shoulders, but he shrugged the lieutenant away. Then he found what he was looking for: Faith Helly's Bible. Hate-Evil Sydall's cipher. He tore it free of the bag, taking his pistols too, and snatched up his sword. Hood and Skellen took him, dragging him physically upwards so that he slid clumsily to his feet. There was no time to return to their own mounts, so the trio pushed their way into the hedgehog as the cavalry of the Eastern Association crashed home. The pikes jutted out to block them, and they veered away, seeking easier quarry, but that was not the end of the danger. Stryker was safe behind the pikemen now, sheltered against the storm, but he knew it was an illusion. Strickland's men muttered, as they witnessed the grinning harquebusiers roll down through the Royalist lines to pick off the weakest units. And quietly, so quietly, they questioned whether this was their fight at all. Because the enemy raiders were numerous and confident, and they all knew that between those spiteful horsemen and the mighty tide of Allied foot, they would stand scanty chance without the support of their own cavalry.

'Hold!' Stryker brayed, though none seemed to heed the call. They were frightened, tempted to break cover and run, and there was nothing he could do to stop them.

He tucked the Bible into his breast pocket and peered through the gaps between the heads of the pikemen and musketeers. The adjacent brigade was in trouble. Like wolves sensing the weakest heifer in a herd, the tawny-scarfed troopers had swirled around its perimeter, maintaining and prolonging their attack because the circle had not been fully formed. Perhaps some of their officers were dead, or simply too frozen by fear to give the right orders, but their manoeuvre to shield against horse had stalled and now they were caught between charging their pikes and presenting their muskets. Holes had opened up, like fissures in a dam, and the horsemen lunged into them; soon the brigade that hitherto had been so well ordered and expertly drilled melted away. In the end, the only thing left to do was run, and so they ran.

'Hold the circle!' Stryker bawled to Strickland's brigade, but he could barely hear his own voice. He could sense men filtering out to the rear, hear the clatter as pikes were discarded, and knew that the formation was beginning to fracture as its neighbour had done.

A massive volley of muskets boomed from the south. Men fell all around. The rebel foot were crossing the ditch now, pressing their advantage as Cromwell's crowing horsemen were unleashed to carve deep furrows into the staggering Royalist blocks. It was too much. Strickland's brigade collapsed, jettisoning weapons and scarves and hats and snapsacks in their desperation to be free of the killing ground. They were making for Wilstrop Wood, but there was at least a hundred paces to cover before reaching the tree line, and there was no chance the fugitives would make it before the rebel cavalry hunted them down.

Stryker, Hood and Skellen bunched back to back. Stryker's pistols were in his belt, for there was no time to load them, and he held his sword out straight, challenging any who might make sport of his slaughter. The rout raged everywhere as the enemy cavalry spurred into the fleeing throng to slash at backs and skulls. Their infantry were on the march now, coming up to support their shattering success. More Royalist brigades were imploding with every moment.

'The wood?' Hood called.

Stryker flinched as a pistol ball whipped between them. 'No! We'll never make it!'

'There!' Skellen snapped. He unslung the halberd from his back, pointing it at a brigade fifty paces to the south-west of their position. 'Lambs!'

Stryker nodded. 'They're standing firm!' The first of the rebel foot were close to their position now, driving blades into the fallen wounded as they swept up the field. Soon their pikes would be jammed into whatever remained of the Royalist units. 'We'll take refuge with the whitecoats!'

'But they will soon be alone!' Hood shouted. 'Stranded!'

Stryker glanced round. 'You're right, Tom, it is a terrible idea. Tell me yours.'

Hood opened his mouth, then hesitated. He did not have to see how many of their routed comrades were already being put to the sword by the exultant cavalry, for he could hear their tormented screams well enough. In the end he simply blew out his cheeks in resignation. 'After you, sir!'

They bolted. Stryker jumped bodies and weaponry, fearing a slip or trip would be the end of him and all the while expecting the thunder of hooves at his back. A corporal ran past him, evidently resolved upon the same course, but the man, younger and fleeter of foot, went down in a welter of blood as a carbine ball shattered the back of his skull. Stryker did not look back. He kept running, sprinting until his legs burned and his chest felt as though it would explode. Up ahead were the whitecoats, Newcastle's Regiment of Foot, and their formation had not been compromised. Their banners of rich red, adorned with the cross of Saint George and the white crosses of the Marquis of Newcastle, called to him, beckoning him to their protection.

He reached the brigade as Skellen bellowed a warning from behind. Stryker turned, just in time to see the flash of a blade stab down at him from the back of a snorting destrier, and he threw himself flat, fingers clawing the mud. He felt the heavy sword slice the air, heard the hiss but felt no pain, and he rolled to the side, scrabbling in the slick filth and pushing himself up as if the ground itself might swallow him.

Then the assailant was gone, too fearful of the poised pikes to linger, and Stryker, Skellen and Hood were hauled into the bristling circle as the rest of Prince Rupert's grand army disintegrated around them.

As the vast Royalist battle line crumbled so the horsemen belonging to the Earl of Manchester and the Earl of Leven, commanded this day by Cromwell and Leslie, gave chase. They spurred into the fraught chaos, slashing at heads and spines, leaning low out of saddles to cleave a fleeing man's neck or snatch the standard from an ensign's desperate grip. And as the men loyal to the Crown – men who had marched all the way from the west coast, men who had held York for so long against such insurmountable odds – turned to run away, the Allied infantry, galvanised by the Earl of Manchester's return and spearheaded by the rehabilitated Major-General Crawford, swarmed into them.

'Parliament!' Captain John Kendrick snarled as he whipped the top of a musketeer's skull away with his sword as casually as if he shelled a boiled egg. 'God with us!' He did not believe in any deity, of course, and nor did he particularly care about any Parliament, but today he would indulge the whims of his new Puritan comrades. After all, he had not expected this. It was, he admitted, something of a miracle.

Kendrick was near Crawford as they advanced. Manchester's Foot, on the extreme left of the rebel line, were already across the ditch when Cromwell struck, and now they wheeled right to come at the Royalists from the west. The huge Scots contingent, away to his right, clambered over the corpse-filled trench and pushed directly north, squeezing the enemy like dogs herding sheep, so that the twin armies of Prince Rupert and the Marquis of Newcastle were now just a single, throbbing multitude. The herd shunted backwards. They had not all capitulated, and those that were tempted quickly learnt that to run meant to be hunted and slaughtered by the whooping cavalry. So they gathered instinctively behind the only brigade that remained entirely intact, a stoically solid block of white-coated men who loaded and fired with impressive regularity from beneath a score of red banners. The whitecoats faced their persecutors as the broken Royalist horde edged north and east, step by anguished step, retiring towards the ancient road that would take them to York. Swarming after them, tramping in their blood-slick wake, was one of the largest armies to have ever been assembled in the three kingdoms.

Kendrick saw his enemies as they were swallowed by the whitecoats. Two he recognized vaguely, the stripling officer and the tall, lugubrious sergeant, but theirs were not the faces that sent so violent a judder through him. The face of the third man – lean and pale beneath a wide-brimmed hat and framed in long, raven-dark hair – was etched on John Kendrick's mind, never to be erased. It was a face that was hard. One of sharp lines, weathered creases and a single, grey eye that seemed to plunge through a man like the stab of a poniard. Perhaps, the Vulture thought, there was a God after all.

Stryker loaded his pistols and slammed them into his belt. It was a strange world, the inner sanctum of a hedgehog, for, though the sounds of battle were undiminished, it was impossible to clearly see what transpired on the outside. Officers and preachers milled at its core below the colours of the various individual companies, while rank upon rank of musketeers formed the first of several concentric circles around them, and three more ranks of pike made the outermost spines that gave the formation its name.

A blast of enemy musketry crackled from beyond the shielding pikemen, punching several back, their spaces filled by the men behind. One ball hit a musketeer who was moving up to present his piece, and he thudded on to his back, his face almost completely wiped away. Stryker retrieved the dropped musket, blowing on the match to keep it alive.

'You said he would come, Lord!'

Stryker spun round. 'Seek Wisdom!'

The elderly priest tugged at his filthy beard and glared skyward. 'I doubted you, Lord, and I am a wretch for it!'

Stryker laughed. 'You linger here?'

'I am no apparition, you ugly English bastard! Of course I linger. I offer these men prayer.' Seek Wisdom and Fear the Lord Gardner frowned suddenly. 'Where is Simeon?' He glanced past Stryker, to Skellen and Hood, and Stryker saw real sorrow in the baby-blue gaze. 'He'd not leave your side easy, boy. Like a bloody mongrel at his master's heel, that one.'

'He is no more,' Stryker said simply.

'Then may he know peace.' Gardner closed his eyes. 'Take him into your arms, Almighty, for he was a good man.'

'Stryker,' a man said, coming to stand beside the Welsh priest. 'Jesu, but you're a grand thing to behold.'

Skellen and Hood offered their hands for Lancelot Forrester to shake in turn, as Stryker grinned. 'Orders?'

Forrester shrugged. 'Stand and fight, old man.' He paused as they all flinched against the tide of a new volley. A teenage herald, not part of the Northern Foot but, like Stryker, part of the hedgehog's new-found jetsam after the rout of his own unit, reeled into their midst and slumped to his knees, winged by a bullet that shredded the cloth at his shoulder. Forrester watched him, unmoved, as he spoke. 'What else may we do? Someone must give those bastard riders pause for thought. The army will seek refuge in York, and we here shall cover its retreat.' He spat between his boots. 'The whitecoats will stand and fight, Stryker, and I am bloody glad to have you with us.'

# CHAPTER 23

The Army of Both Kingdoms fell upon the stranded brigades like an avalanche. Their infantry spearheaded by the Eastern Association swarmed through the acrid clouds, pouring volley fire as they went so that the tightly bunched Royalist foot shivered and shook under the leaden hailstorm, and all the while Cromwell's shattering horsemen harried the men remaining in formation and picked off those who did not.

Stryker fired his musket, the Montero-capped heads of the men in front vanishing in the billow of smoke. He moved back a pace as senior officers howled the command. Retiring in good order was a painstaking business at the best of times, but the enemy horsemen would not let them deploy out of circle, so they were forced to shuffle across their own tangled detritus, moving with aching sluggishness while their southern flank was raked by ceaseless musket fire. The urge to break and run was almost too much to bear, but by placing themselves between the advancing enemy and the York road they might just prevent a massacre, because the rest of Prince Rupert's ruined army was in full retreat.

The battle was lost – they all knew it – but the whitecoats of the Northern Foot were making nuisance enough to prevent the rebel cavalry, Cromwell's brutal warriors, from giving chase. Stryker strode to the rear of the creeping body of men, staring out in the direction of the city. It was difficult to see anything beyond their huge ring of pikes, and the smoke and the darkness made the world all the more opaque, yet one thing was clear; the haemorrhage of Royalist soldiers into the roads and lanes and woodland would be impossible for the enemy to staunch.

Most of the Allied infantry – the Covenanters in the main – were already peeling away from the battle front in pursuit, for they had regiments to spare, but they would not be swift enough to cut off the majority of the terrified Royalists, and plenty would make it back to the safety of York.

Stryker went back to his men. Rupert's routed army would survive, because the whitecoats would protect the routed divisions by sacrificing themselves.

A small field piece erupted somewhere unseen, its iron ball coring the brigade so that a whole file of pikemen was obliterated in an instant. A thickly bearded man, his shoulder emblazoned with the same cross of courage that adorned Forrester's coat, reeled out of the cordon screaming. He collapsed to his knees, guts slithering through his fingers and over his thighs as he scrabbled to gather them with trembling, bone-white hands. Stryker knelt beside him, cutting his bandolier with his dirk. He gritted his teeth as he wiped away the stricken man's entrails, thumbing open one of the powder boxes hanging from the leather strap, and beginning the process of loading the musket.

It was a death of a thousand cuts. Seek Wisdom and Fear the Lord Gardner, black-cloaked and ranting, paced right at the circle's heart, screaming God's power down upon them, beseeching King Jesus to save their souls, to ravage the enemy, to loose the heavenly host and bring all their fiery swords down upon the heads of those who would defy their divinely appointed monarch. But still the whitecoats died. And the rebel horsemen, the famed harquebusiers, swooped around them like a flock of screeching kites at a carcass, slicing at the pikes and wheeling away, bellowing psalms as they launched charge after thundering charge.

Yet somehow the whitecoats kept the shape of their dense block, their pikes on the outermost edges, each spear rammed into the instep of the rearmost foot and thrust up and out at an angle that would catch a horse square in the mouth should it be stupid enough to ram home. The musketeers, squeezing muzzles between the heads of the pikemen, loaded and fired like automatons, throats burning with the gritty plumes they sucked into heaving chests. Yet too many were dying. The Allied muskets coughed as each cavalry charge peeled away, and the Royalists' tight formation made them an unmissable target, to be picked off at will. They fell in their droves, leaving a macabre wake of corpses as the groaning huddle of beleaguered soldiers inched its way across the vicious field.

A musket shot pierced the circle, punching a hole through a drum and killing the drummer. One of the company preachers went down as he waved his Bible at the backs of the defenders, shot through the eye by a horseman's pistol. The edges of the circle were fraying, its stubborn strength dwindling, but still Cromwell's horsemen, intent on destroying this final bastion of resistance, were engaged where they might otherwise have been putting the broken brigades to the sword. That was all the white-coated men could hope for.

Stryker went to fetch another powder box from the severed bandolier that he had dropped beside the gutted soldier. As he bent to it, he noticed a bottle of richly crimson liquid lying beside the corpse. He snatched it up, pulling out the stopper with his teeth, and sniffed the contents. He went to find Hood.

'Get as drunk as you like, Tom. I'll join you.'

Lieutenant Hood's eyes, black-rimmed by soot from the pistol he had been firing out at the thrashing cavalry, peered at the proffered bottle. He smiled, shaking his head. 'I will not, sir. You were right. A copper nose gives a man a stout heart, but a clear head keeps him alive.'

Shouts of alarm echoed on all sides, and they knew the harquebusiers had reformed for another charge. Stryker spat a gobbet of gritty phlegm. 'Nothing will keep us alive.'

'I made a pledge,' Hood persisted, 'to Miss Helly.' A shadow crossed his features, hinting at regret. Stryker lifted the bottle to his own lips. 'As you wish, Tom.' When he had taken a long draught, revelling in the luxuriant claret, he handed the bottle to Skellen. 'You and I, Sergeant.' He fixed his eye on each man in turn. 'A pleasure knowing you both.'

Skellen swilled the wine in his hand. 'It'll be a pleasure dyin' with you, sir.'

As the sergeant drank, Stryker caught a glimpse – fleeting, nothing more; a glimmer of something that struck a chord in his mind. He stared out through the southern face of the circle. Beyond, a large body of the Earl of Manchester's Foot was pressing slowly forwards into the whitecoats' fire. And there, set amongst them, was a company of men who were not clothed in the reds and greens of the earl's units. They wore darker garments in the main, though that was nothing in itself, except that some wore blue cloaks that stretched all the way to the knees and were faced in yellow thread. They were unusual, and, as he stared, he saw that many of their heads were covered by strange hats that were decorated with large, white feathers, and several of their number were draped in thick animal pelts.

'By Christ, he is here!'

Skellen and Hood ran to Styker. He crouched behind the outer ranks and loaded the musket, taking more care than usual, ensuring that his shot would fly true. Then he went into the midst of a row of musketeers, taking his place behind the pikes and screwing up his eye, squinting into the gloom. He saw Janik first, Kendrick's big, moustachioed henchman, and saw too that the fearsome Hungarian trained a musket on his position. Then he sighted the Vulture, black-pelted and glowering, and knew he might never get this opportunity again.

'Now, you ballock-witted oaf!' Captain John Kendrick snarled.

'Not a clear shot.'

'It is as clear as we'll get. Shoot the bastard's head off his shoulders before he slinks back into that hedgehog.'

Sergeant Andor Janik was the best shot in Kendrick's company, and the pair had examined the white-coated brigade every second since first they had spotted Stryker, hoping that he would brave the outer edge of the circle. Now, at last, his shoulders and head were fully exposed. Now was the time.

Janik muttered something in his native tongue as he curled a finger around his trigger. And then he swore, and Kendrick swore too, for they could see Stryker's own musket, and it was pointing at them.

'Take the shot!' Kendrick blurted, suddenly frightened. 'Take the goddamned shot, Sergeant Janik!'

Janik fired.

Stryker pulled the trigger as Cromwell's horsemen launched their charge. Smoke plumed, the heavy stock smacked hard into his shoulder, and he was instantly blind. Air pulsed beside his face and he knew that Janik had fired too, and missed. He dropped the musket, flapping wildly at the smoke, and strained his stinging eye to see what had become of his own bullet.

Kendrick was still standing. Stryker screamed an oath of rage and frustration. His enemy was looking down, as if he regarded his feet, and gradually Stryker realized the shot had, indeed, found a mark. Janik had gone, vanished. Killed. Stryker turned to deliver the bittersweet news to his comrades, and then saw Thomas Hood's body.

The swords of Oliver Cromwell's horsemen clattered against the outstretched pikes like a thousand sticks dragged across a wattle fence. Still the hedgehog did not break. They wheeled away to reform, and every man fighting with the bloody-minded Northern Foot gave a guttural jeer. Almost every man.

Stryker and Skellen knelt beside Hood's prone form. Lancelot Forrester had seen the lieutenant reel back too, but it was too late. Janik's musket-ball, intended for Stryker, had slammed into Hood and the bullet had taken him in the centre of the chest, the soft lead flattening to a wide, destructive disc as it drove a path through flesh and bone. Hood was dead before he hit the ground.

'My God,' Forrester was saying.

Stryker looked up from the lieutenant's wax-white face. But Forrester was not looking at Hood at all. 'Forry?'

'My God,' Forrester said again. He stared northwards, in the direction of the forest. 'It is over.'

Oliver Cromwell had curtailed the last charge deliberately, because all he wanted was to draw the collective gaze of the Royalists for long enough to deploy his dragoons. And now they were in position. His own horsemen had done their job, distracting the musketeers within the hedgehog, and they formed up in their broad, iron-strong line, reloading their pistols for the final time. A messenger brought news, as he prepared his own weapons and summoned his own courage, of the Northern Horse. The only enemy cavalry to have tasted success this day, led by the wastrel George Goring, were returning to the field to find their comrades in deep trouble. He prayed aloud for God to keep their numbers low and resolve feeble, and then he gave orders for a body of his riders to sweep them from the moor.

The dragoons attacked. They were arrayed along the tree line, and they spurred south, getting as close as they could risk to the dogged whitecoats. They drew up as one, dismounted as one, and fired their muskets. Now Cromwell released his horsemen, thundering against the Royalists once again, and they discharged their pistols too. The Earl of Manchester's Foot, pressing up from the ditch, kept up their own volleys. The last of Prince Rupert's brigades absorbed fire on three fronts. And finally, mercifully, gloriously, Cromwell could see that his psalm-singing holy warriors had achieved in the west what Sir Charles Lucas and the famed Royalist horse had failed to achieve in the east: they had broken a fully formed pike circle. God had provided a stunning triumph, for the whitecoats – valiant and resolute – began to fall apart. Newcastle's lambs had come to the slaughter.

Stryker left Hood's body and drew one of his pistols. The volley from the dragoons decided matters, for the hedgehog's north face had not been ready to face such fire, and the pikemen, left exposed against muskets fired at horribly close range, had been savagely flensed. Now the crowing cavalry charged again, but they veered north, curled their run to sweep around to the circle's newly tattered face, aiming for the gaps torn by the dragoons. They careened straight into the block, the fissures wide enough to fit their crashing, snorting destriers, and the heavy hooves kicked at the pikemen, who parted in panic, the range suddenly too close to employ their long spears. As they shied away, more horses plunged into the widening crevices, acting like wedges driven into rotting timber, and the entire circle ruptured.

Horsemen were immediately among them, butchering bloody paths through the melee, their swords and breeches, buff-coats, breastplates and faces spattered in the blood of their prey. A great wail went up, new drums thundered, and then the rebel infantry stormed forwards in waves to support the horse. There had been no quarter asked, and none would be given.

Stryker was barely aware of which way he faced, thinking only of survival. He drew his sword as he fired the pistol, ducking below the arc of a high-swung partisan and shooting the assailant in the face for his trouble. Then he dropped the smoking piece and took the blade in both hands, hacking a green-coated man down with nothing but brute force and desperation. He trampled over the felled soldier, searching for escape but seeing nothing but dead ends.

'God with us!' was the only cry now, and Stryker twisted and turned, cleaving path after path that took him nowhere at all. He slid the tip of his Toledo blade into a man's windpipe, jerking it free to slice it sideways at a passing horse, and rolled clear of the stamping hooves. He was up quickly, dizzy but alive, daubed in mud and the blood of friend and foe. A man armoured in morion pot, breastplate and tassets lunged at Stryker with an axe, aiming to open his belly from stones to sternum. Stryker wrenched himself away, feeling the axe's edge rip at his coat, and, as he slid in a patch of horse dung, he noticed a pike discarded in the morass. He dropped the sword, hefted the shaft that was snapped halfway along its length, and spun, sweeping all eight feet of tapered ash in a wide curve that collided with the axe-man's thigh. The blade, designed only to thrust, failed to penetrate the metal tassets but knocked him off his stride, and Stryker drew back the half-pike, stabbing upwards with all the strength he had left. The tip crunched beneath the Parliamentarian's chin, up through the soft tissue behind his jawbone, and the man's bloodshot eyes rolled up as if staring at the rim of his morion. Stryker released the shaft, leaving it stuck and quivering, and went to find his sword.

'*Stryker!*'

He felt his ears prick like a startled animal. He collected his sword and turned.

Captain John Kendrick ran his tongue slowly over his ghoulishly sharpened teeth. Time seemed to slow. The battle raged all about them, but each man, ten yards apart, stared at the other as though none existed but them.

Stryker pointed his sword at Kendrick's chest. 'You killed Hood.'

Kendrick had a sword in one hand and the other he flexed, letting the metallic fingers, topped by the vicious brass gadlings, clank with grim foreboding. He wiped the sword on his dense cloak. 'You killed Janik.'

Stryker pulled free his second pistol and fired. The shot flew wide. He dropped the weapon and moved forwards, adjusting his sword grip to ensure the shark-skin hilt would not fail. 'You murdered Lieutenant Brownell.'

'A mistake,' Kendrick replied casually, holding up his own sword to beckon his enemy. He winked. 'I was trying to kill you.'

—⁂—

Hidden deep in the woods, Fight the Good Fight of Faith Helly was frightened. Frightened of a Royalist victory without Stryker; of a Parliamentarian victory with the spectre of the Vulture. So she stared at the lengthening shadows, made gloomier by the sepulchral forest, and flinched as flaming tongues licked the bracken where men ran and screamed.

She could not discern anything meaningful in the madness. The battle still raged to the south, but fighting had spread to Wilstrop Wood, and men crashed through the undergrowth, darted round trunks and died in the leaf mulch. There were riders too, helmeted centaurs with bright spurs and dark swords, and they slashed all around, hacking tracks through the wood to cut down whom they may. But Faith did not know to which side any man was loyal, nor whether she would be safe under their white-eyed stares, so she let them pass with sealed lips and a hammering heart. The firelocks guarding the ammunition had long moved away, though they said nothing of their intent, and she had considered following them, but it seemed more sensible simply to hide and pray for nightfall. So she waited and watched and wondered.

It started to rain again: the droplets that weaved through the boughs of her hiding-place were fat and heavy. She decided to move, and gingerly stood up. A horse whickered softly behind her.

'My, my,' a man said. 'What have we here?'

—w—

The rain lashed Marston Moor, mingling with the blood streaking Stryker's blade as it clanged in the air above his head.

The hooked nose of a bare-fanged Kendrick loomed back at him over the cross of steel. He moved as Stryker remembered; incongruous beneath the kinked hump, but somehow neatly balanced. He was weaker than Stryker, but able to deflect and riposte with impressive crispness, and Stryker heaved at him now, throwing him away so that he did not find some sly way to pummel his lone eye with the knuckled gauntlet.

Kendrick stumbled back, breathing heavily. All around them the last pockets of whitecoats were crumbling, falling where they stood, cut like a field of wheat beneath so many scythes, but none paid them notice, leaving them to their private duel. The

Vulture swooped in, darting low to cut at Stryker's ankles, forcing the latter to leap out of range, almost becoming entangled with his own scabbard.

Kendrick straightened, rolling his distorted shoulders. 'Water hemlock, from the New World.' He sneered. 'One draws a yellow liquid from its roots. Looks like piss. Smells worse.'

Stryker's mind went to a tavern in Skipton. 'The poison.'

Kendrick made a clicking noise with his tongue. 'The savages use it.' He swept his blade in the hissing figure of eight he had used to dazzle Stryker at Lathom. 'Jesu, but it is deadly stuff. A drop will do the trick.'

Stryker circled him warily. 'A coward's weapon.'

'As I said, the tainted chalice was not intended for that young peacock's lips.' Kendrick lunged, thrusting at the belly, then whipping the tip upwards to catch Stryker's chin. When he sliced only air, he rocked back, giving himself space to draw the cinquedea. He turned the broad blade slowly to let the raindrops glitter on the wicked steel. 'After that, my place in the service of the Crown appeared rather untenable.'

''Tis a harsh choice to change one's loyalty,' Stryker said, swinging his blade from side to side. 'Unless that loyalty was never truly owned.'

Kendrick blew rainwater from his lips. 'Oh?'

'You are Ezra Killigrew's man. And he, Vulture, is a traitor and a double agent.'

Kendrick laughed. 'Very good!'

'Hate-Evil Sydall was his man too. A Parliament spy, unaware that his master shared secrets with both sides.'

'When Master Killigrew heard we would sack Bolton,' Kendrick returned, 'he feared what Sydall might reveal. Better to eradicate a good agent than risk exposure. But you'll never prove it. And you will die on this field.'

The turncoat jumped in, closing the range and hewing his sword downward in a crushing blow. Stryker parried, staggered back, recaptured his balance only to have to parry again. The second strike caught him just above the hilt, and though the ornate guard turned the edge away, the jarring effect made him sway alarmingly so that his rear foot skidded in the scarlet stew. He took a knee, flattening a palm in the filth to steady himself. His fingers snaked across something hard and smooth. He looked down, registering what he saw, then let it go as he met another blow with a block that only just repelled Kendrick's thrust. He wrenched his body sideways to squirm away from the darting cinquedea. The blade, named for its width, caught him across the upper arm, and he knew he had been saved by the layer of oiled hide. He scrambled to his feet, went on the attack with a half-dozen sharp jabs that Kendrick absorbed without fuss or fluster.

There were horsemen nearby no longer fighting but watching the private performance play out. He hauled air into his lungs as his mind churned. He needed to stall for time. 'I have the cipher,' he said eventually.

Kendrick stopped short, visibly shaken. 'I do not believe you.'

'That is your choice. But I have it, and it is safe.'

'You'll give me that flagon, Stryker, or so help me ...'

'It is no flagon, you dull-witted fool.' Stryker forced a mocking laugh, hoping that the captain would be enraged into a mistake. 'A Puritan like Sydall would entrust his secrets to one place only.'

Kendrick untwisted his features. 'Alone it incriminates nothing. What is a key without its lock?'

'I'll find the lock. You will die now, Vulture, and Killigrew will die later.'

John Kendrick licked his lips. 'That's the spirit, Stryker. But, alas, I am a hard-man. I have been given the power of the Balkan sorcerers and the feathered barbarians of Virginia.' He shrugged, flipped the cinquedea in his hand, and lurched at Stryker. 'I cannot be killed!'

Stryker threw himself to the side, to the place where he had knelt, and there he scrabbled in the mud for the pistol he had so fleetingly felt. Kendrick bore down on him from behind as his fingers hit upon the smooth handle. He snatched it up, twisted, and fired.

John Kendrick stopped in his tracks, baffled as he looked down at the blood pumping from his side. 'You shot me,' he said, utterly astounded. 'But I am a hard-man.' He looked up in amazement. 'You shot me, Stryker.'

Stryker clambered to his feet. 'And now I shall run you through.'

A pistol fired close by, but it was not the one in his hand. The world was spinning and he felt himself fall. Then all was silent.

Stryker woke in darkness. He was curled on the ground, knees drawn to his chest, his side wet and cold where it nestled in the mud. He peeled open his eye. The lids parted stubbornly, stickily, and he guessed they were glued with caked blood. He saw boots pacing around him, fetlocks too. It was all a blur. He tried to sit. His head hurt, and he slumped back down. He waited, breathed through the pain, and sat up again, more slowly this time, happy, at least, that the rain had stopped.

He rubbed his face with cold hands. Calluses scraped his cheeks and he realized that his gloves had gone. He patted his body. His baldric and sword had vanished, his dirk too. The purse that had been strung at his belt had been cut clean away. In panic, he reached for his breast. The book was still there, between coat and shirt.

'They have Bibles, our captors. They need not rob you of yours.'

Stryker forced his aching neck round to peer blearily at the man who had spoken. It was another seated on the ground, one of many, he now realized. Hundreds, unarmed and cross-legged. The voice was one he knew but could not place. 'I was shot,' he heard himself say.

The man hunched behind him nodded. 'Right in the head.'

Stryker stared hard, forcing clarity into the lines that moved in and out like plucked harp strings. He managed to discern a red coat. He saw a wide hat that perched atop thin, sandy hair and a cherubic face. 'Forry?'

Captain Lancelot Forrester smiled, though the gesture barely reached his eyes. 'Fortunately for you, your skull is made of more than bone.' He held up a small, metal dome. 'Where the devil did you get this?'

Stryker gazed for a moment; then he remembered the secrete he had been wearing beneath his hat. 'A gift from a friend.'

'That friend saved your life.'

Stryker slid a hand gingerly to his head and followed the trail of congealed blood to a spot just above his right temple. There was a crusty gash under the tangled hair, and he dabbed it with his fingertips. Then he reached to take the secrete. The bowl-shaped sheet of steel had a pronounced dent on one side, which he fingered in astonishment. 'Jesu.' He looked up sharply. 'Where are we?'

'Marston Field,' Forrester said.

'Hood is dead.'

'Mowbray too. And a great many more.' Forrester pressed his mouth into a firm line. 'I have not seen old Seek Wisdom.' He sighed heavily and sorrowfully. 'We lost.'

Stryker looked around. The prisoners were gathered in a large herd, like cattle, and were being harassed by a ring of musketeers and horsemen. The area was lit by torches held by sentries, and thousands of pale awnings stretched away into the distance like a horde of ghosts. The rebels quite literally held the field. They had made a leaguer of it. Stryker stared at his fellow captives. They had all been stripped of their possessions, no doubt, but their coats remained, and those were a panoply of colours. Tillier's greens, Rupert's blues, some yellows, reds and browns. Maudlin delegates of two proud, annihilated armies.

His scalp burned with sudden brightness, making him wince as he dabbed the injury with numb fingers. 'One of Kendrick's men?'

Forrester's head shook in the gloom. 'One of those bloody horsemen thought to use you for target practice.'

'And the Vulture?'

'Hurt bad, sir,' another, gruffer voice came from the shadows. 'But you did not get a chance to end him.'

Stryker jerked round. 'Skellen?'

'The same, sir.'

Skellen's gloomy face, stained dark from the gash in his scalp, held a new depth of sorrow. He had witnessed many terrible things in the Low Countries, and had long prayed never to see them visited upon English soil. Skellen would never again be the same. Stryker shook the sergeant's huge hand. 'I am glad you live to fight another day, William, truly.'

Skellen let his gaze drift beyond his friend. 'Plenty did not.'

Stryker eased himself round to see teams of men lining up sacks a hundred paces away. With a knot in the pit of his guts, he saw they were not sacks but corpses. They came from everywhere; from the ditch and the woods, from the ridge where the Allied host had converged, to Long Marston in the east and Tockwith in the west. Five armies had clashed on this lonely Yorkshire moor, and the dead numbered in their thousands. They were stripped as they were collected, valuables harvested as waxen bodies were tossed in meshed, crooked heaps upon the back of wagons and brought to the vast line, where some – a fortunate fraction – might be identified. The rest would be dusted in lime and lobbed in a pit.

A thought struck Stryker. 'If I was shot, why did he not make an end of me?'

'I saw what happened,' Skellen said in the matter-of-fact way that was so reassuring. 'I reckoned I would not let that crook-backed bastard reach you. God knows he tried. His men came from everywhere wi' their curly swords.'

'Sergeant Skellen used his halberd, you understand,' Forrester cut in, 'and you know how bloody-minded he can be with one of those in hand.'

'The cap'n, here, came to join my little dance, sir.'

Forrester gave a rueful laugh. 'Had a handful of men with me. Seemed a worthy cause. We'd have fallen in the end, but Manchester's cavalry thought to interfere, thank God. They took us prisoner before the Vulture's flock could chop us to offal.'

'Why did they make prisoner of us?' Stryker asked suddenly. 'The whitecoats were fighting to the last man. There was no quarter asked, and none offered.'

'Cap'n has fedaries among the enemy, sir,' Skellen answered, a hint of the old wryness inflecting his dour tone. A man in the dress of a harquebusier was striding towards them, and the sergeant indicated him with a jerk of his chin.

Stryker looked at Forrester. 'Forry?'

Forrester looked embarrassed. 'This is Captain Camby. An officer in General Cromwell's troop, and a fellow actor. We trod the boards together at Candlewick Street.'

Camby loomed over them, a lobster-tailed helmet in the crook of his arm. He was young and thin, with soberly cropped hair and a deep cut through his right eyebrow. He tried to smile, thought better of it, and settled for a sympathetic grimace. 'A bad business.'

'You won, Captain,' Stryker said coldly.

Camby cleared his throat awkwardly. 'Such effusion of blood is never to be celebrated, sir. Not ever.' He bowed to Forrester and walked quickly away.

Forrester watched him leave. 'You might have been more civil, old man. The poor bugger saved our lives. They'd have butchered every last man found fighting with the whitecoats if it weren't for him. He admired our courage.'

'What happened?' Stryker said, ignoring his friend. 'In the end?'

'The enemy swept the field,' Forrester replied bluntly. 'Our horse rallied briefly under Goring, but they were shattered in a trice.'

'Rupert?'

'Camby says he was not taken, thank God. Newcastle and Eythin appear to have extricated themselves too. Sir Charles Lucas is captured, I'm told. General Tillier with him.' He shrugged, looking around at the human debris. 'And many more besides.'

'I saw Boye killed.'

'Skewered, aye,' Forrester said glumly. 'The rebels are

cock-a-hoop with the news, as you can imagine. They have destroyed Newcastle's grand army, yet they make far greater noise over the death of a poodle.'

'What of Rupert's army?' Stryker asked. He thought of that great wave of men and horses that rolled like gathering thunder all the way from the Irish Sea, taking Stockport and Bolton and Liverpool in such stunning fashion. 'The last stand of the whitecoats did much to delay the pursuit. Most will have made it back to York. Perhaps they shall rally again?'

'The last stand of the whitecoats,' Skellen echoed slowly. The brigade of Northern Foot had been ripped to bloodied rags, and yet not a single man had looked to surrender. 'I have seldom witnessed such valour.'

'They're gone,' Forrester said in a low voice. 'All gone.'

'All?' Stryker asked.

'It is said,' Skellen muttered, 'there are thirty survivors from the brigade, sir. Including we three.'

Stryker felt sick. 'From how many? Two thousand?'

'My friend Camby,' Forrester added weakly, 'saved as many as he could.'

'And God rot him for the saving!' Captain John Kendrick sneered.

All three captives looked up at the pale, black-framed face. Stryker tried to stand, but found no strength in his knees. 'I'll kill you,' he managed to hiss, and could hear how feeble his words sounded.

Kendrick limped closer. Stryker's pistol ball had evidently damaged him, for now his every movement was laboured. 'That fool Camby commands the guards, and he harbours romantic notions of chivalry that would make a reasonable man expunge his luncheon. But I'll take the watch before dawn, and you will suffer.' He sidled in a step, to whisper: 'I want that cipher.'

'You have already turned your coat,' Stryker retorted in sudden panic at the stupidity of the words he had spoken during the battle. 'What concern is it of yours?'

'Our mutual friend will be abundantly grateful for the safe-guard of his reputation,' Kendrick replied, keeping his voice low. 'And I have thought much upon what you said before you shot me. Oh yes,' he added with a grin, 'I have not forgotten. Where else would a Puritan hide it? The answer hit me like your god-damned pistol ball. Where have you hidden it? Does the girl have it?'

'No.'

Kendrick drew breath to rasp another threat, but then he halted. He stared for what seemed like an age, before slowly his lips drew back to reveal the shark-like jaws. 'Wait.' He cocked his head to the side as he regarded Stryker. 'Your hubris glows like the Everton beacon.' Kendrick winced with pain as he turned to click fingers at one of his blue-cloaked hajduks. 'Strip him.'

'You cannot—' Stryker began.

'Search every stinking crevice if you have to,' Kendrick was saying as a pair of his men pushed into the apprehensive herd.

Stryker made to fight the men, but found no strength as they tore away his coat and shook it like hounds with a fox. The Bible dropped to the ground. They pushed Stryker so that he slumped like a rag doll on his back.

Kendrick beamed. 'Huzzah for arrogant men, eh? You believed yourself invincible, so why place something this precious any-where but about your person?' One of the hajduks retrieved the book and tossed it to him. 'I shall kill you, Stryker,' Kendrick declared as he plucked the fluttering object out of the air. 'Slowly, painfully. They call me the Vulture; well I shall make you an *eagle*. The blood eagle, have you heard of it? I will break your ribs and tug your lungs out through your back. They shall drape over your shoulders, like the wings of an eagle, and you will be alive long enough to know every moment of your delicious agonies.' He wetted his thin lips with a flickering tongue. 'I cannot do it here, of course, for these Bible-licking Puritans frown upon such prac-tise. More's the pity. But soon, Stryker. So soon.' He began to walk falteringly away, one hand clutching the prize, the other clamped tight to his wounded side. 'In the meantime,' he called over his twisted shoulder, 'I will find that polecat of yours.'

Stryker's skull throbbed, but he managed to summon the will to heave himself upright. Beyond the mass of prisoners, and behind Kendrick's group, he had noticed the approach of a short column of horsemen. 'Why? You have the book!'

Kendrick halted and turned. 'But I want you to be assured that yours is an end of total defeat.' He waved the Bible at Stryker while his men guffawed. 'Know this; the Sydall whelp will be swived raw, and then she will be gutted like a Christ-tide piglet and left as carrion in a ditch. Because no one defies me, Stryker. No one. Yes, sirrah, I will find her.'

For the first time, it was Stryker's turn to smile. 'Not if she finds you first.'

Faith Helly perched side-saddle on a bay cob that bore notches on its ears and muzzle where blades had cut. She rode through the guard detail, flanked by an escort of a dozen riders on bigger, more intimidating mounts. She was still as slight and wan as Stryker remembered, and yet there was an imperiousness about her he had not before encountered. For the first time, he supposed, she was safe. Truly safe. Her finger, tiny and white, extended towards Kendrick. 'Him.'

'This man?' the rider immediately behind her, large and forbidding on a black destrier, asked sternly. 'You are certain?'

Stryker looked up at him. His face was deeply lined, with a wart rising from the right eyebrow, while his body was bound in leather and iron. He wore no helmet or gorget, so that thick bandaging could be seen about his neck. Stryker was taken back to the cavalry fight below Bilton Bream, and to the man whose head he had so nearly cleaved from his body. He propped a hand against his face, sliding fingers over the scars that would betray his identity. He held his breath as blood rushed in his ears.

Faith was saying: 'May God strike me down if I lie.'

Oliver Cromwell, lieutenant-general of the Eastern Association Army and victor of Marston Moor, pursed his lips as he regarded the hunchbacked soldier wrapped in thick bearskin. 'You are charged, sir, as a murderer and a ravisher of women.'

Kendrick laughed. 'I am a hero of this battle, sir,' he protested indignantly.

'This witness attests to the murder of Godly folk in the town of Bolton-le-Moors,' Cromwell said, gesturing towards Faith. 'You ravished the women there, and you killed the children. There can be no exceptions, lest the favour of King Jesus slip from our good cause.'

'I have seen the light since those terrible days, sir,' Kendrick argued. 'I am a friend to the rebellion now, sir. You would persecute your own friends?'

Cromwell was unmoved. 'If you break God's laws, sirrah, you are no friend of mine.'

Kendrick took a half-step backwards, pushing into the midst of his mercenaries. 'Where is your proof?' he sneered. 'This child's word?'

'Your own words will do,' Cromwell answered levelly. 'I heard the base language with mine own ears, and it is enough.'

'But, sir, I—'

'Place him in irons.'

Kendrick drew his cinquedea, the broad blade twinkling, but it was towards the prisoners that he lunged. Cromwell's escort moved their mounts into his path and he reeled back. 'This man!' He stabbed the air in Stryker's direction with the dagger. 'This man is—'

'Is bereft of the Word of God,' Cromwell interrupted.

Kendrick's mouth flapped wordlessly, thrown by the retort. Stryker could barely hear a thing above his own pulse. His innards tumbled like a butter churn as he waited for the general to recognize him.

But Cromwell had not deigned to look at the multitude of captives. He was staring, instead, at the book in Kendrick's hand. 'Return it forthwith.'

Kendrick shook his head, hugging the Bible to his chest as he waved the cinquedea at the encircling horsemen. 'Fool! This is no ordinary Bible! It is—'

The Vulture fell as one of the harquebusiers kicked him savagely in the face. He writhed, babbling a stream of oaths, as two more of Cromwell's men dismounted to take him in hand. He struggled against them, made to shout at Cromwell once more, but a gauntleted fist slammed into his stomach, folding him double and knocking the wind and the words from his body. Oliver Cromwell was already riding away.

# CHAPTER 24

*Marston Moor, Yorkshire, 3 July 1644*

The Army of Both Kingdoms spent the night on Marston Moor.

Dawn brought only more horror to the land between Tockwith and Long Marston, for with light the terrain itself was finally revealed, its carpet of corpses stretching in all directions, too many for the collection teams to gather during the smallest hours. Half a dozen pyres incinerated the remains of horses and oxen, funnels of filth – thick and yellowish – gouting into the lingering miasma. Locals had come too; some to identify the marbled blue corpses of potential kin, but most to rifle hungrily through snapsacks, breeches, belts and pockets for any item of value. Some of the bodies reached the pits missing fingers, cut away by sharp knives for the plundering of gold bands. All three of the victorious armies officially frowned upon the practice, but on this most grim of mornings none seemed to care.

Stryker and Forrester stood by the edge of Wilstrop Wood. As befitting the dignity of rank, they had been permitted a modicum of freedom, albeit unarmed and under guard, and so they had come to this place, where the ancient trunks were scarred white by bullets, and watched as a squad of halberdiers brought Captain John Kendrick to the hanging tree. A group of witnesses trailed in their wake, led by a bushy-browed provost marshal in a tall, buckled hat and a drummer pounding a slow beat. There were two priests with them intoning psalms as they walked, and at the very back, on her sturdy cob, was Fight the Good Fight of Faith Helly.

Stryker strode closer, his friend following. Their escort, a pair of earnest young soldiers who reminded Stryker of so many who had gone before, tracked them as though they were a pair of dangerous beasts. Still the cracks of firearms echoed for miles as the pursuit of Royalist fugitives went on. The lion's share, he imagined, were inside York, huddling behind the great walls to wonder at their leaders' next move. Most would know that the north of England was now lost.

The halberdiers fanned out and watched in blank silence as three pikemen tossed a long rope over a branch. The looped end flew clear of the bark, dropped and swung gently back and forth in the breeze to join two more ropes on two more boughs that creaked and groaned under the weight of other men – mutineers or thieves, perhaps – who had already met their Maker.

Stryker went to the tree as the noose was pushed over Kendrick's head. He half expected someone to stop him, but it was as though the battle had numbed all their wits. A priest was droning something, and he balked as Stryker approached the prisoner.

'I knew this man,' Stryker said. 'I should like to pray with him.'

The priest glanced at the provost marshal, saw no contradiction in the observing gaze, and nodded: 'Please.'

Stryker went to Kendrick. The turncoat was barefoot, wearing only breeches and shirt. He was pale and thin, his screwed physique pronounced now that his pelt had been stripped away, and his shirt was stained red with the blood spilt by Stryker's sword. Still he sneered. Stryker leaned close, voice kept low. 'For the rape and murder of Bolton's children, and for the poisoning of Heathcliff Brownell, I pray that you choke slowly, Vulture. I pray that your suffering is vivid and terrible. I pray hell's fires consume you for all eternity.'

'A pox on you, whoreson,' Kendrick said, his breath warm and fetid.

'Do you repent, my son?' the priest asked.

John Kendrick grinned his razor grin and spat first in Stryker's face, then again at the scandalized clergyman. 'Fuck your repentance, Bible-swiver! I am a *hard-man*! I cannot die!'

John Kendrick, the Vulture, who had shadowed and tormented Stryker and Faith, hauled against his throttling tether as if he could snap the thick rope with his skinny neck alone. It jerked taut, snapped his body back like a hound on a leash, and his bare, grime-blackened toes scrabbled for purchase as he skittered and choked. Then the drum fell silent. The soldiers, all three powerfully built pikemen, dragged back the rope on the branch's far side, hoisting Kendrick into the air. He kicked and fought, danced the jig, and never once took his eyes from Stryker.

'They found me in the woods,' Faith said. She had ridden to Stryker's side, and looked down on him as the Vulture slowly strangled. 'I told them my name and they took me to General Cromwell.' She shrugged. 'The Hellys are great Puritans.'

'You saved my life,' Stryker said.

'Consider it a favour returned,' she replied simply. Her face took on a sudden shadow. 'Thomas?'

'He fell,' Stryker said, not wishing to elaborate. 'It was quick.' He cleared his throat. 'Where will you go now? To Sussex?'

'I will tarry here awhile. The rebellion is—' she hesitated briefly, then said: '*infectious*. Do not look so shocked, Major. You know my feelings.'

Stryker smiled. 'A rebel heart.'

'Until the day I die.'

Kendrick was falling still now, his tongue protruding past the filed teeth, bleeding where it was punctured by the sharpened points. Stryker looked up at the girl. 'Will you speak to your … friends … of me? Of my intention to destroy Killigrew?'

'I had considered telling all, in the hope that Cromwell would crush Killigrew upon discovering what the man did to Master Sydall.'

'But an agent with the ear of Prince Rupert is more useful than one in the heart of a rebel town.'

'Precisely. The general is Godly, Major, but all men are worldly enough when it suits their ends. He would likely stop you.' She stared at Kendrick's twitching form as she spoke. 'Killigrew was the cause of James Sydall's death, and I would see him brought down without thought of politicking. To that end I will work for your release, for I believe you will find a way to visit justice upon him. You have the cipher. For my part, I pledge to say nothing at all.'

'You have my thanks.'

She shook her head, pushing a hand through the red tresses. 'Do you remember our conversation at that little church? Stydd, was it?'

'St Saviour's, aye.'

'I swore I would never condemn you, sir, and I meant every word.' She leaned down then. The horse was small, and Stryker stood almost at the same height as Faith, so that she did not have to move far to kiss his cheek. 'I am ever your king's enemy, but ever your friend.' Then she was riding away, a dead Vulture hanging still at her back. She glanced once over her shoulder. 'I pray you are not treated poorly, Innocent Stryker. God protect you.'

Forrester came to stand beside Stryker. Both men watched Faith Helly ride away; off to a new life, a life changed irrevocably as theirs had been. A crushing victory had been won by the Parliament and their Scots allies. The Royalist cause was wounded, its forces scattered, and the war in the north was all but finished. But as Stryker turned to look at the corpse of John Kendrick, droplets of piss gathering on his toenails as he swayed, he could, at least, find a little peace. Here, on a sodden field in Yorkshire, his enemy was no more, and another, more dangerous enemy had been discovered. He patted the Bible nestled against his ribs.

He turned back to the guards who would eventually convey him to a dank cell. He thought of Brownell, of Barkworth, Hood and Mowbray, of Vos and all the rest, and swallowed down the lump at his throat. The Battle of Marston Moor was over, and he had survived. He could ask no more.

# ACKNOWLEDGEMENTS

Taking a manuscript from its draft form to something, I hope, worth publishing, is very much a collaborative process, and I would like to thank everyone who has had a hand in bringing *Marston Moor* to the page.

I am particularly grateful to my editor, Kate Parkin, whose skill and insight were once again invaluable in trimming the fat from the original tale, and heartfelt thanks must also go to the rest of the team at Hodder, chiefly Kerry Hood, Francine Toon and Hilary Hammond.

Thanks, as ever, to my agent, Rupert Heath, who has championed the Civil War Chronicles from the very beginning, and to Malcolm Watkins, of *Heritage Matters*, for once again ensuring that there weren't too many mistakes in the final story. I apologise for any remaining errors. They are, of course, my own.

Finally, much love and appreciation to my family. The poor souls have to put up with someone living half his life in 1644. Can't be easy for them!

# HISTORICAL NOTE

*"It had all the evidences of an absolute victory obtained by the Lord's blessing upon the Godly Party principally. We never charged but we routed the enemy. The Left Wing, which I commanded, being our own horse, saving a few Scots in our rear, beat all the Prince's horse. God made them as stubble to our swords. We charged their regiments of foot with our horse, and routed all we charged. The particulars I cannot relate now; but I believe, of twenty thousand the Prince hath not four thousand left. Give glory, all the glory, to God."*

Lieutenant-General Oliver Cromwell,
the leaguer before York, 5 July 1644

The Battle of Marston Moor was a pivotal moment in British history. One of the largest battles ever fought on British soil – probably second only to Flodden Field – it decided the fate of York, secured Parliamentarian possession of the North, realised the impact of the Scottish Covenanter army, and sealed the destruction of both the potent Royalist Northern army, and Prince Rupert's hitherto unbeaten cavalry. But perhaps most significantly, at least in the long term, the victory belonged to the Eastern Association forces, effectively under the command of Oliver Cromwell. Marston Moor was the battle that made his name. It was also a demonstration of how a well-equipped, trained and committed Parliamentarian army could win the war; a perfect showcase for those voices at Westminster calling for the creation of a professional army. In time, the Eastern Association would become the foundation upon which the all-conquering New Model Army would be constructed.

When first I considered writing about Marston Moor, I intended the battle to be the singular focus of the story, a whole novel dedicated to the events of 2 July 1644. But it quickly became clear that by focusing purely upon the battle, I would be neglecting a number of contributing factors that led five armies to converge on a scrap of turf five miles west of York. The book, then, is really the story of three separate historical threads that, ultimately, become entwined: The invasion of the Scots, the siege of York, and Prince Rupert's York March.

The signing of the Solemn League and Covenant (much of which is discussed in the fifth Stryker tale, *Warlord's Gold*) between Parliament and the Scots is one of the major turning points of the First Civil War; the subsequent invasion by a powerful Scottish army ensuring that the conflict would engulf all three of Charles Stuart's kingdoms.

As described in the novel, the Army of the Covenant, under the command of Alexander Leslie, Earl of Leven, crossed the frozen River Tweed on 19 January 1644. Leven's army was significantly smaller than had been contracted for, but remained a powerful force, and they advanced cautiously southwards through Northumberland, hampered by rain and snow, and by significant resistance at their first major objective; Newcastle-upon-Tyne. It quickly became apparent that Newcastle would be very difficult to capture, so Leven bypassed the city, instead occupying Sunderland, a port town with strong Parliamentarian sympathies, and well placed as a base of future operations.

The leading Royalist in the north of England was William Cavendish, Marquis of Newcastle, who left his base at York to intercept the Scots, leaving behind a small contingent of Yorkshire Royalists under the command of Colonel John Belasyse. The Marquis took the bulk of his army to counter the Covenanters, eventually setting up headquarters at Durham. Much of the winter and early spring saw little action between the main armies, the foul weather making roads almost impassable, and neither side was willing to push for a decisive engagement.

When the weather improved at the beginning of April, the respective armies began to jockey for position once more, but news quickly reached the Marquis from further south at Selby. The Yorkshire town was strategically critical. It controlled major routes between York and Hull, and was a defensible crossing point on the River Ouse, making it immensely important to the movement of troops and goods in the area. Belasyse had taken a large portion of his army to Selby to defend it from the county's Parliamentarian faction, led by Ferdinando, Lord Fairfax. There had been a battle: and the Parliamentarians had won, taking the town, huge stocks of munitions and upwards of 1,500 Royalist prisoners (including Belasyse himself). It was an unmitigated disaster for the Royalists. The way was now open for a Parliamentarian advance upon York.

The city was regarded as the capital of the North, and its capture would be a heavy blow to the Royalists, both militarily and in terms of morale. It could not be allowed to fall. Thus, as soon as he heard the news, the Marquis of Newcastle abandoned operations against the Scots and marched rapidly south to its defence. Naturally, the Earl of Leven gave chase, making rendezvous with Lord Fairfax and the Yorkshire Parliamentarians at Wetherby around the middle of April. The combined force, dubbed the 'Army of Both Kingdoms', proceeded to fall upon York, arriving before the city on 22 April. Together, the two armies mustered more than 20,000 men and scores of artillery pieces. For the citizens holed up within the walls, they must have been a truly terrible sight to behold.

And yet York would prove to be a formidable nut to crack, despite the vast horde set against it. Situated at the confluence of the Rivers Ouse and Foss, it commanded the only bridges over the former between Selby and Boroughbridge, making encirclement problematic.

Moreover, the city was fortified by an almost continuous circuit of Roman and medieval walls set upon an earthen rampart and interspersed with small towers, while an outer ring of earthworks and forts stretched beyond the main wall for additional protection. The city possessed four main gates (or 'bars') and a castle that dominated the southern defences, all of which were mounted with powerful guns. There was a quarter-mile gap in the wall to the east of the city, because the low-lying area had been flooded by an expanse of stagnant water known as the King's Fishpond. This had come into being when the Foss was dammed close to its confluence with the Ouse, causing the river behind to form a lake that, though probably quite shallow, would be too broad to cross beneath the defenders' fire. Furthermore, the garrison was well provisioned and contained a full complement of men after the arrival of the Marquis of Newcastle's army on the eithteenth of the month.

Thus, the Army of Both Kingdoms settled in for a protracted siege, fanning out around the city in a large arc, with Lord Fairfax's army to the east and the Scots to the south and west, with the construction of a bridge of boats over the River Ouse at Acaster Malbis to allow communication between the two armies.

The siege dragged on, with the Parliamentarian forces digging into their positions during the next few weeks, until early June, when the third of the region's great powerhouses arrived. The Earl of Manchester led the army of the Eastern Association, with Lieutenant-General Oliver Cromwell in command of his cavalry. Manchester had spent the first half of 1644 securing Lincolnshire for Parliament, and with that task complete, he was free to join Fairfax and Leven, bringing the total number of Allied troops before York to something approaching 30,000. More significantly, the Eastern Association plugged the gap to the north of the city, meaning that York was now completely encircled.

While siege operations continued at York, the most (in)famous of King Charles's commanders was also on the move. Prince Rupert of the Rhine, still basking in the glory he had won by relieving the siege of Newark (described in my short story, *The Prince's Gambit*) marched his army out of its Shrewsbury headquarters in early May, with the ultimate goal of rescuing York from the Army of Both Kingdoms.

In other circumstances, the king's main force, the Oxford Army, would probably have been the natural choice to relieve York, but the course of the war had turned – yet again – in March when the Royalists in the south had been defeated at the Battle of Cheriton. The Oxford Army had, by turns, been thrown onto the defensive, its collective gaze shifting away from events in the north to focus on Oxford itself. This left Rupert to deal with York.

First, though, he had to gather reinforcements and secure Lancashire for troops returning from Ireland. Joined by the Earl of Derby, the county's leading Royalist, and Lord Byron, who brought four regiments of horse and four of foot from his garrison at Chester, they advanced first to Stockport, capturing the Parliamentarian position and securing a crossing of the River Mersey. After plundering the town, and bypassing the well-fortified Manchester, they arrived at Bolton on 28 May. It is here, at the town so staunchly Puritan that folk called it the 'Geneva of the North', that we first encounter Stryker in the book. It is also here that one of the most notorious events of the entire war is played out.

The chief Parliamentarian operating in the area was Colonel Alexander Rigby, who had been laying siege to Lathom House (Derby's seat) until news of Rupert's approach reached him. He abandoned operations at Lathom and took his small army to seek protection behind Bolton's earthen walls. The effect, of course, was that the town – hitherto fairly weakly defended – now possessed a far stronger garrison than Rupert had expected to encounter. The prince's initial attack (formed of four regiments) was beaten back with heavy casualties. This defeat was humiliating enough, but the Royalists' anger turned to rage when, as described in *Marston Moor*, the defenders hanged one of the soldiers taken prisoner during the first assault. It is not clear exactly who the victim was – nor who carried out the execution – but it seems to have been fuelled by the assumption that the man was an Irish Papist. In fact, he was almost certainly English, but a large portion of Rupert's army had recently come back from the war in Ireland. Either way, his summary execution was a fatal error on the part of Bolton's garrison, who faced a furious enemy thirsty for revenge. Prince Rupert ordered a second, larger-scale attack, forbidding quarter to 'any person then in Armes'.

At the second time of asking, the Royalists were successful. As I have described, a group of horsemen were led through the defences by a local man. At the same time, the main part of the army stormed the walls, swarming into the streets to overwhelm Rigby's men. The sack and slaughter that followed is undoubtedly one of the most notorious episodes of the entire conflict. One may dispute the numbers quoted – they range from the hundreds to the thousands – but it seems certain that a shockingly high number were slain from both the garrison and amongst the townsfolk. Nor did the horror stop at looting and killing. Accounts talk of 'barbarous usage of some other maids, and wives of the town in private places, in fields and in woods'. It was one of the few events of the civil wars that came close to the savagery men like Stryker had witnessed on the Continent.

In terms of the story, much of what I describe was reported by survivors, including the murder of James Sydall. He was, it is said, shot twice, and the mocking astonishment of his killer (an unknown Royalist in fact, but the Vulture in fiction) is a matter of record.

After Bolton, Rupert went to Bury in order to meet up with the Northern Horse, under George Goring (of whom his secretary wrote, '*he strangely loved the bottle, was much given to his pleasures and a great debauchee,*' but who was widely regarded as one of the most talented leaders the Royalist faction possessed), while a contingent were dispatched to Lathom House to present the captured colours of Rigby's regiment to the Countess of Derby, who had resisted Rigby's siege so admirably in the preceding weeks.

The prince's next target was Liverpool, its location making it crucial as a landing place for troops returning from Ireland. As retold in the book, Liverpool – protected by a medieval wall and castle – provided a great deal of resistance. The Parliamentarian governor, Colonel Moore, rejected Rupert's summons to surrender, and the incident where the Royalist herald's horse was shot from under him really did happen. Such defiance could only provoke the fiery prince's full ire, and, unsurprisingly, Rupert immediately ordered his artillery to pound the town into submission.

At noon on 10 June, the Royalists assaulted the breach, but were driven back. The writing, though, was on the wall, and Colonel Moore must have realised that he would eventually capitulate. News of Bolton would have reached him, and he surely must have had nightmares of what fate would ultimately befall the defenders. Under cover of darkness, he evacuated the garrison and its stores by sea, leaving the townsfolk to fend for themselves. The second attack met almost no resistance, save a Scottish unit who remained at the castle.

The fall of Liverpool was effectively the completion of Rupert's first objective, the conquest (with the exception of Manchester) of Lancashire. At this point, however, he appears to have been uncharacteristically hesitant. He remained at Liverpool for another week. It is reasonable that he would linger in order to recruit extra troops, but it seems likely that he simply did not know what to do for the best. Should he proceed to York, or turn south to be near the King, who was surrounded by advisers whom Rupert despised?

But everything changed on 19 June, with the arrival of a letter from the King. As related in the book, it was hugely ambiguous, leaving Charles's wishes wide open to interpretation. Historians have argued ever since as to its meaning, but, either way, Rupert decided that it was a direct order to engage the Allied Army at York. The Royalists left Liverpool almost immediately, and were crossing the hills (not called the Pennines until the eighteenth century) by the 23rd. Prince Rupert was now firmly on a collision course with the Army of Both Kingdoms.

Back at York, the Allies had been busy establishing their siege lines and setting up batteries around the perimeter, beginning a full scale bombardment on 5 June. As retold in the book, the Covenanters stormed a trio of outlying sconces, capturing two. The third, at the Mount, was saved by a last minute influx of reinforcements from Micklegate Bar.

As heroic as the action at the Mount had been, the siege-works were now terribly close to the city, and the entire perimeter had been successfully circumvallated. The Marquis of Newcastle knew that his options were now severely limited, and he opened negotiations for surrender. Following a rapid exchange of correspondence, there was an agreement to observe a cease-fire on 14 June, during which commissioners from both sides would meet to discuss terms. As witnessed by Forrester and Gardner, the parley was a failure, ending when the Royalist delegation stormed out of the negotiations without even taking a copy of the Allied terms back into the city. Unsurprisingly, the Allied leaders suspected their wily counterpart had simply been playing for time, and they pressed ahead with plans to capture the city.

By now, though, they understood that York's ancient walls were far too robust to be breached by artillery alone, and a mining operation was initiated at two points: in the south-east at Walmgate Bar and in the north-west near St Mary's Tower. They planned to explode the mines and assault the two breaches simultaneously.

But, on 16 June, the mine at St Mary's was exploded prematurely. Sir Henry Vane wrote the following account of the incident in a letter to the Committee for Both Kingdoms.

"*Since my writing thus much Manchester played his mine with very good success, made a fair breach, and entered with his men and possessed the manor house, but Leven and Fairfax not being acquainted therewith, that they might have diverted the enemy at other places, the enemy drew all their strength against our men, and beat them off again, but with no great loss, as I hear.*"

Vane mentions Lord Manchester, but it was actually Major-General Lawrence Crawford who commanded the St Mary's mine, sending 600 Eastern Association infantry through the breach, without alerting anyone else to the attack. The Royalists counter-attacked in much the manner that I have described in the book, and eventually secured the breach. The attackers were cut off and forced to surrender, suffering large casualties.

Why Crawford exploded his mine in isolation is a mystery. Some accounts blame the weather, saying the persistent rain was threatening to flood the tunnel, thus forcing his hand. Sir Thomas Fairfax, however, was quite clear in his belief that Crawford was, "*Ambitious to have the honor, alone, of springing ye myne.*" I confess, Fairfax's view made it into the book because I found it more interesting. Manchester's collusion, however, is entirely a product of my imagination.

Whatever the real reasons for the abortive attack, the result seems to have been a general slowing in activity by the besiegers. Partly, I dare say, because Crawford's failure took a significant toll on morale, and partly because supplies of powder and ammunition had begun to peter out following so protracted a bombardment. Camp fever was rife, which cannot have helped matters, and then rumours began to circulate of Prince Rupert's approach. All eyes were suddenly looking westward.

With an army now approaching 15,000 strong, Prince Rupert had made swift progress, reaching Denton Hall, the residence, ironically enough, of the Fairfaxes, on 29 June. He then made the first of two moves that completely outwitted his enemies, pushing northwest in a lightning march to arrive at Knaresborough (fourteen miles west of York) the following day.

The Parliamentarians had stationed cavalry to block the southern Pennine passes, and the thrust had entirely outflanked them. He was now within striking distance of the besieged city, and sent an advance guard of cavalry eastwards from Knaresborough to give the impression that he was making a direct play on York. The Allied generals responded by breaking up the siege and mustering on moorland around Hessay and Long Marston with the purpose of blocking Rupert's assumed line of march. On 1 July, the prince again wrong-footed his opponents by taking the main body of his army north-eastwards in an ambitious 22-mile flanking march. He crossed the River Ure at Boroughbridge, continued on to cross the Swale at Thornton Bridge, then marched down the eastern bank of the Ouse to approach York from the north. Late in the evening, Rupert's forces drove off a party of dragoons guarding the bridge of boats over the river at Poppleton, thus securing the only crossing north of York. It was a stunning piece of leadership, leaving the city open to his army while the Allies were left on the far bank wondering how they had allowed the far smaller force to engineer the relief of the city with almost no shots fired.

Most crucially, Rupert could now link up with the Marquis of Newcastle's army, adding at least three thousand new troops to his force in advance of the inevitable battle.

That night, the Royalists made camp in the Forest of Galtres while his cavalry secured the approaches to York. The Marquis invited the prince into York to discuss their collective plans, but it was during this exchange that Rupert, after so many acts of military genius, made what could be regarded as a fatal faux pas. Not only did he decline the invitation, he replied with a brusque order for Newcastle to be ready to march against the enemy early next morning. The prince was technically senior to the marquis, but the latter took offence at the manner of the order. Moreover, his military adviser, Lord Eythin, held a longstanding grudge against Rupert, which must have compounded matters. The poor cooperation between these three leaders would render the Royalist army virtually headless during the fighting of the following evening.

The events of 2 July 1644 unfolded much as I have described, with the Army of Both Kingdoms first marching towards Tadcaster (concerned the prince would actually strike south in an attempt to join with the King) and then returning when they realised Rupert intended to fight. The Allied generals decided to make a stand on Marston Moor, holding the ridge, and urgently recalling their infantry.

The Royalist army arrived on Marston Moor early on the

morning of the 2nd. Prince Rupert had ordered a rendezvous with the York garrison before dawn, but, to his annoyance, the army inside the city were almost deliberately sluggish in their activity. We'll never know if this was directly caused by the terse nature of the prince's correspondence the previous night, but it seems highly likely. The marquis himself arrived at around 9 o'clock, but Lord Eythin did not appear with the main body of foot until around 4 o'clock in the afternoon, by which time the Allies were drawn up in battle order and singing psalms. If Rupert had attacked early, catching the Parliamentarians and Covenanters as they were strung out on the road, perhaps he might have won a great victory. Due to the late arrival of a significant part of his army, he was forced to face the full might of the Army of Both Kingdoms.

The combined Allied army – approaching twenty-eight thousand strong – occupied cornfields on the low northern slope of the ridge running between the villages of Long Marston and Tockwith. Their infantry formed up in the centre in four lines supported by artillery. The first line was comprised of brigades from all three armies, though their exact deployment is a matter of debate, some historians arguing that Fairfax's men were on the right, while others believe they held the centre. I have taken the latter stance based on the available eyewitness accounts. What we know for certain, however, is that Major-General Lawrence Crawford commanded the English contingent and Major-General William Baillie commanded the Scots. Four Scottish brigades, under Major-General James Lumsden, occupied the second line, while Lord Fairfax and the Earl of Manchester led their own brigades in the third. The fourth line was made up of a small contingent of Scots.

As was typical for the time, the flanks were taken up by cavalry. To the west, the Allied left flank, Oliver Cromwell and David Leslie commanded around four thousand horsemen from the Eastern Association and Covenanter armies, while Sir Thomas Fairfax (nicknamed Black Tom for his swarthy complexion) held the right wing of around five thousand.

The main feature of the battlefield was a long ditch, sparsely fringed with hedges, that separated the opposing armies. Prince Rupert deployed to the north of the ditch, positioning musketeers in and around the feature to harass any Allied advance. His own infantry held the centre, though they were massively outnumbered by the Allied troops arrayed opposite. They were arranged in three lines with supporting cavalry, their foremost brigades, under Sergeant-Major General Henry Tillier, made up of the men that had marched to York with Prince Rupert. The remaining lines comprised the units of Newcastle's army that arrived on Marston Moor late in the afternoon.

Rupert's left wing horse was under the command of George Goring and Sir Charles Lucas, while, facing Cromwell to the west, the Royalist right wing horse was commanded by Lord Byron. They too were heavily outnumbered, but Rupert had ordered them to stay behind the ditch to disrupt any charge from the ridge, and it was here, below the place known as Bilton Bream, that the battle of Marston Moor began.

The day of the battle must have been strange indeed for those standing to arms on either side of the ditch. The late arrival of Lord Eythin and the York foot meant that it was already approaching dusk when the two armies had fully assembled. The acrimonious scenes between Eythin and Rupert really did happen, and Eythin was vocal in his criticism of the young general's battle plan. Discouraged, Rupert decided that there would be no engagement until the next day, for time was simply running out. While an artillery duel continued, and the Parliament men sang (the incident with the Royalist officer sent mad by the singing was relayed by an eyewitness), he ordered his army to rest for the night, while the Marquis of Newcastle left the field.

At around 7 o'clock, to the utter surprise of the Royalist troops, Lord Leven, commanding the Allies from up on the ridge, took the opportunity to launch a surprise attack. During the preceding hour, the fight, as described in the novel, had grown into a bitter brawl over on the western flank. The Royalists had identified an advantageous scrap of ground from which to set cannon, and they had harassed Cromwell's harquebusiers mercilessly during the late afternoon. Cromwell had eventually snapped, sending a pair of his own guns forward to form a counter-battery that was escorted by two regiments of foot. By turns, these regiments found themselves embroiled in a firefight with Rupert's musketeers lining the ditch, and it seems logical that more and more troops would have become engaged as the skirmish escalated. Did Leven, watching from his high vantage, always plan to launch a late assault, or did he simply see that the battle had already effectively started? Either way, at around half past seven, beneath a massive thunderstorm, he ordered the rest of his huge army to surge down the slope onto Marston Moor.

Out on Leven's left, where the opposing sides had already made contact, Cromwell led his horsemen towards the ditch, having dispatched Fraser's regiment of dragoons to clear the way. Facing him was Lord Byron, under orders to stand his ground and rely on the terrain for protection. It appears he disobeyed those orders, mounting a charge of his own. Presumably he felt he could gain the upper hand through taking the initiative, but by crossing the ditch he effectively removed any advantage he might have enjoyed. Moreover, his troopers put themselves in the line of fire of the Royalist musketeers stationed in the ditch, preventing them from disrupting Cromwell's attack. Byron's decision was rash and very nearly disastrous, his first line collapsing under the impact of Cromwell's larger, more disciplined force.

As retold in the book, Cromwell was wounded in this exchange, (tradition has it that the wound was inflicted by Colonel Marcus Trevor, but I have given Stryker the task) which coincided with the advance of the Cavalier second line, under Lord Molyneux, to stabilise the Royalist right wing. As Cromwell briefly left the field to have the wound dressed, Major-General Leslie took command in preparation for another attack.

Meanwhile, on the opposite wing, fortunes were reversed, with the Royalist horse having the best of it. Sir Thomas Fairfax's cavalry swept down from the ridge at the same time as his Eastern Association compatriots, but they immediately ran into far trickier terrain. The ditch on the eastern side was a more significant obstacle, and lined by a thick hedge. The only clear crossing point was Atterwith Lane, but it meant that Fairfax's troopers were forced to funnel into its narrow mouth to safely cross. They immediately came under heavy fire from Goring's musketeers, so that by the time they had reached the north side of the ditch they were in considerable disarray. Goring then released his front line of horse, which destroyed most of Fairfax's wing.

One of the most enjoyable things about writing historical fiction is that the truth is so often more interesting – and unlikely – than anything I could make up, and the fate of Black Tom is one such example. He really did manage to break through the otherwise triumphant Royalist line with a small section of his command and chase a group of fugitives almost back to York, on the mistaken assumption that his horse had routed Goring's. When finally he returned to the field, he gazed with horror upon the remnants of his clearly defeated wing. I'll let him take up the tale...

*'returning back to goe with my other Troops, I was gotten in among ye enemy, wch stood up and downe ye Fielde in severall bodys of Horse: so, taking ye signall out of my hat, I passed through ym for one of their owne Commanders, and so got to my Ld Manchesters Horse, in ye other Wing, onely with a Cutt in my cheeke, wch was given me in ye First charge; and a shot wch my horse received.'*

He really did ride from one side of the battlefield to the other, with a slashed face and shot horse, successfully passing thousands of enemy soldiers by simply removing the field sign from his hat!

While this was going on, Goring's front line was off in pursuit of Fairfax's horsemen, and sweeping up the ridge in order to plunder the Allied baggage train. Sir Charles Lucas commanded Goring's second line, and he wheeled right, taking them to threaten the Allied infantry who were now so terribly exposed.

While the horse had been contesting the wings, the foot had been engaged in their own bitter struggle. The Earl of Leven's infantry had advanced quickly down the slope to storm the

Royalist musketeers in the ditch, and the fight developed much as I have described, with the Allies making rapid gains. Crawford – perhaps, as I have suggested, with something to prove after the debacle at the St Mary's mine – led his Eastern Association brigades furthest, swinging to his right as he traversed the ditch to pour flanking fire upon the outnumbered Royalists, who fell back in disorder. The second line of Royalist infantry – bolstered by Newcastle's hardy Whitecoats – moved forwards in a furious counter-attack, and stemmed the tide, halting the Allied advance and throwing the central brigade of Lord Fairfax's men into disarray. As the Yorkshire Parliamentarians fought to reform, they were smashed by a body of Royalist horse (probably Blakiston's, as most of the remaining Cavalier troopers would have been engaged by this point on the respective wings) and panic took hold. They routed, fleeing back over the ditch, and, as the Royalists maintained their momentum, the fear spread like a contagion. Several Scots regiments broke too, both in the front and second lines, and then Goring's cavalry, under Lucas, hit home, striking at the easternmost brigade of Scots foot, formed of the regiments of Lord Maitland and the Earl of Crawford-Lindsay.

To any observer, it must have looked as though there was no way back for the Army of Both Kingdoms, and certainly this perception was held by the trio of lords who shared its command. Fairfax, Manchester and Leven all fled the field on the assumption that the day was lost. The Earl of Manchester did, as I have described, return a little later, so that he was the only one of the three generals to be present at the conclusion of the battle, but, though his arrival must have helped to stabilise matters, this victory, more than any other, was to be won by the lieutenant-generals.

I have already mentioned the impact of the Eastern Association forces at Marston Moor. Their cavalry, as we shall see, had the greatest part to play, and their infantry did an admirable job along the ditch-line, even as Fairfax's brigade collapsed to their right, but one must not overlook the part played by the isolated Covenanter regiments of Maitland and Lindsay. It was their courage, exposed to thick musket-fire and repeated cavalry charges, that prevented the complete rout of the Allied army. If they had collapsed under Lucas's attacks, then surely the rest of the infantry units would have capitulated behind, but they stood their ground, winning priceless time for the reserve lines to move up in support. Though the stand of a certain Royalist brigade is by far the most famous moment of the battle, the stand of Lindsay's brigade is certainly the most pivotal.

Over on the left flank, Cromwell had returned to lead the second charge. This time he used David Leslie's Scots horse to devastating effect. I have taken a slight liberty by giving Leslie a troop of lancers, though there is nothing to suggest that there were definitely no lancers amongst his complement. Whatever the composition of his force, we know that he struck Molyneux's flank as Cromwell attacked head-on. The result was a complete rout, the Royalist right wing utterly shattered.

At this point it is worth considering the whereabouts of Prince Rupert. He had left the field to take refreshment, assuming that there would be no battle until dawn, and it evidently took him a good while to realise what had happened. Returning at the gallop, he ran headlong into the flight of his broken second line, which had comprised his very best troops, his own famed regiment of horse among them. Indeed, he was so shocked at seeing his supposedly invincible cavalry in retreat that he personally intercepted them, shouting 'S'wounds, do you run? Follow me!'

However many he managed to regroup, they were never going to be enough. Rupert was caught up in the general rout, swept away with the rest, and eventually found himself separated from his men. The rumour was that he concealed himself in a bean-field to avoid capture. His dog, Boye, was not so lucky, and the death of the unfortunate poodle became a powerful propaganda tool for the Roundheads in the following months.

It was now, with the Royalist left-wing horse completely broken, and its right wing either off seeking plunder or embroiled in a messy scrap with Lindsay's tough Scots, that Cromwell made a decision that would prove crucial. He did not release the bulk of his own horsemen in pursuit of Rupert's. This seems an obvious thing to do, with a battle still very much in the balance, but the chase was such an integral part of cavalry actions during this period that to keep his force disciplined in the moment of such crushing victory must have taken a will of iron.

What happened next is still a matter of disagreement amongst historians. Many believe Cromwell – having linked up with Sir Thomas Fairfax to learn the news of the defeat on the far side – led his cavalry right the way across the field to destroy the returning members of Goring's original front line. This seems unlikely, given the furious nature of the infantry firefight that was playing out immediately adjacent to Cromwell's position, and I, therefore, have chosen to describe the course of events based around the supposition that Cromwell and Leslie made straight for the infantry engagement.

Cromwell took his well-ordered force into the exposed flank of Royalist foot, overrunning them almost immediately. With the Allied foot pressing from the south and the unchallenged might of their horse rolling in waves from the west, the Royalist brigades ruptured and began to collapse; with one famous exception.

The Marquis of Newcastle's regiment of whitecoats made a last-ditch rearguard action, perhaps because they were simply stranded in open ground, or perhaps in a deliberate move to cover the retreat of their comrades. The area in which this final display of heroism took place has been the subject of much debate over the years, though the traditional site is often named as White Syke Close. It is worth noting that the Close actually postdates the battle by more than a century, and a number of alternative locations have been put forward, but wherever it took place, the final stand of the whitecoats is one of the most famous episodes of the entire British Civil Wars.

Refusing to surrender, they formed a 'hedgehog' behind their pikes (the predecessor of the square formation made famous by later wars) and resisted repeated charges by Cromwell's horsemen, all the while taking musket fire from the Parliamentarian and

Covenanter infantry. Eventually, they broke, the cavalry getting in amongst them and offering no quarter. Several accounts of the final stand have come down to us, and we know that only around thirty whitecoats survived out of a likely two thousand.

Incidentally, one account, written by William Lilly, who was not present but supposedly heard the testimony of a Captain Camby, one of Cromwell's men, states that Camby 'saved two or three against their will.' Captain Camby really was an actor, so it seems highly likely that he would befriend a man like Lancelot Forrester!

The battle of Marston Moor had lasted two hours, featuring around forty-six thousand men and five armies. Almost five thousand men were killed, and many thousands wounded.

The Royalists lost their ordnance, gunpowder and baggage, a hundred regimental colours, and, two weeks later, the city of York surrendered. Thus ended Royalist power in the north of England.

Prince Rupert rallied the survivors and went to Chester in order to raise a new army. It is perhaps no surprise that he kept the king's letter about his person for the rest of his life. The Marquis of Newcastle, accompanied by Lord Eythin, fled to the Netherlands, apparently unwilling to 'endure the laughter of the Court'.

Of the Allied commanders, neither Lord Fairfax nor the Earl of Leven came out of the battle with a great deal of credit, both having fled the field. The lion's share of glory went instead to Oliver Cromwell, whose actions had effectively both started and finished the battle. It was after the battle that he began his start-ling ascent to the top of the Parliamentarian tree. As an aside, for those wondering why I have not mentioned his famed 'Ironsides' in the novel, it may be of interest that the nickname 'Old Ironsides' was supposedly given to him by Prince Rupert as a result of Marston Moor.

During the course of my research, I have read, scribbled over and spilt coffee on a great many excellent histories of the period;

too many to name here. But it would be remiss of me not to acknowledge two. *The Siege of York, 1644*, by Peter Wenham (Sessions Book Trust) was absolutely invaluable to me, as was *The Road to Marston Moor*, by David Cooke (Pen & Sword Books). My heartfelt thanks to both authors.

Marston Moor was, with the benefit of hindsight, the beginning of the end of the First Civil War. But, despite the huge setback of 2 July, all was not lost for King Charles, and there was plenty more fighting to come. And what of our hero? Now a prisoner of Parliament, things are looking bleak, and the summer of 1644 will doubtless prove one of the most testing times of his life.

Major Stryker will return.